GOLGOTHA

GOLGOTHA

LAVIE
TIDHAR

An Apollo Book

First published in the United Kingdom in 2025 by Head of Zeus

9 7 5 3 1 2 4 6 8

A catalogue record for this book is available from the British Library.

ISBN (HB): 9781804543566
ISBN (E): 9781804543542

Typeset by Siliconchips Services Ltd UK

Printed and bound in Great Britain by
CPI Group (UK) Ltd, Croydon, CR0 4YY

MIX
Paper | Supporting
responsible forestry
FSC
www.fsc.org   FSC® C013604

Bloomsbury Publishing Plc
50 Bedford Square, London, WC1B 3DP, UK
Bloomsbury Publishing Ireland Limited,
29 Earlsfort Terrace, Dublin 2, D02 AY28, Ireland

HEAD OF ZEUS LTD
5–8 Hardwick Street
London, EC1R 4RG

To find out more about our authors and books
visit www.headofzeus.com

For product safety related questions contact productsafety@bloomsbury.com

The whole country is no larger than the Principality of Wales—viz., 140 miles long and 40 in average breadth. Small as this theatre of the most stupendous drama in the world's history is, it has never to this day been scientifically or even superficially explored. From end to end are ruins. There are ruins which the Israelites found when first they dispossessed the Canaanites; ruins which date from their own two monarchies; ruins of that long period between Nehemiah and Herod; ruins Herodian; ruins Roman, but post Herodian; ruins Christian; ruins Saracenic; ruins Christian, of later date; and ruins Mohamedan. On every hill-top is a tel, on every hillside is a mound. No traveller, even if there were one found totally ignorant of the Bible and its histories, could put foot upon the soil without perceiving at once that it is a land of ancient story.

From *Our work in Palestine:*
being an account of the different expeditions sent out to the
Holy Land by the Committee of the Palestine Explorations
Fund since the establishment of the fund in 1865
(London: Bentley & Son, 1877)

PROLOGUE

Eve
80,000 BCE

The stars fell down in a shower of gold sparks, burning bright and fleeting in the black canopy of the eastern skies. Eve sat by the fire, the sharp blade of a flint knife in her hand as she skinned a hare. Her son played on the ground nearby, shaping little human figures out of mud. He did not look like Eve, her son. He had his father's narrow face and tall, slender frame.

Overhead the falling stars had faded. A crocodile slid into the water somewhere in the distance. A turtle dove cried out to a mate. Somewhere far away the woolly mammoths roamed. Eve removed the last of the hide from the flesh of the hare. She laid it carefully on the ground. The boy watched her intently, his eyes uncertain.

'I'll be right back,' she said.

She took the carcass to the brook and knelt on the bank and washed it clean. Her nostrils filled with the smell of the mint that grew here in profusion. She stared at her reflection. Sometimes she saw visions, hazy as through heavy rain. She tried to look now, saw a figure stumbling across a wide plain to distant hills, a ground full of skulls. She shook her head. When she opened her eyes, her own reflection stared back at her mutely from the water in the brook. A strong bony forehead, a big broad nose. Her eyes were clear.

In a time so far from now when only her skull would remain, improbably, in a cave in the Carmel mountain, she would be called Neanderthal in a harsh Germanic tongue.

She plucked mint and gathered a handful of acorns from under a tree before she returned to the camp. The others were there, her people and her husband's, and she thought with awe of the first time the two tribes had met, and how strange it was. They were so different from each other, so alien. Her husband's people had come from the north. Tall and gangly, with their small jaws and teeth, their long arms, their curious eyes. They did not speak Eve's language but their own peculiar tongue.

They could have fought each other, she supposed. Weapons they had, spears and knives, but those were for hunting and cooking, not to hurt each other. The other people might have been different, but they were still people, and there was plenty of land.

Land did not belong to the people but the people lived on and with the land. They existed at land's grace. And her husband's strange face was so very haunting, and their eyes met across the divide, understanding each other even when they could not yet share speech.

The fires burned, and as Eve prepared the meal she caught sight of a giant ibex in the distance, a goat on the mountain slope turning its great horned head and looking her way before it vanished into the trees. Eve hummed to herself. The boy played by the fire with his mud people. As the meal cooked they all gathered round, and her husband came and put his arms around her and planted a soft kiss on her head.

'Let's eat,' Eve said.

After the meal she put the boy to sleep and sat with her husband and listened to the night. The air was warm and scented with flowers. She nestled comfortably into his arms, thinking of the time they first joined together, and the consternation of the elders at first until one, a short and wiry woman of Eve's tribe, stopped the discussion and said simply, 'Let them love each other.'

She looked at her boy asleep and wondered what he dreamed. One day he'd grow tall and strong, and find a wife who might be of Eve's tribe or might be of the others, and they'd have children of their own; until there were not two kinds of people but just one.

ONE

THE FOREIGNER
1882

1

The man rode up the steep incline of the hill towards the city. Jerusalem rose above, a thing of dirty white bricks and antiquity. The man carried two pistols on his hips, and a rifle was laid behind him on the saddle. His horse was a fine beast: he had bought the animal two years back in the market in Baghdad, from a Circassian trader who imported the colts from Arabia. The horse whinnied softly, sensing something ahead. The man laid a calming hand on his neck. He watched the two waiting figures without making comment.

Horse and man progressed along the path. There was a cave in the hillside, and in the mouth of the cave stood two men, the first one-eyed and smoking and the other lounging against the stones, tossing a skull from hand to hand. They watched the man approach.

The man stopped the horse when he was some distance away and regarded the two men without an expression.

'Foreigner,' the smoking man said.

'One-Eyed,' the man said, acknowledging him. He nodded to the other. 'Ugly.'

The one he called Ugly looked up and sneered.

'Foreigner,' he said.

The foreigner had been born with a name he no longer used. He had come from the cold lands of the Habsburgs, where snow often fell. He could still remember snow. He considered the problem before him. Ugly and One-Eyed were bandits, of the kind that robbed pilgrims on the way to the holy city and sometimes kidnapped wealthy visitors in the hope of a ransom. The last the foreigner had seen of them was about a month back, when they had all played dice at the mad monk's place in the Armenian Quarter. Then, Ugly had accused the foreigner of cheating.

'You owe us money,' Ugly said. He tossed the skull to the ground and carelessly stepped on it. The ancient skull caved in under his foot.

'Leave now and you may leave alive,' the foreigner said.

'There's two of us,' One-Eyed pointed out. He tossed the remains of his cigarette to the ground. The smell of cheap tobacco was foul in the clean air.

'Where are your horses?' the foreigner said.

Ugly and One-Eyed exchanged glances. The foreigner nodded at the cave.

'You live here now?' he said.

Bandits could never keep anything of value. These two must have fallen on hard times again.

'We just want what's ours,' One-Eyed said, whining now. Ugly moved to one side, One-Eyed to the other, the better to cover the foreigner. It was quiet on the hillside. A lone vulture high overhead circled with more hope than confidence in the outcome.

'I have no money to give you,' the foreigner said.

'All you foreigners are rich,' Ugly said. He spat on the ground. 'Besides, you work for Ahmet Bey.'

'I work for myself,' the foreigner said.

Ugly laughed.

'A slave can dream of freedom, but he is still a slave,' he said. His hand moved to his pistol.

'Don't,' the foreigner said.

'Then give us something,' One-Eyed said.

'I have some food in my bag,' the foreigner said. He kept his eyes on the two of them as he reached behind him and brought forth a small satchel. He loosened it and tossed it on the ground between the two men, where it split open. A couple of oranges fell out and Ugly forgot about his gun as he leaped to stop them from rolling down the hill. The foreigner reached in his pocket, found a handful of coins and tossed those, too, on the ground. One-Eyed fell to his knees to collect them.

The foreigner considered shooting them then, for they had a price on their heads from the Mutasarrif. But bandits were numerous and their value low, and the climb to the city was steep.

'Go in peace,' the foreigner said.

'Inshallah, Foreigner,' Ugly said. He sat back on his haunches and began peeling an orange. The foreigner spurred his horse and they rode on, and soon the cave of the bandits was lost from sight.

The foreigner came riding into Jerusalem through St Stephen's Gate. A bored Ottoman gendarme stood watching the comings and goings and he nodded to the foreigner politely as he passed. Milling before the gate were the usual assortment of small traders selling fruits, vegetables and religious bric-a-brac. Russian pilgrims and British tourists stood in groups, for this was the start of the Via Dolorosa, and the Tomb of the Virgin lay in the valley just below. The Russian women, many of them, wore modest white headscarves. Of the British, who were no fewer in number, the men wore suits and hats, and they looked at the foreigner a little uneasily as he passed. A small Jewish boy with curled sidelocks hawked copies of the weekly *Die Warte des Tempels*, which the German radical pietists published from their new colony outside the walls. The dark Gothic type and the German tongue it carried attracted little business however. The foreigner rode into town.

There were no horse-drawn carts here, for they could not come within the walls. Camels dozed in the shade, sitting on their haunches. Women hung laundry from windows overhead. They looked down on the foreigner and said nothing. He passed a church and then a mosque, a butcher shop where the disembodied heads of goats stared out at him in silent advertisement. Children kicked a ball to each other, a donkey yawned, a slave dashed into the shelter of a tailor shop and vanished inside. On the corner of el-Wad the foreigner passed the Austrian Hospice and, not far from it, the grander Mediterranean Hotel, which was recommended by Thomas Cook & Son and where the more well-to-do European and American visitors preferred to make their stay. The foreigner, however, passed both these establishments, and continued down a narrow, twisting alleyway for some time until he reached a cul-de-sac and a solitary shuttered iron gate in the wall. The foreigner dismounted from his horse and banged on the gate. The sound, the sole one heard in this quiet street, startled a lizard, which darted away in alarm.

'Who's there?' a gruff voice said.

'It's me.'

'Foreigner?'

'Yeah.'

The gate unlocked. The man who opened it stood there with bleary eyes. He had thinning blond hair and a broken nose. His name was Ulric.

'You're back from a job?' he said.

'Yeah,' the foreigner said.

Ulric nodded and didn't ask questions. He moved aside for the foreigner to enter, then went to the horse and led him inside. Beyond the gate was a walled garden and a stone house all but hidden from the outside. The foreigner removed his saddle bags and rifle from the horse.

'I'll take him to the stables,' Ulric said.

'He needs shoeing,' the foreigner said.

'I'll send a boy for the farrier,' Ulric said.

'Thanks.'

'You need food, too?' Ulric said. 'I'll tell Umm Faisal to get a chicken.'

'I'll eat out,' the foreigner said.

'You're not tired?' Ulric said. 'How about a bath?'

'I washed already.'

'A wadi doesn't count,' Ulric said. 'You need hot water, soap.'

'Just look after my horse,' the foreigner said. He went inside the house. Upstairs there was a small, sparse room. He leaned his rifle against a corner and took off his boots. There was a nice view from the window of the roofs of the city. He could see the Dome of the Rock. He wriggled his toes. Then he stuck his head out of the window.

'I changed my mind,' he said. 'I'll take that bath.'

'Only two lira, very reasonable,' Ulric said. 'You need a girl, too?'

'No girl,' the foreigner said. Ulric used to be a dragoman, and selling extras had been his business. It was a habit he never quite got out of. He used to take the tourists out to the ruins near Solomon's Pools. The foreigner didn't know what happened exactly. There had been an incident on Ulric's last expedition, and two of the tourists never returned. Ulric himself had a slight limp since then, a gunshot wound he refused to discuss. He would have no doubt been sent to the executioner were it not for the intervention of Ahmet Bey, who made the whole thing go away quietly. Now Ulric, like the foreigner, worked for Ahmet Bey.

The foreigner waited as the sun fell over Jerusalem. The dying light bathed the dirty stones the colour of ditch water. The air turned cold with the coming of night. When the bath was ready the foreigner went down. He stripped off his clothes and lay in the old copper bath, luxuriating in the hot water. When he looked overhead he saw something surely impossible, a huge streak of bright light crossing the skies like a ship navigating through calm waters. The foreigner watched the light uneasily. It was a great comet, and such things, everyone knew, were heralds of change.

Such a comet was seen after the assassination of Julius Caesar. The foreigner considered whether this was a good omen or bad.

Bad, he decided after a while. There was little change here in Palestine, this backwater of the Ottomans, who had ruled over the land for five centuries already. A new telegraph line had been run into Jerusalem some twenty years ago; the Jews and the Templers had a handful of printing presses; and there was some talk of laying down train tracks to connect Jaffa to Jerusalem, but such talk never amounted to anything. The foreigner had heard the world was changing, that in England there were great factories manufacturing all manner of things on a scale hitherto unknown, belching foul black smoke into the skies. Great steamships sailed the oceans now, bringing tourists from Europe and America to the shores of the Holy Land. In America, too, they had railways, and food that came in cans, excellent gun manufacturers and new miracle drugs that could cure headaches and pains. But little of this filtered through to Palestine other than through the chatter of travellers' tales. Life went on much as it always did. And the foreigner made his living the way a man must.

He used the soap and scrubbed himself clean. The comet lit the sky overhead but the foreigner had lost interest in its omens. When he was done with his bath he dressed again and then put on his boots, the scuffed leather dusty from the road, and he determined to find a shoeshine boy later. They often congregated with the curio sellers and dragomans outside the hotels. He set out into the night and the gate shut behind him. The alleyway was dark. The foreigner wended his way through the narrow streets. An air of whispered delight filled the bazaar as the foreigner passed through, for the tourists, eager for something to do, were out in force, some sitting outside sipping coffee from small china cups, others with the rough local wine that was safer to drink than the water. Street urchins who could have belonged to any number of religions and ethnicities wandered between the tables asking for baksheesh, of which the gentlemen of Mr Thomas Cook & Son often warned against giving. More tourists were arguing with varying degrees of good nature with the sellers of olive-wood crucifixes and Bible covers, silver shekels of dubious provenance of antiquity, mother-of-pearl rosaries and ancient flint pieces as may have been made by the ancients before the dawn of history, and now littered the earth of this land. Isaac the Jew, sitting comfortably on a carpet nearby, did a roaring trade engraving Jehoshaphat pebbles for a crowd of delighted Englishwomen. The engraver worked methodically, inscribing tiny Hebrew words and prayers barely discernible to the naked eye.

The foreigner knew some of these loiterers and hustlers, and he nodded politely here and there but did not stop.

He made his way to the side of the market, where Signor Brutti kept his shop. This Brutti, who true to his name was a big, ugly brute of a man, was an Italian by name only. He claimed to have been with the last of the Sultan's Janissaries, child slaves from the Balkans trained for elite service as the Sultan's guards. But the last of them were disbanded nearly sixty years back, and though this Brutti was old, there was no telling how old he really was. His thick arms were covered in tattoos of a holy nature, and this, too, was his business, for many of the visitors to the holy city desired to put upon their own skins an irrefutable memento from their pilgrimage. As the foreigner entered, Brutti was busy inking and sticking a sharp stick methodically into the arms of a Russian who sat stoically on a low chair as Brutti worked.

'Another Jerusalem cross?' the foreigner said.

'Foreigner,' Brutti said, not looking up. 'A lady has been asking for you.'

The foreigner tensed.

'What lady?' he said.

Brutti shrugged. 'European,' he said. 'She's staying at the Melita.'

'I don't know any ladies,' the foreigner said.

'That's what I thought, too,' Brutti said. The Russian said

nothing. Brutti pricked him with the sharpened stick, over and over, tracing the Cyrillic letters for 'Jerusalem' on the man's arm.

'Nice,' the foreigner said.

'It's a living,' Brutti said.

The Russian said nothing.

The foreigner went past them. He went out the back, into a small, walled courtyard open to the sky. The comet blazed up in the heavens. Nadiya Brutti sat in an English rocking chair by a small fire. She was much younger than Brutti – a daughter, or perhaps a granddaughter, no one knew for sure. She looked up, and when she smiled her teeth were very white.

'The usual, Foreigner?' she said.

There were two customers already lying on mattresses on the ground in the courtyard, lost and gazing up into the skies. The foreigner lay down on an empty mattress. Presently Nadiya got up with a long-stemmed pipe in her hand. She knelt beside the foreigner and applied the stem to his mouth. His lips fastened on the wood and he sucked in a pungent cloud of smoke. His lips slackened and he lay back fully. Again Nadiya applied the pipe, and again the foreigner inhaled. Nadiya returned to her chair and the foreigner looked up into the stars, his weary limbs heavy.

2

When the foreigner opened his eyes an angel stood over him. He knew she was an angel for she was entirely white, and a golden halo surrounded her face. She regarded him with something of a sorrowful expression, and said a name he recognised, but which he no longer used. The foreigner had a mistrust of names. In the Holy Land every place had a plethora of names, like this city, Jerusalem, which was Al-Quds to the Muslims, Yerushalayim to the Jews, and had been at various times Aelia Capitolina to the Emperor Hadrian of the Romans, and long before that was called Uru-Salim, back when a Canaanite god was still worshipped there.

The foreigner had abandoned his own name long ago and in another place. The woman who stood above him had come from that other place, carrying news. She spoke quietly and dispassionately, imparting information that had been given to her.

'If you go to the Holy Land, seek out the son,' she said. 'So I was asked. Tell him...' she hesitated. 'They are dead,' she said, 'but some think of you still. There is a place for you at home, and with the firm. The mother was the last to go, asking for the son, so they said. What happened to him? I said. He left, they said. He was like der wilder Peter, you know.'

The foreigner almost smiled. He remembered the story of Peter the wild boy, Wilder Peter von Hameln, who was found in the woods and was taken to England by a princess. His mother often told him the story, when she despaired of him and his rough ways.

'They said I may find you here,' she said. She hesitated. 'I am leaving for Jaffa tomorrow. In truth I do not care for the Levant, I thought it would be more exciting here, but it is filthy and everyone just wants your money.'

The foreigner wished to tell her everywhere you went the world was filthy and everyone just wanted your money, home even more so than here. The woman looked down on him.

'I heard it told some who come here lose their minds,' she said. 'On encountering Jerusalem they shed their old personas, destroy their papers of travel and remain. Is this what happened to you?'

The foreigner stared up at her mutely. He saw the moue of distaste in the slight turn of her lips.

'Well,' she said. 'I shall tell them you are, still. Servus.'

'Servus,' the foreigner said in goodbye. The woman stared at him in some surprise, then nodded and turned on her heels.

The foreigner sat up slowly once she was gone.

'Another pipe?' Nadiya Brutti said. She rocked in her rocking chair. It made a soft, whooshing sound, back and forth, back and forth.

The foreigner rose to his feet. His head swam pleasantly. He handed the girl coins. When he came through the front room Brutti was working on another pilgrim, tattooing a turtledove on the man's broad chest.

'What did your angel say?' Brutti asked him.

'To let things be,' the foreigner said. He went softly into the night.

He was woken from a dream in which he fled across a wide, desolate plain. A red sky and a dry howling storm that raised dust behind him as he ran. All around him were skulls littering the ground, and they crunched softly under his boots as he ran. Ahead of him, far in the distance, was a tel of antiquity, a huge mound made, too, out of countless skulls in that ancient place of execution. The foreigner's breath rattled in his chest. A shadow rode behind him, laughing with the sound of crashing rocks, but he dared not look back. The mound or tel rose ahead in the shape of a cranium, caves like eyes at the top staring at him in merciless fascination.

The foreigner woke up. He lay on the bed in the room at Ulric's place. His head ached. The knock on the door repeated. It was what had woken him, he realised.

'Yes?' he called.

'Breakfast.' It was Ulric's voice coming from behind the door.

'I didn't ask for breakfast,' the foreigner said.

'It's included.'

He heard a tray placed on the floor, and Ulric's soft tread as he walked away.

The foreigner got up and went to the door and opened it. He picked up the tray and brought it into the room and shut the door. He poured from the fresh black coffee and drank two cups one after the other. It was not like Ulric to offer breakfast. Two fried eggs, a sliced cucumber, sheep's cheese and bitter black olives, and European-style bread from the Frenchman's bakery on Christian Street. There was even a small pot of jam. The foreigner tore a piece of bread and dipped it in the egg yolk. He chewed thoughtfully, then stuck his head out of the window.

'Umm Faisal make it?' he said.

Ulric lay in a hammock in the garden, smoking a small cigar.

'She's experimenting,' he said. 'Maybe we'll get more foreign visitors. Besides, she likes you.'

'No, she doesn't,' the foreigner said.

'You need to eat, Foreigner,' Ulric said. 'You take too much of the red flower.'

'What do you care?' the foreigner said. He had a bad feeling.

'I don't,' Ulric said. 'He does.'

'Ahmet Bey? He was here?'

'He sent his slave to pass along the word,' Ulric said. 'He wants you to come round when you're presentable.'

'I just came back from a job,' the foreigner said.

'As Moses said to the Lord when the Lord told him to lead the Israelites out of Egypt, no doubt, no doubt,' Ulric said. The foreigner withdrew his head. He forced himself to eat. The eggs, one broken and runny, reminded him of the mountain of skulls in his dream. He did not partake of the red flower often, only at the completion of a job. But he had hoped for a few more days in the city to just be.

He ate as much as he could and pushed away the rest. He forced himself to down the rest of the coffee, and after that he felt better. He put on his boots and set out to see Ahmet Bey. The city, awake, was filled with cold harsh sunlight and the sounds of trade and small industry, and the tourists and pilgrims who swarmed through the alleyways like fat flies. A Carmelite monk bumped into the man on his way. In the distance a muezzin called the faithful to prayer. A group of Chassidic Jews stood debating a portion of the Torah in loud Yiddish. A boy in rags stuck his hand out for a coin but the foreigner walked past him. More laundry hanging from baskets. He approached the Tower of David and went around a corner and found the ornate door that led to Ahmet Bey's residence. Two armed Bedaween guards stood watch outside holding ancient muzzle-loading carbines.

'Foreigner,' the one on the left said.

'Musa.'

The guards moved aside. The foreigner went in, to a small courtyard with an orange tree growing in the centre. A bright-green rose-ringed parakeet sat in a cage hanging from the branch of the tree. It stared at the foreigner and said, 'Cocksucker!'

'What?' the foreigner said.

'Two dollar! Cocksucker!' the parakeet said. 'I want him dead!'

'You must forgive my little Ilyas,' a voice said. Ahmet Bey came into the garden. 'I don't know *where* he picks up this kind of language.'

'I wonder,' the foreigner said, and Ahmet Bey laughed.

He was a large man, wrapped in silks and wearing a fine red tarboush which marked him as part of the Ottoman elite. Gold rings adorned his fingers and his moustache was lovingly waxed. Behind him came his chief slave and secretary, Zorik, a small Abkhazian who unlike his master dressed in a fine, light-coloured suit in the English style.

'Sit, sit,' Ahmet Bey said. 'Coffee?'

'I already drank.'

'You eat your breakfast, Foreigner? You are too thin. I need you strong and capable. How was the job?'

'The job was fine,' the foreigner said.

'Indeed?' Ahmet Bey murmured. 'He give you any trouble?'

'No trouble,' the foreigner said. Thinking of a face filled with fear, the man backing away from him slowly, his back to a rock. A vulture circled overhead. The foreigner's gun fired once. The ancient rock splattered with blood—

'Then you must be paid,' Ahmet Bey said.

'At your convenience, effendi,' the foreigner said.

'It *is* my convenience,' Ahmet Bey said. 'Zorik, pay the man his fee.'

Zorik handed over a small bag of coins. The foreigner weighed it in his hand, then shrugged and put it away in his coat.

'Sit,' Ahmet Bey said.

The foreigner sat. He sat cross-legged on the cushions. Ahmet Bey made himself more comfortable across from him. Zorik brought coffee and pastries. He remained standing behind his master. Ahmet Bey had bought Zorik as a child in the slave market of Istanbul, which stood near the Nuruosmaniye mosque. It was a market for female slaves, but children were also sold there. Child slaves were expensive, and Slavs more expensive than Zanj. The boy had been taught to read and write and do arithmetic. An empire like Ahmet Bey's needed an accountant. Zorik knew how much was made and how much was owed, but he kept his hands clean of the knowledge of where the bodies were buried.

'Ulric looking after you?' Ahmet Bey said. 'I heard you visited Brutti last night.'

'Nothing escapes you, effendi,' the foreigner said.

'That is true,' Ahmet Bey said. 'And yet, and yet.' He twisted his signet ring on his finger.

'Is anything amiss, effendi?' the foreigner said. His heart sank.

'It is a little matter,' Ahmet Bey said, and waved his hand as though to shoo away an irritant. 'Please, drink, eat.'

The foreigner took a sip of the bitter black coffee. He nibbled on an almond cake. Custom satisfied, he waited.

'There is a man,' Ahmet Bey said. This was how Ahmet Bey's assignments always began. There is a man. Sometimes a woman. Sometimes a slave, but the foreigner refused to be a yavaci, as those bounty hunters who went after runaway slaves were called. The money was good, but the work distasteful. So Ahmet Bey employed other professionals for that.

Why these men – and sometimes women – elected to escape the clutches of Ahmet Bey remained a mystery to the foreigner, since the result of such an action was invariably delivered by the foreigner himself. He did not ask questions. It was possible that some of these people had merely raised the effendi's ire at some point in time, and thus were doomed to suffer the consequences, some of them ignorant to their very last moment of the nature of their supposed transgression. Others may have legitimately fled, reasoning, rightly or wrongly, that a short freedom, even followed by death, was preferable to remaining under the effendi's control. The foreigner did not enquire. He waited, patiently and a little irritably, for the jobs did not usually come so shortly one after another.

'I must go to Baghdad on business,' Ahmet Bey said. 'Zorik

will remain in Jerusalem to administer my affairs while I am gone. This is but a small matter, Foreigner, and your reward will be ample, I assure you.'

'Of course, effendi,' the foreigner said. 'You are always generous.'

'This man, he was in my employ,' Ahmet Bey said. 'A Jew of the diaspora, a Swiss named Hoffman. He stole something of mine, which I desire to be returned.'

'I see,' the foreigner said. This also sometimes happened. Ahmet Bey desired certain things – papers, objects. Always he maintained they had been stolen from him. The foreigner did not ask questions. On such jobs he retrieved the items before disposing of their owners.

'He *ran*,' Ahmet Bey said. The effendi disliked it when people ran. It offended his sensibilities. 'I wish you to find him. The item he carries is but a small parchment.' He seemed reluctant to go on. The foreigner did not press him.

'He will be hiding out somewhere in the Galilee, if I am any judge,' Ahmet Bey said. 'But try Jaffa and the port, first, in case he is desperate enough to try that way.' Ahmet Bey snorted. 'Of course, I all but own the port,' he said. 'If he did try he would not get far. But I don't think he would be so foolish, and besides...' He fell to brooding. 'No, I doubt he would seek to depart, Foreigner. He will be hiding somewhere close. Find him and, well...' He waved his hand again. 'You know what to do.'

'Of course,' the foreigner said.

Ahmet Bey popped a pastry into his mouth and chewed.

'Delicious,' he said.

The foreigner rose to his feet. The interview was concluded.

'I'll walk you out,' Zorik said. He accompanied the foreigner back to the gate.

'This is Hoffman,' he said. He passed the foreigner a small photograph. A man in a straw hat stared out at the man. He had a thin face wearing a neat, trimmed beard. The foreigner studied the photograph before putting it away.

'This job pays double,' Zorik said.

'Why double?' the foreigner said.

'Because the effendi wants it that way.'

'It's important?' the foreigner said.

'It is to him.'

'Alright,' the foreigner said. 'How are you doing, Zorik?'

'Me? I get by,' the slave said.

'He make you free yet, like he promised?'

'Freedom,' Zorik said, tapping himself on the chest, near the heart, 'is within. Just do your job, Foreigner, and let me worry about doing mine.'

'Fair enough,' the foreigner said. 'Well, I'll be seeing you.'

He went out and the gate closed behind him. Musa, the Bedaween, was smoking a hashish cigarette and looking at the skies.

'Do you see that, Foreigner?' he said.

The foreigner looked up. The comet was still up there, visible even in daylight.

'I see it,' the foreigner said.

'Oh, good,' Musa said. 'I could have sworn it was only me.'

3

The Mughrabi Quarter was a densely populated neighbourhood of small stone houses and twisting alleyways bordered on one side by what the Jews called the Wailing Wall. A narrow alley did indeed run alongside the wall itself, littered with trash, of interest only to those who came there to pray. The foreigner did not pray often and when he did it was not there.

The ground below was littered with caves.

The foreigner made his way slowly through the dank, narrow streets. He bought a pomegranate from a street vendor and carried it with him in his hand. He found the house he required and knocked twice, then waited. Presently the door was opened by the witch's girl. She looked up at the foreigner with dark eyes.

'You remember me?' he said.

She nodded, then smiled when he handed her the pomegranate.

The foreigner entered. The girl shut the door behind him. There were no windows to let in the light. A single candle burned on a rough-hewn wooden table.

'She's expecting you,' the girl said.

The foreigner was not surprised at this. He nodded. The girl lit a second candle, placed it in a holder and handed it to the foreigner. She went to a corner of the room and knelt on the floor. She carefully rolled up the small Persian carpet that covered the spot. It was dusty, the colour of dried blood, and woven in a Herati pattern. With the carpet removed, the girl heaved up the heavy wooden trapdoor. When opened it revealed a dark hole, large enough to let through a man.

The foreigner nodded his thanks. He went to the hole and lowered himself down onto the ladder affixed to the stones. He carried the candle carefully with him. As he descended below the level of the floor the girl shut the trapdoor. The foreigner continued to descend, carefully, until his feet hit hard ground. He let go of the ladder.

He stood in a small alcove. Jerusalem above was an Ottoman construct; down here was the city of old, running throughout with cisterns, aqueducts and abandoned quarries. This was Warren's warren: a maze complex of ancient tunnels and caves breached by the Englishman, Warren, some twenty years back in a futile search for the long-lost treasures of the Second Temple.

Back in Herodian time, the temple served as unofficial bank vault for the riches of the city. Most of its treasure was taken by Titus to Rome. Some, it was said, was sent back to Jerusalem by the Emperor Justinian five centuries later. It was subsequently lost again, if it were ever truly found. Whatever the truth of it, few ventured into the under-city, for it was well known only ghosts and witches dwelt there. The foreigner crawled through a narrow passageway for some time. He reached a shaft in the rock, and a woven rope ladder dangling down it. He climbed one-handed, carefully, and trying not to make a noise, for though few came down, the maze was not unknown to brigands. One could hide in the depths of the city, in this abandoned cellar, until the outside world all but forgot their story.

After climbing, the foreigner reached a level passageway, high enough to stand in. There was ancient writing on the walls, in languages the foreigner could not decipher. He walked along the passage and entered a large cavernous space of great antiquity. The ceiling was high overhead. This could have been a vault once, or a place where grain was stored. The foreigner did not know. He was indifferent to its history. His candle held aloft he progressed along the uneven ground, listening carefully, but all was quiet. At the end of the cavern he found a door. This door had been made in the Jerusalem-of-above, and was of recent vintage. The foreigner opened it, and went into another tunnel where a small light glowed in the distance. The foreigner traversed the tunnel and emerged at last into the witch's abode.

A small fire burned in a circle of stone. Its thin smoke rose high towards a small gap in the rock in which it vanished from sight. A woman, surprisingly young, sat cross-legged on the floor before the fire. She was dressed all in black, in clothes that were freshly pressed and smelled faintly of soap. Her face was of no obvious ethnicity. Her name was Mara, but everyone called her the witch.

She looked up and smiled. Her eyes were bright, her smile gently mocking. She poked at the fire with a stick.

'Foreigner,' she said.

'Witch.'

'I heard you had a visitor,' the witch said.

'Just a ghost from my past.'

'As opposed to a ghost from your future?' Mara said.

'Those are sure to come in due course,' the foreigner said. He sat down on the stone floor, his back to the cave wall. Mara laughed.

'Of course,' she said. 'I expect you will be on your way soon.'

'As soon as our business is concluded.'

The foreigner had ceased to show surprise at the witch's knowledge of his affairs long ago. All she had to do, she told him once, was sit still and listen. And all the secret sounds of the above-ground world filtered down to her in one form or another.

Now the witch added dried leaves to the fire; the smoke grew thicker and sweet-smelling, and as he breathed it in the foreigner felt a pleasant heaviness enter his limbs. One could not rush a chat with the witch.

'Who was this lady?' the witch said. 'The one who came calling on you.'

The foreigner shrugged uncomfortably at this mention of his recent visitation.

'One who married into my former house,' he said. 'They ask about me, I am told. It's to be expected. They like to keep tabs.'

The witch looked at him curiously.

'You come from power?' she said.

'I come from nothing of significance,' the foreigner said. 'That was another life. Mine is here.'

'You were a prince? A duke, perhaps?'

The foreigner laughed.

'Europe is full of princelings and half-witted heirs to non-existent thrones,' he said.

The witch laughed too, the sound more mocking.

'So you are the wastrel scion of some powerful lineage,' she said, 'come to Ottoman backwaters to play with guns, like those cowboys they have in America.'

'I don't *play*,' the foreigner said.

'We all play a part,' the witch said.

The foreigner just shrugged. The smoke turned his mood mellow.

'If you like,' he said. 'Sure.'

'Will you ever go back?' the witch said.

'This is my home now,' the foreigner said.

'Why?' the witch said.

'Because that is what I chose,' the foreigner said. 'Must we go round and round again? Why do you live underground, when you could be overhead, under a sky and sun?'

'I have my reasons,' the witch said.

'And I have mine,' the foreigner said.

The witch smiled politely. She poked the embers with her stick.

'This man you seek,' the witch said, letting the matter go, 'do you know much of him?'

'Only his name,' the foreigner said.

'Hoffman,' the witch said.

'Yes. You know him?' the foreigner said.

'He came to see me,' the witch said.

'I never ask about them,' the foreigner said. 'You know that, Mara. I just do my job.'

'This one's dangerous,' the witch said.

The foreigner frowned.

'How so?' he said. 'Is he a gunslinger?'

'Much worse,' the witch said. 'A dreamer. I believe he has something of value that he carries. I don't suppose…?'

She left the question dangling. The foreigner laughed, surprised.

'Whatever it is,' he said, 'it belongs to Ahmet Bey.'

The witch looked displeased at this answer, then resigned.

'You will not bring it to me?' she said. 'I could make you an offer.'

'I don't need money,' the foreigner said.

'I didn't mean money,' the witch said.

The foreigner looked at her speculatively, then shook his head almost, it seemed, in regret.

'I work for him,' he said. 'Most people do.'

'Not all,' the witch said. 'But be it as it may. I needed to ask.'

For a moment they sat in silence. At last the foreigner reached in his coat and brought out the fee he had been paid. He tossed the bag of coins to the witch, who caught it in mid-air.

'I'll add it to your account,' she said, rising smoothly from the fire. The foreigner stood too.

'Thanks, Mara,' he said.

'What will you do with it all?' Mara said. 'You never spend it.'

'I don't know,' the foreigner said. 'Maybe I'll buy a little homestead by the Carmel, build a house, keep some goats when I retire.'

'Gunmen don't retire,' the witch said.

The foreigner nodded, then left through the door. He made his way back out to the larger cavern. From there he chose a different path, down a low-ceilinged tunnel, then through a narrow gap between two giant slabs of cut stone. Beyond it was another shaft and a ladder going up. The foreigner climbed the ladder and emerged at last into the back of a gloomy storage area piled high with bags of grain. The exit from the maze was hidden behind a stack of ancient cartwheels, misshapen bricks and other detritus of the building trade. The foreigner went through the warehouse and emerged onto a street on the Haram al-Sharif, within sight of the great mosque. In the distance he saw Mehmed Rauf Pasha, the Mutasarrif of Jerusalem, with his retinue, heading to the gate of the mosque. The Pasha was a thin, distinctive man, with a long face, kindly eyes and a neat beard that accentuated his narrow face. As Mutasarrif he was the Sultan's personal envoy to the city. He was surrounded by a group of wealthy citizens. The bankers were in European dress and dangling gold pocket watches, which they took every opportunity to consult. The traders and the land owners were in traditional garb and, like the Mutasarrif, wore a fez as befitted their station.

The foreigner did not move in these circles, but he recognised power, and could count the notables from the Nussaiba, Husayni and Nashashibi families who accompanied the Pasha. The party moved slowly, stopping to speak to the commoners also heading to prayer. The foreigner went the other way. It was time to get out of town.

He returned to Ulric's, where he picked up his rifle and his saddle bags and finally his horse. He left a coin for the bath.

He led his horse out of the alleyway and then rode him down to the Jaffa Gate, where he left him in the care of a man he paid another coin to for the task. He then went into the Deutsche Post, which of the many and competing postal services operating in Palestine was generally considered to be the best. The European powers all had their own postal systems, and their ornate and brightly coloured post-boxes littered the streets of the city. The foreigner, however, did not come to send or receive a letter, but went into the telegraph office. After some hesitation, he sent the message.

THINKING OF YOU STOP NEW JOB CAME UP STOP WAIT FOR ME.

'Would that be all, sir?' the operator said.

'Yes,' the foreigner said. 'Send it to Beyrouth, Syrian Protestant College, care of—' he said a woman's name.

'Yes, sir,' the operator said. 'Sending it now.'

'Thanks.'

'Anything else I could help you with, sir?'

'I have another telegram to send,' the foreigner said. 'Write it down.'

'Of course.'

ARRIVING TONIGHT OR TOMORROW STOP USUAL ARRANGEMENTS STOP KEEP EYE ON PORT.

'Send this one to the office in Jaffa,' he said, 'care of Chazan.'

'Of course, sir. Would that be all?'

'Yes,' the foreigner said. 'Thank you.' He paid the telegraph operator. Then he went out of the post office. The day had lengthened and the road from Jerusalem to Jaffa took most travellers a day to make at moderate pace. The descent from Jerusalem to the plains was in one's favour in that regard. The foreigner found his horse, paid the horse keeper who had looked after it, and rode out of the Jaffa Gate.

4

A deep blue sky stretched out above the foreigner as he rode along the road. White and pink cyclamen flowered in profusion, and red poppies reared their heads here and there beyond the rectangular dressed kurb stones which held up and reinforced the sides of the road. The road itself had been first laid with stones, much of the work done back in the day by child labour, then surfaced over with a layer of lime and earth. Now carriages could travel comfortably all along this main route, while the heavier cargo went through Beit Ur and those on more urgent business – or more eager to avoid the guard posts – used the path that ran through Wadi Süleiman.

The foreigner rode without hurrying, passing through Abu Ghosh, whose powerful clan had controlled the route to Jerusalem for centuries, imposing a toll on the pilgrims. It was only during Ibrahim Pasha's short-lived conquest of Palestine that this right was taken from them. As a result, the clan fought against the Egyptian occupying forces in the Peasants' Revolt, and continued to run their hillside fiefdom until the Ottomans subdued them in a military raid back in the sixties. They still held considerable sway, though, and the foreigner had twice passed through their territories on a job, given free passage through Ahmet Bey's influence.

The road was busy with passengers. The foreigner passed the French mail wagon, then a group of felaheen carrying vegetables on donkey-led carts. A large group of wagons and horses came towards him then, led by a rider in a pith helmet who held aloft a bright yellow flag. The foreigner and his horse moved to the side of the road to let this train of newly arrived tourists pass. These packaged, all-inclusive tours of Thomas Cook & Son were a regular occurrence, some would say nuisance, of the road. On they came, in horse-drawn carriages, an army of porters, guides and cooks following behind. Their usual itinerary, depending on the tides and the availability of steamer ships, was ten days in the Holy Land, and merely a part of a grander tour of the Levant, which took in the pyramids and Alexandria and the obligatory cruise down the Nile. From the Holy Land, some went to Smyrna, others to Istanbul. There were options to suit all budgets.

The foreigner watched as these well-to-do burghers of Liverpool and London, Birmingham and Hull made their way up the mountain to the holy city, where Jesus once trod the Sorrowful Way. Disappointment, he knew, awaited them on arrival. Tourists were invariably let down by the real city, small, provincial and smelling faintly of manure. They resented the tawdriness of the holy sites, the constant requests for baksheesh (as warned about in *Cook's Tourists' Handbook for Palestine and Syria*), the lack of basic amenities (the handbook advised the hardened traveller to bring their own soap), the absence of decent restaurants (though the camp cooks did a decent breakfast of hot coffee and tea, eggs boiled or in omelette, chicken and cutlets) and, in general, the sense of a vague let-down by the whole experience. Thankfully it did not last long, and postcards were available in a variety of fetching designs to send to those unfortunates back home who did not book the tour.

Home was Europe, with its cold rains and snows, its belching factories, the stench of horse dung on the streets as thick as a carpet, its black never-ending smoke rising from a thousand thousand coal fires, its packed tenements and casual brutalities, its grand theatres and palaces, bustling markets and gentlemen's clubs. The Ottomans, the consensus was, had done a crummy job with this place. Elsewhere the world was changing, powered by the great empires of Europe and at their head, rising above all, Alexandrina Victoria Regina, Queen of the United Kingdom of Great Britain and Ireland, Empress of India, in whose image, it was said, the very century was shaped.

The foreigner did not care for the tourists and their notions. He had been in Europe, had seen for himself its squalor and indignities, the harsh future which had been shaped for him in boarding schools and military training. He would have been an officer – a gentleman – a man of wealth and influence under whose pen lives were nothing more than numbers in a column, to be subtracted at will.

His living now, he'd long decided, was more honourable. This land, with its wide skies, its calm sea, could be engulfed, he sometimes thought, between his two arms. To the north the snow-capped Mount Hermon with its ruined Roman temples; to the south the great desert; in between the temperate plains and valleys with their small villages and their handful of towns, where life went on much as it always had. Moments of relative peace in this land were to be treasured. Occupation and war were its more natural state. Ancient Egyptians, Assyrians, Greeks, Romans, Byzantines, Rashiduns, Umayyads and Abbasids, Mongols, Crusaders, Ottomans, even Napoleon, all came and went, and only the land endured. The land did not care one whit for its occupiers, who they were, what they loved. Their blood soaked into the good earth and their bones bleached in the hot sun, and they could not protest, after the fact, could not scream into the storm that this was all worth it.

The foreigner knew why he killed. He did it for money, and because it was an honest job, for there had always been people who needed killing and men who were willing to pay to see it done. In that regard Ahmet Bey was a benign employer, for he murdered sparingly and paid better than most. The foreigner was under no illusions as to his place on the land. He was not born here, but land was just land, while people were people. This land belonged to the Ottomans by name, to the great powers of Europe by political sway and influence, to its tenants by habit and to Thomas Cook & Son by righteous covenant. The foreigner watched the tourists go past and then he rode on.

He did not hurry his horse. Tracking a man could not be rushed and the foreigner did not intend to. The quarry – this Hoffman, whatever his sin may be – would be on the run. He would be panicking, or worrying, for in hiding there was not much a man could do but fear and wait, and the more imagination he had the more he would conjure visions for himself of his end. The more they waited, the easier they were to catch. The foreigner let the horse enjoy the day, which anyway was drawing short now, and the air still cold up here in the heights. It would get warmer as they went down to sea level.

'Gustav!'

The foreigner reined his horse at the call. Coming towards him was a familiar figure – it was Hans Kübler, the butcher's son, from the German village outside the city walls.

The foreigner was known by several names: for the German Templers he was Gustav, for the Bedaween of the southern desert he was known jokingly as Abu al-Bunduqia, the Father of the Gun, so named for the rifle he carried with him. But to most he was simply the foreigner.

'Hans,' the foreigner said. He touched the brim of his hat in greeting. 'How go your affairs?'

The butcher's son grinned good-naturedly. He was young and beefy like the creatures he helped slaughter and clean. 'The End of Days is coming, Gustav,' he said, 'it is not too late to join us and be saved.'

The foreigner nodded. 'So you keep telling me. What if they do not come?'

'Then we shall make Palestine a paradise in waiting,' Kübler said. 'Already our villages flourish in Jaffa, Haifa and Jerusalem. We shall bring civilisation to this benighted land! We have doctors, engineers, hotels and workshops. We make soap, mill flour, and run the post. You will see, Gustav. People will come. It will not be long before the Kaiser's influence extends all over Palestine.'

'No doubt,' the foreigner said. He liked Hans, liked most of the Templers with whom he could speak in his native tongue. They were industrious and polite, and he had more than once taken shelter in their colonies when on a job. Their faith was no stranger to the foreigner than any other, for Palestine attracted believers the way a flower seduces bees. In this land people waited for the messiah the way a resident of London might await the morning train. Sooner or later, they reasoned, it would come. Religion made dirt into earth, it turned the dance of light in water from the physical interaction of rays and liquid into an omen of things to be. It imposed a story over hills and valleys which would otherwise be merely natural phenomena. It named *things*, personifying them. This was the land the foreigner had to move through.

That all these beliefs vehemently disagreed with one another did not cause any of their believers visible distress. Surely only they were right, the others wrong. It had always been thus.

'You have news?' the foreigner said. 'Where do you travel from?'

'I delivered fresh meat to the market in Jaffa,' Hans said. 'Returning now with some glassware my mother ordered months ago. It had arrived on the steamer, miraculously unbroken. She will be delighted, I think. How go things with you, Gustav?'

'I have a journey ahead of me,' the foreigner said. 'Though it should not be too long. Then to Beyrouth, I think, for a while.'

'You have a sweetheart there?' Hans said, smiling. 'The last time I was there the place was all but crawling with Frenchmen ostensibly there for the silk trade. Mark my words, Gustav – the Turks can't ⌐ e this land forever. They are old and weak and Europe is young ⌐ ungry. If not the Kaiser then the French, if not the French the He made a face, and the foreigner laughed.

'I pick a fight with no man,' he said easily. 'Nor would I underestimate our Ottoman friends, Hans. You should watch what you say.'

'I know,' Hans said, still smiling. 'But that's just between you and me. And besides, we are not under their power, you and I.'

This was true, and what made the foreigner so valuable to Ahmet Bey. As a foreign subject, he was beyond the reach of Ottoman law, a part of the devil's bargain that the Ottomans were forced to make with the European empires who helped them in their last war. They *were* weakened, the foreigner knew that. But he also knew they had ruled for centuries, and were not likely to give up their possessions easily.

'I won't make it to Jaffa tonight,' he said ruefully.

'The khan is open,' Hans said. 'Stay there if you are not in a rush. What is your business in Jaffa?'

Hans believed the foreigner to be a sort of dragoman, rough-hewn but ultimately decent: the sort of man sent on business on behalf of a busy employer, to ensure propriety and orderly conduct. At least, if he believed otherwise, he kept the thought to himself.

'The usual,' the foreigner said. 'Tides and trade, the ebb and flow. The Bey likes to keep me busy.'

'Oh,' Hans said, 'I heard some newly arrived Jews established a settlement outside Jaffa a month or two back. They want to turn it into some sort of agricultural commune. Can you imagine?'

'I doubt that will catch on,' the foreigner said. A group of Russian Orthodox pilgrims marched grimly up the slope just then. The men moved slowly and stoically, the women equally silent, all concentrating on the climb and on the long distance still to go. Unlike the British tourists they were without horses or carriages. The British came to gawk, the Russians to pray. They would stay at the hospices and monasteries, not in the hotels. To the tourists they seemed as exotic as the natives.

As Hans and the foreigner watched, one of the pilgrims in the front, an elderly man whose face, deeply lined, showed no expression but for the slightest sign of pain in the way his lips were pursed, slowly crumpled to the ground. From the group of pilgrims there rose a great consternation. The foreigner slid off his horse and ran to help, Hans joining him. Together they rolled the pilgrim onto his back and the foreigner loosened the pilgrim's clothing and checked his pulse, then shook his head grimly.

'I'm sorry,' he said. He had rudimentary Russian. An elderly woman, who had walked behind the pilgrim, burst into silent tears and, kneeling down, struck the chest of the fallen man over and over with her fists before her companions pulled her compassionately away.

'It was his heart,' a young Russian man said, 'we told him it was too hard, the journey, but he insisted.'

'At least he died in the Holy Land,' Hans said. 'This is as close to God and heaven as one can get on this earth.'

The young man nodded.

'We will bury him in Jerusalem,' he said. 'We owe him that. Thank you for your help. I will take it from here.' He shook their hands, one after the other. Then, with three other of the younger men, he lifted the dead man's body and they continued their march up the incline, saying nothing, and soon passed from sight.

'You never know the time of your death,' Hans said as he watched their receding backs. 'This feels like a bad omen, Gustav.'

'I do not believe in omens,' the foreigner said. 'And I must ride on. I will pass by your shop soon, Hans. Send my regards to your father.'

'Will do,' Hans said. 'Ride carefully, friend.'

'And you.'

The foreigner mounted his horse and spurred him on, riding fast now. The path grew narrow and the descent steep, sharp rocky slopes on either side of the road, and in the distance he could see the ruins of an old crusader castle on top a hill. The descent itself was the notorious Bab al-Wady, the Gate of the Valley. The foreigner slowed his horse as they went down. A fortified stone building stood some distance from the road here, one of the thirty-six guard stations positioned along the Jerusalem–Jaffa road. The foreigner could feel the bored gaze of the Ottoman guards on top, watching through the narrow gun slits. There was little cause for their intervention. Some of the stations had been put up as far back as the Egyptian occupation in the thirties.

As the foreigner reached the end of the incline where the valley started he came to another stone building, this one standing alone on the side of the road, where a couple of carriages were already parked and several horses stabled. This was the khan, a much newer establishment, and run by Jews. Beyond it by some distance he could see a sort of canvas town erected, this for the benefit of the Thomas Cook travellers, who made their own arrangements on the way to Jerusalem. Tourists did not stay at the khan.

5

The foreigner led his horse to the stone building. A boy came out and took the horse to the stables. He was short for his age, with a pale, serious face, as though he knew at too young an age about all the world's suffering. The foreigner fell into step beside him.

'How goes it, Samuel?' he said.

'The rooms are sold out,' the boy said, not bothering to look up. 'A party of Christian merchants from Beyrouth who have business in Jerusalem. They brought wine.' He said that disapprovingly.

'Have you come recently upon a man named Hoffman?' the foreigner asked. 'He's of your people,' he added as an afterthought.

'You will have to ask my father,' the boy said indifferently.

The foreigner took out the photograph of Hoffman that Zorik gave him.

'This rings a bell?' he said.

'It's a photograph,' the boy said. 'I wish I could have one made. There is a photographer in Jerusalem but my father says we do not need to make images of ourselves. I disagree but he does not listen to a word I say. I hate this place, you know. I dislike our visitors and have no time to pursue my interest in entomology.'

'Entomology?' the foreigner said.

'The study of insects,' the boy said. 'For example, think of the biblical locust, from which this land suffers to this day. Did you know there are many different species of the insect, though not many of them form themselves into large social groups? The Bible alone lists ten different kinds of locust, and moreover declares it kosher to eat. Perhaps these seasonal plagues could be transformed by an entrepreneurial mind. One could capture and cultivate the insects for food, set up factories to export them as a delicacy to Europe.' His eyes shone. 'The caviar of the Levant,' he said.

The foreigner looked askew at the boy.

'You're a little strange, aren't you?' he said.

'That's what my mother keeps telling me,' the boy said.

The foreigner gave him a coin and went into the khan, leaving the boy to tend to the horse. A comfortable room with a fire burning welcomed him, already busy with travellers who had stopped at the khan for the night, including the aforementioned Beyrouthi merchants. The proprietor, Mr Avigdor, was from an old Jerusalem family, and was known to keep – and to offer at reasonable rates – imported wines from Syria and the Lebanon, as well as whisky, which drew an assorted crowd on any day of the week. The air was thick with tobacco smoke and chatter, the fire kept the chill of the mountains firmly at bay, and the foreigner made his way to the long wooden counter that ran along the far wall. Behind it stood Mr Avigdor himself, a tall, stooped man with arms muscled from the never-ceasing work of managing a khan. Behind him the foreigner could see, through the open door leading to the kitchen, Mr Avigdor's wife at the stove, stirring a pot of spiced mutton stew. The smell made him hungry. Mrs Avigdor was young and pretty, her long black hair tied back. She moved a stray strand of hair from her damp brow as she stirred and the foreigner watched.

Mr Avigdor, raising his head, said, 'Oh, it's you, Foreigner,' without much enthusiasm. Unlike the German butcher's son, Mr Avigdor had a shrewder understanding of what the foreigner did for Ahmet Bey.

The foreigner pulled his attention away from Mrs Avigdor and nodded affably.

'Your son wants to sell locusts to German hausfraus,' the foreigner said.

Mr Avigdor sighed. He placed a tumbler on the counter and poured a measure of whisky for the foreigner, then thought about it and brought out another and poured again.

'You're buying,' he said.

'Sure,' the foreigner said. He put a coin on the counter.

Mr Avigdor raised his glass, the foreigner did likewise, and they touched the sides of their cups together in a gentle tap of salute.

'L'chaim,' Mr Avigdor said.

'Prost,' the foreigner said. He drank. The whisky went down smooth.

'The boy needs schooling,' Mr Avigdor said. He removed the coin from the counter. 'But I am fond of him and do not wish to send him away. You had a good education, back in Europe?'

'The best,' the foreigner said. 'So they told me.'

'And look at you now,' Mr Avigdor said. He poured two more drinks. The foreigner reached for a coin. Mr Avigdor shook his head.

'Thanks,' the foreigner said. He raised his glass in salute.

'L'chaim,' he said.

'Prost,' Mr Avigdor said.

This done, the foreigner slid the photograph across the desk.

'That's Hoffman,' Mr Avigdor said.

'You know him?'

'He stopped by a few nights ago, in a hurry. Said he was going away,' Mr Avigdor said.

'Did he say where?' the foreigner asked.

'No. Is he in trouble?'

The foreigner shrugged.

'I figured,' Mr Avigdor said. 'Listen, we have no rooms for the night.'

'I don't need a room,' the foreigner said.

'You're riding on to Jaffa?'

'In the morning,' the foreigner said. 'I'll just sleep outside tonight.'

'Suit yourself,' Mr Avigdor said.

'I'll take some of your wife's mutton stew,' the foreigner said. 'If that's alright. And a bottle of wine, something decent.'

'I have a nice dry Ksara red,' Mr Avigdor said. 'From the Beqaa Valley. The Jesuits make it.'

'Sure,' the foreigner said. 'I'll take that.'

'Find a seat,' Mr Avigdor said. 'I'll bring it to you. And the food.'

'Thanks.' The foreigner put money on the counter, Mr Avigdor took it. The foreigner went to find a table. There was a seat against the back wall in the corner and the foreigner took it. He never sat with his back to the door. He liked to see whoever was coming.

'Foreigner,' the man on his left said, grinning. He was a grizzled man with a thick beard woven with white, and wore a bandolier across his broad chest. 'Join us.'

'Sheikh Abdullah,' the foreigner said, nodding his greeting in return. The sheikh was the leader of a wandering tribe of Turkomans, those Seljukids who came originally from Central Asia. Some had lived in Palestine since before the crusades, others were more recent arrivals. The sheikh had a fearsome reputation as a warrior. He also liked a drop of the bitter stuff. He had a bottle of whisky in front of him, which he did not offer to share.

'How goes Ahmet Bey's business?' the sheikh said.

The foreigner shrugged.

'The Bey's business is his own,' he said.

'And yet you are abroad, Foreigner. Are you coming or going?'

'Going,' the foreigner said.

'As I thought,' Sheikh Abdullah said. 'As I thought. May God have mercy on your quarry's soul.'

'Do you believe in the existence of the soul?' the foreigner said. 'Considering you have sent your fair share of them to the afterlife, so it is told.'

Sheikh Abdullah laughed uproariously. 'Only those who deserved it,' he said. 'The soul endures, Foreigner. What use are their mortal remains? Only God judges. Do you not have faith?'

The foreigner remembered a time when he was still a boy. A sergeant-teacher, the one they all feared, had caught him by the scruff of the neck for some perceived misdemeanour and dragged him outside to the large courtyard before the school building. A trough of water ran along one side for the animals. It rained, but the teacher was heedless of the rain. The skies were black. The boy squirmed under the painful grasp, the fingers digging painfully into his neck. The teacher dragged him to the trough and pushed his face into the water. He could not breathe. The man's hold on his neck choked him. When he released the boy the boy coughed and cried, and the teacher said, 'You must be baptised, boy, for your sins.'

'I do not know that I have much use for a soul,' the foreigner said.

Sheikh Abdullah laughed again, and the foreigner realised he was quite drunk by now. Mr Avigdor came over then with the promised bottle of wine and a bowl of his wife's stew. The foreigner nodded his thanks and turned his attention to the food. When he later looked back to the counter he saw Mrs Avigdor there, watching him quietly, her face thoughtful and very lovely. The foreigner returned to the food without saying anything. He dipped bread into the last of the bowl and followed it up with a sip of wine, noticing Sheikh Abdullah looking a little longingly at the bottle. The foreigner pushed the bottle towards him.

'Please,' he said.

'I couldn't possibly,' Sheikh Abdullah said. 'Refuse, I mean.' He laughed at his own joke and poured himself a generous helping. His men, sitting around him, said little. They kept watch on the door.

'You are expecting trouble?' the foreigner said. His hand went to rest lightly on the butt of his pistol, under the table.

'No trouble,' Badr, the man on the sheikh's left, said. 'You can relax, Foreigner.'

'Trouble follows him around,' the sheikh said, 'this is why he is always so morose. Good wine.'

The foreigner pushed his bowl away.

'Then what?' he said.

'Just business,' Badr said. He took out a pouch of tobacco and began rolling a cigarette with quick, efficient movements. The foreigner watched. Badr's fingers were stained with nicotine.

'May I have one?' he said.

Badr wordlessly passed him the finished cigarette and began rolling another. The foreigner fished in his pocket for matches and lit up. The rough tobacco singed his lips and he blew out a blue cloud of smoke, feeling a pleasant lightness in his head. When he glanced to the bar he saw Mrs Avigdor again watching him.

The door opened just then, blowing in a gust of cold wind. It was dark outside. A man entered, dressed in travelling clothes, wearing jodhpurs, leather riding gloves and an Alpine-style hat with a heavy brim and dark band. Behind him came two Bedaween. The man took off his hat, looked around, located Sheikh Abdullah and beamed genially. He came over, hand extended for a shake.

'My friend!' he said.

'Monsieur Alphonse,' the sheikh said. He shook the Frenchman's hand. 'Please, sit,' he said.

Badr and his men looked at the two Bedaween. The two Bedaween stared at Badr and his men. The Frenchman, Monsieur Alphonse, waved them away in some impatience. The two men, keeping their eyes on the Turkomans, retreated to a table by the door and sat there watching mutely.

'We are all friends here,' Sheikh Abdullah said.

'Indeed, indeed,' the Frenchman said. 'But one must be careful on these roads.'

'Of course,' the sheikh said.

Monsieur Alphonse looked at the foreigner questioningly.

'He's a friend,' Sheikh Abdullah said, waving his hand dismissively. 'A foreigner here, like yourself.'

'Oh!' Monsieur Alphonse said, pleased. 'Are you French?'

'Habsburgian,' the foreigner said, smiling faintly.

'How wonderful!' Monsieur Alphonse said. 'Well, then, there is no concern here between us gentlemen. Indeed, there is no secrecy as to the nature of my business. I often come and go from the Holy Land. My business takes me all over the Levant.'

'You are a merchant?' the foreigner said, and Monsieur Alphonse laughed.

'In a way,' he said. He rubbed his hands together. The foreigner noticed he hadn't taken off his riding gloves. 'Barkeep!' Monsieur Alphonse called. 'A moment of your time.'

'Monsieur Alphonse,' Mr Avigdor said, appearing. 'You're back so soon.'

'I cannot keep away, Mr Avigdor!' Monsieur Alphonse said jovially. 'You have prepared my room? And a billet for my men in the stables.'

'Rooms are all taken,' Mr Avigdor said.

'Sacré bleu!' Monsieur Alphonse said.

'I will make up a bed for you in the kitchen,' Mr Avigdor said. 'It is the warmest room in the house.'

'That will do admirably,' Monsieur Alphonse said. 'May I trouble you for a small coffee, too?'

Mr Avigdor nodded, then withdrew. His boy, Samuel, came in then and went to stand by their table.

'I want to see,' he said.

'Samuel!' Monsieur Alphonse said. 'I have something for you.'

'What is it?' the boy said. The foreigner wondered if the boy ever smiled.

Monsieur Alphonse reached in his pocket and, with the flourish of a magician, produced a small object in his hand. The boy's eyes widened.

'Is that a *scarab*?' he said.

'I remembered you liked beetles,' Monsieur Alphonse said, smiling happily. He put the small object into the boy's open hand. 'It's late Middle Kingdom,' he said. 'Three and a half thousand years old, give or take. I picked up a bulk lot in Alexandria a couple of months ago.'

'You can see the humeral callosities!' Samuel said. The foreigner was not sure what humeral callosities were. A part of a beetle, he supposed. He looked with interest at the object. It was pale-blue carved stone, roughly the shape of a beetle, with inscriptions cut into the material.

'Is it sandstone?' he said.

'Faience,' Monsieur Alphonse said. 'Egyptian ceramic.'

'It must be rare,' the foreigner said.

'Not really,' Monsieur Alphonse said. 'There were so many.'

'Is this your business?' the foreigner said. 'Antiquities?'

'It is indeed. And with that, gentlemen, shall we get to it?' Monsieur Alphonse said to Sheikh Abdullah and his men.

Sheikh Abdullah nodded. Badr brought out a sack from under the table and opened it. He began laying pieces on the table.

'Very nice, very nice!' Monsieur Alphonse said. The foreigner watched as the Frenchman picked up and examined objects from the table, all the while muttering to himself.

'Beautiful,' he said, holding up a small painted clay vase. 'Hellenistic, early Ptolemaic, I would say. Can you see the artist impression of Zeus there, still so fresh, yes, I will take it—'

He went on in this vein, going over a handful of what were apparently Tyrian half-shekels – 'The Temple's coin, they called it, of course,' Monsieur Alphonse said, 'for the temple tax, you see. Always popular with collectors, the genuine article, I mean, not those awful fakes they make up in Jerusalem these days—'

'No fakes,' Sheikh Abdullah said.

'Quite, quite, my dear sheikh, you always do deliver the goods,' Monsieur Alphonse said. 'Hallo, what's this? Roman glassware?

A little crude, but beautifully preserved. Where do you *find* all of these, my dear sheikh?'

'They are everywhere,' Sheikh Abdullah said. 'You just have to know to look. Here,' he said. 'I brought you something.'

He took out a new object from the bag beside him. The foreigner watched it with interest. It was a ridged flint rock. One side had chipped smooth grooves as if to enable fingers to comfortably rest there. The other side was a sharp, jagged edge like a knife. The foreigner said, 'Could I...?'

He waited for a nod and picked up the knife, if that's what it was. It fit perfectly in his palm, and he tested the edge with the tip of a finger. It was still sharp.

'Ancient humans,' Monsieur Alphonse said without much interest. 'Eighty thousand years, maybe one hundred thousand.'

'They lie about everywhere,' Sheikh Abdullah said. 'In the fields.'

'I can take a bulk lot,' Monsieur Alphonse said, 'if you can have them ready for collection in the port in Jaffa. But there's not much profit in them for me. I could take, say, forty pounds to a hundredweight?'

'Sure,' Sheikh Abdullah said. 'We could accommodate that.'

The foreigner stared entranced at the stone tool. Its very age weighed down his palm. He closed his eyes, imagined lifting the blade, cutting through some ancient beast's hide, stripping the fur from the meat as he hacked—

And for a moment the khan was gone, the air of smoke and fumes, the conversation, Greek pottery and Roman glass, and she was in a cave, the knife in her hand just as sharp as it would be a hundred centuries hence. Dry pine needles covered the floor of the cave and made a soft, homey sound as her husband stepped over them. She looked up at him and smiled, the leather of the gazelle on her knees scraped clean now of sinew and blood, and her husband, with his strange narrow head, his strange long arms, brushed her face with his fingers gently as he went past to tend to the fire—

The foreigner opened his eyes; the vision fled. For a moment he had been elsewhere.

'Can I... Can I keep it?' he said. His voice felt hoarse with disuse – as though he hadn't spoken for a hundred thousand years.

Sheikh Abdullah waved his hand.

'Sure,' Monsieur Alphonse said. 'I have no need for it, myself.'

The foreigner pocketed the ancient knife. The boy, Samuel, lost interest in the display on the table and wandered off, clutching his scarab beetle. Monsieur Alphonse and Sheikh Abdullah began a long negotiation over the various items, each of them seeming to enjoy themselves hugely. The foreigner picked up his bottle of wine and bid them good night, then made his way outside. He had lost interest in antiquities.

6

The foreigner went to check on his horse. The horse nuzzled him and the foreigner patted him on the graceful curve of his neck. The horse suffered the indignities of stables and civilisation but it wanted open country and the speed that came with running wild and free.

'Soon,' the foreigner promised. 'Soon.'

He stepped out under a sky full of stars. In the enormity of night the khan looked alone and desolate, squatting there between valley and hills, a single outpost and bulwark against the night. In the canvas town of holidaymakers only a few torches burned, and someone played 'Greensleeves' on guitar, badly. Smoke rose from the khan's chimney, the light of barn lanterns inside spilling softly through the underside of the door. The foreigner sighed, taking in a breath of the cold, fresh night air, and picked up his bag and carried it beyond the khan to a secluded section between rocks and there he pitched his tent. The great comet was still visible overhead, but the foreigner did not need its faint luminescence to set up camp, and he went through the motions quickly and efficiently. He made no fire for himself. When he was done he sat in the dark, cross-legged, and thought of the vision he had seen, of the strange ancient woman he briefly was. It was peculiar, and he picked up the stone tool again and turned it over and between his fingers, marvelling at its familiarity, at how timeless it seemed to be. As he sat there the last notes of a song faded away. The last of the torches in the camp was extinguished. He watched Sheikh Abdullah and his men, their business evidently concluded, depart the khan and ride off on their horses. Still the foreigner sat unmoving, watching and listening. He was invisible in this spot in the dark. Presently he saw even the light from the khan go out. The smoke from the chimney thinned and dispersed. Only coals would be left burning. In the silence of the night the foreigner heard the soft tread of hooves, and saw two dark figures, mounted on horses, come down from the incline. They moved quietly, and he could not make out their faces. They stopped a short distance from the khan and seemed to confer in low voices. Then, a decision apparently made, turned off the road and vanished into the dark.

Interesting, the foreigner thought. He remained sitting. Somewhere nearby a snake rustled softly as it slithered along rocks still warm from the day's sun. A bulbul called from the branch of a tree overhead, startled, as though sensing danger, then fell silent. The foreigner remained sitting. The back door of the khan opened quietly, and a small dark figure slipped out and closed it behind her. He heard her footsteps, the only sound in the whole of the sleeping world. Then she was there, standing before him, still not much more than a silhouette. It was Mrs Avigdor.

'Foreigner,' she said.

'Miriam,' the foreigner said. He reached out his hand and she took it and he pulled her to him. Her long black hair fell across his face, soft and smelling of smoke and grape hyacinth-scented oil. The foreigner buried his face in the soft crook of Miriam's neck.

'I missed you,' he said.

'They're all asleep,' she said. 'We have to be quick.'

Her hands were on his chest. She pushed him, not roughly, and he let himself fall back. She lay beside him, her closeness with the warmth of the burning coals inside. She reached into his trousers. Her hand was strong and calloused. He quickened under her touch. He went to kiss her but she turned her face away.

'I forgot,' he said. She pulled up his shirt, ran her nails down his naked skin. He squirmed under her and she laughed, then rose and straddled him in one sinuous motion. Her strong thighs gripped him, and she put her hand on his face, holding him captive, then leaned down and bit his lip, so hard that the pain coursed through him and he tasted blood.

'Hey!' he said, and she laughed again, quietly, and her hands reached below his waist again, finding him ready. She lifted cloth and slid onto him and as he gasped she put her hand on his mouth, silencing him. They copulated, quickly and urgently, the great comet passing overhead. Her heat and her need overtook his, and she shuddered and leaned down close to him, her eyes closed, her hands wrapping round his neck as if to choke him. He climaxed then, following her, and she slowly lay on top of him, the both of them spent.

'I shouldn't have come,' she said.

'You should have,' he said. She looked into his eyes, curious, serious, with some regret.

'It's just that you are so ephemeral,' she said.

'What?'

She rolled off him and sat up on the ground. 'You're like a luftl seed,' she said. 'The lion's teeth flower. What do you call it? Dandelion?'

'Löwenzahn?' the foreigner said.

'You have no roots,' she said. 'You just… float.'

'The seeds land and plant roots,' he said.

'Those that make it,' she said. She brought out a couple of rolled cigarettes and handed one to him. The foreigner propped himself up on one elbow, reaching for the matches with the other. He handed her the box and she lit the match, cupping it in her palm so it wouldn't be seen, and lit both of their cigarettes.

'I got them from Badr,' she said.

The foreigner coughed smoke, nodded. He uncorked the bottle

of wine he'd taken from the khan and passed it to her and she took a swig.

'I hate this place,' she said.

'You were born here?' the foreigner said.

'My family has lived here for generations,' Miriam said. 'I wanted them to send me to Germany to study. I showed talent in painting as a child. But girls don't get to go to Europe. When I met Avigdor—'

'Mr Avigdor's name is Avigdor?' the foreigner said, surprised.

'Avigdor Avigdor,' Miriam said.

The foreigner laughed.

'Why is that funny?' Miriam said. 'A name's a name.'

'Oh,' the foreigner said. 'I'm sorry. Go on.'

'When I met him he seemed so… sophisticated. He was born in Safed, the son of an old kabbalist family there. He studied to be a rabbi but he turned away from his faith, I never really knew why. I didn't care. I thought he was going places. That we could go to Istanbul, or Rome, anywhere but here. The world moves so fast elsewhere, and so slowly here… Then Samuel was born, and Avigdor lost the job he had as a shipping clerk in Jaffa, and we had nowhere to turn. This place was a last resort. Now I'm stuck here on the mountain road catering to pilgrims, passing merchants and the occasional brigand like you.' She blew out smoke. 'Why did you have to come here?' she said.

He wondered what he could tell her. There was not much to tell. Miserable childhood, cold rains, huge draughty rooms stuffed with the furniture of long-dead people, more long-dead people staring down on him every day of his life from the walls. One chance to escape, a Grand Tour of the Levant, all paid for. He had been bred to ride horses, handle swords and guns and endure hardship. The things that made a man of his social class a man. He saw the pyramids, he sailed down the Nile. Ancient gods stared down on him disapprovingly in Abu Simbel – just a different version of the family portraits back home. In Alexandria he read a book. *The Last of the Mohicans*, by Fenimore Cooper. He sailed from Alexandria to Acre, an old, walled town with a great fort rising overhead. The foreigner made land in this old crusader town. His first night he was accosted by two robbers, hungry and made fearless by hashish. He killed them both that night, acting out not of well-honed instinct but simple curiosity at what he could do. Then he knew, and he stood over them, the moon overhead, wondering what to do next. He hid the bodies as best he could behind rubbish thrown in the street, stole a horse and fled into the Galilee. He had only a little conversational Arabic. He had no idea where he was headed. But as he rode out that night under that moon and all those stars, the horse moving underneath him, almost a part of him, following a dirt track road into the ancient hills where Jesus first learned to rebel, he felt freer than he ever had.

'I guess we don't feel the same way about this place,' he said.

'Now he says he is going to become a territorialist,' Miriam said.

'I'm sorry?' the foreigner said.

'My husband. Avigdor. You've heard of territorialists? They are Jews who argue for the right of self-determination for the Jewish people. Who say we need a land of our own. My husband said Napoleon, had he succeeded in conquering Palestine, would have declared it a Jewish state.'

'But Napoleon did not succeed in his conquest,' the foreigner said.

'It doesn't matter,' Miriam said. Her cigarette was finished and she dropped it on the ground. She seemed tired now, and a little sad. 'The idea remains. And the Jews of Europe suffer murderous riots and suchlike. Many try to go to America. Others might try to come here.'

'Why here?' the foreigner said.

'Because they can. Because they believe this land was once ours, and could be so again. Avigdor wants us to join with some other like-minded friends of his. They wish to establish some kind of agricultural settlement, to grow oranges and raise sheep. My hands are rough enough from laundry and cooking and washing dishes. I will die on a farm. But he says we must reclaim our land, by working it.'

'I'm sorry,' the foreigner said.

'My boy is only interested in insects,' Miriam said. 'Perhaps it will be good for him with other families, other children. I would leave Avigdor, but where would I go? So I stay here.'

She stared into the dark. The foreigner sat up and tried to put his arm around her. She pushed him off, not harshly, then said, 'I must go back now.'

The foreigner remained seated as Miriam walked away. He saw her shadow, heard the back door of the khan open and close softly. He wondered at these territorialists, who couldn't number more than a handful of people, surely. He corked the bottle of wine, put it inside the tent and went to sleep.

Dawn woke him. A cockerel crowed in the back of the khan, beside the small vegetable patch where Miriam tried in vain to grow cucumbers and tomatoes. The foreigner emerged out of the tent. In the distance, the Thomas Cook tourists were being roused for the journey to Jerusalem. The dragomans went between the tents banging on metal pots. This din was a familiar one on the road. It made the foreigner smile. The smell of coffee and cooking breakfast arose from their camp. In the khan, too, people were waking, already the Beyrouthi merchants were mounted on their horses, no doubt intent on prompt arrival in Jerusalem for their trade. The foreigner watched them depart. He got up and relieved himself behind a pine, then rinsed his mouth with tooth powder. After packing his tent he wandered back into the khan. Mr Avigdor stood behind the counter, adding up numbers mournfully on a sheet of paper.

'Foreigner,' he said, looking up. 'You're still here.'

'I will depart shortly,' the foreigner said.

'Coffee?' Mr Avigdor said.

'Please.'

The foreigner took a table. The Frenchman, Monsieur Alphonse, sat nearby. The foreigner nodded to him politely. The boy, Samuel, arrived then with a tray holding a coffee pot and cup. He placed both on the table before the foreigner.

'Thank you,' the foreigner said. He felt momentarily ashamed before the boy. Samuel watched him with dark unblinking eyes.

'Good luck with those locusts,' the foreigner said.

The boy left. The foreigner drank his coffee. He left a coin on the table. He thought, perhaps he shouldn't have come. He did not see Mrs Avigdor.

He went outside and got his horse. The open road beckoned. In moments, the lonely khan and its occupants were lost behind him.

7

The road to Ramleh was not long, and the foreigner did not intend to tarry there, but fate had other plans. He rode his horse moderately but the horse, sensing the plains, did not wish to trot where it could gallop, and the foreigner did not wish to restrain him. The road, however, was busy with traffic, villagers on their carts, the various and competing postal-service carriages coming and going, pilgrims similarly both coming and going and tourists likewise, not to mention merchants and their cargo, men to guard that cargo, horsemen who went on business known only to themselves, and kids by the side of the road taking advantage of all these goings-on to offer large sweet figs picked from the trees, the last of the summer's prickly pears, goats' cheese and unleavened bread. A group of Jews in long black coats and furred hats walked, chatting animatedly, in the direction of Jaffa; an elderly Englishwoman, cooling herself with a bamboo fan, was carried grandly in a palanquin in the opposite direction. The foreigner had to reign in his horse, as much as he too longed for speed. Beyond the road bloomed autumn crocuses, winter hyacinths and squills, which some call sea onions. Here and there a village appeared, surrounded by sturdy walls of cactuses. As he got nearer Ramleh orchards and vegetable gardens appeared. Behind the foreigner came a cloud of dust and the travellers on the road moved away from the approaching rider with curses. The rider, when he materialised out of the dust, slowed his horse as he noticed him and called out, 'Foreigner!' He was laughing as he did so.

The foreigner said, 'Simeon.' He was wary of this apparition, though not unduly so. Simeon was not a professional killer but a yavaci, that is, a hunter of runaway slaves. As such, he only killed when he had to. The foreigner stared at him in curiosity. Simeon was the son of a Turkish nobleman and a Crimean slave. His father being tender-hearted, he raised Simeon a free man, giving him excellent education in Istanbul and designating him for army service. But Simeon, it seemed, had had other plans. The foreigner was unsure of the exact circumstances of Simeon's exile – he had killed someone, or got somebody pregnant, or some combination of the two – and was sent out of the way to Palestine, where his father reasoned he could cause less trouble. Now Simeon rode side by side with the foreigner, and he tossed him a small bottle, of the sort holding cordial, and said, 'Nadiya Brutti bid me gift you this if I ran into you.'

The foreigner uncorked the small bottle and dabbed a tiny amount of the tincture onto a handkerchief and this he put to his nose and mouth. This diluted opium sent his mind into a pleasant spin, and he put away the handkerchief and bottle both and nodded his appreciation.

'You knew I would be on the road?' he said.

'Relax,' Simeon said. He seemed in good spirits. He was a huge man, his bare arms covered in tattoos of birds, reptiles and invertebrates, so that he looked almost like a human bestiary. 'I heard you were out on your master's orders once again.'

'I have no master,' the foreigner said.

'All men must serve a master,' Simeon said. 'Yet all must have their pride.'

'I only work for him,' the foreigner said.

'As do we all,' Simeon said, 'from time to time. Though I am on an unrelated mission, as it happens. A matter of some faithful servant, many years in happy servitude, who snapped last week and killed his master in the bath just as the man was reaching for the soap. A tragic story. The family, of course, wish not only revenge but the return of their property, for the poor fool, no doubt terrified at what he had done, took to his heels. In truth I think the sons are only too glad of the way things turned out, for they stand to inherit a considerable fortune. Perhaps the slave will be rewarded… If not here then in the afterlife. I am bid bring him back alive, at any rate. And so – shall we ride together?'

'I'm going to Jaffa,' the foreigner said.

'As am I,' Simeon said. 'Though I doubt my quarry will be there.'

'I doubt mine will be, either,' the foreigner muttered. 'But one must check.'

'One must be methodical,' Simeon said, nodding. 'I am glad you are not in my business, Foreigner, or I would have competition I scarcely want or need.'

'Your business is safe from me,' the foreigner said.

They rode on companionably. Ramleh came into view then, a pleasant town of low stone houses, surrounded by a thick fence of cactuses, with tall palm trees and minarets dotted here and there in the thicket of the town.

As they rode in through the gate the bells of the Franciscan monastery rang for prayers, and from across the street came the matching cry of a muezzin from a mosque. A small market welcomed the travellers, selling local tomatoes and olives, garlic and oil at one stand, soap from the small local factory at another. Already there was a fresh group of tourists who had just arrived and were walking around in search of sustenance and local colour on their way to Jerusalem. Nor were they short of it, for standing apart from the other stalls of the market was one booth manned by a peculiar individual, a man in a dirty cassock, with hair long and matted in braids. When he smiled, which was often, his mouth flashed with its abundance of gold teeth, and when he raised his voice, also often, it carried easily throughout the market.

'Brothers, sisters, heed my words!' the man cried, raising his arms dramatically. 'For the coming of the shepherd is proclaimed! To hasten his arrival the conditions must be met, starting with the building of the Third Temple in Jerusalem! I am but a poor man, but God has given my life meaning, to hasten the return of our lord! Give generously, O pious pilgrims, for the society for the second coming of which I am but a humble servant! Oh, it's you, Foreigner,' he said, letting his arms drop as the foreigner and Simeon, having dismounted, arrived at his stall.

'Brother Titian,' the foreigner said in greeting.

'Up to your old tricks again, old man?' Simeon said, smiling.

Titian smiled back, flashing his gold teeth. All who knew him knew that this was how he liked to keep his fortune (such as it was), for he often said the mouth was the strongbox of the body.

'Raising money for a noble cause,' Titian said.

'Build the temple yet?' the foreigner said.

'We shall be laying down the foundation stone any day now!' Titian said loudly, as a woman came by to look. She stared with interest at the model of the temple, made out of papier-mâché, which Titian had on display.

'Are you a monk?' she said.

'Madame, I was the personal secretary to His Holiness Pius IX!' Titian said with absolute authority. 'For years I toiled by his side in Rome as he set the Immaculate Conception into dogma! It was he who said to me, he said, "Titian, go forth to the Holy Land, go ye to the town from which hailed Joseph of Arimathea! And there beseech the good folks, the faithful of the Christian faith, to help build the temple so you may usher the dawn of the new age, and hasten the arrival of our saviour!" Amen, sister! I accept pounds, franks and liras as well as hotel coupons.'

He looked at her expectantly.

'And this will go towards the temple?' the woman said, hesitating.

'What else?' Titian said. 'Just look at me, good lady. I am but a poor brother, an ascetic with no earthly needs of my own. All I do I do for our lord.'

The woman rifled in her purse and handed Brother Titian an English sovereign.

'God bless you,' Titian said. He made the money disappear.

'God bless you, Brother,' the woman said. She walked on, to look at soap.

'A moment of your time, Brother?' the foreigner said.

'To every thing there is a season, and a time to every purpose under the heaven,' Titian said. 'Ecclesiastes. What profit hath he that worketh in that wherein he laboureth?'

'Depends on what information you can give us,' the foreigner said.

'Buy you a coffee,' Simeon offered.

'That is kind of you, Brother Simeon,' Titian said piously. 'But my only reward is simple hard cash.'

The foreigner smiled despite himself, and he took out the photograph and showed it to Titian.

'Hoffman,' Titian said without missing a beat.

'You know him?' the foreigner said, surprised.

'He's bad news, Foreigner.' Titian hesitated. 'I had a run-in with him a few months ago where he became quite agitated and rude. He called me a crank and a phoney. Accused me of preying on the gullibility of others! Can you believe it? This was after I sold him a map that decisively shows the final resting place of the lost treasures of the Second Temple.'

'Decisively,' the foreigner said.

'Quite so! We almost came to blows.'

'Did he pass through here recently?' the foreigner said.

'He did, Foreigner. And in a hurry, too. There is no one who passes through Ramleh, called Arimathea in ancient times, of which I am not aware. I thought nothing of it when I saw him, but now I take it he has done something to offend the higher power in Jerusalem?'

'He has indeed,' the foreigner said, and Brother Titian sucked his teeth in consternation.

'May God have mercy on his soul,' he said, crossing himself.

'Did he say where he was heading?' the foreigner asked.

'Alas, we were not on speaking terms,' Titian said.

'What of a slave, somewhat elderly, goes by Dmitry?' Simeon said. 'Would have come through here only recently. Has a bald patch on the left side of his head from an old wound—'

'Dmitry, of course,' Brother Titian said. 'A gentle soul. He stopped to chat a while, quite distraught. It seems his master has had some sort of accident.'

'Knifed in the bath,' Simeon said. 'By the slave's own hand.'

'Well,' Titian said. 'Nobody's perfect.'

'Did *he* say where he was heading?' Simeon said.

'Alas,' Titian said. 'But the road leads to Jaffa, so one may make a reasonable assumption.'

'Here,' the foreigner said, handing him a coin.

'Only a grush?' Titian said.

'I'll get you next time,' Simeon said, patting his pockets theatrically and coming up empty. 'For now, consider this handsome sum as coming from both of us.'

'With men like you,' Titian said, 'it's no wonder the second coming is taking so long.'

Simeon laughed and slapped the con man on the back. Brother Titian flinched but recovered his good spirits. Turning his back on the two men, he raised his arms to draw the attention of the tourists before they departed, and began to sing, in a high, reedy voice: 'Gather, sinners, where you may! Celebrate this coming day! He who died shall live again – the beginning, not the end! Oh, Jesus! Jesus is saving me!'

'Titian has never been any further than Damascus,' Simeon said as he and the foreigner walked away. 'I don't even think he's a Christian.'

The foreigner shrugged. 'Everyone must make a living. His seems as honest as any.'

'Less honest than some,' Simeon said. They stopped at a place where an old Bedaween man had a small fire burning, and paid for coffee and khubz, the fresh unleavened bread the old man baked on a small, portable clay oven. The foreigner picked at small, sour olives. He spat out the pits. A mangy dog came and whined at them for scraps, and Simeon kicked it, not hard, until it went away.

8

It was not yet midday. The foreigner and Simeon rode the ancient King's Highway, and the foreigner, idling in the saddle, thought of all those who had passed on this road before. Slaves once carried stones to the temple. Romans came to raze Jerusalem to the ground. Crusaders came to lay their own claim to the city, and on and on they went, a silent army of ghosts, their ethereal forms raising dust into the clear air. And who came before? he wondered. What ancients, their names, if they ever had them, once trod here, bygone cave people and the like? Their remains were everywhere, and he once again fingered the flint knife he was given, and thought of who might have once used it. This was the land of the dead, traversed still by the living. Now Simeon said, 'Whoh, whoh,' and the foreigner, aroused from his daydream, similarly reined in his horse, for blocking the road before them there came a great herd of goats.

Goats, the foreigner knew, were like locusts. They swarmed and ate everything in their path. He cursed, and Simeon laughed, and together they sat atop their horses and watched the herd. Boys ran on either side of the animals, shouting when need be to keep the animals in place. Behind them came camels, the men in keffiyehs covering their faces against the dust. One of the camel riders, noticing the two men, drove his beast towards them and hailed them with a cry.

'Who is that?' Simeon said. 'Abu Karim, is that you?'

'The Angel of Death and the Angel of Tears,' the Bedaween said. 'Azrael and Cassiel riding together abroad. An ill omen, the sight of you brings.'

'A bit dramatic, old man,' Simeon said, laughing. 'Since angels are not known to be hindered by the appearance of goats.'

'Ah, but these are not just any goats,' Abu Karim said. 'For like the Gerasene pigs their souls are those of demons!'

'All goats are demonic,' Simeon said. 'Just look at them.'

'Indeed they are,' Abu Karim said. 'Indeed they are. Yet I am fond of them.'

'Where are you heading?' the foreigner said. Abu Karim turned his shrouded gaze on him.

'Foreigner,' he said. 'We are to the fertile fields near Lydda, I think, for the goats are hungry.'

'Goats are always hungry,' the foreigner said.

'No doubt, you speak truth,' Abu Karim said. 'I could sell you one, should you wish. You could turn a profit, taking it to the market in Jaffa.'

'How long have you known us, Abu Karim?' Simeon said. 'Do you mistake us for goat traders?'

'Take a goat for your sins,' Abu Karim said. 'As Leviticus says, so you may be absolved.'

'But I have not sinned,' Simeon said.

'All men sin,' Abu Karim said.

'I'm not buying a stupid goat!' Simeon said, his temper flaring.

The foreigner smiled. The idea of this trade tickled him.

'You are right,' he said. 'No man is above judgement, come the final days, and when my time comes, as it surely must, I would feel lighter in my heart if my sins did not weigh quite so heavily against me. How much for the goat?'

'I'll do you a good price, Foreigner,' Abu Karim said.

They haggled briefly, but the foreigner's heart wasn't in it, and he tossed Abu Karim a gold Napoleon as Simeon shook his head in exasperation.

'You see?' Simeon complained. 'This is why they call you Foreigner, man. You are worse than those British tourists.'

'Add it to my list of sins, then,' the foreigner said. 'But I have my heart set on this goat.'

'I suppose we could eat it, if the need arises,' Simeon said. 'Or get a doe, at least, so you may milk it.'

Abu Karim whistled. A boy rushed over, was given his orders and ran off again. He came back leading a young goat on a string. The goat stared up at the men on their horses and snorted derisively.

'He is young and tender,' Abu Karim said. 'He will take on your misdeeds for some time to come.'

Apparently he wasn't joking about using the animal as a scapegoat.

Simeon laughed then, his good humour restored. 'I will slaughter the damned thing myself,' he said.

'You will not,' the foreigner said. He accepted the string from the boy and tied it to his saddle. 'I was never allowed a pet when I was a boy,' he said.

'Goats are not pets, they're pests,' Simeon said. But he shrugged.

The last stragglers of the herd passed, and the road was once again clear. Abu Karim raised his hand in goodbye.

'Ma'a salama,' he said.

The two riders, now accompanied by the kid goat, continued on their way.

It was noticeably warmer now, the cold mountain air dissipating like a bad dream, and a humid wind now blowing gently from the fast-approaching sea. The horses chafed at their pace. The kid goat trotted happily enough along, baying disdainfully from time to time at the riders, the horses or the poor condition of the world in general. The first orange trees came into view, the smell of citrus perfuming the air, and the foreigner felt a gladness lifting in his heart. Jerusalem brooded on its mountaintop, wrapped within its walls like an old man with a blanket clutched against the night. Soon the first snows would fall on the ancient white stones. But here on the plains it was still the end of summer. The skies were a wide expanse of blue, the orange trees heavy with fruit, and it felt good to be down from the mountains, down on the plains. The comet, it was true, was still in the sky, but it was unremarked upon, this great celestial mystery becoming just another detail in the background of the world.

'Hold on,' Simeon said.

The foreigner did not need telling. He saw them too. A roadblock was erected in their path, and it was guarded by soldiers.

'Unusual,' he said.

'You think they're there for us?' Simeon said.

'Why, have you done something wrong lately?' the foreigner said.

Simeon shrugged uncomfortably. 'You never know,' he said.

They rode on.

'Halt,' a soldier said when they got to the roadblock.

'Yeah, yeah,' Simeon said. 'Who's in charge here, soldier? Because it sure as hell isn't you.'

'I am,' a man said, and he stepped out of the shade of an olive tree and stood watching them with a faint, dangerous smile. He was a thin man, not tall, with a thin moustache and black receding hair.

'Colonel Ali,' the foreigner said. He dismounted and went to shake the officer's hand. 'I apologise for my friend here.'

'Foreigner,' the colonel said. 'Where are you coming from?'

'Jerusalem,' the foreigner said.

'And going?'

'Jaffa.'

'On what business?' Colonel Ali said.

The foreigner shrugged. The colonel smiled a smile as thin as a blade.

'I see,' he said. 'And the big one?'

'Runaway slave,' Simeon said.

'You have the paperwork?' Colonel Ali said.

'Sure I do.'

'Let's see it,' the colonel said.

Simeon slid off his horse. He presented the documents without further comment.

'The murder in Jerusalem?' Colonel Ali said. 'My men are searching for him, too. You are wasting your time.'

Simeon laughed. 'No,' he said. '*You* are wasting my time.'

The colonel gave him back the documents. The foreigner took the opportunity to untether his new goat. The kid goat nudged him with his horns, not roughly, and went to chew on a patch of grass by the side of the road. Colonel Ali considered this interaction and said, 'Do you have papers for that goat?'

'Did you just make a joke, Colonel?' the foreigner said, surprised. He had known Colonel Ali Bey for some time now, but had never considered the man to have a sense of humour. Ali Bey was an anomaly. An efficient member of an old and rigid imperial force, a man whose superiors considered incorruptible and therefore, on the whole, of no use. And so he was shunted here, to a backwater province where he could do no lasting damage – though the foreigner never believed that story. His opinion of Ali Bey was that he was efficient, ruthless and ambitious, and therefore a dangerous man. Now he regarded him warily.

It did not escape the foreigner that the colonel regarded him in much the same way.

'I like neither of you being out here,' Colonel Ali said.

'That much is clear,' Simeon muttered.

'But I suppose I can't stop you,' Colonel Ali said.

'What *are* you here for, Colonel?' the foreigner said.

'You know two ruffians who go by the names One-Eyed and Ugly?' Colonel Ali said.

'Sadly, I do,' the foreigner said. And he thought again of the two shadows he saw the previous night, turning off the highway at the khan. He'd thought little enough of it then. 'What have they done this time?'

The colonel's smile, when it came again, was the same expression of compressed violence.

'Just looking to have a word,' he said.

'About?' the foreigner said.

'The whereabouts of a Swiss national.'

'Oh?' the foreigner said, as casually as he could manage.

'Would *you* happen to know anything of his whereabouts?' Colonel Ali said.

'Whose whereabouts?' the foreigner said.

'Fellow by the name of Hoffman,' Colonel Ali said.

'What did he do, this Hoffman?' the foreigner said.

'What does anyone do here?' Colonel Ali said. 'Other than get into trouble?'

'Is he in trouble, then? This Swiss?' the foreigner said.

'You tell me, Foreigner. You tell me.'

The foreigner shook his head.

'I'm afraid I know nothing of who he is or where he went,' he said truthfully.

'Well,' Colonel Ali said. 'If you hear anything, you let me know. You're free to go. Both of you. And your goat.'

The goat said, 'Baaa,' and urinated on the spot under the olive tree where the colonel had stood. The foreigner pulled it by the string and climbed back on his horse. He was keen suddenly to get away. The soldiers opened the roadblock.

As the foreigner and Simeon rode away, the foreigner had the uncomfortable awareness of all those men with guns at his back, and he fought against the urge to turn back and look.

9

Two months earlier, Ahmet Bey had summoned the foreigner to his house. Zorik had roused the foreigner from a pleasant dream at Brutti's, where he was spending some of his hard-earned cash.

'Boss wants a word,' Zorik said. 'Are you ready to work again, Foreigner?'

The foreigner grunted and sat up from the mat. Nadiya Brutti regarded both men from her rocking chair with evident disinterest – this was not the first nor, she likely reasoned, the last time such an exchange took place in her establishment.

'Ready and eager,' the foreigner said, 'for it has been a long while since the last job you gave me. I thought the effendi's enemies were numerous.'

'Well,' Zorik said, not unreasonably, 'you have ensured there are a few less of them walking around in the world, Foreigner.' He extended his hand and the foreigner accepted it, and rose to his feet with some effort.

'The effendi has no shortage of enemies,' he said and smiled goofily.

'We'd better sober you up first,' Zorik said. 'Nadiya, can you get some coffee in him?'

Nadiya rose from her rocking chair, vanished into the interior of the building and returned shortly with a small clay jug. The foreigner stared at it in revulsion.

'This isn't coffee,' he said.

'Better than coffee,' Nadiya said. She placed her hand on the bottom of the jar and lifted it gently so that the foreigner was forced to drink.

After he drank it, the foreigner convulsed violently and threw up against the stone wall. This took some time, but then he felt better.

'What is it?' Zorik said interestedly.

'Old family recipe,' Nadiya said.

'Might it be possible to purchase?' the slave said.

'No.'

'Oh,' the slave said, taken aback. The foreigner guessed that as Ahmet Bey's emissary he wasn't used to hearing the word very often.

As Zorik and the foreigner left, Nadiya slipped a bottle of cordial into the foreigner's hand.

'Only take a little at a time,' she said.

He nodded, then followed Zorik. When they got to Ahmet Bey's house the foreigner was made to wait in one of the inner courtyards as the effendi attended to other, more important meetings. Ahmet Bey was not native to Jerusalem but then, who could truly claim to be more than a passing nomad in a city that had sat there for thousands of years, burned to the ground on numerous occasions, and had been occupied, taken and retaken by every great power of the ancient world? No, Ahmet Bey had *made* Jerusalem his own, had slid in like a boning knife between the thin and oh so unappetising ribs of the city and cut with judicial jurisprudence. The Mutasarrif may have been Istanbul's representative; the great families of Nussaiba and Husayni, Nashashibi and Khalidi, the native holders of old wealth, land and power; but Ahmet Bey wove his spider's silk around them all, and even those road pirates of Abu Ghosh bowed under his influence.

At least, this was the speech Ahmet Bey liked to give, and the foreigner had heard it more than once. The effendi's real business was just that – business, the selling of any and all things and the acquisition of wealth.

'Horses, slaves or bullets,' Ahmet Bey liked to say, 'Damask roses or Persian carpets, none of them have any value in themselves. The value of a thing is low in one place, high in another. Transport it across from one to the other and you have made your fortune. The Nabateans controlled the spice routes and made their fortune off cinnamon and nutmeg. The Persians levied tax on the silk that passed through their kingdom and made their money without ever handling the stock itself. I am a modern man, Foreigner. Times are changing, the old alliances shift. There is value in land for the people who live on it, but land is a thing that is easy to lose and hard to keep. People want *things*. Palestine is frankly something of a shithole. But it's a magnet for rich Europeans who like to look at ruins, and if it's a thin bone it is one with marrow to be sucked out all the same. To me it is just a piece of a bigger picture. *You* understand. You come from wealth and power, the second paid for with the first. And it amuses me that you serve me now and do my bidding. No, don't protest. We help each other. I give you protection and the opportunity to do that which you desire. There is something in your psyche that is broken and doesn't feel. Killing for you is a way to feel alive, I think. Or perhaps you just enjoy it. Whatever it is, you are reasonably good at it, and you hold a foreign passport, which makes you valuable to me. We make a good team.'

The foreigner waited in the quiet courtyard. He did not think the effendi was right. He did not enjoy killing, but it was true he didn't mind it either. He had been bred to it back in Europe, and as Ahmet Bey said, he *was* reasonably good at it, so it seemed a decent a line of work than many, and certainly better than some. He wouldn't stick at it forever, he thought. There was a girl in Beyrouth, and he could buy his own land, make a home, raise children and pigs. Presently Zorik returned, and behind him came the effendi.

'Ah, Foreigner,' Ahmet Bey said. 'Glad you could join us.' He did not bother sitting down and the foreigner stood as soon as the effendi came in. This was to be a short meeting, he understood.

'There is an American,' Ahmet Bey said, and he said it with slight displeasure. There were not many Americans in the Holy Land but they were backed up by a powerful government backed up in turn by gunboats, and so it was that one had to be careful with these interlopers from across the sea. Americans had their own ideas about things. 'Dickson by name and though American by blood he is native to Palestine by birth, and lives now in the European settlement in Artas. I want you to find him and, well, you know. Before you are done with him, you must tell him the blood is for the blood already spilled. He will understand.' Ahmet Bey snapped his fingers and Zorik hurried over with a plate of rahat lokum for his master. Ahmet Bey popped one of the sugared jellies into his mouth and chewed with a mournful expression.

'I am only the broker on this one, you understand,' he said. 'This is some real blood money shit.'

The foreigner nodded, though he did not really care one way or the other. The interview concluded, he let Zorik escort him outside.

'He is young, this Dickson,' Zorik said, 'and may be wise to your coming. You know how they say, when the effendi so much as farts in Jerusalem they smell it in the valleys.'

'If he runs, I'll find him,' the foreigner said. He did not intend to tarry and, after bidding Zorik farewell, retrieved his horse and rode out on the road to Bethlehem. He left the city through the Jaffa Gate and passed first through the Valley of Rephaim, that is to say, the valley of wraiths, where he stopped briefly at the German colony to talk with the butcher, Kübler.

'Yes,' Herr Kübler said, after the foreigner had good-naturedly paid for some sausages, 'I know the place in Artas, but it is nought to do with our people. A British convert started it, fellow by the name of John Meshullam. It's set on land abandoned in the past by its villager owners who owed blood money to a family they murdered some years before. Meshullam stepped in to pay their diya to the Pasha, allowing the owners to safely return. In exchange for his generosity he asked for half the land to be leased to him, and there he established the settlement. A worthy enterprise, though few live there now, I think. Old Meshullam's dead and so is that American lady.'

'American lady?' the foreigner said.

'Clorinda Minor, her name was,' Herr Kübler said. 'A firebrand she was, too, from Philadelphia, and quite rich. She died in the Holy Land, of quite a painful cancer, and her bones are buried here. But those who came with her fled back home after the trial.'

'What trial?' the foreigner said.

Herr Kübler shook his head. 'A painful episode,' he said. 'And best left forgotten. If you do find worthy Christians in Artas do send them my blessings, won't you, Gustav? And tell them their brethren in Jerusalem think of them still. Enjoy your sausages.'

'That I will,' the foreigner said.

It was not a long ride to Bethlehem. The foreigner did not tarry at Rachel's Tomb and did not care for the Church of the Nativity. The picturesque views of the terraced gardens of fig trees and vineyards, and the sight of a young shepherd leading his flock along the steep incline to the town, did not move the foreigner to reverie. It was a mostly Christian town, the Muslim Quarter having been destroyed by Ibrahim Pasha in the thirties, and the local wine was both cheap and in abundance. The foreigner did not follow the road into town but skirted it and continued on his way, and in another hour of moderate riding he reached the Pools of Solomon.

This ancient water reservoir, of much interest to the tourists who flocked there, was built by Herod to provide a supply of water to Jerusalem. There were three large cisterns made of ancient marble masonry, and already the foreigner could see some of the tourists swimming in the lower pool, while others camped outside the ruined fort, or khan, of Saracenic origin, which towered overhead. The foreigner led the horse down the incline, past the pools, and in short time reached a temperate valley in which sat a small Arab village surrounded by biblical ruins. Past the village the foreigner found the path to the European colony, which sat apart from its neighbours in a pleasant grove of fruit trees and abundant vegetable gardens. He saw several carts, well-maintained, which ferried their produce to Jerusalem, and a stable with some half-dozen horses, none thoroughbred, and several donkeys.

A boy came out of a modest stone house, one of several in the settlement, and stared at the foreigner.

'I'm looking for Dickson,' the foreigner said.

The boy kept staring at the foreigner.

'Is that your horse?' he said at last.

'Yes,' the foreigner said.

'Nice horse,' the boy said. 'We ain't got a horse like that.'

'I noticed,' the foreigner said. 'But you don't need a horse like mine.'

'Dickson has a good horse,' the boy said.

'Where's Dickson?' the foreigner said.

'He ain't here, mister,' the boy said.

'Do you know where he went?'

The boy shrugged.

'South,' he said.

'What's in the south?' the foreigner said.

'Desert,' the boy said. 'I think. I've never been anywhere.'

A woman came out of the house then, rushing to the side of the boy. She relaxed when she noticed the foreigner's European countenance.

'Can I help you, sir?' she said.

'He's looking for Dickson,' the boy said.

'Dickson's not here,' the woman said.

'That's what I told him,' the boy said.

'Do you know where he went?' the foreigner asked.

'South,' the woman said. 'I think.'

'Anywhere in particular?' the foreigner said.

'He often goes in search of lost cities,' the woman said, evidently more helpful than her son. 'There are quite a few in the desert, according to Dickson.'

'What does he do in them?' the foreigner said, surprised.

'He prays to God,' the woman said. 'Also, they hold treasures, though he never found any. You could ask for him in Hebron, though it is late to ride there now, and the road can be dangerous at night. I will be glad to offer you accommodation here.'

The foreigner looked at her speculatively, then looked at the boy and shook his head.

'I don't mind night riding,' he said.

He left them there still watching as he rode away, and for all he knew they were still standing there now, with nothing else to do but wait for the End of Days and the Second Coming of the Lord.

10

Night fell swiftly over the hills. Jackals howled in the distance but both man and horse were used to their sound. The road to Hebron was poorly maintained, though the Ottoman authorities in recent years had made a moderate attempt to improve at least the first part of it. The horse did not mind the rough terrain and the foreigner was happy to be riding under the stars, though he kept his gun loosely on his lap in case of trouble. No trouble came, and after another two hours of slow riding the foreigner decided to make camp for the night. He found a copse of pine trees on a rise beside some ancient ruins and made himself comfortable, the ruins – whether ancient synagogue, Roman temple, Abbasid fort or merely a shepherd's hut – hiding him from sight of the road. He built a small fire and cooked the sausages he had bought from the German. They reminded him of home, and he found himself strangely missing the old country all of a sudden, a feeling he seldom experienced but which came upon him from time to time, like a false memory of a gentler, kinder childhood.

He fell asleep beside the embers in their ring of stone, his gun by his side, and when he awoke it was past dawn already. He covered the remains of the fire with dirt and mounted his horse and in two more hours of steady riding reached Hebron. Like most towns in this part of the world it had been destroyed and rebuilt numerous times since antiquity, being first a Canaanite town, then the site of

King David's exile and the place of Absalom's revolt, then Greek some centuries later when Alexander swept through the land like a figure out of myth. Later still it was razed to the ground by one of Emperor Vespasian's more enthusiastic officers. Whoever held it, the people patiently rebuilt and waited for the next round. It got its modern name, al-Khalil, meaning the Friend, under Saladin. Now it was a pleasant enough edifice of stout stone buildings with domed roofs, but lacking a modern hotel. The foreigner rode through a gate that had no walls and entered the town. He found the souk and sat himself down in a place serving coffee which stood between a shop selling glass trinkets and a Jewish butcher's. The proprietor of the café, whose name was Abu Adnan, brightened when he saw him and said, 'Foreigner! As-salamu alaikum.'

'Wa-alaikum as-salam,' the foreigner said.

He waited, watching the souk and listening to the thump-thump-thump of the butcher's knife as it cut through bone. A cat dozing in the sunshine opened one eye and looked at the foreigner and then closed it again, indifferent. Presently Abu Adnan brought him coffee and bread and sheep's cheese and two hardboiled eggs. The foreigner ate, for he was hungry. When he was done he said, 'I am looking for an American by the name of Dickson.'

'I know the man,' Abu Adnan said, for he knew the comings and goings throughout Hebron. 'He stayed here three nights ago, in the house of a Jew who rents out rooms to visitors. He was gone by morning.'

'Heading south?' the foreigner said, remembering what the woman and child had told him in Artas, and Abu Adnan nodded.

'He speaks good Arabic and has friends among the Bedaween of al-Naqab,' he said, meaning the southern desert.

'A competent rider?' the foreigner said, calculating, and again Abu Adnan nodded.

'How will I find him?' the foreigner wondered aloud.

'You may ask some of the Abu-Mahfouz,' Abu Adnan said, 'they graze their herds near the Beersheba ruins.'

'I know the place,' the foreigner said. He went to use the commode and upon his return filled up his skins with water for the hard road ahead. He stepped over the cat.

'Go in peace, Foreigner,' Abu Adnan said.

'We both know that's unlikely,' the foreigner said.

Three days in the mountains followed. The foreigner liked the clear high air, the cries of larks and chiffchaffs, the quiet solitude of the unpaved paths. The road did not continue past Hebron, the trees grew tall and ancient, and once, as he urinated near a stream, a leopard silently appeared and stared at him from the other side of the water before yawning and turning away. Here and there were small villages, and from time to time the foreigner could also hear the gunshots in the distance that signified a hunting party out and about, for the mountains, like the Hula Valley in the north, were favoured by gentlemen of the hunt for their abundance of wildlife. The foreigner had once or twice, before he came to the employ of Ahmet Bey, led such expeditions himself as a guide, though he did not approve of the senseless slaughter of the animals. There were bears in the woods, and here and there wolves, but they did not bother the foreigner and he did not bother them.

He emerged out of the mountains at last onto the desert plains and as he rode the land became parched and vegetation sparse, and the sun beat down without mercy. It was not long before he spotted the ruins of what had once been Beersheba, one of those lost, abandoned towns this Dickson was apparently so interested in.

Beyond its hill the foreigner saw a camp of large tents and camels grazing and he rode towards the camp.

Dogs came out barking at him, and after them streamed children who looked up at him with big curious eyes. The foreigner saw a herd of sheep in the distance and men on horses rounding up the sheep. He waited. A woman came out of the largest tent, her face covered, and stared at him and then said, 'Abu al-Bunduqia.'

'Umm Sayed,' the foreigner said, and she said, 'You remember me?'

'How can I forget?' the foreigner said. Some three years back the effendi had sent him out here on a job that went bad. The foreigner had carried out the job to completion but he was caught soon after. The men who caught him hurt him at first and had intended to kill him in the desert, and it was Umm Sayed who interceded on his behalf and negotiated for his life, then tended to him. Once he recovered he understood the debt that this had placed him under. Umm Sayed then requested him to carry out a job on her behalf, which involved a man who was then living in Baghdad. The foreigner, in time, had done what she had asked of him, and the deed was done. Blood, in Palestine, had to be paid with blood.

'What brings you back here, Abu al-Bunduqia?' she said.

'I am searching for a man named Dickson.'

'That,' Umm Sayed said, 'is bad news for Dickson.'

'I'm afraid so. He is a friend to your tribe?'

'He is a friend.'

'Then I am sorry. I should not have asked,' the foreigner said.

Umm Sayed shrugged. 'You can ask,' she said. 'I can't promise you an answer.'

'He is here?' the foreigner said.

'No,' she said. The riders from the herd came close then and hailed the foreigner and he returned their greetings. He did not mention Dickson again. The Bedaween welcomed him into their camp and the foreigner sat with them, sharing their food.

'I will not tarry here,' he said when the meal had concluded. 'My business is elsewhere.'

'What is your business, Abu al-Bunduqia?' Sayed, the son of Umm Sayed, said.

'Nothing that need concern the Abu-Mahfouz,' the foreigner said. He rose smoothly, and offered Sayed a gift of a tobacco pouch he had brought along, which Sayed smelled in appreciation before passing it to one of his men to put away.

As the foreigner went to his horse Umm Sayed followed him out.

'There is an ancient city some two days' ride from here, deep in the desert,' she said quietly. 'Called Abdah or Avdat. You know it?'

'I know of it,' the foreigner said.

'You can find your way there?'

'I am not sure,' the foreigner admitted.

'The al-Tarabin roam that part of the desert,' Umm Sayed said.

The foreigner nodded.

'Thank you,' he said quietly. Umm Sayed watched him as he rode away, but he did not look back.

The land changed again. Deep desert. Gazelles and hyenas watched him from a distance as he passed. Even the animals were the colour of the desert. The foreigner hid from the sun in the daytime, rode when the air cooled, the stars lighting his way. The horse never complained, and the foreigner shared his water with him, sparingly, but though the desert seemed to be empty of any sign of human life it was not. Here and there the foreigner came across ruins and the remains of ancient highways, and from time to time, too, he saw tents and herds in the distance, but he avoided the Bedaween for now, for the tribes of al-Naqab, while hospitable to strangers, were sometimes at war with each other in a series of shifting alliances, and he resolved not to mention his purpose here again. The Bedaween recognised no political authority or border but roamed as they had done for centuries between the Arabian peninsula and Palestine, inhabiting the Sinai desert and the wilderness of Zin. The foreigner rode south, south, and on the second day came across a small party of men of the al-Tarabin tribe at an ancient well, and there he filled up his water and exchanged greetings and gifts, and was told the place he sought was not far. He followed their directions and shortly before sunset beheld ahead of him the lost city of Abdah, an extensive set of ancient ruins on a hill.

The foreigner did not hurry but watched, and he could see there was indeed a horse tethered there, beside the columns of some long-ago temple to a deity not worshipped anymore in this land, and he knew too that he was seen by the man he came to find. Nevertheless he at last approached, if cautiously, and climbed the hill as the sun set over the miles of empty desert. He held his gun loosely in his grasp.

'Stop where you are.'

A man who had to be Dickson stepped out from behind a column, and he too was holding a gun, which he aimed at the foreigner.

'I wish you no harm,' the foreigner said.

'I could have shot you on your approach,' Dickson said.

'Perhaps,' the foreigner said. 'But then again, that would be murder, and you don't strike me as a murderer, if you don't mind me saying so.'

'What is your purpose here?' Dickson said.

'I heard of this ruined town and was curious,' the foreigner said. 'It belonged to the Jews?'

'Edomites,' Dickson said. 'That is to say, Nabateans. It was dedicated to their king, who they believed to be a god and who is buried here. A German named Seetzen visited here some eighty years ago. This used to be a way point on the Incense Route to the port in Gaza.'

'You know much about history?' the foreigner said.

'I like to contemplate God in these places,' Dickson said. 'Where there is not the hubbub of the world to distract me. The old people did not know the true God but they understood divinity, I think. It is easy to see God when you are out here in God's creation.'

'May I dismount?' the foreigner said. 'My name is Gustav.'

'I'm Dickson,' the man said. He lowered his gun. The foreigner knew his kind. Dickson did not want to believe him his murderer. The foreigner climbed down from his horse.

'May I share my food with you?' he said. 'I don't have much, but what I have is yours.'

Dickson nodded. They sat on upturned blocks of stone and shared a meal of hard cheese, dry bread and olives. The stars came out over the desert, harder than diamonds and more numerous. They scattered like gems across the dark skies. The foreigner daubed a piece of cloth with the tincture that was Nadiya Brutti's gift. He put it to his face and breathed deeply.

'Laudanum?' Dickson said. 'Are you in pain?'

'I was, before,' the foreigner said. 'They gave it to me for the pain and I took a liking to it.'

'That will happen,' Dickson said. 'You should wean yourself off it.'

The foreigner shrugged. 'I have few vices,' he said. 'This one seems harmless enough.'

They sat in silence, and the foreigner was considering when he should do the job when Dickson spoke again.

'Did Ahmet Bey send you?' he said.

'Who?' the foreigner said, feigning innocence.

'Do you know why they want me dead?' Dickson said.

'Who?' the foreigner said again.

Dickson nodded. The foreigner considered shooting him there and then. He did not generally care for the cause or reason which led to his being where he was. His was just a job to do. But something in Dickson's face in the pale starlight arrested his hand.

'There were several families who travelled from Philadelphia to the Holy Land in the fall of 1851,' Dickson said. 'Their leader was a woman named Clorinda S. Minor, the devotee of an American preacher who failed to predict the Second Coming. Unlike most of the preacher's adherents, Clorinda did not lose faith. She just figured her preacher got the date wrong, and set about moving her small congregation to Palestine, where they would be more effectively able to hasten Jesus' return.'

'Like the Templers?' the foreigner said.

'Very much so,' Dickson said. 'And indeed when they arrived in Palestine, they went straight to John Meshullam's colony in Artas. Well, Clorinda and Meshullam soon had a falling-out – they both had rather strong personalities. Every quarrel has more than one side to it and, as is generally the case with Palestinian quarrels, there are many more sides than two.'

The foreigner nodded.

'The Americans moved to a new place near Jaffa, already worked by another German family, the Steinbecks. They were joined there by a new arrival from Massachusetts, a man named Walter Dickson and his family, and in short order the Dickson boys married the Steinbeck girls, and for a while all was well. Clorinda died—'

'In great suffering,' the foreigner said, and Dickson looked up sharply.

'You have heard the story?' he said.

'No,' the foreigner said. 'Just something I was told once, in passing.'

'She died in great suffering, yes,' Dickson said. 'But the Steinbeck-Dicksons remained, and worked the land, and their children were born, and for a time all was well.'

He rubbed his eyes, as if the story brought about painful memories.

'I will spare you the more vile details of what happened,' he said. 'It is true the settlement – it was called Mount Hope, and lay between Jaffa and the Musrara river – had disagreements with its Arab neighbours, and that had built up over time. On the night of the eleventh of January, 1858, five men came to Mount Hope to settle those slights, real or imagined. They broke in and murdered Friedrich Steinbeck, wounded Walter Dickson, and raped Mary Steinbeck over and over, as well as her sister-in-law. Finally they robbed the house of what money there was to be got and fled.'

'Steinbeck,' the foreigner said. 'That is a curious name.'

'It was shortened from Grosssteinbeck,' Dickson said. 'You do not seem shocked by my story.'

'Such things happen,' the foreigner said. 'Were you there?'

'I was away in Jaffa that night. I was only a child.'

'It must have been hard,' the foreigner said. 'I take it there is more to the story?'

Dickson nodded.

'There was a trial,' he said. 'Eventually. This was an attack on the Western powers, after all, on the citizens of great nations. Such an insult could not be tolerated. The American and Prussian consuls both became, in effect, detectives, trying to track down the culprits, who fled. The American consul threatened the Ottomans with some gunboat diplomacy, though the captain of the nearest vessel, moored in Alexandria, saw no immediate reason to intervene. But enough effort was expended to bring the men to justice. Four were given prison time in Acre. A fifth, it was said, was handed over to the American gunboat when it at last arrived, and was hung unceremoniously from its mast. In truth the fifth criminal, and actual murderer, was never brought to justice.'

'I see now,' the foreigner said.

'The Steinbecks left for America, where they eventually settled in California. The Dicksons left too, but I stayed behind. I had been born here and this was my land just as it is anyone's, I reasoned. I was stubborn even in my youth.' Dickson smiled. A scorpion scuttled across the sand but neither man paid it any attention. 'But blood begets blood, and no one in this land ever forgets...'

'I was told to tell you this,' the foreigner said, and he rose then, and pointed his pistol at Dickson. 'I was told to tell you this is for the blood.'

'Will you make me one promise, my friend?' Dickson said.

The foreigner hesitated.

'In my house in Artas, behind a false back in the wardrobe beside the bed, there is a bag of money,' Dickson said. 'It is not a lot, but it is a respectable sum. Will you take it in payment? And if you pass by the place that was once Mount Hope, seek out the family of one Abd el-Sallam and despatch them from this world, so that the diya is paid in full. Would you do that for me?'

The sound of the gunshot filled the still air of the desert. Dickson collapsed slowly onto the sand, there in the ancient, ruined city, and lay there to become one more dead amongst the many.

'Sure,' the foreigner said. 'Why not.'

11

'Why are we stopping?' Simeon said. They were not far from Jaffa now.

The foreigner pointed.

'See those houses over there?'

'Look abandoned,' Simeon said. 'What about them?'

'Used to be called Mount Hope,' the foreigner said.

'That's a stupid name,' Simeon said.

'Are you going to give me a hand or not?' the foreigner said. 'I promised someone to do a job near here.'

'I have a slave to catch, Foreigner,' Simeon said. 'I don't have time for your nonsense.'

'We both know your slave isn't going anywhere,' the foreigner said.

'Fine,' Simeon said, 'but I'm not killing anyone for you.'

'Wouldn't dream of asking,' the foreigner said. 'This won't take long, anyway.'

They turned their horses and followed a dirt path, past the houses, and soon came to a village. The foreigner explained what he needed. He stayed back as Simeon rode in. Soon he was laughing with the some of the locals, enquiring for his missing slave and handing out small coins. It was a while before he came back, and as he passed the foreigner he said, 'Second house on the left as you come in, the one with the orange tree growing in the back garden.'

The foreigner nodded his thanks. He climbed off his horse and tied it to the tree with a knot that was quick to release, the goat with it, and then he went quietly to the village from the back and climbed over a low stone wall and then entered the house Simeon had indicated. After all, he had gone back to Artas and taken Dickson's money which was right where Dickson had said it was.

There was an old man sitting in a chair and a woman tending him, and they both looked up as the foreigner entered but he shot them before they could speak. The retort of the gun was loud in the small room and a shadow detached itself from a dark corner and tried to run – it was a boy, not yet thirteen. The bullet caught him in the back and he fell and did not rise again, and the foreigner left the way he came, quickly, and got his horse and the goat and he fled from that place.

He caught up with Simeon three miles away where the road bisected two orange groves.

'It's a distasteful job you do,' Simeon said.

'I do not understand blood feuds,' the foreigner complained, and Simeon laughed.

'Then you will never truly be of this place,' he said.

They continued on their way and soon the foreigner smelled the sea air and heard the cry of gulls, and in two more miles they came to Jaffa.

'Hoffman,' the foreigner said. 'Do you know him?'

'Of course I know him.' Hardegg said. Hardegg ran the Jerusalem Hotel. He was also the American vice-consul for Jaffa. He was bald and bearded, with a thin face and somewhat prominent ears. The hotel was a beautiful European-style building on the edge of the German colony and a little outside the city

proper. It advertised biblical simplicity and evangelical purity.
A piano player in the salon played Brahms.

'Did he stay here?' the foreigner said.

'Hoffman always stays here when he's in Jaffa,' Hardegg said.
'He is a good man, Hoffman. For a Jew.'

Hardegg's father was the co-founder of the German Templer
movement. He had dedicated his life to the Holy Land. He had
died three years earlier and was buried in Haifa. The foreigner
came to the Jerusalem Hotel first, because most Europeans who
passed through Jaffa stayed at the J, and Hardegg had a reputation
for knowing everyone.

'When did he last stay here?' the foreigner said.

'He was here a few days ago,' Hardegg said. 'Do you want a
room?'

'No,' the foreigner said.

'We are pretty full,' Hardegg said. 'All booked for tomorrow,
American party coming in on the steamer. But I can do you a
room for tonight at a reasonable rate.'

'I'm fine,' the foreigner said. 'But thank you. How long was
Hoffman here?'

'A couple of days,' Hardegg said.

'Is he still in the city?'

'I don't think so,' Hardegg said. 'But it's possible.'

'How did he seem?' the foreigner said.

'Seem?' Hardegg said.

'Worried? Afraid? Excited? Happy?'

Hardegg shrugged.

'Hoffman's not the most sociable fellow,' he said. 'Keeps to
himself. He didn't seem any different than usual. But I didn't see
much of him. He goes into town mostly. What he does there I am
sure I can't say.'

'Anything else you can tell me?' the foreigner said.

Hardegg shrugged again.

'He always pays on time and he never takes whores to his

room,' he said. 'And if you say that of a man, what else is there to say? He is a good man, Hoffman, for a Jew.'

The foreigner nodded. He went into the salon. A few of the guests were sitting on comfortable chairs, reading month-old copies of the *Vossische Zeitung* and the *London Illustrated News*. Two men were playing chess and smoking cigars. A group of four pious women in a semi-circle sat together working at needles. The foreigner went up to the bar where the Zanj bartender poured him a measure of American whiskey.

'Omar,' the foreigner said, nodding greeting.

'Foreigner,' Omar said. 'What ill wind propels you into my salon?'

'Hardegg paying you well?' the foreigner said. He sipped the whiskey.

'Better than most,' Omar said. 'But one can always stand to make a little extra.'

'You know a man named Hoffman?' the foreigner said.

'You're not the first to ask for him,' Omar said. He poured himself a glass of whiskey too and raised it as though admiring the colour.

'No?' the foreigner said. 'Who else?'

'Colonel Ali,' Omar said.

'Is that so?' the foreigner said. 'Do you know why?'

'I do not,' Omar said.

'Do you know where he went?' the foreigner said.

Omar downed the whiskey and placed the empty glass on the wood counter. 'Your health,' he said.

'So, no?' the foreigner said.

'No,' Omar said.

'So what *do* you know?' the foreigner said.

'He always pays on time and never takes whores up to his room,' Omar said.

'What does that mean?' the foreigner said.

'Figure it out,' Omar said.

'He has a girlfriend in town?'

Omar pursed his lips.

'Boyfriend?' the foreigner said.

Omar raised an eyebrow.

'Man of few words, aren't you,' the foreigner said. He drank the rest of his whiskey.

'Here,' he said. He left a Napoleon on the counter.

Omar made it disappear.

Jaffa wasn't a bad place. The smell of citrus trees filled the air, and the sounds of the sea washing against the untamed shore, and the cry of seagulls, were calming to the foreigner's soul. The city itself rose in an untidy gaggle on its hill overlooking the sea. It had been walled before but the walls were taken down in recent years and the stones used for the new buildings that spilled out beyond the city proper. Not far from the hotel was a Muslim cemetery. Fishermen's boats sat on the sandy beach and fishing nets were strung up to dry. The foreigner walked over and he took off his boots and socks and waded into the water. He liked the sea. He stared out to the horizon, where a couple of ships hovered far away. Jaffa had no natural harbour, and the ships could not dock there. He took in a deep breath of sea air and let it out slowly in an exhalation of relief. He had not particularly cared for the killings earlier.

'You want to go fishing, mister?' a boy said, appearing on his left. The boy looked at him speculatively. 'Can take you out there, you could catch a grouper or mullet, cook it for you on the fire right here on the beach, we take tourists out all the time.'

'Do I look like a fucking tourist?' the foreigner said. He was annoyed at his momentary peace being interrupted.

'I mean, yes?' the boy said. 'I heard you gave old Omar at the J a Napoleon.'

'What's it to you?' the foreigner said.

'What are you looking for?' the boy said.

The foreigner sighed. 'I'm looking for a guy called Hoffman,' he said.

'Oh, him,' the boy said. 'Yeah, I know him.'

'You know where he went?' the foreigner said.

'No, but I know who you can ask,' the boy said. 'Is that worth anything to you?'

'I'll give you a shilling,' the foreigner said.

'That's too little,' the boy said.

'Then fuck off,' the foreigner said, and he turned his back on the boy so he could go back to looking at the sea. The wet sand felt nice between his toes. He took in another deep breath, let it out slowly. Tried to empty his mind—

'Are you still there?' he said.

'Yeah,' the boy said.

'What are you doing?' the foreigner said.

'Thinking.'

'It's a take it or leave it kind of situation,' the foreigner said. 'I really don't care all that much anymore.'

'I *could* use a shilling,' the boy said.

'So?'

'I'm still thinking.'

'Can you do your thinking somewhere else?' the foreigner said. 'I'm trying to take in the sights.'

'You're kind of on *my* beach,' the boy said.

'Fair point,' the foreigner said, 'but I have a gun.'

'Fair point,' the boy said. 'So?'

The foreigner turned and glared at the boy.

'You're not going to go away, are you?' he said.

'Don't reckon I will, no,' the boy said.

'I'll give you a sovereign,' the foreigner said, defeated.

'See?' the boy said. 'Classic tourist.'

★

The town sprawled on the hill, its houses solid, its streets narrow, its population mostly Muslim and its churches filled with ghosts. It had not been that long since Napoleon came at the head of an army, sacked the town and murdered thousands only for his soldiers to come down with the bubonic plague. Practical as ever, the man who was then known as General Bonaparte stuffed the plague sufferers into the Armenian monastery and ordered his physician to poison them with opium. Whether the story was true or not was hard to tell after nearly a century, but the legend endured, and after all, the ghosts of French soldiers were merely the latest to haunt the ancient town. Jaffa had stood before Mohammed, before even there were Jews; it was old, dirty, unkempt and vital, and the foreigner followed the boy up the hill and along a narrow alleyway between two stone walls and to a door on which the boy knocked twice, then stopped. He put his hand out, palm open, and the foreigner, after some hesitation, gave him a coin.

'Be nice to her,' the boy said. Then he ran off.

No one came to the door. The foreigner knocked, more loudly than the boy. He could hear movement inside.

'Come on,' he said, 'open up.'

'Who is it?' a voice inside said.

'A friend,' the foreigner said.

'You sound handsome,' the voice said.

'One way to find out,' the foreigner said.

The door opened a crack. The foreigner kicked it and went in, grabbing the person inside and pushing them against the wall.

'Oh,' he said, surprised, for the figure seemed for a moment to be a beautiful young woman. Then her robe fell open and he saw the smooth, hairless chest and realised she was of the third gender, which some called butterfly. 'I beg your pardon,' he said.

He let her go. She pulled back her robe and smoothed her long black hair that fell down on her shoulders.

'You're a rough one, aren't you,' she said. 'Shut the door, would you? You nearly took it down.'

'Sorry,' the foreigner said. He went and shut the door.

'Well, sit down,' she said. 'He warned me someone would come.'

'Hoffman?'

'Yes,' she said. She sat down on a stool and reached for a box and opened it and began to roll a cigarette with the tobacco. 'I love him, you know. And he loves me. He said he would come back for me, when it was all over.'

'I don't know his business,' the foreigner said. 'I just need to know where to find him.'

'He wouldn't tell me,' she said. 'He was scared of someone like you. Do you have a name?'

'They call me Foreigner,' the foreigner said, and she snorted a laugh.

'That figures,' she said. 'I'm Juzfin.'

'That figures,' the foreigner said, and she laughed again.

'Are you going to kill me?' she said.

'No,' the foreigner said. 'Could I have one of those?'

She passed him the cigarette she had rolled and started to roll another.

'I just want to know where he went,' the foreigner said. 'I take it he's not in Jaffa anymore.'

'It's hard to hide in a place like Jaffa,' Juzfin said. 'He only came to say goodbye.'

'He didn't try to get on a steamer?' the foreigner said.

She shook her head. 'He knew they'd be watching the ships,' she said, 'but he had no intention of leaving. He has his business to finish here first.'

'What business?' the foreigner said, and she shrugged.

'He was going to be very rich,' she said. 'Then he was going to come back for me, so we could get married.'

'But you're a man,' the foreigner said, and then thought about it and said, 'and he's Jewish.'

Juzfin shrugged.

'We could still be together,' she said. 'It didn't have to be all official like.'

'I just want to know where he went,' the foreigner said.

'Are you going to smack me around so I'd tell you?' she said. She lit her cigarette. 'I don't know where he went. He had some friends in the coffee house near the souk.'

'Which one?' the foreigner said.

'Suleiman's, by the water fountain,' Juzfin said. 'The one the Europeans like.'

'You think he'll come back for you?' the foreigner said. He got up to leave.

'I think he's a dreamer,' Juzfin said. 'This is all this land is good for. Dreamers like us. But what's a girl to do but dream?'

The foreigner left her there to her thoughts. She seemed an enterprising sort of girl. He figured she'd be fine, when it came down to it.

12

As the foreigner made his way down to the souk he ran into Chazan. The Jew was portly and looked out of breath.

'Foreigner!' he said, patting his sweating forehead with a chequered cloth.

'Chazan, where have you been?' the foreigner said. 'Did you not get my telegram?'

'I was out of town with Mr Amsalek,' Chazan said.

'The British vice-consul?'

'The very same,' Chazan said mournfully.

'For what reason?' the foreigner said.

'A murder outside town,' Chazan said. 'Three felaheen shot dead. An old man and his wife, plus a boy. The old man had only recently come out of a twenty-year stretch in Acre.'

'So?' the foreigner said.

Chazan mopped his brow. 'Blood feud, in all likelihood,' he said. 'It's no matter to the vice-consul in any case, but Amsalek likes to take an interest. He's from an old Jerusalem family. We had a wasted journey. I am sorry I wasn't here to welcome you. Did you make any progress?'

'Some,' the foreigner said. 'You kept your eye on the port?'

'For Hoffman?' Chazan said. 'Yes. I already had word from Zorik. I know Hoffman, of course. He came and went through here on the regular. But I have not seen him in some weeks.'

'Someone must have an inkling where he went,' the foreigner said. He had to admit to himself he was getting a little exasperated with the whole thing. Jaffa had that effect on him. Maybe it was all those oranges. 'I just need a direction.'

'He did hang out with those new Jews,' Chazan said.

'What new Jews?' the foreigner said.

'There's been a bunch came over recently,' Chazan said. 'After the pogroms in Russia. You've heard of the pogroms?'

'Vaguely,' the foreigner said.

'They were bad,' Chazan said.

'So?' the foreigner said.

Chazan shrugged. 'So some new Jews came on the ships this year. They have new ideas.'

'Territorialists?' the foreigner said, thinking of Mr Avigdor back at the khan and what Miriam – Mrs Avigdor – told him. 'They want to settle in Palestine and all that? Work in agriculture?'

'I suppose,' Chazan said. 'They tend to meet at the coffee house by—'

'The fountain,' the foreigner said. 'Suleiman's.'

'Right.'

'I was just on my way there,' the foreigner said.

'Good, good,' Chazan said. 'Well, I will go home, unless you need me further.'

'I'll be there when my business is done,' the foreigner said. 'I already left my horse in care of your stable hand. Also a goat.'

'A goat?' Chazan said.

The foreigner considered. He could not really keep the goat, he thought. You could not be a hardened killer and travel with a goat. It just made everything more difficult.

'For dinner,' he said, somewhat regretfully.

Chazan nodded.

'The wife will be pleased,' he said. 'I'll see you later.'

The foreigner watched Chazan ride off on his donkey, swaying on top of the small, sturdy animal. Chazan's roots also ran deep in this land, but he was no agriculturalist. He was in shipping. Chazan had a dream of selling Jaffa oranges across the world. It seemed a stupid dream to the foreigner but then he didn't particularly care for oranges.

The souk was lively at this hour. It was shortly after dusk, lanterns were hung from poles and the newly arrived tourists took in the sights while the women of the town gathered to draw water, exchange gossip and scope out the men. One called out to the foreigner, making the others laugh. He tried to ignore their attentions.

Suleiman's by the fountain wasn't much to look at. Wooden benches and tables were busy with customers, some local and some foreign. A group of novice monks from the Latin monastery were getting drunk at one table, while some of the local merchants, unwinding after the day's work, sat sipping coffee from small china cups and smoking sheeshas. At a third table sat a group of men in Western suits and hats, talking intensely, some drinking coffee and others local Bethlehem wine. The foreigner approached that third table. A Babel of languages filled the air: Arabic and Yiddish, Russian and English, Turkish and German and French all proliferated. The foreigner saw Colonel Ali some distance away, sitting with a carpet seller, while Simeon was squatting on his haunches chatting to an orange fruit seller at another stall.

'Mind if I join you?' the foreigner said to the table. He did not wait for an answer but sat down as the others on his bench shifted to accommodate him. At the head of the table sat a rather eccentric-looking Englishman, bald on top, with a long thick beard and prominent eyebrows, who said gravely, 'Welcome, sir. We were just discussing oranges.'

'Of course you were,' the foreigner said miserably.

'Consider,' the Englishman said. 'The Jaffa orange, so ubiquitous that you could not imagine the land without it! And yet it is a foreigner, a Chinese one at that, brought across the world by the Portuguese and acclimatised here. As it is with fruit, so it is with people. If anyone can lay claim to this land it's the Jews, for they have the oldest claim. And the messiah would not come lest the Jews return to Palestine. Name's Oliphant,' the Englishman said. 'Laurence Oliphant. Formerly on Her Majesty's Diplomatic Service. I was attacked by a ronin in Japan once. That's a rogue samurai. They have these funny little cousins of the orange there in a region called Satsuma. Easy to peel. This is my wife, Alice.'

'How do you do,' the foreigner said. He stared at Alice Oliphant. She looked back at him in amusement, a small smile playing on her face, her large eyes studying him as if deciding on her next meal.

'I'll fuck any non-believer to purify their soul,' Alice said.

Oliphant smiled benevolently. The man on Alice's other side flinched as though in pain. There was an empty bottle of wine in front of him and another that was half-full.

'And this is my secretary, Naftali,' Oliphant said. 'A very talented poet.'

'Naftali Imber,' the man said, extending his hand for a shake. 'How do you do. What name do you go by?'

'They call me Foreigner,' the foreigner said, and Oliphant laughed.

'But we are all foreign here,' he said. 'Until we're not. Just like the orange.'

'If you say so,' the foreigner said. 'Have you been in Palestine long?'

'Oh, no,' Oliphant said. 'Recent arrivals. I've taken a house in Haifa, but we like to get about.'

'You look like a non-believer,' Alice said, still looking at the foreigner hungrily. 'If you have a room we could go fuck later.'

'I'm sorry,' the foreigner said, 'this is your *wife*?'

'We are devotees of the prophet Thomas Harris,' Oliphant said. 'Were, I should say. The man was a crook. But his teachings were true, and we believe that sexual congress, if divorced from beastly desire, can act as a powerful spiritual cleanse for the heretic's soul.'

'And you?' the foreigner said, turning to Imber. 'You're a Jew?'

'Naftali is too pure,' Alice said. 'His soul is beautiful. We could never have congress.'

'Never?' Imber said pathetically. Alice turned her smile on him. 'Darling boy,' she said.

The foreigner noticed the others at the table were talking amongst themselves in a mixture of Russian and Yiddish, and were not paying much attention to the peculiar British lord, his wife and his secretary. No doubt they'd heard the lecture already.

'Excuse me,' he said. 'Do you know of a man named Hoffman?'

The others turned to him then.

'What about him?' one of them said.

'I'm looking for him,' the foreigner said.

'Why are you looking for him?' the other man said.

'I have a message for him,' the foreigner said.

'Give me the message,' the other man said, 'if I see him I'll pass it along.'

His friends laughed. The foreigner felt himself grow irritated. His fingers itched on the butt of his gun. But he couldn't shoot people just for being rude. Not in public, anyway.

'Who are you, exactly?' he said.

'We're with the Palestine Pioneers,' the other man said. 'We've come back to our ancestral land. We've only just arrived, but we intend to purchase some land and work it until Palestine flowers again like it did of old.'

'Hear, hear,' Oliphant said.

'You wish to become felaheen?' the foreigner said, amused. 'Have you worked in agriculture before?'

'I haven't,' the other man said. 'But how hard can it be?'

The foreigner laughed.

'Is Hoffman with you?' he said.

'Hoffman understands our goals,' the other man said. 'Who are you, exactly?'

'Just a friend of his,' the foreigner said.

'You don't seem like his friend,' the other man said. 'I do not know where he is, anyhow, but he was going to help us find suitable land in the Galilee. He said he knew people there.'

'The effendi said he would hole up in the Galilee...' the foreigner said.

'Who?' the other man said.

'Never mind. Have a good evening, all of you. Ma'am.'

'Goodbye, stranger...' Alice Oliphant said dreamily. Imber, sitting beside her, had finished the second bottle of wine and looked up at the foreigner a little blearily.

'Buy me a bottle and I'll recite you a new poem I wrote,' he said.

'I don't much care for poetry,' the foreigner said.

'Our hope is not lost yet – the two thousand years' hope!' Imber said. 'To be a free people in our own nation, the land of Zion and Yerushala'im.'

'Is that it?' the foreigner said.

'I'm still working on it,' Imber said. 'I'm calling it *Hatikva*. That means—'

'The hope?' the foreigner said.

'How did you know?' Imber said. 'You speak Hebrew?'

'A lucky guess,' the foreigner said. 'You know what they say.'

'What?' Imber said.

'Hope in one hand and shit in the other,' the foreigner said, 'and see which one fills up first. Goodnight.'

As he walked away Simeon joined him.

'Any luck?' he said.

'The Galilee, I think,' the foreigner said. 'I'm tired of asking questions in this town. They're all lunatics around here.'

'That Englishman's lady's tasty enough, though,' Simeon said. 'I met her earlier. She has a thing for sinners, and I have a thing for sin. We might make some sweet organ music tonight.'

The foreigner shuddered. 'She's a fanatic,' he said. 'And I do not understand those new Jews, either.'

'They're a desperate people,' Simeon said. 'And desperate people will hold on even to an impossible dream. My slave, too, seems to have run off north. I think he might be trying to reach Beyrouth. He'd better not make me go all that way. But I might keep you company at least partway for now.'

'I'll meet you outside the Jerusalem Hotel tomorrow morning, then,' the foreigner said.

That night the foreigner tossed and turned under Chazan's roof. The goat meat in his belly disagreed with him. He dreamed again that he was running across a vast plain, heading to the place of skulls, but then the skulls started raining down from the skies, splintering when they hit the earth, and the awful sound they made woke him. For a moment he didn't know where he was. It was dark and the sound in the distance, rhythmic and heavy, was of waves breaking against jagged rocks. Then he remembered this was Chazan's house. Amongst the rocks in the sea below was one where King Cepheus was said to have chained his daughter Andromeda as sacrifice for a sea monster. In the end she was rescued by Perseus, who married her. Which seemed unfair to the sea monster, when all was said and done, but it couldn't complain, what with Perseus having slaughtered it. There wasn't really a story, the foreigner thought, that didn't end in bloodshed. At least, none that were worth telling. He listened to the waves and the silence of the city around him, staring into the dark.

He wondered at the people he met. People always left where they came from and looked to start a new life. He had done the same. But he was happy with his lot. This was what he had wanted. There were things other people took for granted: honour, sacrifice, the love of one's nation. But people were just people, whether they were Prussian or Japanese, and all the land was just one land at the end of the day. The foreigner did not see the point of sacrifice. Was it not better to live than to die? In Ahmet Bey he'd found a suitable employer, for the effendi shared the foreigner's lack of conviction about such nebulous things. All anyone could do was live, eat, shit and dream, and finally breathe out a last breath. It all happened in the blink of an eye. Everything else felt like someone was just trying to sell you a carpet you didn't need. His mind wandered, and at last he fell asleep, and in the morning he could not remember having woken up in the night at all.

13

Simeon was already outside the J when the foreigner arrived on his horse. It was just past dawn, the sky clear, the fishermen on the beach returning with their haul. The foreigner could smell fish cooking on coals.

'Did you congress with the English lady?' he said.

'A gentleman never tells,' Simeon said, smirking. 'Shall we ride? I'd like to make haste going north.'

'Yalla,' the foreigner said.

He spurred on his horse and the creature, happy to be put to the task for which God had made it, streaked across the open land, Simeon following behind whooping and hollering. They rode through gardens and orange groves and crossed the Nahr al-Auja over an old wooden bridge, the water of the river rushing below them. From here on it was open land for a while, and they made good progress before reaching the great forest that covered much of the ancient Plain of Sharon, which pharaohs long dead once held in their sway. The woods were pleasant with thick old oaks, but the going was slow and the foreigner was glad they had set off early. There was no road here and he wondered if they shouldn't have followed the coast road to Haifa for a while first. They followed natural paths in the wood and came to a swamp which they had to cross carefully, and the foreigner cursed at the mosquitoes that swarmed here, knowing they were malarial.

He had had the fever twice, and each time was bad, his limbs weak and his mind clouded. He was grateful for modern medicine and whoever it was who'd discovered quinine. The second time he had had the fever was also in the north. He had ridden to Haifa, a pretty little seaside town, and there all but collapsed at the door of the Carmelite Monastery of Stella Maris. Here the monks tended to him, for they had a small hospital attached, as the foreigner emptied the contents of his stomach from both ends at once, not even able to feel humiliation at this lack of control but simply letting his body expel its evil spirits. It had taken him some time to recover fully from the ordeal.

'Little buggers,' Simeon said, slapping the mosquitoes on his arms irritably.

Soon they came across a group of Bedaween chopping wood, their great charcoal kilns belching smoke into the air. The Bedaween of the plain often came into the forest to make coal. The foreigner greeted them cordially enough, and let them see his pistols and his rifle, and their mukhtar laughed and wished him and Simeon well on their way. This was no place for Thomas Cook & Son tourists to visit.

The foreigner and Simeon made good progress through the woods, and they camped that night by a small wadi. Simeon sat with his feet in the water and fished, and the foreigner gutted and cleaned the catch and cooked the fish on their fire. After they had finished their meal the yavaci lit a cigarette and the foreigner took a soothing breath from his tincture of opium and they sat peacefully and looked into the flames.

'It's a job with not much future in it,' Simeon said. 'Hunting slaves. They're going to outlaw slavery soon enough. They've already done it in America, you know.'

'I heard,' the foreigner said, poking at the embers with a stick. 'They had a big war there and everything. I don't agree with your work, Simeon. I don't think I ever told you. I think every man should be free.'

'Then you're an idealist, my friend,' Simeon said. 'But it doesn't matter. I will have to find another line of work, I suppose.' He blew smoke into the air above the fire. 'Perhaps I could be a dragoman, take tourists out on excursions and the like. Sleep with the women, the pretty ones, and tell the men stories of my adventures. The money's not bad and it's a lot less hazardous than running around in the woods after an old slave who's probably succumbed to malaria by now.'

'I suppose I could join you,' the foreigner said. 'If the killing business ever goes sideways. We could start our own firm to take on Thomas Cook.'

Simeon laughed and stretched himself on the ground.

'Best get some sleep,' he said.

The foreigner slept, but he was troubled, and he awoke in the night, and went soundlessly into the trees. He had had a vague sense that in their course through the forest they had been followed. He moved cautiously in the dark, retracing their path for some time, but could see no sign of any pursuers and so he urinated against a tree and returned to camp.

In the morning they rode again, making good time, and by the late afternoon were suddenly out of the woods and into sunlight. It was a beautiful day. The sun shone the way it can shine only over the Holy Land. They were in a temperate valley that seemed untouched by human hands. Blades of wild grass and za'atar swayed in an almost imperceptible breeze. The air was warm and perfumed with the flowers called Harbingers of Autumn. The foreigner gave a whoop of joy and spurred his horse into a gallop. Simeon followed suit, and the two men thundered across the plain until man and horse became one and all that mattered was speed—

Gunshots have a way of echoing in an open space.

This one rolled like thunder, the sound bouncing off the distant hills, startling a group of pheasants into an undignified run and making a deer burst out of hiding and flee across the weeds into the safety of the nearest wadi. The foreigner reigned his horse sharply, turning as he lay low against the horse. As he turned he saw Simeon, with a surprised look on his face and a hole in his forehead, slide quietly from his own horse and fall down with a muted thud. The foreigner cursed, slid off his horse as it slowed, and pulled out his gun. He scanned the hills but could not make out where the shot had come from. He crawled across the grasses to Simeon.

The bounty hunter was dead, there was no doubt about it. His glassy eyes stared into the same blue skies he had ridden under only moments before, but no longer saw a thing. The foreigner cursed, for he had not expected an ambush, and he kept looking for the shooter but could not see a damned thing. All this while Simeon was just lying there being useless and looking like a wax figure. The foreigner had almost *liked* Simeon. He had to wonder if the shot was meant true or if it had been aimed at him and missed.

Another shot didn't come, however. The foreigner raised himself slowly, anticipating a bullet at any moment, but none came. He wasn't sure what to do. He would have to report this, which was a hassle he had not anticipated. And then there was Simeon's horse, too, to consider. The sky was so blue. He could have done with clouds and rain just about then, some fog ideally. He felt too exposed out there in the open. He called Simeon's horse to him and then, straining with the weight of the giant Turk, pulled the corpse up under the arms and tried to load it onto the horse's back. The horse shied away; Simeon dropped like a bag of rocks; the foreigner cursed and tried again. It took him a few tries before he succeeded. Now Simeon flopped over the saddle and was in danger of falling off again, so the foreigner secured him to the horse with rope and at last he was satisfied that it would hold him.

The foreigner got back on his own mount and rode on, pulling Simeon's horse behind him. The yavaci's heavy corpse lay across the horse's back, Simeon's head dangling from the side and looking up into the heavens. The foreigner couldn't even spur the horse into a trot, the rhythm would no doubt make a mess of the corpse.

He just wanted to get out of that valley. He entered a small wadi and followed the brook with some relief, searching the pine trees above for hidden assailants. He tried to figure out where he was. West of Jenin, south of the Esdraelon. There was nothing for it but to keep going. He followed the wadi, found a secluded spot and tethered both horses to a tree. He left Simeon in the saddle.

The foreigner carried his pistols as he doubled back, moving cautiously until he reached the valley again. He circled it in a clockwise direction, moving methodically and quietly over the hills, making sure to reduce his profile behind trees. He expected either to run into trouble, or that the shooter would be long gone. Instead, going over a rise, he saw a series of low caves in the side of a hill and an old man sitting beside a fire singing happily to himself as he made coffee.

'All the bad things, they go away,' the man sang, 'ifrit or djinn or evil men, bang bang! Bang bang! I shoot them dead,' and here he laughed crazily and stirred the black powder of the coffee into the water. Sitting beside him was a new long-barrelled rifle. The foreigner tried to move as quietly as he could but a dry branch under his foot cracked, betraying him. He stepped forward with both his pistols extended and said, 'Don't even think about it, slave.'

The old man froze, his hand almost touching his gun. He looked suddenly pitiful sitting there by his fire.

'I spared your life, effendi,' he said. 'I have no quarrel with you.'

'You killed my friend,' the foreigner said.

The old man spat.

'Simeon was no one's friend,' he said. 'Are you a yavaci, too? You will take me back to Jerusalem to be hanged, or worse? You owe me a life, effendi.'

'That is true,' the foreigner allowed.

'You could have kept riding,' the old man said. 'You didn't need to come back.'

'I felt I owed Simeon,' the foreigner said. 'Also, I do not like being shot at. No. Keep your hands away from that rifle.'

The old man's hand twitched, as though he considered disobeying.

'Just be done with it, then,' he said. 'I was a faithful slave for so many years. I'd had enough there in the end. But I knew they'd catch up to me sooner or later.'

'Where were you trying to get to?' the foreigner said. 'Beyrouth?'

The old man shrugged. 'Tyre,' he said. 'I figured I could get a boat from there. I always wanted to see Paris.'

'Go to Damascus,' the foreigner said. 'And I will tell them you headed to Tyre.'

'Why would you help me?' the old man said.

'You said I owe you a life,' the foreigner said. 'And you're right. I have no fight with you, old man.'

'It's no use,' the old slave said. 'It's all under Ottoman control. There's no escape for me.' He reached for the gun, picked it up and aimed it at the foreigner. 'I'm sorry I have to shoot y—'

The foreigner fired twice. The slave fell back, the rifle slack in his hands. Twin red flowers bloomed in his chest. The foreigner crouched beside him.

'Why?' he said. 'I would have let you go.'

'Fuck… you,' the old slave said. Then he died.

It was a good death, the foreigner had to admit. He figured the old man was crazier than he'd thought. Crazy enough to kill his master and make a run for it, smart enough to kill Simeon when the yavaci came for him – crazy enough to commit suicide by gunman there at the end—

'Oh, come *on*!' the foreigner said.

He couldn't just leave the old slave there. And he didn't have a horse—

He went looking and found an old donkey tied up at the bottom of the hill, blissfully chewing on thistles. The foreigner untied him and led him up to the caves. He put out the fire and poured out the coffee un-drunk. Then he picked up the old slave – a much easier job than Simeon – and put him without ceremony on the donkey.

Finally he tied him up with some rope. He looked through the old man's saddle bags and in the bottom of one found a stack of British pounds and these he kept to himself. The rest of it was just clothes and one gold watch with a faint inscription on it that said *Feebes* in faded English lettering. The foreigner couldn't think where the old slave got it, but neither did he care. He didn't bother taking it.

He led the donkey back the way he came. He found the horses where he'd left them. By this time it was getting late. The foreigner had hoped to reach the Plain of Esdraelon before sundown but that was not to happen. He would have made camp for the night but he now had two corpses to carry and corpses did not last long in the hot weather of the Levant, even this late into the year.

He sighed and got back on his horse and his small train of grisly cargo followed behind him.

14

Under starlight and a deep black sky the foreigner rode and the dead followed him. The road did not treat the dead well. Simeon was beginning to look distinctly... peaky. And the old slave's donkey kept braying in complaint at his cargo. Nevertheless the foreigner pushed them on, along low hills and through wooded copses, over small brooks and through fallow fields. Eventually a sort of road appeared, and he could see lights in the distance, and then he heard the cry of 'Halt! Who goes there!' and knew he had found Lajjun, which lay just a mile or so from Tell el-Mutesellim – what the Jews called Megiddo and the Christians Armageddon. It seemed appropriate to bring the dead there.

'Don't shoot,' the foreigner called out. 'I have Simeon the yavaci with me and his killer.'

'Who is that there, Foreigner, is that you?' the cry came back. 'We had word you might be coming this way.'

'Word?' the foreigner said. 'From who?'

'Colonel Ali, may God bless him with good health!'

The foreigner peered into the dark.

'Osman,' he said, 'is that you?'

'So it is, Foreigner! Don't move. What is that upon your horse yonder?'

'It's a corpse, Osman.'

'Whose corpse, please, Foreigner?'

'It's Simeon's,' the foreigner said.

'May God in his infinite mercy take pity on his soul!' Osman cried. 'And who is that upon the donkey?'

'A runaway slave Simeon was chasing. I think his name was Dmitry.'

'His name is of little significance,' Osman said. 'How came he to be in this condition?'

'I had to shoot him,' the foreigner said. 'In self-defence as he was reaching for a rifle.'

'I see, I see. And Simeon?'

'The slave killed him with a long shot as we came out of the woods,' the foreigner said.

'Ya Allah!' Osman said.

'I felt compelled to bring them both to the authorities and give a true account of what transpired,' the foreigner said.

'You are wise, Foreigner, wise beyond your years.'

The unseen Osman barked orders. The foreigner heard movement in the dark and soon found himself surrounded by soldiers. Their guns were aimed at him and he raised his hands to pacify them.

'You are armed, Foreigner?' Osman called.

'Two pistols, on my belt, and a rifle behind me,' the foreigner said. 'I also have the yavaci's guns and the slave's.'

'So much violence,' Osman said. He materialised out of the darkness at last, shaking his head sadly, a small, intense man in a crisply ironed uniform. 'Hand the weapons slowly to my men.'

'May I dismount?' the foreigner said.

'Slowly.'

The foreigner got off his horse with some weariness. Before he could reach for his pistols they were taken from him, then the rifle. A soldier turned him round and patted him down, removing the knife strapped to his left leg and the one he had on his belt.

'My, my,' Osman said.

'You know me, Osman,' the foreigner said. 'You know who I work for.'

'If you speak truth, Foreigner, you will not be harmed,' Osman said. 'But I serve the Sultan in Istanbul, not the effendi in Jerusalem.'

'I speak the truth,' the foreigner said.

'Come,' Osman said. He barked more orders at his men, to take the animals to stables and the dead to the doctor to write out a certificate. The foreigner, feeling naked without his guns, followed Osman without protest. There was not much left of the town, he saw – the stone buildings in ruins, and only the khan standing still by the stream – but Osman's men had erected tents and a fence, and had lanterns hanging from poles to provide illumination for this orderly and well-kept camp. Lajjun was named for the long-vanished Roman legions and had since ancient times been a useful spot, high on its hills, for any occupying army to watch over this rich and fertile territory of the valley the travel guides called the Jezreel. Like every other place in Palestine it had had multiple names at multiple times. Names were ever-changing across the map of that land.

In Osman's tent his subaltern prepared coffee while Osman gestured for the foreigner to sit.

'I am not saying I don't believe you,' he said. 'Your coming here in good faith supports your story and does you credit – indeed, had you not done so and I were to find the bodies it would have made life quite difficult for you.'

'I am well aware,' the foreigner said.

'Your master's reach is wide,' Osman said, 'but this valley belongs to the Sursocks of Beyrouth, and they are not to be fucked with.'

'They bought the entire valley?' the foreigner said, surprised.

'They did,' Osman said, 'and told the Bedaween to fuck off into the bargain. They may be absentee landlords, but they like to keep an eye on their possessions.'

'I see,' the foreigner said, for he indeed saw now why Osman was there and why the camp was so well-kept and the man's uniform so beautifully pressed. 'I thought you served the Sultan in Istanbul,' he said.

'I do,' Osman said, not smiling. 'And the Sursock family is much in his grace, Foreigner. Your master's reach into this valley is limited.'

'Look,' the foreigner said, irritated now, 'I have no designs on this godforsaken place. I am merely passing through and have no desire to dawdle. Simeon and I were travelling together from the Bab el-Wadi to Jaffa, and elected to join forces on our journey north. I could not have conceived that an elderly slave was such a sure hand with a rifle, and neither did Simeon or he wouldn't be lying here dead and unmourned. I did right by him and went to find his murderer. I would have taken him alive but the old slave was mad and would not come willingly. I wasted half a day carrying both of their useless carcasses here, much like the Good Samaritan.'

'That is not exactly how the tale goes,' Osman said, 'and there are still some Samaritans living in Nablus to this day who might take exception to your comparison. Nevertheless. I have no reason not to believe you, but I must make inquiries. You will be my guest for tonight.'

'Your prisoner, you mean,' the foreigner said.

Osman did laugh at that.

'You have been a prisoner before, I'm sure,' he said. 'But no, you are a guest. I will simply keep your weapons until such time as they can be returned to you.'

'And the dead?' the foreigner said. Osman's subaltern brought over coffee and Osman drank before replying.

'They must be sent back to Jerusalem,' he said. 'You might even be in for some money. That slave Simeon was chasing had a blood price on his head.'

'I don't want that kind of money,' the foreigner said, and Osman shook his head.

'Money is money,' he said.

The foreigner slept well enough. In the morning he rose early and stood on the hill overlooking the Esdraelon. The entire valley was spread out before him, fields crowned here and there by small villages, the sun falling on blades of golden wheat beyond count, and beyond them the foreigner could see the Nazarene hills upon which Jesus once trod, light of foot and with the voice of the Lord echoing in his head. The valley was pretty. He was eager to get the hell away from it.

He watched as a line of dust rose on the horizon, resolved itself into a rider at full gallop. In the daytime he could make out the wooden observation towers of the camp, and heard a signal called out. Osman came out of his tent as the rider approached. The soldier on the horse dismounted and saluted before handing Osman a note. Osman read it and nodded.

'It's from Colonel Ali,' he said.

'What does it say?' the foreigner said.

'That he is on his way. He will be here by noon.'

'Then he had left Jaffa not far behind me,' the foreigner said.

'So it seems.'

'He was looking for this slave,' the foreigner said.

'That is so,' Osman said. 'No doubt he'll be pleased.'

'May I go?' the foreigner said.

'Let us wait for the colonel,' Osman said. 'I can offer you breakfast, effendi.'

'It's effendi now, is it?' the foreigner said. 'What was the price on the head of that slave?'

Osman shrugged.

'Enough to buy you breakfast,' he said.

The foreigner did not mind waiting. Hoffman wasn't going

anywhere. He'd get another day to live, another day to fear what was coming. He'd be holed up with the Jews somewhere in the Galilee, the foreigner thought. Tiberias or Safed, most likely. He'd be easy to find. Palestine was a hard place to really hide in. He ate his breakfast. He watched Osman at the head of his soldiers as they went on their morning patrol. He watched Armageddon rise less than a mile from the camp, the ancient tel on top of it. More ruins. It was always ruins, it was why tourists came to Palestine in the first place.

By noon he saw the dust raised by several riders. They were joined by Osman and his men and all returned to camp together. The foreigner stood as Colonel Ali rode in.

'Colonel,' he said.

'Osman tells me you've been busy,' the colonel said.

The foreigner retold his story. Colonel Ali nodded when the foreigner was done.

'It's a shame about Simeon,' he said. 'But I suppose this is always the danger in this line of work. That old slave, though, he had hidden talents.'

'It was probably just a lucky shot,' the foreigner said.

'There is a reward on his head. You wish to claim it?'

'No,' the foreigner said. Colonel Ali nodded.

'Wise,' he said.

'Then I am free to go?' the foreigner said. He was suspicious of Colonel Ali. The colonel had given no indication he was heading north when they last met. Yet here he was, and must have been close behind the foreigner and Simeon.

'Where do you wish to go?' the colonel said.

'I'll ride to Nazareth first,' the foreigner said.

'I can offer you an escort,' Colonel Ali said, and the foreigner would have laughed but he knew better than to offend the colonel.

'I think I'll manage,' he said, then, 'Oh, did you succeed in your mission of capturing Ugly and One-Eyed?'

'Not yet,' Colonel Ali said. 'I have reason to believe they are in the vicinity, however.'

'Is that so?' the foreigner said, discomfited. He wondered if it was coincidence, but he did not believe in coincidences. Nor did he forget that Colonel Ali, too, was looking for Hoffman.

'I do not like your business,' Colonel Ali said. 'But it is clear events transpired as you told them. The bullet in Simeon matches the slave's gun, and you clearly shot the slave. It was nice work. You can go, but watch your step as you do. An old slave may not be the only one wishing to take a shot at you out here.'

The foreigner shrugged at that, and Colonel Ali laughed, a short sound with no humour in it.

'You think it is your land to play in like in a sandbox,' the colonel said. 'Because of the Capitulations. But it is not. It's ours.'

'Yes, Colonel,' the foreigner said. He did not wish to argue. The truth was the Ottomans were weak and had been for some time. They'd only kept this part of their empire thanks to the intercession of the European powers – hence the Capitulations, the special privileges European citizens now enjoyed. So Colonel Ali could kiss his behind. But he didn't say that, of course. The colonel could be terrifying.

The foreigner was silent as they gave him back his guns. He felt better when he strapped his pistol belt back on. He looked down on Simeon and the slave as they lay in waiting on their stretchers. Simeon's face looked puffed and broken. The slave looked more at peace. Soldiers picked up the stretchers and put them into the back of a carriage for the journey back to Jerusalem.

Osman came out as the foreigner went to fetch his horse.

'Be careful,' he said.

'Of what?' the foreigner said.

'The colonel wants what you seek,' Osman said. 'And for good reason. So watch out.'

The foreigner didn't ask why Osman was telling him. He was rattled – which was no doubt the point. Osman did not act on his own behalf. So the message came directly from the colonel.

'I'm just taking in the sights,' the foreigner said, and Osman looked at him almost sadly before he turned away.

15

There were people after him, he knew that now. Ugly and One-Eyed were hiding somewhere on his path, and Colonel Ali had his own agenda. Now the foreigner knew why he was allowed to go. He was just the hare to run before the hounds. He was surprised at this, for usually Ahmet Bey's sway held strong over Palestine. So whatever it was that Hoffman had done or stolen, it was valuable enough to make other forces pay attention. The foreigner contemplated this as he rode through the Esdraelon. As peaceful and calm as this land seemed it was a nest of scorpions, small and nasty, the sort that got into your boot when you weren't looking. Well, he thought, he would just have to stomp them if and when they came.

Villagers harvested wheat. Buffalos grazed in the sun. The foreigner rode towards the distant hills.

It was a nice easy ride and the foreigner did not wish to tax his horse. They were both of them pleased to be back on the road again. The Bedaween and Turkoman tribes which had roamed here for centuries must be unhappy with the land sale, the foreigner thought. But this was the way of the world. The effendis had the power and the nomads just had to go around them, the way the water in a brook must go around the rocks. He patted his horse affectionately. Onwards they rode through the valley.

The climb up to Nazareth was steep. Sheep grazed on the slopes, and a small group of Bedaween gathered za'atar from the wild plants that grew in profusion. The foreigner soon saw the town rise overhead, and the horse picked his way unerringly between the old oaks that grew there. Stout stone houses appeared, and gardens enclosed in fences of prickly-pear cactuses. The bells rang out from the Church of the Annunciation. It was a pretty scene. Thomas Cook tourists were already camped on the north side of town where their porters had set up tents and their cooks were busy cooking. The foreigner rode into Nazareth.

He did not intend to stay long. He wanted to see if he was being followed. He watched the approach into town for a while when he was out of sight. He saw two mounted figures climbing the path but they did not make an attempt to go up into town and vanished in a copse of trees. The last time he saw them, Ugly and One-Eyed did not even have horses. If it were them then they'd either stolen them or were supplied by someone else. He remembered the witch had asked about Hoffman. Too many people, it seemed to the foreigner, were after this Hoffman, when all *he* wanted to do was find the guy and do his job. It was vexing. He didn't care what Hoffman carried. The witch had called Hoffman a dreamer. The foreigner did not care for dreams. He reached in his bag and felt the sharp edges of the flint knife that Sheikh Abdullah, the antiques robber, had let him keep. When he closed his eyes he could almost see her again, that ancient woman in her cave, looking at a pool of water and finding a strange, almost inhuman reflection. There had been different kinds of humans living in this land once, he thought; he must have read it in a book.

He did not intend to stay in Nazareth long. He went to see Dr Vartan, the Englishman. Dr Vartan was not really an Englishman. He was an Armenian from Istanbul who studied at the American school there and later joined the British Army as an interpreter during the war in Crimea. He studied medicine in Edinburgh and married a Scotswoman, and instead of a honeymoon the newlyweds took off to Palestine to start a hospital.

If anyone passed through Nazareth the good doctor knew about it. He looked up without much enthusiasm when the foreigner entered the infirmary and said, 'Foreigner.'

'Dr Vartan. Good afternoon.'

'It was until you turned up,' Dr Vartan said. The foreigner had come to him twice before, once with a gunshot wound in his leg and another time with malaria, and the doctor looked after him both times, but he did not like the foreigner and he was not shy about making that known. That was fine with the foreigner. He had no need to be liked. He just wanted to ask his questions and get out of town.

'I'm looking for a man named Hoffman,' he said.

'Why should I help you?' Dr Vartan said.

'I will be honest with you,' the foreigner said, which was the sort of thing people often said when they were about to lie. 'I think there are worse people than me looking for this Mr Hoffman, and perhaps I could help him.'

The doctor looked at him with new eyes and said, 'You support the Jewish cause?'

The foreigner was not sure what the Jewish cause was at first, but then he realised the doctor meant the return of the Jews to Palestine, because what else could it be? And he remembered the new Jews he had met in Jaffa, and he said, 'Yes, exactly. I was just discussing this with my new friend, Lord Oliphant, and his charming wife the other day.'

'Oliphant!' Dr Vartan said. 'He is an impressive man. He came to see me and my work here not a month past. He took a keen interest in the hospital.'

'Oliphant wishes me to find Hoffman,' the foreigner said. 'To help him. For, you know,' he lowered his voice, 'the cause.'

'I am not one of those who believe the Jews must return to Palestine to hasten the Second Coming of the Christ,' the doctor said.

'Oh,' the foreigner said.

'I wish to heal the sick and convert lost souls to the Gospels,' Dr Vartan said. 'But Oliphant—'

'Is an impressive man,' the foreigner said.

'Yes. Well, I cannot offer you much help, in any case,' Dr Vartan said. 'He did pass through here, but whether he went to Tiberias or Safed I couldn't tell you. He came and went in something of a hurry, and I only heard of it through one of my patients who spoke with him briefly about his horse.'

'He has a good horse?' the foreigner said.

'*Had* a good horse,' the doctor said. 'It was roughly treated and could not run fast by then, I understand. He passed through here a few days ago. The horse might have gotten him to Safed, but it would not have got him any further than that, I don't think.'

'I'm much obliged to you,' the foreigner said, and he left quickly after that. It was not too far to Tiberias and he could try there first. He bought a lamb shashlik that was cooking on coals outside the Latin Convent and ate it standing up, the grease from the fat running down his chin. A tourist couple went past and stared at him curiously and he thought how odd he must look to them, with his pistols and unkempt appearance, until he heard the wife say to her husband wistfully, 'Oh, he's so *authentic!*' The foreigner finished his meat and rode out of Nazareth, and he thought of Jesus and how he led his disciples into the Galilee and into endless troubles on their way.

The road to Tiberias was hilly, with a few small, prosperous villages dotted here and there. The first one the foreigner came to, called Reineh, had an elaborate and very old sarcophagus standing by the side of the road, where it was used by the villagers as a water trough. The tourists sometimes made their excursions via Mount Tabor instead of by this much easier, shorter route. Tabor was an oddly shaped mound rising suddenly out of the earth where in ancient times Sisera fought and was defeated by the Israelites, and where much later on the Transfiguration of Jesus took place. Whoever passed through Palestine fought over Tabor at one time or another, from the Emperor Vespasian to Napoleon. There was also a good view from the top, if you were into that sort of thing. The foreigner had been once just to take a look. He did not much care for the Galilee, which was like a nation unto itself and where half the runaway slaves of the sort Simeon had chased ran to in the hope of vanishing.

In due course the foreigner passed the Horns of Hattin, where Saladin at last defeated the crusaders and watered the ground with the blood of the Templars. The ride itself was pleasant here. The horse broke into a canter along a level ridge of hills, and the foreigner reflected on how pleasant it was to travel without a second horse and donkey behind them both carrying dead men. For a moment he thought of the young goat he had thoughtlessly bought and then, almost as quickly, discarded for the slaughter. He would have liked to have had the kid goat there, he realised, and he felt a pang of loss he couldn't quite explain.

At the end of the ridge, and with the sun not yet setting but low in the sky, he came abruptly upon a sheer drop down and beheld below him the Sea of Galilee, with smoke rising from campfires along the shore and a few fishing boats out on the lake. Far in the distance was Mount Hermon dusted in snow, while down on the shore there squatted the town of Tiberias, which looked more pretty from a distance than it did on actual approach. The lake sat nestled in a basin some thousand feet below him. The foreigner now began the slow descent with his horse and about halfway down the slope came across a Bedaween encampment. He slowed as he went past, dogs streaming out to bark at him, the women watching him from the cooking fires. The foreigner shouted a greeting. A man with a rifle strung over his shoulder raised his hand in return, and the foreigner rode on. He did not wish to dawdle.

He reached Tiberias by sundown. The city had only a partial wall. It was much damaged in the earthquake back in '37, the foreigner knew, and people still recalled that terrible night when the ground opened up and the houses came down. A lot of people died that day, in both Tiberias and Safed. Now the city seemed dark and a little menacing to the foreigner as he rode in. If Jerusalem was mixed, Jaffa Muslim and Bethlehem and Nazareth Christian, this town was for the Jews. He saw them now, black-clad and strange, with their wide-brimmed hats and long side curls, going about a business the foreigner did not understand. This was a town for praying and debating old texts, its people living on the charity of their brethren in Europe and America. The foreigner did not wish to tarry here unnecessarily but if Hoffman had gone to the Galilee it would be amongst his people that he would seek to hide. The foreigner wondered how best to go about his business. The looks he got were not overtly hostile but they were not friendly either, and few lights illuminated the darkening streets. He rode to the lake shore and sought the Latin Convent, where he saw a Franciscan monk in his distinctive habit standing by the gates.

'Brother Humilis!' the foreigner said, with some relief, for he knew this monk and that made things easier.

'Foreigner?' the monk said, peering up in surprise. He was young, and often went on missions across the Holy Land, which is how the foreigner had first met him. 'But what on Earth brings you all the way to Tiberias?'

'I am glad to see you,' the foreigner said, and the monk brightened in delight and said, 'And you, my friend! Do you seek shelter for the night?'

'I do,' the foreigner said. 'Do you have many visitors?'

'Not tonight,' Brother Humilis said. 'Few come here, and even the tourists seem to avoid the town. I blame the guide books. They call the town filthy and claim it is full of fleas. What nonsense,' he said, scratching himself.

'I am searching for a man who might have come here,' the foreigner said. 'A Jew named Hoffman.'

Brother Humilis shrugged.

'I have not met him,' he said, 'but then again, he would not have come to us. Does he have kin in town?'

'I don't think so,' the foreigner said.

'Is he a devout man?' Brother Humilis said.

'I do not think so,' the foreigner said.

'They are mostly devout here,' the monk said. 'You could ask in one of their many schools or synagogues.'

'Would they tell me?' the foreigner said.

'It depends,' Brother Humilis, 'on what your intentions are with this Hoffman.'

He looked shrewdly at the foreigner. Brother Humilis had more than an inkling of what the foreigner did for a living. The foreigner sighed and climbed off his horse.

'Will you look after him for me?' he said.

'Of course,' Brother Humilis said. 'I could keep you some supper, too, if you'd like. Lentil stew tonight, and some good bread.'

'Sure,' the foreigner said. He wondered if he should not go to bed and resume his mission in the morning, with the daylight, but he felt compelled to go on and so, if with some dampened spirits at the prospects, he left his horse to the Franciscan's care and went once more into the night.

16

Tiberias was the sort of town where people went to bed early, and often on an empty stomach. There was trash in the streets, a stray dog stared at the foreigner as he passed row after row of small dismal houses. He needed to find out if Hoffman was hiding out in Tiberias but if it wasn't bad enough that the Jews weren't all that friendly, they weren't even homogenous. There were Ashkenazi Jews and Sephardi Jews, all from different lands, some of whom spoke the common Arabic and others a language of their own called Ladino, while many were subjects of the German, French, Russian and British powers, and those spoke Yiddish or other tongues. Of the Sephardi Jews many were Maghrebi, and some Algerian, and others were from Turkey, and anyway they all disagreed with each other on obscure articles of faith and city ordinance. It was enough to give anyone a headache. The foreigner headed to the market and saw yeshiva boys – as those Jewish schools were called yeshivas by the Ashkenazim and kutabs by the Sephardim – hanging out in groups outside, and they eyed him with suspicion. The foreigner let them see his guns and they subsided, but took to muttering amongst themselves, and as the foreigner went deeper into the town they followed him at a distance.

The main market itself was closed at this hour but a handful of shops remained open, amongst them a shop selling religious books and manuscripts and a place that served tea where many of the older men sat at long tables with guttering candles on them. The foreigner went into the book stall first, where a black-clad Jew behind the counter looked up at him and seemed friendly enough.

'Are you lost, friend?' he said in German.

'It is so nice to hear a familiar tongue,' the foreigner said. 'Do you sell only bibles?'

'Oh, no,' the bookseller said, 'I have the Talmud and Rashi and the Rambam and a lot more besides. What is it you're after?'

The foreigner said, 'I am looking for a friend of mine, who is one of your people, and I wondered if he came here, for I think he must like books. He is an engineer.'

'We do not get many engineers here,' the bookseller said, 'I'm sorry to say. Does your friend have a name?'

'His name is Hoffman.'

'Hoffman,' the bookseller said. 'Hoffman. There was a Hoffman family who lived here back in the sixties but they went back to Breslau years ago. Was he perhaps a relative?'

'I don't know,' the foreigner said.

'Ask in the tearoom,' the bookseller said. 'The men from many of the congregations meet there of an evening to discuss the affairs of the day and take a drop of something warm. They do soup and whisky there.'

'Soup?' the foreigner said.

'Chicken on a Thursday, if God is willing, but otherwise just broth. We are a poor people.'

'And the whisky?' the foreigner said.

'Strictly medicinal,' the bookseller said.

'Thanks,' the foreigner said.

'Good luck,' the bookseller said.

The foreigner stepped out. The boys were still out there, he knew, looking for trouble. The foreigner didn't want trouble. He just wanted to do his job. He went into the tearoom. All eyes turned to him and the murmur of conversation ceased. The air was scented with the smell of soup and cigarette smoke. The foreigner tipped his hat and said, 'Just a poor traveller seeking a moment of respite, if you please.'

A small man who must have been the proprietor hurried over, wiping his hands on a dirty cloth.

'You're not Jewish,' he said. 'And you carry pistols.'

'Only to defend myself on the road at night,' the foreigner said. 'I am hungry and I smelled your good soup.'

'The soup *is* good,' the proprietor said. 'My wife makes it.'

'It is chicken?' the foreigner said.

'Some bones and carrots, but it will warm you through,' the proprietor said, evidently taking pity on the foreigner. 'Come, sit. You want something to drink?'

'I would not refuse.'

'Sit,' the proprietor said.

The foreigner sat, joining a table where men of different ages all sat together, now back to talking animatedly but in low voices with each other. A small bowl materialised with a spoon. A small glass likewise, and the proprietor poured him a measure. The foreigner downed the drink and almost choked, and the man beside him laughed and said, 'It takes a real mensch to drink this poison. Ah, what I wouldn't give for a real Highland scotch!'

'Put hair on your chest!' the man opposite said, also amused. 'I'm Rabbi Simcha,' he said. 'This is Rabbi Nachson. Who might you be, stranger?'

'Gustav,' the foreigner said.

'And what is your business, Gustav?' Rabbi Simcha said.

'Let the man eat first,' Rabbi Nachson said. 'You came from afar?'

'Lajjun,' the foreigner said.

'From the Jezreel!' Rabbi Simcha said. 'That's a long way in one day.'

'Not too long, with a good horse,' the foreigner said. He tried the soup. It was watery.

'You have a good horse?' Rabbi Nachson said.

'I travel for my master,' the foreigner said. 'He is an effendi in Jerusalem and works me hard. It is his horse. I am sent to find an associate of his, a Mr Hoffman.'

'Why, is he lost?' Rabbi Simcha said.

The foreigner shrugged.

'I do not know his business,' he said. 'Perhaps he got into some trouble and needs help.'

'And are you the kind of man to offer such help as needed?' Rabbi Nachson said. 'You seem a little rough around the edges, if you don't mind my saying so.'

'Yet he clearly has breeding, too,' Rabbi Simcha objected. 'You are Austrian?' he said.

'A long time ago,' the foreigner said, smiling.

'Eat, eat,' Rabbi Simcha said. 'How is your soup?'

'It is delicious,' the foreigner said.

'You see?' Rabbi Nachson said. 'He is a liar!'

The foreigner tensed, but both rabbis burst out laughing and the foreigner smiled too, and put down his spoon.

'Shmulik,' Rabbi Nachson said, 'bring us another drop of your firewater!'

The proprietor reappeared, frowning disapprovingly.

'Please keep your voices down,' he said; but he poured them all another round of drinks. From down the table there appeared a box of tobacco. Rabbi Nachshon rolled a cigarette; Rabbi Simcha passed. The box was offered to the foreigner, who accepted it and rolled one for himself. They lit up using the candle on the table and added more smoke to the already smoky atmosphere.

'It is very convivial,' the foreigner said.

'We do our best,' Rabbi Nachshon said. 'Our life here is hard, but spiritually rewarding. There is no Israel without us, holding on to the old, holy places.'

'Israel?' the foreigner said.

'Eretz Yisrael,' Rabbi Simcha said. 'This land. This is what it has always been. We keep it for God, who put us here. We maintain it with our prayers.'

'About this Hoffman,' the foreigner said, 'would you happen to have come across him? He is a Swiss engineer.'

'An engineer?' Rabbi Simcha said. 'We are all students of the Torah here, Gustav, not...' He waved his hand. 'Dam builders,' he said.

'I thought he might have passed through here,' the foreigner said.

'And does he wish to be found, this Hoffman?' Rabbi Nachshon said. 'You will forgive us, Gustav, but in our experience it is never a good thing when a goy comes asking for a Jew.'

'I mean him no harm,' the foreigner said. 'He was working on behalf of my employer in Jerusalem, and has gone missing. My employer is worried.'

The two rabbis exchanged glances, and Rabbi Simcha shrugged.

'Has anyone here come across a Hoffman?' he called loudly to the room. Heads turned, more shrugs were offered, and the men returned to their talk.

'Try Safed, perhaps,' Rabbi Nachshon said.

The foreigner nodded, thanked them, and rose. He left a handful of coins on the table.

'You will not stay for another drink?' Rabbi Simcha said. He was bright of eye and red of face now.

'I'd better not,' the foreigner said. 'Thank you for your hospitality. Auf Wiedersehen.'

'Auf Wiedersehen, Gustav,' Rabbi Simcha said.

The foreigner stepped back out into the night, the remnants of the cigarette in his mouth. Above him were the stars, but he could no longer see the comet that had passed there and for a brief moment he missed the sight. He walked back through the narrow streets and came across the same group of yeshiva boys who had been evidently waiting for him, and saw that they were armed with clubs and stones.

'You have no business here,' a tall boy said. The foreigner again let them see his guns, but it did not dissuade them, and they closed on him. He knew he could not shoot a bunch of boys. The first of the clubs caught him on the shoulder and a sharp pain erupted all down his arm. The foreigner gritted his teeth and swung with his other fist as he spat his cigarette in the tall boy's face. He felt a satisfying impact as the boy's face snapped back from the punch but then the others were on him, raining blows with hard rocks in their hands, and the foreigner fell from them and tried, too late, to reach for his pistols.

'Get away! Ver farvalgert!' a woman shouted. The foreigner dimly saw her. He was lying on the ground. She appeared out of one of the houses. The boys hesitated, just enough time for the foreigner to painfully reach for a pistol. He fired once in the air. The sound exploded in the quiet street. The boys scattered and the woman retreated back into the safety of her home. The foreigner cursed and stood up slowly. One arm felt numb and his side hurt. He limped back to the Latin Convent.

'What happened to *you*?' Brother Humilis said after he let the foreigner in and locked the gate. 'You look like you were in a fight!'

'I *was* in a fight,' the foreigner said. He winced. 'Not a very fair one,' he said.

'Come, sit,' Brother Humilis said. He helped the foreigner remove his upper garments and examined him critically.

'You took a few knocks,' he said, 'but you should be alright. I have a bandage somewhere...' He rummaged around and returned with a moderately clean piece of gauze which he wrapped carefully around the foreigner's ribs. 'It can be a rough town after dark,' he said.

'Could have fooled me,' the foreigner said.

'Were you otherwise successful in your endeavour?' Brother Humilis said.

The foreigner shrugged, then winced. That hurt.

'I'm not sure,' he said.

'You didn't find your man?'

'I don't think he came here,' the foreigner said. 'I asked around and if they were hiding him they made a good display of not showing it.'

'Tricky people, the Jews,' Brother Humilis said. 'You can't trust them.'

'But you can trust a man to lie a certain way,' the foreigner said, 'and this was not the case here.' He yawned, feeling tired and a little irate. 'I've seen enough men lie,' he said.

'Best get to your sleep, then,' Brother Humilis said. 'Though I saved you some soup.'

'No more soup,' the foreigner said.

Morning. Pain. Bright sunlight hurt his eyes. The cry of lake birds from the window. Mosquitoes had bitten him in the night. Fishermen outside, the smell of cooking fish on coals, boats being readied with dragomans leading their tourist charges for a picturesque ride across the lake where Jesus once calmed a storm.

Hoffman wasn't in Tiberias. Perhaps he wasn't anywhere at all. What if there was no Hoffman? Would the foreigner be doomed to wander this land from one end of it to the other, endlessly, through its snowy mountains, pine forests, ancient caves where ancient skulls proliferated, past ruined temples, synagogues and mosques, a blue sea and a dead sea and a red sea and deserts and plains and hills, as though God had taken every bit of geography there was to be had and tossed it all together heedlessly like a child at play?

No, the foreigner decided. The universe had to have at least a semblance of order, just as empires did. Take the Ottomans, for instance. They didn't do much with the place but they kept it functioning. So was the world. It didn't make a whole lot of sense but it had to make *some* sense. So Hoffman would be somewhere, and not very far now, the foreigner thought. There weren't that many places left to run.

Safed, he thought. If he were a Jew that would be the place he'd run to.

17

The foreigner rode along the lake shore and all the way around to Tell Hum, which some said was the ancient Capernaum and some said wasn't. The huge ruins of some ancient synagogue built out of white stone jutted out of the overgrown shrubbery and a few tourists milled about admiring the antiquities. The foreigner turned south, and up a steep hill, the horse unprotesting and the air turning cooler again by degrees as they climbed the steep road to Safed.

As he looked back he could see the lake below and the Hermon in the distance, and a bird flying over the lake and the small boats that bobbed in the water, but what drew his eye were the two mounted men, too small from this height to make out clearly, who seemed to still be pursuing him. It was three hours' ride from Tell Hum through the mountains before the foreigner reached Safed, the city very pretty from a distance and its houses cascading in neat rows down the mountainside. The ruins of a great citadel stood forlorn on one hill, broken down from the same earthquake in '37 that had also killed so many down in Tiberias. Here it had thrown house over house and buried the living in rubble. The earth had killed many that day. Land, the foreigner thought, could be vindictive. But there was no trace of that tragedy now. A few horses and donkeys followed the steep routes and many of the houses were painted blue as if the skies here were lower than anywhere else on Earth, and it was said if one could not speak to God in Safed one could not speak to him anywhere. The foreigner had long ago given up on looking for God, but he had not given up on looking for Hoffman.

The town was divided into a Jewish Quarter and a Muslim Quarter and the foreigner went to the Muslim Quarter first, where they spoke with a Damascus accent, and he went to the house of Abu Latif.

Abu Latif wasn't in when the foreigner arrived. A boy came out for the foreigner's horse and said, 'He went to the village.'

'What village?' the foreigner said.

The boy just looked at the foreigner like the foreigner was stupid and didn't bother to reply to that.

'He left you a message, though,' he said.

'A message?' the foreigner said. 'Did he know I was coming?'

'He received a telegram from Jerusalem to look for a stranger in town,' the boy said.

'And did he find him?' the foreigner said.

'I did,' the boy said. 'It wasn't hard. Strangers stick out here. You sure do.'

'What's your name?' the foreigner said.

'Salim,' the boy said. 'And you're the foreigner who kills people for Ahmet Bey.'

'You know this how?' the foreigner said.

'My father talks,' the boy said. He considered. 'He trusts me.'

'Where is this other stranger, then?' the foreigner said.

'He rents a room from a widow in the Jewish Quarter,' the boy said. 'He does not come out much but seems to spend most of his time inside. It is as if he is waiting for something.'

'Or someone?' the foreigner said. 'Someone like me?'

'It's possible,' the boy said.

'Does he seem worried?' the foreigner said.

The boy shook his head. 'He bought some books in town and paper and pens,' he said. 'And he works indoors, mostly.'

'Does he have a horse?' the foreigner said.

'The horse he came in on was no good,' the boy said. 'He sold it. This is how I found him, you see. I went looking for the horse. A man might hide but a horse needs stabling.'

'So he has no horse now?' the foreigner said.

'I didn't say that,' the boy said.

The foreigner tried to mask his annoyance with the boy but it fooled neither of them. The boy grinned.

'He bought a new one,' he said.

'From who?' the foreigner said.

'My father.'

'I see,' the foreigner said. 'Good horse?'

'It's a good horse,' the boy said.

'Can you take me to this stranger?' the foreigner said.

'If I do, will you kill him?' the boy said.

'That's not for you to worry about,' the foreigner said.

'It's what my father said you'll do,' the boy said.

'Is it a problem for you?' the foreigner said.

The boy considered. 'Murder is wrong,' he said. 'What right do you have to take somebody's life? Besides, he seems harmless, this stranger.'

'Is he armed?' the foreigner said.

'Armed? I don't think he is,' the boy said. 'Is it not wrong to kill a man when he can't even defend himself?'

'You think like a boy,' the foreigner said. 'Killing isn't noble but neither is it a deviation. It is just a thing that nature does, and every moment people kill or are getting killed. Animals kill and fungus kills and no God in his heaven judges them.'

'But this is murder, what you plan,' the boy said.

The foreigner looked at him, amused. 'You think there are degrees of killing?' he said. 'You really *are* a boy.'

'What if I refuse to help you?' the boy said.

The foreigner shrugged.

'Then I will find him myself,' he said. 'It's what I do. And like you said, foreigners stick out in this kind of place.'

The boy considered.

'What will you give me if I help you?' he said.

'The arrangement is between your father and the effendi in Jerusalem,' the foreigner said. 'I was not even aware of it, so it has nothing to do with me.'

'But we can make our own arrangement,' the boy said. 'After all, my father's gone to the village and this effendi of yours is far away in Jerusalem.'

'Very well,' the foreigner said. 'I can give you a Napoleon.'

'One Napoleon?' the boy said. 'For a man's life?'

'Well, then,' the foreigner said. 'What price a life, boy?'

'An English ten-pound note,' the boy said.

The foreigner whistled.

'You value your services too highly,' he said.

'I'll throw in a goat,' the boy said. 'We have plenty.'

'No more goats,' the foreigner said, 'not for all the sins in Palestine. I'll give you two sovereigns.'

'Ten pounds,' the boy said.

'Is that too high or too low for a life, I wonder?' the foreigner said. 'I will give you five pounds, after you lead me to him. Or don't, and I'll go myself.'

'I suppose when you put it like that,' the boy said, 'it seems any life is only worth what one is willing to pay for it.'

'So we have a deal, kid?' the foreigner said.

The boy nodded.

The sun had set by the time they went into the Jewish Quarter. The stone houses' blues deepened to black, and the smell of cooking foods wafted out of open windows and courtyards. The town was pleasant, with flowers growing here there and scenting the air, and as the foreigner climbed one terraced street to another it was on the roofs of houses that he trod. There were many people out in the streets, the men in black and the women with their heads modestly covered, and none of them paid much attention to the foreigner and the boy. An air of supressed festivity suffused the crowds, but when the foreigner questioned him about it the boy just shrugged.

'There,' the boy said, stopping. He pointed to a house with a light burning in the window. 'This is the widow's place.'

'And he is inside?'

'You can see him,' the boy said, still pointing. The foreigner watched and indeed could now make out the silhouette of a man bent over a book at the table inside. He nodded and fished in his pocket for the five-pound note.

'You won't hurt him, will you?' the boy said. 'You'll make it quick?'

'It depends,' the foreigner said. 'He has something I need.'

'What is it?' the boy said.

'I have no idea,' the foreigner said. He gave the boy the money and the boy stared at the note for a moment, undecided, before he snatched it from the foreigner's hand and ran off.

Night settled over Safed. The foreigner felt conspicuous in his road clothes and he was hungry besides, and the streets filled with Jews carrying lanterns that bobbed up and down in the dark. It was no doubt one of their many festivals. The foreigner kept a watch on the window but the figure at the table did not move and perhaps he had slumped asleep over his books. The foreigner didn't know. It had been a long day, his ribs still ached from last night's beating, and he was hungry. He abandoned his post, reasoning there was no hurry, and went a short distance down the street until he saw a hand-drawn sign that said, in both Hebrew and Latin letters, *Restoran – Esn*. He followed the sign down an alleyway and into a small courtyard where three low wooden tables were placed in the dirt and low chairs beside them, and a fire burned, and an old woman stirred a pot. She turned when he approached and looked him up and down and said, 'Bist a goy?'

'Bist a Yid?' the foreigner said, and the woman laughed

toothlessly and motioned for him to sit. The foreigner sat. The place was empty but for a small boy, sitting by the fire at the woman's feet, who drew circles and lines in the dirt with his finger.

The woman brought the foreigner a plate. It was a stew of some sort, he saw, filled with beans and chunks of potatoes and bits of beef. It was good. A browned hard-boiled egg came with the stew.

'Vas iz das?' the foreigner said.

'Tsholent,' the woman said.

'Es iz gut,' the foreigner said.

The woman smiled toothlessly. The foreigner ate. The boy drew in the dirt.

'What's his name?' the foreigner said, pointing to the boy.

The woman followed his finger, shrugged.

'David,' she said. She pronounced it Dah-vid.

'David,' the foreigner said.

'David,' the boy said.

'Er iz a kenig,' the woman said.

'He's a king?' the foreigner said, thinking he'd misheard.

'David,' the boy said.

The woman shrugged.

The foreigner finished eating and he let out a belch. The boy laughed at that. The woman said, 'Iz dot gut?'

'Gut,' the foreigner said.

'Gut,' the woman said. She took the plate away.

There was a commotion down the alleyway then. The foreigner rose, alarmed, and saw a horde of black-clad Jews stream past and into the small backyard. They ignored the foreigner and the old woman and lifted the small boy on their shoulders and cried, 'Moshiach! Moshiach!'

The boy looked bemused but also resigned to this. The men carried him on their shoulders out of the courtyard and down the alleyway and then they were gone from sight.

The foreigner said, 'Should I go after them?'

The old woman shrugged.

'Abi gezunt,' she said.

The foreigner left some money on the table. He went back out onto the street. People congregated around a small dais not far from where he stood. He went over. The boy, David, sat on a makeshift throne draped in red velvet. A man poured oil on his feet.

'What the hell,' the foreigner said.

'They're anointing him,' a voice said. The foreigner turned and he saw it was a man whose face he recognised from somewhere, but he didn't know where. Then he realised it was from the photo he carried, and that the man was Hoffman.

'Hoffman,' the foreigner said.

'I know Ahmet Bey sent you to kill me,' Hoffman said.

'How do you know?' the foreigner said.

'The boy told me.'

'Abu Latif's boy? That little shit,' the foreigner said. 'I gave him five pounds!'

'Then you *were* overcharged,' Hoffman said. 'Listen, let's go find somewhere quiet to talk. These guys will be at it for a while.'

Just then another group of Jews in different hats came. They seemed angry. They started to shout at the ones doing the anointing. Men started pushing each other. The foreigner nodded.

'Lead the way, then,' he said to Hoffman.

18

The Citadel of Safed lay ruined and abandoned in the starlight. It was quiet here. Hoffman picked his way through the broken stones like he'd been there before and he knew the way.

'It was terrible when the quake hit,' Hoffman said. 'I heard stories from some of the survivors. One of them still wakes up screaming every night, he was only a boy then.'

'Tell me why I shouldn't just kill you?' the foreigner said to Hoffman. The man's quiet confidence irritated him.

'Ahmet Bey charged you take what I have from me before you do,' the man said. 'But that you will not have by force.'

'Most things can be got by force,' the foreigner said. He considered. 'Why did they anoint that little boy?' he said.

'Who can say?' Hoffman said. 'There are a lot of sects here, some of them mystical. They believe him the messiah, perhaps. For every generation there must arise a candidate, a Khristós, Christ, call it what you will. He must be a boy of the line of David, the king, and if he is successful he shall gather the scattered people of Israel back to their ancestral land and rebuild the temple in Jerusalem, and usher in a new age of peace.'

'You people have been waiting for the messiah for a long time now,' the foreigner said.

'Two thousand years, give or take,' Hoffman said. 'It's not very long. Perhaps this time it will be different.'

'The Hope,' the foreigner said, remembering suddenly the drunk poet in Jaffa. 'You're a believer, then?'

'I believe the times are changing,' Hoffman said. 'In Europe Jews are agitating for auto-emancipation, for nationhood. Conditions there are bad. They will come here. They have already started. As for the rest, I might have an idea about that. Ah, here we are.'

They were inside an almost intact room, but the roof was gone and it was open to the skies. A table and two chairs had been set there, and the foreigner could see signs of a campfire. Hoffman removed a pack from his shoulder and took out a half-full bottle of slivovitz and two glasses. He set them on the table and poured.

'What is that for?' the foreigner said.

'I have a proposition for you,' Hoffman said.

'You knew I would come,' the foreigner said, re-evaluating. He had thought Hoffman would be cowering in his hiding place. But the Jew had other plans all along.

'I knew the effendi would send someone like you,' Hoffman said. 'I need a partner.'

'A partner for what?' the foreigner said.

'For an expedition. You see, I made a slight miscalculation or two when I set about my work. I took the patronage of Ahmet Bey out of desperation, which was not optimal but was necessary at the time. Unfortunately I had made other overtures too. You are not the only one coming for me, Foreigner.'

The foreigner thought of the two shadows who had been dogging his moves. 'I thought they were coming for *me*,' he said.

A smile hovered at the corners of Hoffman's lips. 'You must have made enough enemies, I presume.'

'Not really,' the foreigner said. 'The effendi has enemies. Me, I'm a friendly enough guy. Why do you call me Foreigner?'

'The boy said that is what you are called.'

'That boy sure talks a lot,' the foreigner said. He took the glass of slivovitz and raised it to his lips, considering.

'I do what the effendi asks,' he said. 'This is how I am tolerated here. You ask me to turn my back on him, and that is a deadly mistake.'

'Nonsense,' Hoffman said, raising his own glass. He downed it quickly and filled it up while the foreigner was still considering his. 'Ahmet Bey is nothing but a middling businessman. A successful one, yes, and with good connections, but there are people out there who could eat him for breakfast. He only seems big in such a small place.'

'And what you have is so valuable as to offer protection?' the foreigner said.

'It is enough for you to make what you want of yourself,' Hoffman said. 'But it will be dangerous, getting it.'

'What is it, then?' the foreigner said.

'Can I trust you?' Hoffman said.

'Let's assume not,' the foreigner said. 'For the moment, at least.'

Hoffman laughed.

'Very well,' he said. 'Look.' He reached for a stick from the blackened fire. With that he began to draw on the table.

'We're here,' he said. 'We go down the lake, then down the Jordan, to the desert that lies here…' He marked an X on the spot, then tapped it with the stick.

'It's there,' he said.

'What is?' the foreigner said.

'The treasure,' Hoffman said. His eyes shone.

The foreigner thought of all the useless antiquities lying all about the land and he sighed inwardly but he said, 'What treasure?'

'The treasure of the temple,' Hoffman said. 'What do you think Warren was looking for under Jerusalem back in '67? It was looted by the Romans, and Titus himself took the treasure to Rome. There were almost one hundred items, which were put on public display. When the Vandals sacked Rome they took the treasure to Carthage, but when Belisarius defeated the Vandals in his turn he took the treasures back to be kept safe in Byzantium. Are you with me so far?'

'Sure,' the foreigner said. 'I like a good story as much as the next guy.'

Hoffman smiled thinly.

'Procopius, the historian, then tells that the treasures were sent by Justinian *back* to Jerusalem for safekeeping,' Hoffman said. 'They went to the Nea, the then-new, opulent church Justinian had built. But the church fell to the Persians only a few decades later and was lost.'

'And the treasure?' the foreigner said, interested despite himself.

'It was taken from the Nea to the nearby Monastery of the Cross,' Hoffman said. 'Which still stands, more than a thousand years later. There the monks guarded it, and it was said they buried it in a secret place. I believe I now know the exact location of that place.'

'And how do you know that?' the foreigner said.

'I am an engineer,' Hoffman said. 'Just like the men who built the Nea and the Monastery of the Cross. I was hired by the Orthodox Church to undertake preservation work at the monastery. In the course of my work I uncovered some of the ancient tunnels the monks used in bygone days as escape routes. Wonderful workmanship. I surmised they would have travelled in one such tunnel out of the city to carry the treasure. I was allowed access into their library and there I studied many of the ancient manuscripts, until I found the map.'

'A map,' the foreigner said.

'Yes,' Hoffman said.

'To the lost treasure of the Second Temple,' the foreigner said.

'Yes. You don't believe me?'

The foreigner drank his slivovitz. Hoffman, grinning, filled up his glass again. The foreigner said, 'It's a tall tale.'

'It's true,' Hoffman said.

'You have seen it, then?' the foreigner said. 'This treasure?'

'I did not,' Hoffman said. 'This is where you come in, my friend. I propose we travel there together to find it. It is a dangerous route and a dangerous place, and there are people after me for a promise of gold. I knew Ahmet Bey would never keep me alive if he had the map. Why would he? He would merely sell it on, and quietly, and grow ever richer and more powerful. But you – a man like you – you don't owe fealty to mammon. You like adventure, and this is an adventure – with a great reward at the end of it!'

'What would you do with it if you found it?' the foreigner said. 'The treasure?'

'Share it with the world,' Hoffman said. 'It will serve as a promise to the many Jews of the diaspora, whether they are believers or not. That the time is nigh to return to our ancestral land.'

'You're a fanatic,' the foreigner said.

'Not at all,' Hoffman said. 'I'm a pragmatist. Hush. Have you heard something?'

The foreigner stilled. He put his hand on his gun. It was quiet in the abandoned citadel. Hoffman was not as confident as he appeared. He was a desperate man. And his story was absurd. And yet...

The foreigner thought of gold.

They moved cautiously through the dark night and the streets seemed full of hidden threat. The kabbalists or whatever they were had gone, and the streets were suddenly deserted. They went to the widow's house, where Hoffman got his few belongings. From there they went to Abu Latif's. The boy was sitting in the courtyard and he said, 'I see you found each other.'

'I need my horse,' the foreigner said.

'And mine, please, Salim,' Hoffman said.

The boy went and got the horses.

'I thought you were going to kill him,' he said to the foreigner.

'Still might,' the foreigner said, and Hoffman laughed – his confidence in his plan really did seem rock solid. The foreigner had to admire such conviction, even if it was unwarranted.

They mounted their horses and Hoffman said goodbye to the boy. The foreigner did not, and the boy stuck his tongue out at him as they rode away. The two riders did not speak. They departed the city in the night and the horses stepped cautiously down the slope. The stars overhead illuminated little. The foreigner felt exposed. He kept his rifle ready on his knees as they rode. A half hour out of Safed and lower down the hills they came to a small copse of trees. The foreigner slid down beside his horse and walked with the horse providing him cover from the darkness of the trees and as they got closer he slapped the horse's rump and the horse bolted.

A shot rang out in the night. The foreigner was already moving fast, running in a crouch into the wood. He saw a shape ahead of him and raised his rifle and fired while still running. The shape fell. The foreigner ran to it and saw a man lying in the dirt unmoving and he thought, it was a lucky shot.

'Foreigner?' Hoffman called out. 'What is happening?'

The foreigner cursed him silently and then he heard Hoffman making a strangled cry. The foreigner stepped to the edge of the trees and peered out. He recognised the man holding Hoffman with a gun to his head – it was Ugly.

'I just shot your partner!' the foreigner called. He moved quick as Ugly's gun fired at the place where the foreigner had been. The foreigner crouched low and peered through a shrub. He was lying on pine needles. They smelled pleasant. He tried to get a bead on Ugly.

'I'm going to kill the engineer,' Ugly said. 'You're working with him now?'

The foreigner didn't reply. Hoffman said, 'I am sure we can be reasonable about this, Ugly. I am not—'

'Shut it,' Ugly said. 'You owe her a debt, Hoffman.'

'I owe the witch nothing!' Hoffman said. 'The find is mine!'

'You made a lot of promises to a lot of people,' Ugly said, 'and now One-Eyed's dead, too. There's always a price, Hoffman. There's always a p—'

He screamed then, for the foreigner had pulled the trigger and the bullet caught Ugly in the shin and he dropped his pistol and let go of Hoffman in his hurry to clutch his leg. The foreigner would have finished him then but Hoffman took hold of Ugly's pistol and he pointed it at the bandit with unsteady hands and he said, 'Then let this be the price, that I have spared your life tonight.'

The foreigner stepped out of the trees.

'It would not be sensible to let him live,' he said.

'Let me live!' Ugly said. He lay on the ground moaning and holding his leg.

'The witch sent you?' the foreigner said.

'She was helping him,' Ugly said. 'She wants what he knows. The treasure.'

'Hoffman,' the foreigner said, 'go find their horses, will you? They would be tied up somewhere nearby.'

'What do we need their horses for?' Hoffman said.

'We could trade them for passage,' the foreigner said. He turned back to Ugly. 'Why would the witch entrust this to you?' he said. 'No offence.'

'We work for her from… time to time,' Ugly said. 'Look, are you going to help me or what here? I need help—'

The foreigner saw Hoffman had gone off. He knelt beside Ugly.

'Oh, no, no, don't,' Ugly said.

'You know how it is,' the foreigner said. His hands closed on Ugly's throat. Ugly tried to fight but the foreigner pressed down and eventually Ugly stopped kicking and his hands fell uselessly by his side.

The foreigner searched him quickly. In a hidden pocket sewn into the lining of Ugly's shirt he found the coin he knew was there and palmed it. He couldn't say why he took it, only that Ugly wouldn't need it anymore. Then the foreigner got up and went back into the wood for One-Eyed's corpse but he could not find it and he cursed his own stupidity. However his bullet connected it hadn't finished the second bandit.

'Hoffman?' he cried. 'Hoffman!'

'What!' Hoffman said. He came back into the clearing leading a single horse. 'There was only one,' he said. 'Hey, what happened to Ugly!'

'It happens like that sometimes,' the foreigner said. 'It's tragic.' And he picked Ugly up by the feet and began to drag him into the cover of the trees.

19

A year earlier, Ahmet Bey had sent the foreigner down to the Dead Sea on a job. He was woken up at Ulric's. He went to the effendi's house. Zorik welcomed him into the courtyard. There was a cage with a songbird inside it hanging from the old tree. It was before the effendi acquired his swearing parakeet. The foreigner tapped the bars of the songbird's cage. Zorik followed the sound, said, 'They never last long, the birds.'

'Where's Ahmet Bey?' the foreigner said.

'He is not joining us today,' Zorik said.

'Why not?' the foreigner said.

'This is a delicate matter,' Zorik said. He looked uncomfortable, which in itself was odd. Not much affected his cool. 'Ahmet Bey wishes you to go down to the Bahr al-Mayyit.'

'The Dead Sea?' the foreigner said. 'I hate it down there.'

It was hot as hell there in the summer, and it was summer then.

'What you like or dislike is between you and your priest, if you have one,' Zorik said. 'The effendi needs you to do this for him.'

'Then let him tell me himself,' the foreigner said.

'He won't,' Zorik said. 'It is a matter of pride with him.'

'Why?' the foreigner said. 'What's so special about this man he wants dead?'

Zorik hesitated.

'It isn't a man,' he said. 'It's a woman.'

'A woman?' the foreigner said. 'Why would Ahmet Bey wish to kill a woman?'

'Why do you suddenly ask questions, Foreigner?' Zorik said.

'Because I was not asked to kill a woman before,' the foreigner said.

'Man, woman, what's the difference?' Zorik said. 'Dead's dead.'

'What did she do,' the foreigner said, 'break his heart?'

Zorik shrugged.

'Will you do it or not?' he said. 'I have other things to get on with here.'

'Yeah, sure, what the hell,' the foreigner said. But he wasn't happy about it.

He played cards at the mad monk's in the Armenian Quarter that night. The mad monk may well have been Armenian, no one knew for sure. He wore a dirty cassock and his place was a crumbling stone shopfront between a church and an abattoir. There were several men around the wooden table and a bottle of whisky in the middle of it. A couple of hung lanterns provided the only illumination. Ugly said, 'Raise,' and pushed all his coins in. This was back when Ugly and One-Eyed were flush, having reputedly robbed a money changer with a shipment of gold on his way back from Damascus.

'Call,' the foreigner said. He pushed his pile in and flipped over his cards. Ugly cursed and One-Eyed looked less than happy, too, even though it wasn't his money.

'You ever kill a woman?' the foreigner said, considering.

'A woman?' Ugly said, momentarily forgetting about his losses. 'Sure. Who hasn't?'

'Once or twice,' One-Eyed said. The foreigner had forgotten that people were always killing women hereabouts, over family honour and things like that. But it was hardly a crime.

'I might have a job for you,' the foreigner said.

'Oh?' One-Eyed said. It was hard to tell who was the brighter of the two, One-Eyed or Ugly. It was possible, the foreigner thought, that they were equally dim. Which did not make them any less dangerous – if anything, more so. They didn't have to think too much before they shot someone.

'On the Bahr al-Mayyit,' the foreigner said. 'You know the area?'

'Know it well,' One-Eyed said. 'We'd need camels.'

'What's in it for us?' Ugly said.

'That money you just lost,' the foreigner said, and the mad monk, listening, gave a short, braying laugh.

'I'll split my pay with you,' the foreigner said. He saw Ugly and One-Eyed exchange a glance, and Ugly shrugged.

'Sure,' he said. 'We weren't doing anything anyway.'

They set off the next day, on three patient camels hired from the Bedaween outside the Jaffa Gate. These were not the famed racing camels of Arabia and the Sinai, but plain old beasts, good-natured – as far as camels went – and slow, and the foreigner took time to settle into their strange gait, for he did not like camels. The descent from Jerusalem into the desert was rapid. One moment there were trees and shrubs and then there was sand, and the land sloped ever downwards as the heat rose. The foreigner felt the pressure in his ears. The road was not terrible and they passed a group of English tourists and their dragomans making the climb up to Jerusalem on the way.

'It used to be you could get away with anything down there,' Ugly said, and One-Eyed nodded and said, 'Especially on the south side of the sea. It wasn't safe for anyone.'

'So what happened?' the foreigner said, for he did not know the area well.

'The Ottomans put a garrison in Es-Salt,' One-Eyed said. 'It was a ruined fort but they'd rebuilt it and now maintain order under the Pasha of Damascus. I'm not saying you can't get up to mischief there, because you can, but they don't make it easy anymore.'

'I'll bear that in mind,' the foreigner said—

On and on they rode, until a shimmering lake arose in the distance below them, a perfect silver mirror around which nothing lived. The heat was intense by then. They entreated the camels go faster. The foreigner wasn't sure where the woman went. Her name was Sister Agnes and she was a nun. Why the effendi in Jerusalem wanted a nun dead was anyone's guess. The foreigner felt bad about the whole thing. Women always died so men could have adventures. They died for saying the wrong thing or not saying anything, for the food being too hot or too cold, for voicing an opinion or for liking the wrong person. Sometimes they were just in the wrong place at the wrong time. That was just how it went. They were like those scapegoats that took everyone's sins upon them. When they got to the shore the salt sparkled in the sunlight like thousands of diamonds. They circled the lake northwards and it wasn't long before they came to the place where the Jordan fell into the lake. A short ride from there was the Pilgrims' Bathing Place, where Jesus was baptised, and the foreigner and his two companions rode there. By then it was late afternoon and cooler, and the banks of the Jordan were awash in green vegetation, and turtledoves and nightingales sang in the jujube and osher trees, which were also called Apple of Sodom. Something moved in the bushes then and Ugly and One-Eyed were after it in pursuit, and two shots rang out, and the foreigner saw a wild boar fall, crying pitifully as its blood seeped into the mud. Ugly commanded his camel sit and climbed down, and he went to the boar and shot it again in the head, then looked up happily.

'We'll eat well tonight,' he said.

That night around the fire, the pork crackling as it turned, the foreigner considered this life was not so bad. There were no trains and roads and factories, no big cities, nothing but the skies overhead and the Jordan burbling gently as it flowed. It must have been much the same when Jesus trod this same ground, though he was probably absent the pork. One-Eyed stretched himself beside the fire and turned the meat over gently round and round. Ugly reached into a hidden pocket and came out with a small object that caught the light as he flipped it, up and down, up and down.

'What's that?' the foreigner said.

Ugly tossed it to him and the foreigner caught it. He looked at the coin in his palm. It was clearly ancient, but well-preserved, as though it had sat untouched in a pot in the ground for centuries. There was a ship's anchor on one side and a star on the other.

'It's a Widow's Mite,' Ugly said. 'You know, like English pennies but for ancient Jews. It's called a pruta. It's from the time before Jesus, when a Hasmonean king ruled Judea. It's got his name on it. Ten of these could get you a loaf of bread back then.'

'Where did you get that?' the foreigner said, fascinated despite himself.

Ugly shrugged. 'Found it one time,' he said. 'On a job. It was just lying there on the ground. It's my lucky coin. I always keep it with me.'

The foreigner looked at the coin again, thinking how strange it was someone would have given it in change in a shop in Jerusalem or somewhere all that time ago, and how even stranger it was that Ugly kept it. Then he flipped the Widow's Mite back to Ugly, who caught it and put it away again carefully. They ate the pork, and Ugly and One-Eyed went off to one side and were soon asleep. They lay together like husband and wife, and the foreigner thought how you could never really know anyone. He didn't sleep but got up and went, very softly, along the river until he came to the bathing place. Pilgrims slept alongside the river, some in tents, others under the stars. The foreigner wished to go into the river in the dark and wash himself clean and be baptised. He didn't know why he was there. He'd agreed with Ugly and One-Eyed that they'd go in the morning and finish the job.

He found Sister Agnes standing on the water's edge. She was

dressed all in white, and her hair too was white and fell down to the small of her back. She turned when she heard his approach and offered him a beatific smile that he found unsettling.

'I knew he would send someone,' she said. 'But I didn't think my angel of death would be so handsome.'

The foreigner blushed, he didn't know why. 'You should step away from the water,' he said, 'the current can be strong here.'

'How would you do it?' she said, not heeding him. 'Have you thought about it? A strangling, a shooting, a drowning? Did he instruct you with a final message to say to me before the deed is done? I heard he does that, sometimes.'

'Why does he want you dead?' the foreigner said. 'What have you done?'

'Done?' she said, looking at him in surprised. 'What's done got to do with any of it? Are you yet a child, to think violence needs a reason? All it needs is a spark.'

'But why?' the foreigner said, 'I don't understand.' He felt very weak then, before her.

'I could tell you I tried to show him the errors of his way,' the nun said, 'and that he didn't like it. But I'd be lying. I found something he wants, but I will not give it to him.'

'What is it?' the foreigner said. A bird called in the reeds, her voice sad and alone. The air was still. He felt afraid.

'Old treasure,' the nun said and smiled, 'like in all the best old stories.'

She spread her arms and for one impossible moment she seemed like a white bird to him, and he thought she would fly. Then she fell backwards into the water, her arms spread out like on a cross, and the foreigner had been right – the current *was* strong there that night. The nun did not fight it. She bobbed once under the water and did not rise again, and the foreigner watched helpless as she washed away.

★

In the morning, they sought the nun's body. It had drifted out into the Dead Sea, where it floated above the water, buoyed by the salt.

'We still get our cut, though, right?' One-Eyed said, watching the small pale figure drift away to the horizon.

'Sure,' the foreigner said. He felt tired. The heat was already unbearable. The corpse would rot, never sinking. Or perhaps the salt would help to preserve her until she got caught in some reeds on the other side of the sea. He didn't know.

'Is Ahmet Bey looking for some sort of treasure?' he said.

Ugly shrugged. 'Who isn't?' he said.

20

Two riders and three horses went down to the shores of the Sea of Galilee, and the foreigner wondered where One-Eyed went and if this was the last they'd see of him. He'd buried Ugly in a shallow grave and covered him with pine needles. It seemed as nice a final resting place as any. He kept the Widow's Mite.

Once on the shore they tied up the horses and tried to get a little sleep until dawn. The foreigner was tired. When he slept he dreamed again of that strange prehistoric woman and her flint knife, watching the new people come. He woke up in a sweat, a mosquito bite swelling on his forehead. He removed all his clothes and waded into the lake, burying his head under the cool water. When he rose back up for air he was laughing.

The sun rose and early morning light glinted on the surface; and for a moment it could have been any time in any century, and the foreigner was set adrift from time and caught in the wonder of the day. Then a barge came gliding across the lake, with two burly Tiberian fishermen pushing it, and a group of tourists standing uneasily on the flat surface of the barge, gawking. One of the fishermen called out, 'Ya Allah, Foreigner, are you naked? Put some clothes on!'

The foreigner laughed and he waded out of the water and stood with his back to the lake as he let the sun dry his skin. The tourists gasped and the fishermen cursed him and the foreigner shook his behind at them and laughed uproariously until he woke Hoffman, who stared blearily and said, 'I can see your willy.'

'I've not washed in some time,' the foreigner said. He waded back into the water with a piece of soap and washed himself thoroughly and when he came out again he sat and watched the rising sun and only then did he get dressed again. In the meantime the tourists disembarked to take in the sights, for the ruins of Chorazin were an hour's ride away and *Cook's Tourist Guide* described it as 'the most delightful place in Palestine'. Already the dragomans were coming along the shore with horses for the visitors.

'We had best get on,' the foreigner said to Hoffman. He strapped on his guns. Hoffman was already waiting with the horses. The foreigner spoke briefly to the older of the two fishermen, and soon money changed hands and Ugly's horse was handed over. The foreigner did not need the money but he needed the horse even less.

They rode out, following the shore on the eastern side of the lake. The foreigner figured it would be safer that way, away from the outstretched hand of the Mutasarrif in Jerusalem. There were few settlements but for some fishing villages and they made good time, and green rolling hills passed them by. Halfway along the lake they saw a ruined city on a hill above and Hoffman said longingly, 'This could be Hippos, one of the famous cities of the Decapolis, perhaps we should stop to have a look?'

'It's all ruins from here on,' the foreigner said, and he spurred on his horse and Hoffman, after hesitating a moment, followed. Onwards they rode, until the lake ended. They headed south and soon came to the Jordan as it departed the Sea of Galilee and wended its way to the Dead Sea through a series of rapids. It was not a great river like they had in Europe, no Danube or Rhine, just a little stream that got itself entangled in tales of miracles and wars.

'You are probably wondering about the treasure,' Hoffman said. He took out a small metal case from his pocket and opened it to reveal a compass, which he then held horizontal in his palm as he squinted. 'We should turn off from the Jordan shortly and begin our ride to Jerash,' he said.

'Is the treasure in Jerash?' the foreigner said.

'It is not,' Hoffman said. 'But it would be a good place to rest, and I have long wished to visit it. I hear the ruins are very impressive.'

'You like ruins,' the foreigner said.

'I like the past,' Hoffman said. 'But my dream is that one day all this land will be rebuilt anew. Imagine paved roads and comfortable towns, gas lamps on every corner, shops providing all the necessities of civilisation, palaces of culture to offer the latest performances of Mozart and Bach! It could be very beautiful, I think.'

'You would turn it into a little Europe,' the foreigner said, amused.

'You like it the way it is?' Hoffman said, and the foreigner said, 'I do.'

'All things must change,' Hoffman said. 'These are modern times.' He looked at the foreigner critically. 'You may play at being a native,' he said, 'but you belong in the industrial age, Foreigner. You can be master or subject, and I know which one I'd prefer to be.'

'I was groomed for mastery,' the foreigner said. 'I ran from it. Here I get to live by my wits and my gun.'

'Your gun won't fell an army,' Hoffman said, 'and your wits will addle sooner or later, if someone doesn't put a bullet in you first. Don't you have something to *live* for?'

The foreigner thought of the woman in Beyrouth, and of his dream of a little farm – and he wished then that he had sent her another telegram, before he left. She would be waiting for him, but no woman waited forever. And he was filled with a melancholy he couldn't quite explain, as though things were coming to an end in a way he had anticipated for some time without knowing.

Perhaps he had an inkling of his own mortality, as all men must from time to time. He didn't know. He shaded his eyes as he gazed beyond the Jordan. A column of dust was rising in the distance and coming closer.

'I do not like this,' he said, and he motioned for Hoffman to follow him up the hill and away from the river. They hid momentarily in a copse of ancient oaks. The foreigner watched in silence and he saw a small column of soldiers arrive at the banks, led by an officer, and he let out a sigh, for the officer was Colonel Ali. Behind the colonel came four mounted soldiers. A sixth horse came behind, upon which lay the unwilling frame of one One-Eyed, bound hands and foot and draped like a sack in an undignified fashion over the saddle. As they reached the Jordan they stopped, and the men left their horses to drink from the river. They gathered round the colonel, and the foreigner saw that one of them was Osman, who he had last seen in Lajjun. No doubt they had followed behind the foreigner since he left the Esdraelon; and poor One-Eyed ran straight into them in his flight. The soldiers crouched in the mud as Colonel Ali drew a map with a stick. He looked up and over the Jordan and for a moment the foreigner had the irrational notion that the colonel was looking directly at him.

'We should put some distance between us and them,' he said to Hoffman in a whisper. It was not that Ali and his men could hear them from this distance; but the foreigner was spooked.

Hoffman nodded. They led their horses out of the trees and along a dirt path until they reached a valley between two low hills and well out of sight of the soldiers. Here they mounted their horses and rode, first at a trot and then at a gallop, east of the Jordan and south. The land rose gradually away from the river, the greenery growing more sparse. There were nomads in the distance but no villages the foreigner could see as yet, and soon he was confident they had left the colonel and his men well behind. It depended how much they knew or suspected. They had tracked him this far, knowing he would track down Hoffman. Now they would be in pursuit. The ride was hard, the horses panting now, and Hoffman looked worse for wear though he never complained. The foreigner did not think they would make Jerash. Ruins lay here and there – a temple, a citadel, an ancient inn, piles of stones and eerily standing columns holding up nothing but the skies. It got dark, the horses were tired, there was no sign of pursuit. The foreigner said, 'Let's stop here.'

It was a narrow gorge with a small brook and if they lit a fire it would be masked by the rocky walls. Hoffman said nothing. He slid off his horse and just lay on the ground. The foreigner climbed down too. He let the horses free. They drank greedily from the brook, then wandered a short distance away to pick at grass poking out of the ground. The foreigner built a small fire. The sun had gone. The night was cold and above them were thousands of stars. There was no other sound but the crackling of the fire, and the foreigner thought again of the hard wooden walls, polished to a gleam, of his childhood, and how much they were like prison bars.

He thought of hunting but he did not want to make a sound with his gun to attract attention. Though there were few villages it did not mean there were no people. He boiled water from the brook and added a handful of lentils and a few chunks of salted beef and a pinch of dried herbs and spices. It was peaceful there, under the stars. His stomach rumbled pleasantly.

'You are probably wondering about the treasure,' Hoffman said. It was the second time he'd said it. The foreigner glanced his way. Hoffman looked wan in the light of the fire, and there were beads of sweat on his brow. He was not a man used to a hard ride and must have been in pain, but he did not complain.

The foreigner said, 'Not really,' and stirred the pot.

'The inventory was written on a scroll of copper,' Hoffman said, 'not on parchment or papyrus. It was meant to survive down the centuries. It listed gold, silver, many of the holy objects. Precious stones as were set into the Urim and Thummim, the breastplate of the High Priest. A man who could find such a treasure would not just be rich – he would be immortalised for the find.'

The foreigner considered. It sounded fantastical, but he believed Hoffman in so far as that Hoffman himself was a believer. The foreigner knew there were always treasures in the ground. In Egypt there were stories of vast tombs under the earth filled with gold. But the foreigner also knew many of them were robbed over the long centuries. He and Hoffman would merely be the latest in a long line of antiquities robbers. He took out the flint knife and closed his fingers around it and closed his eyes. Again he thought he could hear her, that ancient woman to whom it once belonged. Her bones must have long ago turned to dust, and only this tool endured as a reminder that she once existed. She held a baby in her arms. The baby was strange, with the prominent brow ridge of her people but with a chin like that of the newcomers. It was a hybrid baby, and she sang to it in her arms.

'What are you doing?' Hoffman said. The foreigner opened his eyes. Hoffman was looking at him strangely.

'I keep having these visions,' the foreigner said. 'Of people who lived here before.'

'Ancient humans?' Hoffman said. He came and sat by the fire and poked the embers with a stick. 'Yes,' he said. 'Strange creatures they must have been.'

The foreigner thought of the woman with the baby in her arms. She did not seem strange to him. But he was disinclined to discuss it further with Hoffman.

21

A couple of hours' ride from their encampment the next day brought them to Jerash. The foreigner stared in some awe at the valley below, for the ruined city still stood here, in the wilderness, like a testament to the power and majesty of the empires that once held sway there. It was a square mile bounded by broken city walls. Inside it were the ruins of grand temples, theatres and public baths, while a long colonnade composed of hundreds of still-standing columns bisected the city, terminating in a great coliseum that still stood half-broken, bereft of its last gladiators and lions.

'Antioch on the Golden River!' Hoffman said. 'Alexander built her, the Jews occupied her, Trajan built roads for her and Hadrian himself once trod these ancient streets! Imagine what this land once was, Foreigner. What it can be again.'

The foreigner scanned the city. Beyond the ruined walls he could see a more modern hamlet, with smoke rising and cattle grazing, but he noticed these living residents did not go near the old city. He scanned the streets but could discern no other movement within, and still he was troubled by the thought there was something there lying in wait for them.

'Why are we here?' he said.

Hoffman looked uncomfortable.

'I haven't been entirely honest with you,' he said, 'when I told you I knew the location of the treasure. They were wily, those who hid it. The bulk of it is buried near the Dead Sea. There is another, secret scroll buried in Jerash – Gerasa, it was then. The city had not yet fallen to the Sassanids. The monks had scattered clues all over the old cities of the Decapolis, this much I know. No doubt many of them were lost forever. But my hope is the scroll is still here, and it should lead us not just to the vicinity of the treasure, which I already know, but to the exact spot where it is buried.'

This was, the foreigner now realised, just another fool's errand; and he cursed himself for going along with Hoffman. It was not too late, perhaps, to simply kill the man and report back to Ahmet Bey in Jerusalem. But the effendi would already be aware of the foreigner's betrayal, and besides, once the decision *had* been made, the foreigner realised he had no desire to depart from it. He had served long enough. Whatever happened from here on, it would be on his own terms and not a foreign master's, no matter how powerful that master was.

'I'm not even mad at you, Hoffman,' he said. 'I'm more mad at myself. If you find this scroll, will it lead you to another scroll, and then another, and another? No wonder no one's found your treasure in two thousand years! It doesn't exist.'

'Have some faith!' Hoffman said. 'Listen, we'll go down there, it should be a simple matter for me to find it. I just need you to make sure we are not interrupted by those vultures coming for us. But it does not look like we were followed.'

The foreigner scanned the ruined city again but he could see nothing to raise alarm. They rode down into the valley and passed through a broken gap in the walls where a gate might have stood in centuries past. The foreigner kept a wary eye, the rifle resting in his lap. It seemed too quiet to him. In other times he might have found the quiet peaceful, but not just then. They rode down the colonnade. There were houses on both sides, walls and roofs caved in and only the foundations remaining. The foreigner said, 'What are we looking for?'

'There was a temple to Zeus near the forum,' Hoffman said,

consulting the notes in his lap. 'Listen, Foreigner. The treasure is buried on the east of the Dead Sea, in the gorge of the Wadi Mujib. I have told you everything, now. This is a very great secret. Many have sought the treasure, but it is safe.'

'You don't know that it's safe,' the foreigner said. 'Others could have found it before us.'

'Not without knowing the exact location,' Hoffman said, with a confidence the foreigner did not share. But he felt himself uplifted. It was hard *not* to be seduced by the idea. A fortune, and a place in history, and the girl in Beyrouth who was waiting for him... What would she think of him then? He would be not just a killer but someone important in his own right, not by birth and heritage. He let the dream of it lull him.

The temple, when they found it, rose above the city on a low hill, commanding a view of the forum. Its roof had long vanished but its columns rose from their base of stone into the sky as though defying the elements. Hoffman muttered to himself and squinted against the sun as he looked over the lost and sleeping city. The foreigner, too, watched. He thought he saw a shadow detach itself and move furtively in their direction, but when he looked again he could not make it out. It was hot. Perhaps he was imagining things.

'Well?' he said.

'I just wanted to get a good view,' Hoffman said. 'That must be the Temple of Artemis over there – can you see it?' He pointed to the distance, where the remains of a temple much like the one they stood in rose on a hill. 'And there's the hippodrome where they must have had the chariot racing.' He pointed again in a different direction. The hippodrome lay just beyond the temple, a large oval space, still retaining terraced seats – it must have been quite impressive once. The foreigner waited. Hoffman climbed off his horse and measured steps through the rising columns.

'This would have been a Christian monastery back when the monks came here,' he said. 'They would have stayed here, perhaps, after they had buried the treasure. They would have been relieved, having done their job, but also conscious of the changes that were coming. They needed to hide the key, somewhere where it could survive however long it took. There must have been a library here then, of course. But libraries have a habit of catching fire. The scroll says – this is something of a rough translation, you understand – "The scroll lies in the convergence of the Golden River, between Artemis' wildness and Zeus' roar, where the nymphs of old frolic."' He turned to the foreigner, grinning. 'Isn't it obvious?' he said. 'It's in the nymphaeum.'

'What the hell's a nymphaeum?' the foreigner said.

'The water supply,' Hoffman said. And he turned his horse and rode off.

The foreigner cursed, knowing this was all folly. Lost treasures and secret maps and old monks. He chased after Hoffman. It was not far through the ruins to the water works. They still stood, and looked impressive. A monumental fountain stood before them, though dry now. It was semi-circular and topped with a concrete vault. The water would have fallen down from the stone lion heads overhead. The etched faces of nymphs, no doubt beautiful once, stared at them from the stones. Hoffman almost fell off his horse in a hurry. He paced and measured, muttering to himself. The foreigner, too, climbed off the horse. He kept the gun ready, alert for any trouble. It was very quiet still. The river flowed beyond the ruins. The horses were thirsty again. Hoffman traced the path of the aqueduct. He was an engineer. Here and there he pushed at the heavy stones as though expecting them to spring open a secret door, but none materialised, and he went back to muttering.

'A conquering army might destroy much of a city, if it has to,' he said after a while, 'but the water supply would be last to fall. Think of the Pools of Solomon outside Jerusalem, still in use. The monks came here, I am sure of it. I just need time.'

The foreigner waited. The long afternoon drew on. The foreigner cat-napped in the shade of an old wall. He woke up to shouting and thought the attack he'd been expecting had finally come, but when he ran out it was only Hoffman, barefoot and dripping wet. Hoffman was waving a copper scroll in his hand.

'It was elementary!' he shouted. 'Don't you see? It's—'

A gunshot sounded, awful and loud in the still air. A flock of rock pigeons took to the air and Hoffman hit the ground.

'Someone's shooting at us!' he screamed.

'He's shooting at you!' the foreigner said. Hoffman crawled on the ground to a fallen column and hid behind it. The foreigner saw a shadow move overhead over the scattered stones of Jerash's public baths. He took a shot. The figure vanished.

'Who's there!' the foreigner called. 'Osman, is that you?'

'You killed Ugly, you bastard!' the reply came. The foreigner fired again, the bullet hitting rock. He scanned the ruins, searching for where the shooter would go to next.

'One-Eyed?' he called. 'It wasn't personal, it's just business!'

A shot hit the wall next to the foreigner, chipping the concrete. A shard hit the foreigner in the cheek, drawing blood. He cursed and heard One-Eyed's laughter.

'So is this!' he said.

'Colonel Ali let you go?' the foreigner shouted. 'You know he'll kill you when he's finished with you!'

'Just toss me the map and I'll keep you both alive!' One-Eyed shouted back. He was behind a wall, not far from them now. Hoffman looked at the foreigner helplessly from behind his hiding place. The foreigner made a *stay there* gesture.

'What map?' the foreigner called. He went between two columns and along a row of fallen masonry, crouching low. He could hear One-Eyed moving somewhere ahead. He peered through a crack between the stones and saw One-Eyed. He aimed the rifle at the moving target. One-Eyed had his back to the foreigner, evidently still keeping watch on the spot where Hoffman hid and where he believed the foreigner still was.

'I know all about the treasure!' One-Eyed shouted and the foreigner fired, letting the trigger go nice and slow. The shot hit One-Eyed in the leg and One-Eyed fell. The foreigner shouted, 'Drop the gun, One-Eyed, or the next bullet's the last!'

One-Eyed groaned. He tossed the gun away and stayed lying down. The foreigner leaped up and over the stones and in moment stood over the bandit, the rifle trained on One-Eyed.

'The nun,' the foreigner said.

'What?' One-Eyed said. 'Listen, Foreigner, you've got to get me some help!'

'Sister Agnes,' the foreigner said.

'The one you killed in the Jordan?' One-Eyed said.

'I didn't kill her. She drowned herself,' the foreigner said. Thinking again of the woman in white and how she fell into the water, arms spread out, seeming so at peace.

'If you say so.' One-Eyed winced in pain. 'I need a tourniquet.'

'She was after this treasure too,' the foreigner said. 'You knew, all this time?'

'People are always looking for lost treasure, Foreigner,' One-Eyed said. 'It's the Holy Land. You *shot* me!'

'Hoffman?' the foreigner called. 'You can come out now. Bring some cloth.'

He waited as Hoffman appeared, still barefoot and wet. Dry sand clung to him where he'd lain in hiding.

'Just shoot him,' he said.

'I think he's right,' the foreigner said to One-Eyed, almost apologetically. 'It's easier that way.'

One-Eyed whimpered. The blood from his wound flowed. It fed the dry ground. One-Eyed looked up at the foreigner with his one eye, not really comprehending at first, not really believing this was how it ended. Then it came into his eye, slowly, that understanding.

'It won't do you any good,' he said. 'They're here.'

'I know,' the foreigner said. Then he shot One-Eyed.

22

'We need to go,' the foreigner told Hoffman. 'We need to go fast.' All this sound of gunshots was like raising a flag right here between the nymphaeum and the river and the Temple of Artemis. The foreigner knew what had happened. Colonel Ali released One-Eyed the way one lets a captive animal go to seek out its kin. Draw them out into the open so now the soldiers could close in on the kill.

'Just give me a minute,' Hoffman said, 'I need to put my boots on.'

'Where is the scroll?' the foreigner said.

'Don't worry about the scroll,' Hoffman said, laughing. He sat on a fallen plinth and pulled on his boots one after the other. 'Fuck me!' he said. 'What was that!' He scrabbled at his left boot. 'Get it off me, get it off me!' he screamed.

The foreigner rushed to Hoffman's side. He pulled the boot and upended it, and a small yellow scorpion fell out and scuttled under a rock. Hoffman fell to the ground. He looked up at the foreigner with a terrified expression on his face.

'What is happening to me?' he said. His face was rapidly swelling up.

'You were stung by a scorpion,' the foreigner said. He knelt next to Hoffman. 'They don't always kill you,' he said. Hoffman's eyes were white. He was having a reaction to the poison, the foreigner saw. He'd seen such swelling before. This was not good. He shook Hoffman and said, 'Where did you put the map? Hoffman, where did you put it!'

Hoffman tried to speak. His lips had swelled grotesquely and his skin looked red and taut, almost boiled. He clutched at his throat. The foreigner said, 'God damn it, Hoffman, where did you hide it!'

Hoffman tried to point, then gave up. He fell on his back, clawing at his neck, trying desperately to breathe. The foreigner thought maybe he could poke a hole in Hoffman's neck into the windpipe, let him breathe that way. But even as he thought it Hoffman was expiring, and the foreigner knew nothing he could do would help against the poison. There were no doctors here. He watched until, mercifully, Hoffman's struggles ended.

The foreigner stared at the dead engineer.

'Shit!' he said.

Hoffman couldn't have hidden the scroll very far away. But now the foreigner could hear the measured clip-clop of horses, not hurrying, coming along the colonnade. He cursed again, but quietly. He searched Hoffman's body and found his passport and some money and the photo of a girl it took him a moment to recognise – it was Juzfin, from Jaffa. The foreigner stared around him and then he saw one of the lion's mouths was open and something inside it caught the light. He jumped for it and pulled down the scroll, almost crying in triumph. He stared at the unfamiliar writing. It didn't matter, he thought. He'd find someone to interpret it. He felt a rush of excitement and then heard Colonel Ali call, 'Come out, Foreigner! I only want the engineer!'

The foreigner thought, Is that so? He dragged Hoffman's corpse along the dry dust to where the horses waited. He pulled Hoffman up but the engineer was heavy and the foreigner was tired. At last he got him on the horse and then he slapped the horse's behind and the creature bolted, riding straight towards the colonnade and

Colonel Ali and his men. The foreigner mounted his own horse and crossed the river, then galloped away from there as fast as he could. He heard gunshots and laughed.

'No point shooting a dead man!' he screamed. He tried to circumnavigate the town but a rider appeared on his left, flanking him, and let off a warning shot, and the foreigner realised they had already hemmed him in. He swerved past the hippodrome and entered the city through the south gate and aimed for the ruins of an impressive amphitheatre as a second rider appeared on his other side and he saw it was Osman.

'There's no running from here!' Osman shouted. 'Just give us the map, Foreigner, and we'll cut you in on it!'

They'd cut *him* in on it? the foreigner thought in sudden fury. The gold was *his*, it was he who travelled for it, who killed for it, who spent years of his life in the Holy Land fashioning himself into a weapon, all leading to *this* – *his* moment in the sun. He whooped against the skies and fired his pistol at Osman, then thundered into the old Greek theatre.

'Come and get me if you think you can!' he screamed.

He was in the orchestra before the stage. Rows of seats cascaded above him, all empty, only a mute crowd of ghosts perhaps lingering. Were they Greeks or were they Romans, were they rebellious Jews or were they Persians? What did they last watch here, *Medea*, *Antigone*, some tragedy by Seneca? The centuries had exhaled the last of the words and buried the actors, turned the chorus into bones, rotted the costumes. Only the stones remained, waiting for a troupe to come back one day and put on a show again. Well, he will put on a show today, he thought, giddy with it. He held his rifle at the ready, not sure where they would come from first. Something moved in the upper reaches of the amphitheatre and the foreigner fired his rifle and saw a soldier spin, wounded. He laughed and fired again, spinning the man like one of those Jewish spinning tops from that holiday of theirs. The soldier fell, but now a second appeared from under the arches and he fired at the foreigner, once, twice, missing him both times by inches, and he took shelter behind the stones.

'Give up, Foreigner!' the soldier shouted.

'Who's that, Osman, is that you?' the foreigner shouted back, taking cover.

'We just want the map!' Osman called back. The foreigner turned with some unexplained instinct to see a third soldier creep up behind him. They fired at the same time. The soldier staggered back. The foreigner felt pain explode in his arm. The bullet went clean through. He emptied his revolver at the soldier with his other hand and the soldier fell. Now there were only Colonel Ali, Osman and the one remaining soldier, by the foreigner's count. The horse was nervous. He did not like the gunfight. The foreigner rushed Osman's position. He fired at Osman but missed. Osman had not expected the move. The foreigner thundered out of the theatre and back along the colonnade and ran up against Colonel Ali and his remaining soldier.

'Stop right there, Foreigner!' Colonel Ali called. The foreigner cursed, spurred on the horse and took a path through the ruins, heading south. They followed behind him, knowing they had him now, knowing they did not need to rush it. The horse galloped, the foreigner's arm hurt. Three horses followed behind him. He could outrun them, he knew. But not for very long.

The sun was setting. The ancient city was at his back, the skies growing red, the wind was warm as the foreigner rode south. He could still make it, he thought. Lose the pursuit, get to the Dead Sea, find the place in Wadi Mujib.

The crack of a gunshot. The horse jerked, lost his footing, fell. The foreigner rolled with the horse. The horse thrashed on the ground in pain, hooves flailing. One hit the foreigner as he tried to get away, a kick like Satan's, winding him. He crawled away. The chasers were gaining ground on him. He could just give in, he thought woozily. He picked up his pistols and fired at them to slow them down and then he turned and ran.

This was how it was always going to end, the foreigner thought, staggering across the land under the darkening skies. Behind him his horse lay dead or dying, the trail of bodies: Simeon and the slave Dmitry, Ugly and One-Eyed, Hoffman, the soldiers whose names he didn't even know. He thought of the gold buried somewhere in the desert, so much gold he'd need a cart just to carry it. This was what he had always wanted, he realised then, ever since he was a little boy. He reached for something, found the flint knife and his fingers closed on it and he smiled. He raised the knife. Land wasn't land until people died on it, until blood watered it; and he wondered suddenly if he had it all wrong, if land didn't need anything like that at all, but just something like love, even compassion.

But those, he thought, were in short supply; and blood was easier.

The foreigner fled across the plain under the darkening skies and with a dark joy in his heart, and the men on horseback chased him. In this manner he vanished from history – and what did it matter, anyway? He was only a foreigner.

TWO

BURTON
1948

23

The telephone ringing woke him up and for a moment Burton didn't know where he was. Black night pressed against the windows of the police station. Some gunfire in the distance, but it was sporadic and soon stopped entirely. The office was thick with cigarette smoke, the sound of typewriters, another ringing telephone, a group of seconded soldiers helping to move a stock of a guns and ammo from the armoury to load onto trucks to go to the harbour.

'Yes?' he said thickly into the phone. 'This is Burton, CID.'

Hassan Abu Omar, passing by the desk with a tray, wordlessly handed Burton a coffee. Burton nodded thanks.

'Burton,' the voice on the phone said. 'This is Gray.'

'Sir,' Burton said, sitting to attention. Gray was the new inspector general, an ex-commando who'd fought in the war. They'd brought him in to replace old Rymer-Jones, who now had a cushy job back in London as police commander in the West End.

'There's been a murder,' Gray said.

Burton almost laughed. In the last six months even the pretence at some semblance of order had been abandoned. The last few years had been hard enough. But when Britain officially requested to end its mandate in Palestine, and the new United Nations voted to partition the land, the Jews and the Arabs started going full tilt at each other and hadn't stopped since. Six months of war against which Burton and his men had to fold up three decades of police work. Murder was a thing he would have investigated back when it still meant something, when policing still meant something. But all there was out there was chaos and death now.

'Sir?' he said.

'The German Colony,' Gray said. 'I need you up here.'

Gray hung up. Burton stared at the phone. The IG shouldn't be anywhere near a crime scene, he thought. The police had no business even keeping order anymore. Their instructions were to close up shop and make an orderly withdrawal before the deadline, now just a week away. The ships anchored in Haifa harbour, waiting to be loaded with the hundreds of thousands of tons of military stores that had been accumulated in between two world wars, and the thousands of army and police personnel who needed to be evacuated from Palestine. Burton downed the bitter coffee and lit a cigarette as he stood.

'Hassan,' he said, 'who's still here?'

'Cohen and Paddy,' Hassan said.

'Tell them we need to go.'

Hassan nodded. Burton went outside, the fresh air reviving him. Haifa was in semi-darkness all around him, the lower city almost abandoned now as its residents had fled to Egypt and Lebanon after the Haganah takeover of the city two months back. Only the port still blazed bright, and the ships in the bay looked like festive fairy lights as they waited for their cargo of weapons and men. Almost peaceful, he thought. More sporadic gunfire in the distance cut his reverie short. He dropped his cigarette and ground it underfoot, thinking longingly of a hot shower and a fresh bed. One week to go till evac, and no one was getting much sleep.

'Sir,' Cohen said, appearing from the direction of the car pool, keys in hand, 'where are we going?'

He was a thin tall Jew in crisp ironed khakis and a pencil moustache. His wife was expecting a baby any day now. Behind

Cohen came Paddy Cooper, the Irishman – he'd joined the force back in '46 after serving in the Italian campaign during the war. He wasn't much more than a kid.

'We'll take two of the armoured cars,' Burton said. 'Cohen, you and Paddy take the second vehicle, me and Hassan will go in the front.'

'Sir,' Cohen said, a little reproachfully. Officers weren't supposed to drive up front. The first car was always going to hit the IED or ambush fire or the half dozen other horrors that awaited a police officer in this benighted land. But Burton had lived here too long. He remembered Palestine when it was still *manageable*. He was only a kid when he himself joined, back in '29, when the recruitment film he'd watched back home, in black and white, offered good pay, good weather and a bit of adventure in the Orient. These days he just felt ancient.

They got into the cars. Hassan drove, Burton beside him, Cohen and Paddy following behind. The cars were small and light and their armour offered little protection. The guards opened the gates to let them out onto the Kingsway. Burton looked back. Police HQ had still not recovered from the Stern Gang bombing the year before. Burton wasn't there that day but he saw the damage, the wrecked officers' mess, the shattered windows, the blackened remains of the truck that had been packed full of explosives; and he knew one of the constables who'd died that day. Hassan drove calmly, his eyes alert and scanning the empty road. Haifa sprawled along the slopes of the Carmel, and Burton remembered with some nostalgia his early days there, when all he had to worry about was telling the taxi drivers to keep their car horn usage to a minimum because the commissioner did not like the noise.

They drove up the mountain and came shortly to what remained of the German Colony. Handsome houses built in an old European style, a tree-lined main road that was very pleasant in the daytime. Burton remembered the German Templers who used to live there, big, beefy second and third generation settlers in the

Holy Land who kept clean, tidy shops and were always cheerful and polite. Back in the thirties they flew the Nazi flag proudly above those same houses, and when Britain got entangled in the war there had been no choice but to deport the lot of them, and the houses had lain empty for a while.

'There,' Burton said, pointing, but Hassan was already slowing down. The house sat on the end of the lane and was the only one lit up from within. Police cars were parked around it and now Burton's small convoy joined them. He stepped out, wondering what the hell he was doing there, and saw the IG's black car and a military jeep that gave him an uneasy feeling. That meant the army was also involved.

'Burton,' he said, not bothering to flash a badge. A young Arab constable looked up guiltily from the cigarette he was rolling and said, 'They're all inside, sir.'

'Who is?' Burton said, but the constable just shrugged and went back to his tobacco pouch. Burton went up to the house alone. Of his men, Cohen and Paddy were talking in low voices, while Hassan sat apart reading a pocket book in French. The Palestine Police Force had always prided itself on having Jews, Arabs and British officers all working together. But even this was coming to an end now, Burton knew. Everyone had to pick a side; pick a side or leave. He went into the house.

It was a scene of considerable opulence that welcomed him on entry. Paintings on the walls, encased in thick gold frames, showed tableaux of the Holy Land and the Near East by a variety of painters: a huge Moses on Mount Sinai facing the Lord, by Gérôme; a Bedouin encampment in the Wells of Moses, by Taylor; the Dead Sea as viewed from Masada, by Lear; and many others. The floor was thickly carpeted in Persian rugs, and the eclectic collection of furniture was equal parts Queen Anne and late Ottoman bijou.

Much of it, Burton saw with dismay, had been torn and thrown about in a seeming fit of frenzy. Books scattered on the floor, paintings pulled from their frames, cupboards opened and drawers emptied. Near the cold fireplace he could see the unmoving shape of a large, elderly man in a robe lying limply on the floor, his head resting in a pool of congealing blood. A group of men stood around the corpse talking in low voices.

'Ah, Burton,' a voice said. Burton looked up to find Detective Jack Smith of the CID, looking a little apologetic.

'Sorry to drop you in it, old boy,' Smith said.

'Jack,' Burton said. 'Are you in charge here?'

'No one's in charge here, old boy,' Smith said. 'It's a bleeding mess is what it is. But they asked for you.'

'Care to fill me in?' Burton said. The men around the corpse looked his way and he recognised not only the IG, Gray, but also Major General Hugh Stockwell, of the 6th Airborne Division, who was in charge of the port and the British evacuation effort. Burton was surprised to see him involved. A recent arrival, Stockwell was simply there to carry out his job. He had no patience for the game of Arabs and Jews. Two months back he informed both sides in Haifa that he would no longer take pains to maintain order beyond his core responsibility for the harbour and British interests. This resulted in a quick, decisive fight for the city between the Jewish Haganah and the local Arab militia, ending with Jewish victory twenty-four hours later, and beginning the mass exodus of Arabs from the lower city. Stockwell was not popular with the police force, who seethed in private about what they considered an all but criminal dereliction of duty. Yet Burton supposed Stockwell was right. They could hold the line no longer here.

Burton nodded to the officers, and they went back to their quiet conversation.

'I got called in around two hours ago,' Smith said. 'I mean, we're still the police, damn it.'

'It was a phone call?' Burton said. There were not that many phones in use, certainly not in private—

Smith nodded to a telephone still standing on a hand-carved footstool in the hallway.

'Who called it in?' Burton said.

'The houseboy,' Smith said. 'He's in the kitchen, you can talk to him later.'

'What did he say?' Burton said.

'Said he came back from an errand to find the house trashed and his master dead. Blunt force trauma to the head – my words, not his. Someone hit him with a fire poker, then dropped the murder weapon next to the corpse.'

'Fingerprints?' Burton said, and Smith laughed. There was not much humour in it.

'Lab boys are all packed up to go home,' Smith said. 'And the files are either in boxes or destroyed. You know this, Burton.'

'I keep forgetting,' Burton said. 'I keep thinking we're still real police.'

He pulled out his packet of Woodbines, offered it to Smith, who accepted a cigarette. Burton lit them both up.

'So then what?' he said. 'Who's the stiff?'

'One Isaac Samuelsohn,' Smith said. 'Antiques dealer. He's had this house for about a year.'

'Alright,' Burton said. 'So someone tried to rob him.'

'Nothing seems to be missing,' Smith said. 'Well, not quite nothing.'

'Come on, Jack. Why am I here? Why are *you* still here?' Burton nodded at the officers and said, 'More importantly, why the hell are *they* here?'

'Sorry, old boy,' Smith said. 'I tried. Thanks for the gasper.' He walked past Burton and straight out of the door. Burton saw Gray coming over. He saluted. Gray saluted back.

'Good of you to come out,' Gray said. 'We have a case for you.'

'Sir,' Burton said, 'I don't know how I can solve a murder when I have no crime lab, we have no courts, and we don't even have a prison.'

Only two weeks earlier a Jewish force that could have been Haganah or IZL or Stern Gang fired mortar at Acre Prison leading to all the inmates escaping.

'I don't need you to solve a murder,' Gray said, a little impatiently. 'I need you to find a missing person.'

'The victim's right there, sir,' Burton said. 'All he needs is a box... Oh.' He cursed Smith quietly. 'There was someone else?'

'It appears there was,' Gray said. 'We need you to find her.'

'Her, sir?' Burton said.

'It seems Mr Samuelsohn had a house guest,' Gray said. He went back to the corpse and Burton followed reluctantly. He looked at the victim. Isaac Samuelsohn lay on the carpet in his robe and slippers, the wound in his head no longer bleeding. He had bushy white eyebrows and a pale, waxy skin. He did not look pretty in death. The MG, Stockwell, nodded curtly to Burton.

'You fill him in yet?' he said to Gray.

'Not fully,' Gray said.

'I have to get back to the port,' Stockwell said. 'I am missing a shipment of Sten guns, two armoured vehicles and about a warehouse worth of rifle ammunition, and that's just tonight.'

'They'll be long gone by now,' Gray said.

'There's more thieves here than on Brick Lane,' Stockwell said. 'I wish I could court-martial half the force in Palestine. No offence.'

'These are strange times,' Gray said. 'And the men...' He hesitated. 'Some of them still *care* what happens here,' he said.

'Anyone I catch selling weapons *will* get a trial,' Stockwell said, without much conviction. Burton tossed his cigarette into the empty fireplace. Stockwell turned his attention on him.

'Gray tells me you know the lay of the land here,' he said. 'You've been here, what, twenty years?'

'Joined up in '29, sir,' Burton said. 'I was only a kid. Missed out on the Great War, wanted to see some action. First job I had was directing donkey traffic on the waterfront, sir.'

Stockwell didn't smile.

'We have a situation,' he said.

This was evident, Burton thought, or none of them would be there.

'According to the houseboy,' Stockwell said, 'this antiques merchant – what is his name again?'

'Samuelsohn,' Gray said.

'This Samuelsohn had a house guest,' Stockwell said. 'Unfortunately for us – for you, Burton – she appears to be missing. The houseboy said she was here when he left. Her room was upstairs. Her effects are still there. There are signs of a struggle. She may have been kidnapped by the perpetrators, whoever they were. That is indeed our working hypothesis.'

'Who is she?' Burton said. 'Do we know?'

'Jack Smith conducted the preliminary investigation,' Gray said, stepping in. 'He carried out a cursory check of the property when he realised who she was, at which point he had the good sense to call me. He'll go far, that man. I of course filled in the major general, so we could convene at the scene.'

'I don't have time for this,' Stockwell said. 'This is one more headache than any of us need.'

'Indeed,' Gray said.

'Who is she, sir?' Burton said.

Gray handed him a passport.

'Smith found it upstairs,' he said.

Burton flipped it open. The first thing he saw, of course, was that it was British. The pale face of a woman in her twenties, somewhat sharp-featured yet not unlovely, stared back at him from the details page.

'Eva Finer, born '21,' he said. 'That makes her what, twenty-seven?' He scanned the rest of the biographical information quickly, then shrugged.

'Who's Eva Finer?' he said.

Gray sighed.

'You don't study your *Debrett's*, do you?' he said.

'Eva Finer is the favoured cousin of Lord Melchett,' Gray said. 'And the fiancée of the son of the Marquess of Reading.'

'Ah,' Burton said.

'Old Anglo-Jewish family,' Stockwell said. 'They have ties to both the Rothschilds and the Sassoons by marriage.'

'I was not aware,' Burton said.

'She's often in the society pages back home,' Stockwell said, a little disapprovingly. 'We had no idea she was in Palestine, nor why. It is rather confounding, frankly.'

'Is she a Zionist?' Burton said.

'If she is, we have no file on her,' Gray said. 'I spoke to the political lads but they were not aware of her either.'

'Melchett,' Burton said. 'Doesn't he have a villa out on the Sea of Galilee?'

'The old Lord Melchett built it, yes,' Gray said. 'I even went there once. Lovely place.'

'Oh?' Stockwell said. 'What were you doing there, Gray?'

'The young Lord Melchett was visiting and hosted a party for the top brass,' Gray said. 'The family's made significant investment in Palestine over the years.'

'So they are Zionists,' Stockwell said, in something like an accusation.

'I suppose so,' Gray said. 'But they're still nobility, Hugh.'

'Did you meet this Eva Finer while you were there, sir?' Burton said.

'If I did,' Gray said, 'I certainly don't recall.'

'I do not need this headache,' Stockwell said again. 'Listen, Burton. Can we trust you to find her?'

'If one of the Arab factions did it they may be holding her hostage,' Burton said. 'In that case we should get a ransom demand very soon.'

'Or her chums in the Haganah,' Stockwell said. 'Or IZL or the Stern Gang. Christ, man. I'll be glad when we leave this place.'

'We don't know she was connected to anyone,' Gray said.

'Can you do it, Burton? I'm told you're good at asking questions. And you have your own informants, don't you? On both sides?'

Burton stared at the antiques dealer's corpse on the floor. Trying to find a missing person in Palestine in the midst of war, when law and order no longer had any meaning, was like trying to find the proverbial needle in the haystack, he thought. But he knew both of his superior officers knew it too, and he knew this wasn't a request, it was an order.

'I'll do my best, sirs,' he said.

24

The lights of the waiting ships twinkled in the harbour and somewhere in the distance Burton heard the sharp retort of gunfire again, but he'd grown so accustomed to it now that it barely registered. It was agreed he could keep Hassan, Cohen and Paddy on secondment – a sign of how much the brass valued this job, because all hands were needed in this final week. Burton was keenly aware his men would not have a job past Friday. This would be their last assignment together. He didn't know what Cohen and Hassan had planned. They were both good men and he'd never found fault with them, but their people were now at war, and both men were fighters – they would fight for their people, and against each other, he knew. As for Paddy, rumour had it that he had a Jewish girlfriend in one of the kibbutzim, those strange socialist communes that had sprouted all across Palestine in the years of the British mandate – would he leave her behind? Take her with him?

Burton didn't know what he himself would do. The Met in London were looking for good, experienced men, and there was the new police force in Kenya, of course – he'd get by whatever happened, he supposed. There was always a need for a good policeman across the empire's dominions. Morton, the guy who'd shot Yair Stern, the leader of the Stern Gang, back in '42, serving in Nyasaland now. Burton wasn't sure he was rea home to Britain. London after the war was a cold, dreary sort of place, and many of the buildings lay in ruins. It would take years to rebuild the city.

He thought with some longing of his first few months in Palestine. He was just a kid, unused to the heat, the discipline, the barracks. Everything felt new and exciting, the cacophony of languages on every street corner, the unfamiliar shouts in Arabic and Hebrew, English and Russian and French, Armenian and Yiddish. The smell of oranges seemed to be everywhere, so sweetly scented – though the way people treated their donkeys was a travesty, in Burton's eyes. He abhorred cruelty to donkeys.

He was in Tel Aviv one day, that new Hebrew town the Jews had built in the sands beyond Jaffa. Its wide avenues and white stone Bauhaus houses were in stark contrast to their Arab neighbour, and that day the Jews celebrated the festival of Purim. They were gathered out in the streets, many of the children in outlandish costumes, the adults passing cups of wine and kosher wishniak, for on Purim alone they were commanded to drink to insensibility. Cars honked incessantly, and from the factories came the sound of sirens, not in alarm but in joy. The noise was deafening all the same. The blue and white flags of the Jews were waved from rooftop to rooftop, and it was then that, raising his eyes to the skies, Burton saw something surely impossible, a huge shape gliding across the heavens, high above, its shadow sailing over the crowded rooftops with their jutting poles that resembled ship's masts, over balconies crammed with people, over flower shops and bakeries, and it took him a long moment to make sense of this ethereal apparition.

It was the Graf Zeppelin. The giant airship glided majestically in the skies of Palestine, its engines muted, silvery and shining in the late sunlight, its name clearly visible on its side. It seemed like an omen, a harbinger of the future, a better and more hopeful one; and as Burton watched, his heart lifting, thousands upon thousands of tiny pieces of confetti fell gaily from the skies and down on the crowds, on hats and cars and cats and people.

All that evening, almost drunk with it, Burton patrolled the streets, welcomed into people's homes, offered food and drinks in this strange new town in this strange new world. Palestine was all change, the Jews arriving from all the places to which they had once dispersed, and the sound of construction was everywhere in Tel Aviv.

He stared out at the dark city now and thought of that Graf Zeppelin only a few years later, after the Nazis came to power, when it bore the swastika proudly on its fins. Then the Hindenburg disaster in '37, and that was the end of those behemoths of the sky.

He thought now how hopeful he had been, and how naïve. The more the Jews kept coming the more the Arabs resented their presence and their future plans, the more they clashed. The Arabs demanded independence from the British, a Palestine to call their own. The Jews demanded what was promised to them, too, a Jewish land in their ancestral home.

The PPF tried to keep the peace, its policemen drawn from both the Jewish Yishuv and the Arab population, commanded by British officers, and for a long time, he thought now, for a long time they had kept, if not the peace, then order. And there was pride to be had in that.

Perhaps it could never have been, Burton thought now. But he was older and wearier, more used to the cruelties and indignities that people so casually inflicted on each other. The younger him had looked up to the skies once, and dreamed.

'Hassan,' he said, 'you and I will speak to the houseboy. Cohen, you will search the girl's room again. Smith is good, but he might have missed something. Paddy, get Mr Samuelsohn's corpse removed, but be discreet about it. The brass want this kept quiet.'

'Does he have next of kin, boss?' Paddy said.

'I don't know,' Burton said. 'Find out if you can.'

'We can still use the morgue in HQ,' Paddy said. 'I'll stash him there as a John Doe.'

Burton nodded. It was as good an idea as any. The rest

of the houses in the German Colony had their lights out. Perhaps they were unoccupied. Or maybe the residents were hiding. But someone would be watching them. Someone was always watching.

He went back inside, Hassan following. They found the houseboy in the kitchen. He was a young man, quite handsome, rocking in a chair with eyes a little vacant.

'Detective Smith gave him something to calm him down,' Hassan said.

'Tell me everything from the start,' Burton said to the houseboy. The houseboy didn't reply.

'What is his name?' Burton said.

'Ali,' Hassan said.

'Ali,' Burton said, 'tell me what happened.'

'I don't know what happened,' Ali said.

'You worked here how long?' Burton said.

'One year,' Ali said. 'Two more with the effendi in Jerusalem before that.'

'You worked for him that long?'

Ali shrugged. 'He was good to me,' he said.

'What did he do, Ali?'

'Bought and sold antiques,' Ali said. 'We were always coming and going. Paris, London, Cairo. Our shop in Jerusalem always had so much old stuff. So much. What we have here is only a little, in the house. A few pieces he liked.'

'Why did you move here?' Hassan said.

'The harbour,' Ali said. 'He needed to be near the harbour.'

'To send off the stuff?' Hassan said.

Ali shook his head, no.

'He was bringing it all in,' he said.

Burton and Hassan exchanged a look.

'Bringing what in?' Burton said.

Ali shrugged.

'Antiques go out,' Burton said, 'not in. Hassan, you know of anyone importing antiques?'

Hassan laughed.

'What good will they be here?' he said.

'Then what was he doing?' Burton said.

'I don't know,' Ali said. 'I miss our shop. It was full of beautiful things.'

'When did this start?' Burton said. 'This importing? The same time you moved from Jerusalem to Haifa?'

'I suppose so,' Ali said. 'Maybe a few months earlier, he was winding down the shop, taking a lot of meetings, a lot of phone calls, but he didn't tell me anything.' He started to cry. 'I don't know why anyone would do this to him,' he said.

'Tell me about the girl,' Burton said, deciding to change tack.

'Miss Eva,' Ali said. 'She came about a week ago. The effendi told me to prepare the room for her.'

'Did she seem worried?' Hassan said. 'Afraid?'

Ali shook his head. 'I didn't see much of her,' he said. 'She and the effendi would take lunch together sometimes. They often argued.'

'About what?' Hassan said.

'I don't know. They spoke English between them. But it was nothing out of the ordinary. They argued like Jews argue, you know—'

Burton almost smiled. 'Lots of loud voices and waving hands?' he said.

Ali nodded. 'There is no cook anymore, he left with his family to Beirut when the trouble started. So now I do the cooking and cleaning too. I just served dinner. I don't know what I will do now.'

'Do you have family, Ali?' Hassan said.

'I have an uncle in Jenin,' Ali said. 'But I barely know him.'

'Go to Jenin, Ali,' Burton said. He felt bad for the houseboy. But this was the way it went. One had to make their own way in the world. He said, 'What was Miss Eva doing in Palestine, Ali?'

'I don't know, sir,' Ali said. 'I told you everything I know.'

Burton tapped Hassan lightly on the shoulder and Hassan

nodded. Burton left him there, but he doubted Hassan could get anything more out of the houseboy. He climbed the steps to the second floor, admiring more curios and paintings – here, too, ransacking had taken place, as though the invaders had searched, desperately and brutally, for something they couldn't find.

But what? he thought. The paintings and antiques were the valuables here. Perhaps Samuelsohn hid gold or cash about for use in his business. But that would be in a safe somewhere, not behind a painting. He went into the guest room and found Cohen still going through Eva Finer's effects, of which there were precious few.

'A credit letter drawn from Feebes to the Anglo-Palestine Bank in Jerusalem,' Cohen said, holding up a paper.

'Feebes?' Burton said. 'That's a private bank. I heard the king has his account there.'

'I've never been to England, sir,' Cohen said, a little reproachfully. 'I also found a return ticket for the steamer. It appears she came via Cairo.'

'So we know she's wealthy,' Burton said, 'and that she came by sea. That doesn't get us very far, Cohen.'

'I'm sorry, sir,' Cohen said. 'I don't know why she was here or who took her. Our best hope is that we receive a ransom demand.'

'Is that likely?' Burton said.

'I don't know, sir.'

'She must have friends, acquaintances,' Burton said. 'She wouldn't have been sitting here the whole time. The IG said she is engaged.'

'Engaged does not mean married, sir,' Cohen said. 'Especially when your fiancé is safely across the sea.'

'You think she had a boyfriend, Cohen?'

'I'm sure I can't say, sir.'

A book of old maps was splayed open on the table. Burton picked it up, shook it, but nothing fell out and he let it fall closed on the table. Another book, titled *Beetles of Palestine: Volume 1*, by an S. Avigdor, had dark rings on its cover as if someone often used it as a coaster. There was no cup there now, but rather a curious object, an ancient flint knife made who knew when, back when some vanished ancient people lived there. Burton picked it up—

And for a moment the room vanished. Overhead the stars fell in a shower of gold sparks. The fire burned low in its ring of stones. The boy lay curled asleep by the embers as the woman hummed a low, voiceless tune. She looked up, troubled, as if recalling a dream she once had—

'Sir?' Cohen said.

'What?' Burton said. He put the flint knife down on the table. Looked around the room again, momentarily disoriented. But these things happened to him from time to time.

'Clothes?' he said.

'A few dresses, hats. Practical shoes,' Cohen said.

'Alright,' Burton said. They went downstairs. The corpse was gone, the carpet rolled. Paddy stood leaning against a post.

'Load-bearing,' he said.

Smart, Burton thought. He hadn't thought to check for hollow walls.

'What about the safe?' he said.

Hassan came to join them.

'See for yourself, sir,' he said.

They traipsed to Samuelsohn's study. It was on the ground floor and surprisingly utilitarian. The desk had been searched expertly, Burton saw, the drawers pulled out carefully. The shelves were emptied of their books and folders. A small safe was set in the wall. It lay open and empty.

'Why search the rest of the house?' Burton said.

Paddy shrugged.

'I know those old dealers,' he said. 'They're crafty. He probably hid his cash all over the place.'

'How much cash could an antiques dealer have?' Burton said. 'This doesn't make sense. Why kill him, too, when he opened the safe for them? They must have come in as soon as the houseboy left. They were watching the house. They beat or threatened the old man and he opened the safe for them. At that point they got what they came for. So why kill Samuelsohn? Why take the girl? Why ransack the house?'

His men looked at each other. Paddy shrugged. Hassan said, 'Unless they were looking for something else. Something other than money.'

'Something more valuable?' Cohen said.

'Maybe,' Hassan said.

'Or they were always after the girl,' Paddy said. 'And everything else's just a distraction.'

They were good men, Burton thought. He hoped he could still rely on their loyalty.

'Cohen, Hassan,' he said, 'you go down to the harbour, see what you can learn about Samuelsohn's business. Paddy, you come with me.'

The men saluted. Outside the street was dark. Most of the houses had lain empty since the Germans were deported, Burton knew, but still. He kept having that uneasy feeling of being watched.

'Where to, boss?' Paddy said.

'Let's try the casino first,' Burton said.

25

There was no gambling at the casino, despite the name. It was a nice modernist building on the sea in one of the new Jewish neighbourhoods and had a swimming pool attached that was popular in the summer. Back in the old days Burton often came to the casino. There was a bar and a dance floor and a restaurant. It was open even with the recent fighting, and swarming with Brits who had nowhere else to go. Paddy parked and they went in, and Burton thought with some longing of Ruth, a Jewish informant he had once and with whom he'd had an affair. She never forgave him for Operation Agatha in '46, when British forces swooped on the Jewish kibbutzim, confiscated their hidden caches of weapons and arrested many of their fighters. Burton was just doing his job. And he had liked Ruth. He had been as much her informant as she had been his. That was how this job worked, that was what people didn't understand – you had to have a give and take. And just because you were on opposite sides, you didn't have to let it get personal. Though of course, it did get personal with Ruth. But that was just the way it was. Like the song in the barracks went, all the girls were Haganah.

The Haganah was what the Jews called their main paramilitary organisation. Which meant the Defence. They were serious about building their new-old homeland and serious about keeping it. They'd been promised it by the British but they didn't trust the

British one bit. So they kept stockpiling guns, and training – and they were the reasonable ones. The IZL were worse, and the Stern Gang even worse than them, common terrorists who blew up buses and murdered innocent civilians and a fair number of cops. When Morton shot Stern no one at the PPF gave a fuck it was in the back. Only the year before the IZL kidnapped two sergeants, Martin and Paice, and strung them up in a eucalyptus grove near the new Jewish city of Netanya. When the police came to cut them down to give them a decent Christian burial, at least, they realised too late the corpses had been booby-trapped. When Burton found out he felt sick, even after everything he'd seen. And some of the men, vowing revenge, went on a rampage in Tel Aviv, beating up Jews, smashing shop windows and shooting dead five people, all discipline lost. The two sergeants were buried the next day at the military cemetery in Ramleh, next to so many others who'd given their life for the empire.

Ugly times, Burton thought. Paddy followed him into the casino. People were dancing, the air thick with smoke. The girls young and lovely. Some were from the NAAFI, some ATS, nurses, support staff. Mixing between them and the soldiers and officers were plenty of the locals, men and women both. Burton scanned for faces he knew. Haifa had grown so much in the twenty years he'd served in Palestine. And all the people he knew kept dying.

'Almog,' he said, in some relief at spotting a familiar face. He was pretty sure Almog was high up in the IZL, but he used to be in the CID with Burton back in the day, and they'd always got on reasonably well.

'Burton?' Almog said, feigning surprise. 'What are you still doing here? Haven't you heard? The Mandate's over.'

'Not for another week,' Burton said, and Almog laughed. Burton had to smile too, it sounded so stupid.

'Buy you a drink?' he said. 'For old times' sake.'

'Sure, why the hell not,' Almog said. 'Got a lot to celebrate these days. We're going to have our own country back on Friday, after all, after two thousand years.'

'How'd you do it, Almog?' Burton said. 'How'd you keep going all that time?'

'It's the hope that keeps you going, Burton,' Almog said. 'It's the hope.'

'Like that song of yours,' Burton said. 'Two whisky sours,' he said to the bartender.

'They do better ones at the Piccadilly,' Almog said.

'Do you know anything about an Isaac Samuelsohn?' Burton said.

'Isaac? Why?' Almog scanned Burton's face. 'What happened to him?' he said.

'Would anyone have reason to harm him?' Burton said.

'Isaac's a good man,' Almog said. 'A patriot.'

'Can you be a patriot for a country that's not even there yet?' Burton said.

'It's there already, Burton. It's there in all but name.' Almog sipped the whisky sour. 'What happened to him, Burton? Is he dead?'

'Afraid so,' Burton said.

'What happened?' Almog said.

'You don't know?' Burton said.

'You think we had anything to do with it? He's one of ours, Burton.'

'His house was burgled and he was killed with a blow to the head,' Burton said.

'Those bastards,' Almog said. 'He wasn't a young man, he never did anyone any harm. We'll find out who did this.'

'This is what I'm trying to ascertain,' Burton said.

'Why?' Almog said. 'You're leaving in a week.'

Burton sighed. He wasn't sure how much to tell Almog, only nothing remained much of a secret in a small town anyway, and he needed help. He said, 'Do you know an Eva Finer?'

Almog's face closed up and he said, 'Is she dead too?'

'Missing,' Burton said.

'I never met her but I know who she is,' Almog said. 'Her uncle was a great supporter of the cause. We'll name a town after him one day.'

'What's your plan after withdrawal?' Burton said.

'We accepted partition,' Almog said. 'It's the other side who hasn't. We'll have a country. We'll defend it, whatever happens.'

'War, then,' Burton said.

'We're already at war, Burton,' Almog said. 'We won't be expelled from our land again. Not this time.'

'What of the people who were here before you?' Burton said, and Almog shrugged.

'They can stay in peace,' he said. 'Or they can leave.'

'Very noble,' Burton said.

'Nobility has nothing to do with it. Listen, Burton, I didn't know about Finer. It's certainly not any of our doing, if that's what you were thinking. Isaac Samuelsohn was a good man. And the Finer broad's connected. No, it's some Arab gang.' His face twisted in hatred. 'They'll pay for it, I can assure you.'

'I need to find her, Almog.'

'Could be al-Kaff al-Aswad,' Almog said.

'The Black Hand? Come on,' Burton said. 'They haven't been active since the Great Revolt.'

'Oh, they're still around,' Almog said. 'Could be the Army of the Holy Jihad, or the Arab Liberation Army, who gave us hell last month in the Jezreel, or those fuckers from the Arab Legion who are supposed to be working for you.'

'The legion's under British command,' Burton said.

'So?' Almog said. Which Burton had to admit was a fair point.

'But those are organised,' Burton said. 'This feels more...'

'Criminal?'

'It has that feel to it,' Burton said.

'The Latifs from the Galilee, they're still active around here,'

Almog said. 'The Turkomans are not above armed robbery and kidnapping still. The Abdul Razak gang—'

'They're all in prison,' Burton said.

'No one's in prison anymore,' Almog said. 'And your lot burned half the criminal records so that people could have a, what did you call it? A second chance.'

Damn it, Burton thought. Almog was right. Surely the withdrawal could have been managed in a more... *orderly* fashion than this? The country was swarming with the criminal element: smugglers, robbers, simple murderers... A second chance indeed.

'Anything else you can tell me?' he said now. They'd both finished their drinks.

'I don't know where she is,' Almog said. 'I will do my best to find out.'

'Leave it to me,' Burton said. 'I don't want you making trouble.'

Almog laughed.

'You're just a guest here now,' he said, 'and an unwanted one at that. Thanks for the drink.'

Burton watched him leave, wondering if they were ever friends. He went and met up with Paddy back by the car.

'Well?' Burton said.

'I worked my contacts,' Paddy said, 'but no one knows or, if they do, they aren't telling.'

'Someone must know the girl,' Burton said. 'What she was doing here. I got the sense Samuelsohn was definitely up to something fishy, the way Almog clammed up when I mentioned him.'

'Almog has a book filled with all the signed photos of the famous people he met,' Paddy said. 'He showed it to me once. Why did he leave the CID?'

'It depends who you ask,' Burton said. 'But he's a cold-blooded killer. Still. He was a decent policeman once.' He lit a Woodbine and passed one to Paddy without being asked. It was going to be a long night, he thought. A long night in a long week. It felt like it would never end but all things ended, Burton thought. They just seldom ended well.

'Listen, do you really believe the idea of an Arab gang?' he said. 'Haifa's held pretty tight by the Haganah now. I don't think an Arab could fart in this town now without getting a Haganah gun pointed at him.'

'Don't know, boss,' Paddy said. 'Could be some inter-insurgency thing. Remember the Saison?'

'The hunting season,' Burton said. 'That was ugly.'

'Exactly.'

It was after the Jewish terrorists assassinated Lord Moyne in Cairo. Moyne was the minister of state in the Middle East, and his murder was one step too far against the empire. Too far for anyone. The Haganah declared open season on the IZL. For three months the Haganah gave information to the CID on the location of IZL members, some of whom they kidnapped and held themselves. It almost came to an intra-Jewish war; but after a few months all three organisations formed a unified alliance instead.

Burton needed something. With each passing moment the girl would be further out of reach, the chance increasing of Eva Finer coming to a fatal end. There would be questions in parliament, there would be inquiries – heads would roll, he knew. And he had a pension to keep.

Just then the radio went off and Paddy went to answer it.

'It's Cohen,' he said, 'they found something in the harbour.'

It was a short drive along the shore. Floodlights searched the dark roads against attackers and in the distance Burton saw with some sadness the ruins of Haifa East, the train station built by the Ottomans that had linked Africa, Europe and Asia. It had been bombed by the IZL two years back, and the main office of Palestine Railways had burned down more recently, in the battle for Haifa. Burton could still remember what it was like in its heyday, the passengers coming and going from Damascus, Kantara and Istanbul. Now it was just another broken monument to the folly of war.

A row of trucks waited at Palmer Gate. They were packing everything up – even the telephone system's copper wire. Which the Bedouins were stealing faster than the signallers could take down. Though Burton heard the signallers went into business by themselves, and most of the recovered material ended up sold across the border in Egypt... Well, only the other day a detail sent to Sarafand to destroy some turrets had been offered a hefty bribe not to carry out the job. The men from the Royal Electrical and Mechanical Engineers refused and did their job diligently, only to be ambushed on their way back to base, with the loss of all men. Doel, McCarthy, Rigby-Jones, all dead. Good men, but being honest was dangerous in Palestine.

Paddy drove to a side gate and Burton flashed the guards on duty his ID. He stared in some awe at the stacked containers, the stevedores moving about even at this hour, the forklifts driving up and down the ramps and the alert soldiers standing on duty – 'We built this place, damn it,' he said.

'And now you have to give it away,' Paddy said; and it didn't escape Burton's notice he said *you*, not *we*.

'There's Cohen,' Paddy said.

26

They parked near one of the warehouses. Cohen and Hassan ambled over.

'Sir,' Cohen said, saluting.

'What do you two have?' Burton said.

'We spoke to the customs officer, sir,' Hassan said. 'It was quite revealing.'

'Well?' Burton said.

'According to customs, Mr Samuelsohn was importing artwork for a new museum he was going to build right here in the city,' Cohen said, handing Burton a sheaf of papers. Burton scanned them. The letterhead read *Samuelsohn Imports/Exports Inc.* on *behalf of the Samuelsohn Museum of Jewish Art, Main Street, German Colony, Haifa.*

'What the hell is the Samuelsohn Museum of Jewish Art?' Burton said.

'That's the thing, sir,' Hassan said. 'It does not appear to exist.'

'Really...' Burton said.

'The museum was bringing in regular shipments, sir,' Cohen said. 'All above board with the paperwork.'

'Mostly through Marseilles,' Hassan said.

'Big crates?' Burton said.

Hassan smiled.

'A lot of sculptures, apparently,' he said. 'Large, heavy things.'

'And valuable,' Cohen said. 'Strictly do not touch, do not open.'

'I see,' Burton said, who was indeed beginning to. 'Did they ever catch him at it?'

'There was an incident about a year ago,' Hassan said. 'The crane cable snapped as it was moving a crate to the dock. It dumped a bunch of alabaster statues on the ground which broke on impact and—'

'Let me guess,' Burton said. 'They were full of guns?'

'Got it in one, sir,' Hassan said.

'And this wasn't dealt with?' Burton said.

Hassan shook his head. 'Mr Samuelsohn was happy to pay for the… misunderstanding, sir.'

'Handsomely,' Cohen said, with the mournful tone of voice of a man who never even considered guns could be illegally smuggled through the port. Burton gave him a sharp look.

'What happens in this new state of yours next week?' he said.

'Sir?' Cohen said.

'Is there a government?' Burton said. 'A police?'

'There will always be a police, sir,' Cohen said. 'There must always be order. There must be order above all things.'

'And who will serve in this new police force of yours, Cohen?' Burton said. 'They'd need experienced officers, no?'

'That is a matter for next week, sir,' Cohen said.

Burton once again wondered if he could trust any of his men. He wanted to believe he could. But he wasn't so sure.

'These guns were for the Haganah, correct?' he said.

'Who else?' Hassan said with some bitterness. 'They've been flooding the country with weapons for years.'

'Only to defend ourselves,' Cohen said, and Hassan gave a surprised, disbelieving laugh. Even Paddy smiled at that one.

'Another reason to kill Samuelsohn?' Burton said.

'A week before the withdrawal?' Hassan said. 'Why now? Anyway, sir, we found out some more. May we go inside?'

Burton followed Hassan into the warehouse, where a very

miserable-looking official was waiting for them on a chair, smoking nervously from a cheap pack of Egyptian cigarettes.

'Look,' the man said. 'I told you everything, what more do you want me to do? It doesn't matter now anyhow, or I wouldn't have told you shit.'

'Sir, this is Mr Mansour,' Hassan said. 'He's a Druze,' he added as an afterthought.

'Yes, yes, so I'm a Druze, so what?' Mr Mansour said. 'What are you suggesting? Your men here are very rude, sir,' he said to Burton. 'I am very busy. The major general relies on me, sir!'

'He does, does he?' Burton said. 'Tell me what you told my officers, please, Mr Mansour.'

'What is there to say?' Mr Mansour said. 'It was all on the level, sir. Tip top paperwork and never a problem.'

'And the guns?'

Mr Mansour shrugged.

'So maybe he was smuggling guns,' he said. 'Someone came and took them and after that it was back to business as usual.'

'Someone came?' Burton said. 'Who?'

'Jews, I suppose,' Mr Mansour said. 'These things happen in a big port like ours. If we had to stop for every little bit of smuggling we'd never get anything through.'

'Did you tell him what happened to Mr Samuelsohn?' Burton asked.

'No, sir,' Cohen said.

'Why?' Mr Mansour said. 'What happened to Mr Samuelsohn?'

'He was killed earlier tonight,' Burton said. 'Murdered.'

'How do you say?' Mr Mansour said to Cohen. 'May his memory be a blessing?'

'Yes,' Cohen said.

Mr Mansour nodded. Some colour had left his face.

'He was a good man,' he said. 'He did not deserve that.'

'Who told you it was alright to cover up the smuggling?' Burton said.

'Told me? Nobody told me,' Mr Mansour said.

'What about your supervisors? The British officials?' Burton said. He was getting annoyed.

Mr Mansour shrugged.

'It was understood to be a mistake,' he said. 'Someone taking advantage of Samuelsohn's deliveries. We were assured precautions would be taken. And some money changed hands, for our trouble, you understand.'

'You didn't mind that these were guns for the Jews?' Burton said.

'Mind? Why would I mind?' Mr Mansour said. 'I have no trouble with the Jews.'

'And if there's a war next week?' Burton said.

'The Druze won't get involved,' Mr Mansour said. 'Besides, who do you think will run the port from next week if not the Jews? And Mrs Mansour still needs me to bring home the bread.' He laughed a little dry laugh to himself.

Burton wasn't sure he understood the Druze but then again he wasn't sure anyone did. They lived in villages on the Carmel and had done so for centuries; they had their own religion, which they kept secret, not only from strangers but within their own communities as well; they got on pretty well with everyone unless they didn't, at which point they were more than happy to get into a scrap. There were Druze all over the Middle East, in Syria and the Lebanon, but they did not admit converts, so their numbers were small.

'I'll tell you what I told your men, too, sir,' Mr Mansour said. 'I did not like the look of the people who came to pick up the shipments from time to time. Mostly it was, I may as well come clean with you now, mostly it was Haganah and well, one can turn a blind eye. Sometimes there were smaller shipments though, sir. At those times Mr Samuelsohn never came in person, and the people who did come were not like the others. They were...' He hesitated. 'What's the Yiddish word for it?' he said. 'I learned it from Mr Ganz in accounts… gonif,' he said. 'They looked like gonifs.'

'Thieves?' Burton said.

'You said it, not me,' Mr Mansour said.

'Anyone you recognised?' Burton said.

'Yes, maybe,' Mr Mansour said.

'Well?' Burton said. 'This isn't time for games, Mr Mansour. A man is dead.'

'I don't want any trouble,' Mr Mansour said. 'Fine, I'll tell you. It means nothing to me anyway. There were two of them, an Arab and a Jew. The Arab was from the Latifs, and the Jew is named Waldman.'

'David Waldman?' Burton said sharply. 'Didn't we arrest him a couple of years ago, Hassan?'

'That's right, sir,' Hassan said. 'Drug smuggling. Eight bottles of cocaine worth five thousand pounds in his hotel room, and sixteen drums of hashish in a warehouse in the lower city, plus a small amount of Turkish opium. But the case didn't go to trial.'

'Why not?' Burton said.

'I'm not sure, sir,' Hassan said. 'There were all kinds of big accusations thrown around at the time. The IG – it was old Rymer-Jones then – even fed the story to some journalist from *Ha'aretz*. There were all kinds of claims, of a joint Jewish-Arab organised crime gang, some dozen traders implicated across the major cities – but then nothing happened.'

'The evidence went missing,' Paddy said.

'What?' Burton said. 'I'd not heard this.'

'You were away at the time, sir,' Hassan said. 'That business in Cairo. Anyway, it didn't amount to anything and it went away.'

Burton wanted to believe the police was above corruption and criminality, but two decades into the job he knew better. So someone high up was backing these people. He said, 'Thank you, Mr Mansour.'

The Druze nodded curtly and got up to leave. 'I have a lot of work still to do, sir,' he said. 'But I hope you catch whoever did it.'

'Me, too,' Burton said. 'Me, too.'

But all of a sudden he wasn't so sure that that they would.

'Do we think this supposed Waldman gang was involved, then?' Burton said. They stood outside smoking. He could smell the stink from the oil refineries nearby. The oil flowed in the pipe from Iraq all the way to Haifa. It was the line the old Special Night Squads patrolled, commanded by that lunatic, Captain Orde Wingate. Burton had ridden with him once. He didn't like thinking about that time. Wingate's methods were unsound.

'Samuelsohn's little operation must have been winding down,' Hassan said. 'The Haganah hold Haifa now and as soon as you – the British, I mean, sir – leave they will take control of the harbour.'

'No more gun smuggling,' Burton said.

'No, sir,' Hassan said, perhaps bitterly. 'They could bring them in legit then.'

'And that's a problem for Samuelsohn,' Cohen said, picking up the through-line, 'because his... *civil* partners don't give a shit about the weapons, pardon my French, sir, but who*ever* takes control in Palestine eventually—' here he shot Hassan a sharp glance, 'they still won't permit drug trafficking, not since you – I mean, the British, sir – passed the Dangerous Drugs Act and applied it to all your dominions.'

'So they wanted to keep the operation going?' Paddy said.

'Either that or they just wanted to make up for their losses by robbing Samuelsohn,' Hassan said.

'If there really is a gang,' Cohen said.

'The other one was a Latif,' Burton said. 'Almog mentioned them earlier too, the Latifs.'

'Powerful family, sir,' Hassan said.

'Where can such men be found at this late hour?' Burton said.

'Not in their beds, boss, likely as not,' Paddy said.

'The Piccadilly,' Cohen said. 'That great cesspool into which all the loungers and idlers of the empire are irresistibly drained.'

'You've been reading your Conan Doyle!' Burton said, and Cohen gave a shy smile.

'Always trying to improve myself, sir,' he said. 'Did you know he was first translated into Hebrew by Jabotinsky?'

'The agitator?' Burton said, surprised. 'The Revisionist rabble rouser. He was before my time.'

'A great Zionist leader, sir,' Cohen said, 'and a one-time officer of the Royal Fusiliers, lest we forget. He was not a half-bad writer in his own right, either. He began translating detective stories when he was incarcerated in Acre Prison.'

'What was he doing in prison?' Burton said.

'As you said, sir,' Hassan said. 'He was a rabble rouser and an agitator.'

'Gentlemen, please,' Paddy said. 'No one gives a shit about this Jabotinsky, whoever he was. We have a job to do.'

'Let's try the Piccadilly,' Burton said. 'As far as we know, they carried out the job, have the girl stashed up somewhere safe and are out celebrating.'

'If we're lucky,' Paddy said.

'If we're not,' Hassan said grimly, 'she's already dead.'

They drove up the dark mountain. The night felt hushed, the lights few, an anticipation of danger and bad things to come. Cohen and Hassan followed in the second armoured car.

New, still sparsely built neighbourhoods here. One beacon of light in the dark – a handsome new-build two-storey hall, loud music wafting on the breeze. It had its own parking area and this, like in the casino in the lower city, was packed. Burton measured out civilian cars and army jeeps and trucks that had been covered in recent days in protective shielding.

'How does the song go?' he asked Paddy now.

'The song, boss?' Paddy said.

'You know damn well what I mean.'

'Oh, that one.' The Irishman smiled. 'Fifty pounds just for a Sten gun, it's the same old ruddy line, he's a hook-nosed robbing bastard, and he comes from Palestine!'

It was sung to the tune of 'My Darling Clementine'.

Now Paddy warmed up as he went. 'Half a million for a Churchill, bring along the crew as well! Haganah will make you captains, better pay than IZL! Piccadilly on Mount Carmel, all the girls are Haganah, where the BM did do business, propping up the fucking bar!'

Burton stepped out and lit a fresh Woodbine. The night would never end, he thought. A couple were making out against a cypress tree in the dark. Somewhere in the distance a dog barked. Inside the Piccadilly a band was massacring 'Midnight Serenade'. Cohen and Hassan stepped out of the second car and fanned out and into the shadows.

'They make *you* an offer, Paddy?' he said. 'Money for guns, make you a captain too?'

'Boss!' Paddy said.

'I don't even care,' Burton said. 'It doesn't matter anyway, not anymore. I just want to know where your loyalties lie on this.'

'I'm with you until we find her,' Paddy said, losing the smile. 'After that, that's my business, Burton.'

'Fair enough,' Burton said.

27

The couple in the shadows were making hurried sounds now, and Burton averted his eyes as he caught a flash of pale thighs and buttocks. He went into the Piccadilly, Paddy following behind.

The lighting inside the Piccadilly was dim, the smoke in the room flavoured here and there with the illicit smell of hashish, for everyone knew the police weren't going to be catching any more smugglers and there was no clarity just who would be keeping the law by next week. Or even whose law would be kept. Still, it offended him. He was still a policeman. This was still his beat.

Voices went lower when Burton stepped in. Couples danced close on the dance floor, on the bar men with guns looked over his way and laughed, then looked away. IZL. Six months ago they wouldn't have dared. A couple of British officers in uniform at one table with pretty young girls and an official-looking man in a chequered shirt who was negotiating something quietly. The officers looked up, saw Burton, nodded without much interest and went back to their business. God, but he hated the Piccadilly. It was vice on open display.

'Do you see Waldman?' he said.

'I think it's that shady little fucker on the balcony with the Arab,' Paddy said, pointing. Burton raised his eyes, saw a small, thin man he recognised as Waldman. Short haircut, a small scar on his cheek invisible in the bad light, but Burton knew it was there. The man with him was a little taller and with a little more mass, a little darker, eyes clear and scanning the dance floor below. He looked their way and his eyes met Burton's.

'Shit,' Burton said. 'He made us.'

'That's Latif, boss,' Paddy said. 'Samuil Latif, Sami to his friends. Which he ain't got none, on account of he's a sneaky little fuck too. Middle boy of the Latif children. His older brother owns the smuggling routes from Lebanon through half the Galilee—'

'I'm aware, Paddy,' Burton said. He watched the two of them. An unlikely pair. Latif was whispering urgently to Waldman, who looked their way too. Burton made for the stairs. The two men overhead stood. Paddy headed for the second set of stairs, blocking their escape.

'Keep it calm,' Burton said, to no one in particular. Waldman and Latif looked both ways and picked Burton over Paddy. They came towards him. He put his hand on the grip of his gun in the holster.

'Just want to have a word, boys,' he said, or started to. Waldman was there before Burton could quite *see* him. Somehow he had closed the gap between them, and light hands touched Burton on the chest, and then Waldman *shoved*. Burton, too surprised to react, lost his balance. He fell hard, trying to roll into a ball as he landed and not quite managing.

Waldman and Latif ran past him.

'Boss!' Paddy shouted. Burton groaned, hoping he hadn't broken anything. Everything hurt. Paddy ran to him, then past him, chasing the two men. No one else made a move to either help or intervene. Burton heard a door bang open and the sound of a toilet flushing. Jack Smith came out of the bathroom doing his belt up. He looked up, red-faced, in surprise. The armed men on the bar also turned to look, smirked and looked away. The two army officers at the table with the girls stared down their pints. Burton dragged himself upright, pulled his gun from its holster and limped out of the Piccadilly.

As he stepped out he heard two gunshots in rapid succession and dropped to the ground. Paddy shouted, 'Stop!' Burton saw two figures holding a third down – Cohen and Hassan, with Waldman twisting under their combined weight. A figure streaking into the dark must have been Sami Latif, getting away. Paddy chased him and they both vanished from sight.

'Stay down, damn it!' Cohen said, and he dealt Waldman a kick. Hassan pushed him down and both policemen wrested Waldman's hands behind his back before Hassan was finally able to put cuffs on him. Cohen gave the now-prone Waldman another kick – 'This one for the trouble,' he said.

'Fuck you, Cohen,' Waldman said. 'You're nothing but a pisher and a thief. Ough!'

'Stop kicking him, Cohen,' Burton said. He limped over, then swung a kick that connected with a satisfying thud with Waldman's side.

'That's for pushing me,' he said.

'Sorry, Burton, I didn't realise it was you,' Waldman said. 'I didn't do anything. You've got the wrong man.'

Paddy came back, breathing heavily.

'Lost him,' he said. He stood over Waldman then kicked him suddenly and with force. Waldman yelped again.

'That's for making me run,' Paddy said.

Burton lit a cigarette. The first drag was the best, the rough smoke burning his lungs in a pleasant way. He felt light-headed. They all needed sleep.

'Take him back to HQ,' he said.

The telephone ringing woke him up and for a moment Burton didn't know where he was. The first fingers of dawn light tapped urgently on the windows of the police station. In his dream he fled across a lifeless plain under a red sky, and all about him were skulls. Burton popped an aspirin. His mouth tasted disgusting.

'Yes, sir,' he said into the receiver. It was Gray on the other side. 'We have a man in custody. Yes, sir. He'll talk.'

He went into the bathroom and washed his face and ran toothpaste around in his mouth until it stopped tasting like a pub carpet. Cohen came in then. He looked tired. They all did, Burton thought.

'Well?' he said.

'He's sweating,' Cohen said.

'Good.'

They'd stuck Waldman in an interrogation room and left him there to contemplate the errors of his ways. Burton washed his hands and shook them dry. He went to see Waldman.

Waldman was a sorry sight. He was not allowed to nod off. He sat tied up in the chair. Hassan watched him from behind the desk.

'So, nu, Waldman?' Burton said. 'Tell us everything, why don't you?'

Waldman twitched.

'I have nothing to say to you, Burton,' he said. 'I didn't do nothing.'

'You did something,' Burton said. Waldman blinked nervously. He knew what was coming.

'Just let me go,' he said. 'Come on.' His voice had a needling quality.

'Where is she, Waldman?' Burton said. He nodded to Cohen. Cohen sank his fist into Waldman's stomach. All the air left Waldman's lungs and he let out a muted gasp. Cohen held the chair steady so Waldman wouldn't fall off. Burton did not like these methods, they were unsavoury, but this was an unsavoury sort of place, Palestine. He thought, for the first time, he might be happier when he was elsewhere. He'd spent too long here. Next week Palestine will be someone else's problem, and he might be happier in Kenya, where everybody's problems were simpler. He hoped. Truth was, you had the same problems everywhere.

'Come on, Waldman,' Burton said tiredly. 'You know how this goes.'

'What are you going to do to me, Burton?' Waldman said, wheezing. 'You're out. Out and gone. You have no court and no prison, you have no authority here. Nothing you can do but slap me around a little.'

'No one's going to miss you, Waldman,' Hassan said quietly. 'No one's going to miss you if you're gone.'

'You can't do that,' Waldman said. He looked at Burton beseechingly. 'Tell him you can't do that!'

'I can't,' Burton said. 'But those two can do whatever the hell they like, at this point.' He went to Waldman and put his hand gently on Waldman's shoulder. Waldman flinched.

'Think about it,' Burton said. Then he left Cohen and Hassan to it.

When he came back a half hour later Waldman was on the floor and his face was a mess. Burton lit the first cigarette of the new day. He was trying to cut down.

'Well?' he said.

'What do you want to know?' Waldman croaked.

'Let's start with Samuelsohn and the port,' Burton said.

Waldman coughed.

'Help him up,' Burton said. Cohen and Hassan lifted the chair and set it back. Waldman coughed blood.

'He was fucking his houseboy,' Waldman said.

'That's what you had on him?' Burton said.

'Initially. Enough to muscle in on what he was doing.'

'What *was* he doing?' Burton said.

'Smuggling guns,' Waldman said. 'But I bet you already knew that.'

'So he was working for the Haganah,' Burton said. 'You didn't worry they'd come for you?'

'Only if they knew what we were up to,' Waldman said. 'Besides, there was no harm. The product just rode along. A few bottles of cocaine weigh a lot less than a fucking machine gun.'

'How come you didn't go to prison the last time we caught you?' Burton said, remembering. 'We had you cold.'

'Everyone's greased,' Waldman said, and tried to smirk. It sat poorly on his ruined face. 'Guess it's too much to expect protection this late in the game, though. Everything's up in the air.'

'What about you, Waldman?' Burton said. 'Are you a Zionist?'

'Am I?' Waldman looked surprised. 'Of course,' he said. 'Why do you think I'm in Palestine and not, I don't know, New York someplace? I do my bit for the cause.'

'But you work with Arabs,' Cohen said.

'Business is business,' Waldman said.

'Tell us about tonight,' Burton said.

'Tonight?' Waldman said. He blinked nervously.

'Last night, then,' Burton said. 'You broke into Samuelsohn's house?'

'I don't know what you're talking about – no, don't!' Waldman screamed. Cohen, fist raised, looked questioningly at Burton. Burton shook his head and Cohen lowered the fist.

'I ain't saying shit without guarantees,' Waldman said.

'What sort of guarantees?' Burton said, a little amused.

'What are you going to do if I tell you? If I... cooperate?'

'Keep you on ice for a couple of days and let you go,' Burton said. 'Like you said, I don't have judges or jails. Next week you'll be somebody else's problem.'

'And if I don't tell?'

Burton shrugged. Hassan said, 'People have been known to commit suicide in police cells before. Always tragic, when that happens.'

'You wouldn't,' Waldman said. 'You're still cops.'

'Only for another week,' Hassan said.

'Where is the girl, Waldman?' Burton said. He nodded to

Cohen. Cohen smashed his fist into Waldman's face. Waldman screamed.

'My nose!' he said. 'You broke my nose!'

'Where the fuck is Eva Finer?' Burton said.

'We sold her, alright! We sold her!'

There was a sudden, heavy silence in the room. The four policemen around the prisoner, all suspended, a four-pointed star, turning.

'Who did you sell her to, Waldman?'

Burton wasn't sure which of them had asked it. He didn't trust himself to speak.

'I will take you to them,' Waldman said.

'Bedouins?' Cohen said.

Waldman nodded. 'Only as couriers,' he said.

'Destined where?' Hassan said.

'Beirut, Cairo. Somewhere where they like their meat white,' Waldman said. Paddy took out his gun and silently put it to Waldman's head.

'Don't,' Waldman said. 'Or you'll never have her back.'

'He's lying,' Hassan said. They all looked at him.

'About what?' Burton said.

'I don't know,' Hassan said. 'It just doesn't fit.'

'You promised you'd let me go,' Waldman said. 'If I told you.'

'Where are these Bedouins?' Burton said. 'Paddy, remove your gun, damn it. You're not going to shoot him.'

'I really, really want to, boss,' Paddy said. But he holstered his gun.

'We made the handover at the foot of the Carmel,' Waldman said. 'They took her in a jeep. Their main camp's in the Jezreel.'

'You know where?' Burton said.

'I know,' Waldman said.

'And Latif?' Burton said. 'Where is he?'

'I don't know,' Waldman said. 'We're only business associates. All we wanted was the money. The girl was a complication but we thought, why not turn it into an opportunity? It wasn't personal, Burton. Girls go missing all the time in this damned country and no one cares. They're just girls.'

'This one's not just anyone,' Burton said.

28

'Why should I bloody help you?' Hansen said. Hansen was police in title only. He was one of the fresh bodies parachuted in by Gray and the lieutenant general, Fergusson, who were both fucking cowboys, if you asked Burton. Burton kept those sorts of thoughts mostly to himself. Gray was his superior officer and Burton followed orders, but he didn't like what men like Hansen did. Hansen was SP, special squad, the sort that only the year before got in trouble for the extrajudicial execution of a Jewish boy, Alex Rubowitz, whose crime was hanging up posters in support of the Stern Gang.

'The orders came from the top, Hansen,' Burton said. The special squads were former commandos, Royal Marines and SAS forged in the heat of battle in the Second World War who found it hard to adjust to civilian life. Gray brought them in to fight fire with fire against the Jewish terrorists who just kept killing police officers. But there still had to be due process, Burton thought. All these guys ever did was move fast and shoot.

'We're fighting the Jews, not the Arabs,' Hansen said.

'This isn't *about* that!' Burton said. He hated arguing with Hansen. 'This girl's going to be sold in the fleshpots of Cairo if we don't mount a rescue operation.'

'And she's important why?' Hansen said.

'She's connected,' Burton said. 'She's a lady.'

'Ah, so it's *political*,' Hansen said. It was like trying to explain equations to a Rottweiler.

'It came from the top,' Burton said again.

'Well, sure,' Hansen said. 'Me and the boys haven't been out for a ride in a while. Near Nazareth, you say?'

'The Esdraelon,' Burton said. 'But we can't go in all guns blazing, we need to get her out alive.'

'We should wait for tonight,' Hansen said. 'We won't have the element of surprise in the daytime.'

'They could move her by then. We should move now.'

'Bedouins get up early,' Hansen said.

'Then we should get going.'

Hansen laughed. He slapped Burton on the shoulder.

'Don't get your knickers in a twist,' he said. 'Ready when you are.'

'My boys are ready,' Burton said.

'Your *boys* are no use in an operation like this,' Hansen said.

'We're coming with,' Burton said.

'Then stay out of the way,' Hansen said, 'and try not to get shot.'

They assembled in the courtyard. Waldman was left back in his cell, safely locked away. Hansen's men rode armoured cars and fast jeeps. Burton and Hassan followed, Cohen and Paddy behind. Hassan drove. The city woke up around them, its skies a startling blue, a fresh blanket hung up to dry above the rising ancient mountain adorned with green. It could be so god-damned *beautiful*, sometimes, the Holy Land, Burton thought. As if all the wars and occupations had left not even a scratch upon its skin.

Twenty years in this place and it was like, sometimes, he didn't know it at all.

They drove in a convoy, skirting the mountain. Down past the place the locals now simply just called the Check Point, driving north, fast and armed, Burton knowing they were watched, identified, but also that no one was going to mess with them, that this was, just about, a land under their mandate. They took a turning past Yokneam where a lone Jewish farmer was out in the field on his tractor; past a turning into the woods of what was not too long ago the Templer settlement of Bethlehem of Galilee. He saw aeroplanes overhead, back from patrol and heading to RAF Ramat David nearby. Another turning and he remembered where he was – down past these windy hills, between the Arab villages was a kibbutz, Trashim, it was there Ruth lived still. They'd arrested both her men back in '46 and sent them to the camp in Cyprus. He'd have tried to warn her, but she was too stubborn, and they hid too many guns on that damned kibbutz. Those stony hills were good for hiding bodies.

Along and through the hills they went, a column of dust, down to the Esdraelon or Jezreel, which the Jews owned now, having bought the lands from the Sursocks in Lebanon back at the turn of the century. On and on they rode under a calm blue sky and a rising sun and the bulbuls sang in the trees. Past Armageddon and into the heart of the valley, the hills of Nazareth rising in the distance.

'There,' Hassan said, pointing.

Burton could see it now too. A Bedouin encampment of tents, a herd of sheep and goats, and tethered camels, and in between the tents third- and fourth-hand jeeps and trucks, salvaged from who knew where, fuel drums piled up away from the camp.

Fast and hard, now. It was the only way the special squads knew how to be.

They were already awake in the Bedouin camp. The cooking fires already burned. Kids were playing outside. They looked up at the sound of the vehicles coming at them. The cars fanned out. The special-squad men, used only to war, came alive then. Bedouin men came running out of the tents. There were guns in their hands. The kids vanished to shelter, the men opened fire, the squaddies fired back. Burton saw a young man fall with a shot to the head, another drop his rifle as his arm exploded in a red haze. The cars overran the camp, the squaddies jumping out, shouting, the rest providing them with covering fire from a distance.

'Stop the car,' Burton said. 'God damn it, they are going to kill everyone in there. I said, stop the car!'

Hassan hit the brakes. Bullets pinged off the light armour. Burton eased the door open. He crawled out, a gun in his hand, feeling faintly ridiculous. He was too old to play cowboys and Indians.

He was too old for a lot of things, he thought; maybe too old for Palestine.

He crawled towards the camp. He couldn't see much but he could hear the gunshots and the screams. It reminded him again of going on that tour with Wingate back in '38. These were Wingate's methods, only back then the officers he trained were all young Jews who took his training with them into the resistance. The mad bastard used to walk around in the nude and bite into onions like they were apples, the juice running down his chin. Brutality was the first and only rule of Wingate's commandos, and he took what he developed here and applied it in Ethiopia and then Burma, during the war, before someone finally, mercifully shot down his plane over India. A mad old bastard but he was like a god to the Jews he trained. Burton crawled on, then rose to a crouch and ran into the smoke.

'Face on the ground! Don't fucking move!' Hansen was screaming. There were bodies lying all around Burton, a dead woman stared up at him from a ditch, in front of the tents the squaddies were pushing men face down into the ground.

Burton went into the first tent he came to and peered inside. Frightened children looked back at him and he withdrew. He knelt beside one of the captured men.

'Where is the woman?' he said.

'What woman?' the Bedouin said.

'The Jew woman,' Burton said. 'Al Yahudiya.'

'Don't know shit about a Jewish woman,' the Bedouin said. Hansen knelt on the other side of him from Burton.

'Where is she, you fuck?' he said.

'I don't know anything about a J—'

The gunshot made Burton jump. The Bedouin's head exploded the way Burton had seen a melon burst once. He said, 'Jesus, Hansen!'

But Hansen wasn't listening. He was already crouched by the next prisoner in the line, the still hot gun held to the man's temple.

'Where is she, you fuck?' he said.

'Please,' the man said. 'Please! I don't know anything about a J—'

Hansen fired again. Burton's gun was out at the same time and he was pointing it at Hansen.

'Stop that, now!' Burton said.

'Don't ever point a gun at me, Burton,' Hansen said. His gun pointed at Burton now, and he looked too casual about it, Burton thought. 'Don't ever fucking p—'

'There's some more of them, there's some more of them, get d—!' someone screamed to the beat of fresh gunshots.

Burton didn't hear the explosion. A giant punched him from behind, the force of it lifting him up in the air, helpless like a doll held in the hand of a vicious child. It raised him and tossed him and finally, with indifference or contempt, slammed him down into the ground, far beyond the screams and the fire. Before he lost consciousness he saw the fireball of oil drums as it rose like a biblical curse, devouring the Bedouin encampment and anyone in its wake.

'Burton? Burton, can you hear me?'

Burton opened his eyes and the world came blearily into focus. Everything hurt, but he was still alive. He was lying in a field of snow. No, not snow. White ironed bedsheets. They did not feel as cold. He realised he hadn't seen snow for a long time now, only when he'd visited the Hermon. He could remember snow falling in his childhood, falling softly on the streets and houses, on the

grey brick buildings and the omnibuses back in London. But
Palestine was too hot for snow.

'Who?' he said. He tried to focus. A youngish man with an eye
patch covering his left eye sat by his bedside.

'Dayan?' Burton said. His voice was hoarse. 'What the hell are
you doing here?' He tried to sit up, failed. 'Where is here?' he said
after a while.

He knew Moshe Dayan from the Orde Wingate days, the
Special Night Squads. Later they put him in Acre Prison for gun
running but let him go during the war so he could serve. Dayan
joined up with the Australian 7th Division, lost his eye to a Vichy
sniper over the Litani. He was the sort of guy, Burton knew, who
thought the law only applied to other people.

'I'm in charge in Haifa now,' Dayan said. 'For the Haganah.
Someone has to figure out what to do with all the abandoned
property in the city. Make sure there's no looting.'

It was in the last intelligence briefing Burton had read. He
would have laughed if it didn't hurt so much.

'You're in *charge* of the looting?' he said.

'Appropriation,' Dayan said. 'Listen, Burton. Did you find it?'

'Find what?' Burton said. 'The girl?'

'Not the girl, you fool,' Dayan said. 'Listen, I don't have long. If
you found it and you're holding out on me you're going to regret
it. But I'm willing to split it with you, old boy. For old time's sake.
You'll be a rich man by the time you leave Palestine.'

'Found what, Dayan?' Burton said. 'What the hell are you
talking about?'

'The map,' Dayan said.

'What map?' Burton said.

'The map to the treasure,' Dayan said.

'The map to the – what?' Burton said. 'That old story?'

He wanted to laugh again.

He'd forgotten Dayan's other hobby – the man was obsessed
with antiques. They lay everywhere, after all, and all you had to do

was dig. From end to end were ruins. And Dayan well knew the value of old, buried stuff. He was always making deals for pocket money, and there was more than one Brit who worked with him for that same reason.

'That's just a stupid story,' he said. He wanted to explain to Dayan how stupid it all was, how he thought so even the first time he'd heard it, one night around the campfire, with only the stars God made overhead. But he was lying in a hospital bed and he had more important things on his mind, like what had happened, and where was the girl?

'The fuel drums,' he said. Whispered. 'They went up in flame. The explosion... Did anyone live?'

'I heard one of your men died,' Dayan said carelessly. 'But he was an Arab.'

Burton closed his eyes, the pain catching him afresh. He'd seen so many die over the years. But every time it hurt as though it were for the first time.

And he had liked Hassan.

'The girl,' he said. 'Did we find her?'

'She wasn't there,' Dayan said. 'Listen, Burton. Forget about the girl. She doesn't matter. I need that map! I would have had it but someone stole it. Stole it and murdered Samuelsohn to get hold of it. Don't be like Morton, looking over your shoulder for the rest of your life. Just do the right thing. Hand it over.'

'I don't... have it,' Burton said. His voice felt to him as if it were coming from very far away.

'Then find it, old boy,' Dayan said, and he put his hand on Burton's shoulder, his fingers pressing into Burton's flesh. 'Find it and bring it straight back to me. You won't be sorry if you do.'

His hand slackened. When Burton opened his eyes again, Dayan was gone, as though he had never been there at all. The sun pressed against the closed shutters of the room. Burton listened to the silence.

He thought about treasure.

29

The wanted man's name was Zorkin, though he went under a variety of aliases. He also went by Sorkin and Ziskind, and was sometimes called Al Ghul. His real name and origin were shrouded in mist. He was a horse thief and a murderer, a trafficker in people and drugs and an occasional grave robber – at least when there was money in it. Since Palestine was nothing but one giant grave of the ancients, there was plenty to rob. Despite the long list of charges, nothing ever stuck to Zorkin. Witnesses tended to turn up dead.

'I want you to go see the witch,' Cairns said. Cairns was head of the Jewish Section of the CID. This was back in 1938, in Jerusalem, at the height of the Arab Revolt. The next year Cairns would be assassinated by the Irgun with a remote-controlled explosive. But Burton wasn't to know that then.

'Why the witch?' he said, groaning. He was out too late the night before with the boys at Fink's on King George Street, and his head hurt. It had been a fun night, considering. Jack Smith, who was only a constable then, did card tricks to impress the girls. But Burton got stuck talking to Golda Meyerson, one of the higher-ups in the Jewish leadership of the Yishuv. She was not unattractive, but unfortunately married, with two children, and she kept badgering him about the importance of establishing a Jewish state in Palestine while pinching half his cigarettes. It took Burton forever to get away.

'The witch says she knows where Zorkin is headed,' Cairns said. He was a good man, and if he tended to be heavy-handed with some of the Jewish prisoners it was for a reason. They were still hunting for Stern back then. It was before Morton had shot the bastard. No one in the CID was sorry when they heard the news.

'Zorkin's a ghost,' Burton said. 'That's why they call him Al Ghul.'

'They call him a ghoul because he leaves such gristly remains behind him,' Cairns said, not amused, and Burton was reminded of what it was like working in Palestine, a place where witches and ghouls walked the streets just like ordinary men and women.

'Sir, yes, sir,' Burton said, making a passable attempt at a salute.

He hated going to see the witch. Fortified with an aspirin and a glass of soda – what they called gazoz here – from the nearest kiosk, Burton set out. The ancient stone buildings hemmed him in, a camel dozed in the shade of a sweetshop, where men sat outside drinking coffee from tiny cups. They looked up at his passing, then looked away. Monks walked past him in the opposite direction. A beggar child came up to him and said, 'Hey, mister, give us a grush.'

'It's ten mils, it's not a grush anymore,' Burton said, but he tossed him a coin all the same. Some of the locals still used the old Turkish names for the new money. The five, ten and twenty mils coins had a hole through them and some of the locals took to stringing them through to make necklaces. It turned giving change into something of an art form, which no doubt was half of the point.

It was chilly walking the streets here. Jerusalem was cold, up on its mountains, nothing like the cities of the plain that were warm even in winter and boiling hot in the summer. Some of the men preferred the cold of Jerusalem, but Burton had had enough of the cold back in England.

He lit a gasper as he walked. The Dome of the Rock rose overhead. A group of Chassidic Jews clad in black went past him, going in the opposite direction. Somewhere a muezzin was calling the faithful to prayer. A donkey stared at Burton without expression and let out a gentle fart.

'And a good day to *you*,' Burton said, and the donkey snorted and swished his tail against the flies. Burton came to the maze of lean-to houses and narrow alleyways that was the Mughrabi Quarter. Laundry hung from lines overhead. He stepped over a puddle of dirty water then cursed as a motorbike sped past, almost knocking him over. As the bike ran through the puddle the water shot up and splashed Burton and he cursed again, almost dropping his cigarette. There were more and more bikes in the old city now. Jerusalem itself spread out far beyond its walls now, new Jewish neighbourhoods sprouting like blue and white anemones after the rain. Out there were cars and telephone lines and printing presses putting out book after book in Hebrew, a language barely spoken in two thousand years and which Burton was now forced to struggle with, along with Arabic, in order to be an effective policeman. His boss, Cairns, spoke Hebrew fluently. The Jews were always putting out books now. They even had detective stories.

He knocked on the door when he found it. A sullen young girl opened it and stared at him.

'Yes?' she said.

'I'm here for the witch, Adele,' Burton said.

The girl stood there still, not saying a word. Burton said, 'She's expecting me, Adele. Just move aside.'

The girl considered. Burton sighed and reached in his pocket.

'Here's a pound,' he said.

The girl took the coin. She covered it with the palm of her other hand, then opened both to show him the coin had vanished.

'That's very good, Adele,' Burton said. 'Do it again.'

'Give me another coin,' the girl said.

'Make it reappear,' Burton said. 'Making a coin disappear is only half the trick.'

'Making things disappear is the *only* trick,' the girl said. She stepped aside. Burton went in.

He hated coming here. Palestine had an underworld and then it had an *under*world. People were always trying to sell you charms to ward off the evil eye, saints' relics or amulets blessed by holy rabbis and imams. Here, in this dark, dank room, only a single candle burned, and Burton had heard that though the candle obviously changed over time the flame was passed from taper to taper, unbroken, over decades. The witch was *old*. And it was said that there had always been a witch in Jerusalem.

'Through there,' the girl said, pointing.

'I know the way,' Burton said.

The girl shrugged.

'You paid the fare,' she said, 'so you can go and no spirit shall harm you.'

'I'm not here about spirits,' Burton said. 'I'm here about a ghoul.'

With *that* cutting remark (it was the best he could do under the circumstances of his hangover) he went to the hidden opening, but when he tried to pull it open nothing happened.

'Made some changes,' the girl said. She pressed a button on the wall and unseen engines whirred to life. A trapdoor opened in the floor, a row of electric lights blinking into being one by one down below.

'Fancy,' Burton said.

He lowered himself into the hole, holding on to the metal rungs of the ladder. Down and down he went, until his feet touched dry stone. He walked down the tunnel, the glow of the electric lights fading behind him until he was once more in the dark. He turned on his torch (he always made sure to have fresh batteries) and shone it at the path. It was never easy to find the witch.

This was the Jerusalem-of-Below, the old-old city. The last

people to carelessly come here in search of treasure were the members of the Parker Expedition of 1909. For two years, a group of Edwardian Eton boys, accompanied by a Swiss psychic, dug recklessly in the holy sites, convinced by a Finnish poet that he'd cracked a secret code embedded in the Bible that revealed the location of the lost treasures of the temple. When they finally – and even more recklessly – smuggled themselves into the Al-Aqsa mosque in order to continue digging, a riot broke out. Some said they *had* found the treasure, and smuggled it successfully out of the Holy Land, others that they didn't. Whatever the truth of it, they had had to decamp Jerusalem in a hurry and return to a life of aristocratic service. Montagu Parker, their nominal leader and second son of the Earl of Morley, had served with distinction during the Great War, if Burton recalled correctly.

Parker's Place, the men called it now; though no one entered the under-city willingly or easily, and the police had no sway over the ancient tunnels. The witch ruled here as she always had.

He took a turn and another; climbed hand and foot over boulders; crouched along a narrow old aqueduct, then through a breach in the wall and laboriously up a rope ladder, then crawled through a narrow space and emerged at last into a wide cavern. He stood there for a moment, breathing heavily, then lit a cigarette. When he shone the light over the walls he saw they were covered in ancient graffiti, and someone had laboriously etched a penis into the stone.

At the end of the cavern he found a door. He sighed and opened it, then walked down a final tunnel and into a small but not uncomfortable room. A fire burned in a circle of stone, and Burton could smell the pleasant scent of hashish. The witch sat in a high-backed chair, reading a book. She put it down when Burton entered.

'Burton,' she said.

'Mara.'

She smiled. Burton stole a glance at the book she was reading and saw it was a novel by Agatha Christie. He said, 'You had something you wanted to tell me?'

'You're always in such a hurry,' she said. 'Give me one of your Woodbines.'

Burton shook the pack out of his pocket and offered it to her. She accepted the cigarette like an offering and lit it with a coal from the fire, which she picked with her bare fingers. She regarded Burton as she drew in smoke and blew it out. It vanished into the small gap in the rocks high above. She tossed the coal away as an afterthought.

'I would have liked to go to London,' she said. 'See the young princess – what is her name?'

'Elizabeth,' Burton said.

'She would be queen one day?'

'I suppose so,' Burton said.

'It must be nice, to be queen,' the witch said. 'I can still remember when there was another woman on the British throne. Empress of India, too, she was.'

'Just how old *are* you?' Burton said.

'Old enough,' the witch said.

Burton shrugged. 'Whatever you say, Mara,' he said. 'I was told to come see you about Zorkin.'

'That grave robber,' the witch said. 'Yes. We have a mutual interest here, Burton. He stole something of mine.'

'What's that?' Burton said.

'Nothing much. A trifle,' the witch said. 'But I'd like it back. It's a map of some sort, a reproduction of one at any rate.'

'A map of what?' Burton said.

'Nothing important,' the witch said.

'You know where Zorkin's hiding?' Burton said.

'I know he joined forces with Ali Siksik,' the witch said.

'The Butcher of Jaffa?' Burton said, taken aback. 'Jesus.'

'Don't say that name here,' the witch said sharply. 'Nothing good comes from men who rise from the dead.'

'We've been searching for Siksik,' Burton said. 'He murdered his boyfriend and then every witness we managed to find.'

Siksik was a giant, the son of an effendi from Jaffa. Though from a good family he had a bad habit of killing people. The boyfriend he murdered was found by a passer-by, chopped up into parts and rolled up in a bloodied sack left on the Ajami Road. Siksik then shot and killed three of the witnesses and promptly vanished. The CID managed to track him down to the Syrian border, where he was hiding in a watermelon cart. They finally subdued and arrested him and brought him back to face trial, only for Siksik to saw through the bars of his cell and escape, all without the terrified wardens lifting a finger to stop him. Since then he was in the wind.

'They are hiding out in the Cave of the Abyss in the Galilee,' the witch said. 'Near the village of Alma. You will find them there, but you must be careful, they have many men and terrorise the nearby villages.'

'What cave?' Burton said. He didn't know from caves.

'It's old and deep,' the witch said. 'A good place to hide. There's a fig tree marking the entrance.'

'And in exchange for this, what do you want?' Burton said.

'I told you,' the witch said. 'Zorkin has something I want. An old map, of no use to anyone. It was lost for many years. If you bring it back to me I would be grateful.'

Burton stared at the witch in suspicion, but she merely looked up at him with innocent eyes. Burton tossed his cigarette into the fire.

'Sure,' he said. 'Why the hell not.'

He traversed the way out of Parker's Place and when he got back to the surface he breathed in a lungful of cold, fresh mountain air and let the sun touch his face. He did not trust the witch. Some said Mara was the selfsame witch who had once raised the prophet Samuel's spirit on behalf of King Saul. But people said all sorts of things.

30

'Cohen, sir,' the young constable said. He was standing to attention by the jeep, as thin as a rake, with a pencil moustache sitting oddly on his boyish face. He looked like he'd only just learned how to shave. 'I'm to take you to Captain Wingate, sir. He is expecting you.'

Of all the things Burton didn't want to do, chasing Zorkin into the badlands of the Galilee was second only to having to work with 'Mad' Wingate and his Special Night Squads.

But the order had come down from on high, from the IG himself. Wingate might have been eccentric but he was highly effective, and his men knew the terrain well. His methods were not for the squeamish but he got results. And so on. 'Just go and let them do what they do best and bag us a couple of useful bodies,' Cairns said. 'Nailing both Zorkin and Siksik will buy us a lot of local good will. You might even get a promotion out of it, Burton, if you play your cards right.'

'I'm more likely to get myself killed,' Burton said. 'Sir.'

'Well,' Cairns said, 'if you do it will be in the service of the king, eh? So cheer up and get on with it, man.'

So Burton went home and shaved and had a two-hour sleep and when he got back to HQ it was to discover this Cohen waiting for him in the yard. Burton checked that he had the arrest warrants, he had an orderly make a coffee, he smoked a Woodbine and finally, in the face of Cohen's patient good cheer, had to give in and get in the jeep.

'I need to make a stop in Jaffa,' Burton said.

'Why Jaffa, sir?' Cohen said.

'Because I said so,' Burton said.

'It's just that the captain is waiting for you, sir,' Cohen said, 'and the captain doesn't like waiting for anyone.'

'I'm sure he can entertain himself until we get there,' Burton muttered. They drove out of the Russian Compound; the old city walls shone a dirty white in the sun. Cohen beeped at a donkey blocking the road. A car full of Russian Orthodox priests in black robes, with thick square beards, went past them going towards the old city, along the new avenues with shops like Nussbaum's Photographic Studio and Blau's Bookshop and Furniture Moldovan, the new cafés in the European style, and a pretty girl walking her small dog on a leash who looked up and smiled. Cohen almost blushed.

'You have a girlfriend, Cohen?' Burton said.

'I have a sweetheart in Haifa,' Cohen said.

'Is that where you're from?' Burton said.

'Yes, sir.'

Along the paved and surfaced Jaffa Road, and it was hard to imagine ancient armies had once marched here, ancient Jews had carried temple tax, and what was the witch talking about a map Zorkin stole from her? Burton didn't believe a word of it. Flowering cyclamen, pretty. They drove through Abu Ghosh and down the Bab al-Wad and the old Ottoman fortifications, many fallen into disuse, and the little khan at the bottom where the mountains met the valley.

'Married?' Burton said.

'Not yet,' Cohen said. 'But I hope to make an honest woman out of her yet, sir.'

The air turned warmer, the fields stretched out and away from them, in a grove of olive trees men sheltered in the shade, their faces hidden, and Burton had a moment of unease – it could be Arab marauders, it could be Irgun terrorists, it could be—

But it was just men sheltering from the sun, and Cohen drove their jeep on, oblivious, the vehicle bobbing along the road, the sun shining, until a herd of goats swept across the road and blocked their passage.

'Move!' Cohen shouted. 'Get out of the way!'

Burton squinted. Behind the goats came men on camels, and Burton made a calming motion for the young constable. He ambled out of the jeep, then stretched, enjoying the sensation. The goats moved past him, indifferent, the sharp smell of their bodies filling the air.

'Ibn Karim?' Burton said, shielding his eyes with his hand. 'Ibn Karim, is that you?'

The old Bedouin riding stopped his camel and considered the man below.

'Burton Effendi,' he said. 'You're out of your jurisdiction today.'

'Why, are you worried, you old rascal?' Burton said. 'Are you smuggling guns again, Ibn Karim?'

'Guns?' the Bedouin said, mortally offended. 'I am a goat herder, nothing more, just as my father was before me and his father before him.'

He was the grandson of old Abu Karim, who was hung by the Turks back in '16 during the Great Revolt. His father, Karim, was the only man put on trial for the crime of holding a stolen monkey, having been caught with said monkey on the Syrian border. This was before Burton's time but he'd heard the stories. He'd had his run-ins with Ibn Karim before, but quite liked the man, who had the same casual attitude to British law and order as the average burgher of Whitechapel or Soho.

'I am not here for you,' Burton said. 'Not today, anyway. I'm after a bigger quarry.'

'Oh?' Ibn Karim said. 'Tfadal, Burton, come sit, we'll have tea while the goats cross and you can tell me all about it.'

Cohen at the wheel looked irritated. Burton hid a smile. He nodded and Ibn Karim made the camel sit down – a series of odd foldings that never ceased to surprise Burton when he saw it – he could never quite get used to camels. The camel leered at Burton with big yellow teeth. Ibn Karim barked orders. A barefoot boy ran over with a pot and cups. The tea was made with sage leaves. They sat on the ground, cross-legged, and Burton accepted a sugar cube to drink the tea through. He liked the Bedouins' tea.

'Your boy there,' Ibn Karim said, nodding to Cohen in the jeep. 'A Jew?'

'Special Night Squads,' Burton said.

'Allah!' Ibn Karim said. 'That Wingate Effendi is the devil himself, they say.'

'He gets results,' Burton said uneasily.

'That he does, that he does,' Ibn Karim said. 'They say he is a big lover of the Jews, that he is training them to one day take over.'

Burton nodded. The same mutterings had been heard in HQ. For now Wingate wasn't questioned – the pipeline from Iraq was too tempting a target for Arab insurgents and the SNS patrols had significantly reduced attacks on the precious flow of oil. For now, Wingate could do what he wanted.

'Who is this man you are hunting?' Ibn Karim said.

'Zorkin,' Burton said. Ibn Karim spat on the ground.

'That horse thief,' he said.

'Do you know him?' Burton said.

'Only by reputation,' Ibn Karim said. 'He used to visit with the Bani Sakher but he double-crossed my cousin Moussa and used his knowledge of our camps to come at night and steal the horses. I heard he is hiding out in the Galilee now.'

'I heard that too,' Burton said.

'There is no use capturing him alive,' Ibn Karim said. 'Put a bullet in him and it is God's work you will be doing, Burton Effendi.'

'We have such a thing as magistrates, Ibn Karim,' Burton said. 'We have such a thing as justice.'

The old Bedouin laughed at that.

'Of course you do,' he said. 'You have your justice.' The words seemed ambiguous. 'Come then, Burton,' Ibn Karim said. 'The herd is passed. Go on your way in peace.' He whistled for the boy as he rose. The boy ran over, holding a young goat on a string. The goat tottered behind him.

'Take this goat,' Ibn Karim said, 'let it be my gift to you, as a token of our friendship.'

'You know I can't accept gifts, Ibn Karim,' Burton said. 'And I have no need for a goat.'

'You would be so impolite as to refuse?' Ibn Karim said. 'Take the goat.'

'What do I need with a damn goat?' Burton said. But he knew Ibn Karim was right. He reached in his pocket and came back with an unopened packet of Woodbines and this he handed to the old Bedouin.

'For our friendship,' Burton said.

Ibn Karim put the pack to his nose and breathed in appreciation.

'British tobacco,' he said. 'You honour me with your gift, effendi.'

Burton looked at him suspiciously, but if Ibn Karim was making fun of him he kept his face straight. It was as much of a joke he was playing on Burton as forcing the young goat on him. One day, Burton was sure, he'd get a handle on this place; but not today. He pulled the goat by the string and led it to the jeep.

'Don't say anything,' he muttered to the young constable. Cohen tried and failed to hide a smile. The goat jumped into the back of the jeep. Burton got in the passenger seat and said, 'Just drive, god damn it.'

'It's a sin goat, sir,' Cohen said.

'A what?' Burton said.

'A, how do you call it? A scapegoat?' Cohen said. 'We call it a Sa'ir la'Azazel, the hairy one given to Azazel. Every year on Yom Kippur the High Priest would have selected the fate of two goats. One was for God. The other would be imbued by the priest with all of the confessed sins of the people of Israel, and the goat would then be sent into the desert and thrown from a cliff to be broken on the rocks.'

'Seriously?' Burton said. 'That's where the expression comes from?'

'I believe so, sir.'

'You know your Bible, Cohen?'

'I try to study it when I can, sir. Is that book not why your government has supported the Jews' ambitions in Palestine? There can be no Jesus without Jews, after all.'

'And you are, what?' Burton said. 'A Zionist?'

'I'm a policeman, sir,' Cohen said.

'And don't forget that,' Burton said. The goat bleated. It shoved its small face into Burton's and he pushed it away, but gently.

Burton sat back and closed his eyes.

'Just drive,' he said tiredly.

Tel Aviv, less than an hour away, was modern and airy. Along the wide avenues furniture shops proliferated. Polished wood cabinets, tables and beds spilled onto the sideways. Burton knew they came with the latest Jewish refugees from the Nazis. Unable to take their money with them as they fled, they were reduced to shipping these old movables to be sold at cut-rate prices. Burton didn't know about the Holocaust back then – how could he? All he knew was that that Hitler fellow was causing no end of trouble over in Germany.

'There,' he said, pointing to the new police building. They'd driven past the German Colony to Jaffa, where the clock tower erected to celebrate the Sultan's jubilee still ticked the hours under the hot sun, a sole remnant of the vanished Ottomans. They drove through the police station gates and Cohen parked. Burton smelled the sea, heard the cries of gulls in the distance. He went into the office and found Tashy Thompson at his desk. Tashy stood up smiling.

'Burton!' he said. 'What brings you to this neck of the woods?'

They'd served together in Jenin. It was and remained a hotbed of Arab unrest, where the police went armed and ready for trouble. Burton could still remember one attack when it was just him and Tashy against a mass of rebels. Only Tashy's cool under duress, and his Lewis gun, had saved them that day.

'I need the papers on Ali Siksik,' Burton said.

'Siksik? You have a lead on him?' Tashy said. 'Then I'm coming too. That bastard's a name in my book, Burton. I want to cross him out.'

'I'll be glad of the help,' Burton said. 'I'm having to go to the SNS on this one, Tashy.'

'That chap Wingate?' Tashy said. 'I like the way he works. Let me get the warrant and a proper gun. That Siksik's built like a shit brickhouse.' He went off, whistling cheerfully. That was Tashy all over. Solid as a rock. Sound as a pound. Burton waited by the jeep. Tashy came over. He started to laugh.

'When did you get a goat?' he said.

The kibbutz of Ein Harod stood in the Esdraelon Valley surrounded by orderly squares of patchwork fields. It was itself an orderly if primitive arrangement of tin huts set in neat rows like flowers planted in the ground. Trees grew between the houses and dirt roads ran between the buildings.

Burton followed Cohen's directions to the army camp that sat adjacent to the kibbutz. Officers ran drills as soldiers in khaki shorts stood at parade. Burton hit the brakes and the wheels threw dust into the air. He climbed out, the goat following, and lit a cigarette.

'Sir, this way,' Cohen said. He led him through the tents to a large command tent pitched into the earth, from which emerged a thin, intense-looking young man with clean-shaven cheeks and a good head of hair.

'Burton,' he said. 'I've heard a lot about you.' He put his hand out for a shake. 'Orde Wingate. Welcome to the outfit.'

Burton shook his hand. 'Heard of you, too,' he said, and Wingate laughed. 'What can I do for you?' he said.

Burton handed over the papers. Wingate glanced at them but it was clear he was satisfied. Here was a man given to action, not petty bureaucracy.

'We shall set off at night,' Wingate said. 'It's best to catch them just before dawn, when they will be at their weakest. Why do you have a goat?' He knelt on the ground and patted the goat in question, who butted his head affectionately against Wingate's hand. Wingate scratched the goat behind the ear.

'It's a long story,' Burton said.

'All the good stories usually are,' Wingate said. 'Come, I'd like for you to meet the men.'

The men in question, Burton thought, were in truth little more than boys. In their khaki shorts and their short-sleeved shirts they looked like truant schoolboys on a day out. But he saw the purpose in their eyes, and the practised, orderly way they moved, and he thought, Wingate is forming the start of a Jewish army here, and right under our bloody noses too.

'Dayan,' Wingate said, introducing a young man with a twinkle in his eyes – he reminded Burton of a street hustler straight out of Seven Dials.

'Sir,' Dayan said, saluting Burton in far too casual a fashion.

'This is Yigal, Yigal Allon,' Wingate said, introducing a fresh-faced man of not more than twenty. 'They're two of my top men, Burton. They'll get your Sorkin out of that cave for you in no time.'

'Zorkin,' Burton said.

Dayan and Allon exchanged glances.

'You know him?' Burton said.

'Only by reputation,' Allon said.

Burton could tell they were hiding something. But it didn't really matter, not then. Back then they only had rudimentary files on these men at CID.

The day was hot. Burton rested in an improvised hammock made out of an old bedsheet and strung up between two poles. Wingate wandered up and down the camp in the blazing heat, stark naked and biting into a raw onion as if it were a pear. No one seemed to notice.

'The man's bonkers,' Tashy said.

'They say he's a military genius,' Burton said groggily. He was uncomfortable in the hammock, which kept sagging lower and lower to the ground.

'Don't look much like one,' Tashy whispered.

'Not to dream is to slip back,' Wingate said. 'Slip back! The present is in this sense a dream, as is the future and the past.'

'Say what now?' Tashy said. But Wingate paid him no heed, while Burton closed his eyes so as not to see the captain's bollocks flopping in the hot dry air.

'To live rightly is to achieve a proper blending of the present, past and future,' Wingate said. 'Or rather only the last two, for the present in this sense does not exist.'

'Amen, brother,' Tashy said.

Burton tried to drown away the captain's voice. He slept fitfully through the long, slow afternoon.

At two hours past midnight they rode out into the Galilee.

31

Burton tossed and turned in the hospital bed. In his dream he was running across a lifeless plain, the sky burning a lurid red, and under his feet were uncountable skulls, some human, some rodent-sized, others of some species which were like people but different from them, long and low and with a prominent ridge, and he knew in his dream that they belonged to the old people, the ones who vanished into the mists of time. He ran towards a distant place, a Golgotha, and the scent of gunpowder and death was in his nostrils.

'What is this place?' he whispered. A man ran beside him, a man in last century's clothes, twin guns at his hips, a wide-brimmed hat on his head.

'It is where all things eventually go,' he said in English. He had a foreign accent, maybe German. 'But it is not your time yet.'

'Who are you?' Burton said.

'A ghost.'

'I was wrong about Samuelsohn's murder,' Burton told the ghost. 'I have to go back to the beginning.'

Dry and brittle bones crunched underfoot as he ran. The sky burned red. Burton fled across the lifeless plain.

'Boss?'

He opened his eyes. Dim light in the hospital room. His head still hurt. He didn't know what time it was. Another ghost stood by his bedside, looking worried.

'Hassan?' Burton said.

'Yes, boss,' Hassan said. He wore a cast on his right hand and one side of his face was blistered and red.

'But they told me you were dead!' Burton said.

Hassan frowned. 'Who did, sir?'

'The one-eyed man told me,' Burton said.

'Dayan?' Hassan said. 'I saw him skulking around earlier. Never trust a one-eyed man, sir. I was only injured in the blast, same as you.'

'Paddy?' Burton said. 'Cohen?'

'They're both fine. So are you, sir, at least that's what I overheard the doctor say. You just needed the rest.'

'What I need is a cigarette,' Burton said, and Hassan smiled.

'That's what I thought, sir,' he said. He fished in his pocket with his unbroken hand and brought out a packet of Fatimas. It had a veiled woman on the front. Burton could have cried. Hassan tossed the packet on Burton's chest. Burton opened it, shook out a cigarette and put it between his lips.

'Did you get matches, too?' he said.

Again Hassan reached in his pocket. He brought out matches and tossed them to Burton. Burton lit up. The thick fug of smoke rose into the air and hovered above them. For a long moment Burton was silent, letting the rush of the nicotine course pleasingly through him. For the moment, it seemed, they were both still alive. It was worth savouring.

'That was foolish, what we did,' he said at last.

'We acted on information received, sir, that was all,' Hassan said.

'Waldman lied to us,' Burton said. 'He sent us into a trap.'

'So he did, sir,' Hassan said.

'I didn't think he had it in him,' Burton said. He pushed himself off the bed and stood up groggily.

'Either way, sir, the girl's still missing,' Hassan said. 'And we still need to find her.'

'It seems almost pointless, doesn't it, Hassan?' Burton said.

'Sir?'

'In the middle of all... this,' Burton said. 'The withdrawal. Where will you be next week? On the run from the Jews? Or fighting them?'

'I think we can live together, sir,' Hassan said. 'There is enough land here for the both of us.'

Burton laughed. The ash from his cigarette drifted to the floor. He thought of his dream, of the place he was running to. He said, 'You're a dreamer, Hassan.'

'What would the world be without dreamers, sir?' Hassan said. 'You should get dressed now. Cohen and Paddy have gone back to check on Waldman. He'll soon be singing a truer tune. And your ass is hanging out of your hospital gown. Sir.'

'Huh?' Burton said. 'Oh.' He scratched himself. 'I suppose you're right,' he said. The dream still lingered. He found his clothes folded on the dresser by the bed. The hospital was quiet. He dressed slowly, still hurting from the explosion, but he knew he was going to be fine. It's why he never married. He'd seen too many good wives left without a husband, too many good men shot or blown up in service in Palestine.

'Nothing but skulls,' he said.

'Sir?'

'Never mind,' Burton said. 'You must stay here and rest, Hassan. I'll drive back to HQ.'

'I am good to go, sir,' Hassan said. 'It is only a cast.'

'Don't be ridiculous, man,' Burton said, 'you're on medical leave until further notice.'

'Until Friday, sir?' Hassan said. 'You might as well retire me right now.'

Burton looked at the man. He could understand the dedication. It got you that way, the job. It took over, and that's how you ended up banged up and alone in a hospital room, no wife, no kids, no idea what you'll be doing next week when the job, the only thing that ever mattered to you, was over.

'I'll drive,' Burton said.

'We were going into the Galilee under cover of deep night,' he told Hassan. 'There was me, Tashy Thompson, Wingate and his merry men of the SNS. And the goat.'

The wind blew warm. There were no lights. The car sped towards distant Haifa. There was a sense of tension in the air, an anticipation. It was all so calm, but trouble could flare up at any moment.

'Why the goat, sir?' Hassan said.

'For the sacrifice,' Burton said.

The night had been warm then too, the heat of the day dissipating into a pleasant atmosphere that grew almost but not quite cold as they approached the cave. What had Ruth once quoted to him, when they lay in bed in some anonymous hotel in the city after lovemaking? 'In the endless summer I experienced a drop of autumn in between'. Ruth never struck him as a poet, she was too practical, too hard sometimes. She said the Jews in Palestine could not afford to be soft, not anymore. That land could only be reclaimed with blood.

He'd liked Ruth. He had hoped she liked him too, but there was never love between them, theirs was a pleasurable transaction, secrets for secrets, sealed with a hasty fumble and a drink. Or so he tried to delude himself. To admit he had stronger feelings was to invite nothing but heartache.

'The cave, when we finally found the entrance, seemed abandoned,' Burton said. 'We'd parked the jeeps two kilometres back and made our way there on foot, so as not to alert the gang to our presence. Wingate's men moved silently and very fast. He'd made them into good soldiers. We crouched in the bushes and watched for a while. There were two guards on duty stationed in the shadows, and it took us a while to spot them. Wingate sent two of his men and they snuck up behind them and disabled them without a sound.'

'Disabled, sir?' Hassan said.

'Wingate's methods were questionable,' Burton said, remembering the queasy feeling he had when the guards dropped noiselessly to the ground. It was knife work that did it. 'But he got results.'

'Then what happened?' Hassan said. He frowned as he watched the road. They drove without lights. 'How does it connect with our case, sir?'

'I'm getting to that,' Burton said. 'Once the guards were eliminated, Wingate sent in my goat.'

'Your goat, sir?' Hassan said.

'Sent to Azazel,' Burton said, wincing as he recalled. The young goat went happily enough, not knowing its probable fate. The men of the SNS crept behind the animal, for goats could find their way even in the dark and on uneven ground, and it was reasoned that the appearance of a goat would lull Zorkin's gang's suspicions, allowing for a quick strike – the element of surprise, Wingate called it.

The plan worked. The path down into the cave was steep, the air growing colder and more humid the deeper they went. Once, Burton had to stifle a scream when a small leathery thing flew at his face. He struck at it helplessly and it fell to the ground – it was only a bat. The place was crawling with them. As the ground evened they had to move cautiously, following the goat, who picked a path through the fields of stalagmites that grew in profusion from the floor. Visibility was dim, but a distant glow, the remnants of the gang's fire perhaps, provided just enough illumination for Burton to imagine what a magnificent sight the place might be with proper lighting. It was like an Aladdin's Cave.

The cave was wide and the ceiling high, a sense of open space here deep under the ground. The gang made their camp in an even bit of ground near one of the distant walls. The goat made for them, stumbled over sleeping bodies and baaed.

This was when things went wrong.

A huge figure, whom no one had noticed, detached itself from the shadow of the wall where it had evidently been taking a piss. Ali Siksik, his very size giving his identity away, gave a shriek of pure outrage and with one hand still holding his member he used the other to fire at the approaching men.

Burton dropped to the ground as Wingate, heedless of the bullets flying in the dark, gave the order to attack. The men of the Night Squad didn't need to be told twice. Gunfire erupted, sleeping gang men jumped out of their bedrolls, scrambled for their weapons and were mowed down. Ali Siksik, seemingly impervious to bullets, fired back and vanished behind a rock.

'I've got him,' Tashy said. He was on the ground next to Burton. 'I think I can go round and catch him from the back.'

'Don't be a hero, Tashy,' Burton said, but his friend grinned and began to crawl purposefully away. Bullets flew back and forth, the gang members taking up defensive positions, the men of the Night Squad advancing and firing in precise, coordinated bursts wherever they identified a weakness.

'Zorkin!' Burton shouted. 'Come out with your hands up and tell your men to put down their weapons!'

'I'm not giving it up!' Zorkin shouted. He was hiding somewhere in the deep recesses of the cave. 'You tell the witch the treasure's mine!'

'What fucking treasure!' Burton shouted back. There was a short silence.

'Burton, is that you?' Zorkin said. 'I heard of you.' His voice had a wheedling quality. 'They say you're a fair man. Get me out of here alive and I'll give it to you. Just don't let these vultures kill me! I didn't do anything.'

'Come out in peace and I'll take you in alive,' Burton said. 'I don't know anything about a treasure.'

'But *they* do,' Zorkin said. 'Those men you brought with you. They want to kill me!' He sounded desperate.

Burton stole a glance sideways. He saw Dayan and the other fellow, Yigal Allon, crouching as they came to talk to Burton.

'Do you know anything about this treasure?' Burton said.

'They say he has a map, sir,' Dayan said.

'A map?'

'To the treasures of the Second Temple, sir,' Dayan said, as if it were obvious. 'If we could only find it...' His eyes shone. 'It would prove it, don't you see?' he said earnestly. 'That this land is ours.'

'This is ridiculous,' Burton said...

'The treasure of the Second Temple, sir?' Hassan said. Haifa was in the distance, the streetlights illuminating the mountain and the ships in the harbour glimmering like pearls. 'That sounds like, what are those books for kids you have in England? *The Famous Five*?'

'Like *Five on a Treasure Island*, yes,' Burton said, smiling. 'But that wasn't even out yet when this happened.'

'Were they serious, sir?' Hassan said. 'About the map?'

'I think they were,' Burton said. 'It's not impossible. People *do* find buried treasure here all the time. Coins and things. Gold. Dayan went on to become quite notorious for grave robbing and selling antiques on the black market, but we could never prove anything.'

'I remember, sir,' Hassan said. 'But this is just a fairy tale, no? Do you really think it connects with our present investigation?'

Burton rubbed his face. 'Do I think Mr Samuelsohn was murdered for a map that may or may not exist, for a treasure that may or may not be real?' He stared out of the window at the approaching city lights.

'People have died over far less in Palestine,' he said. 'All the stories here are fantastical.'

32

A dark shadow crept along the walls, pistol extended. Its target was just ahead, the huge shape of Ali Siksik, the Jaffa murderer, his back to the shooter, presenting an irresistible target. Burton could just about see what happened next, from the corner of his eye. Tashy, creeping along the wall. Siksik, turning suddenly, a machine gun in his hands, his face a rictus of – what? Fear? Triumph?

Tashy's finger closed on the trigger just as Siksik fired—

'Tashy, no!' Burton screamed.

Tashy Thompson fell. Siksik leaped out of his rock shelter, raining bullets on the SNS men. Burton dropped, crawled to Tashy as all hell broke loose again. Any attempt at talking Zorkin into custody in peace were over. He found Tashy lying there, blood pouring out of his stomach.

'We'll get you out, Tashy,' Burton said, 'I promise.'

'Just… nail him for me,' Tashy said. He tried to smile and coughed blood instead. Burton took the blood-stained pistol…

Then he ran blindly into the firefight, screaming vengeance.

'By the time it was over Zorkin was dying,' Burton said. 'I'd got to Siksik but it still took three men to take him down. The rest of the gang fled or were massacred. The wounded were shot where they lay. Made it simpler, I suppose. The goat vanished back up the slope and made his escape from the cave. Somehow he had survived all the shooting. As for Zorkin, I only saw him for a moment, after all that. He lay between the stalagmites like a fallen king, his face smeared with blood. I could see the whites of his eyes.

'"Where is it?" Dayan kept saying. He was standing over Zorkin, shaking him. "Where is the map, damn you?"

'"Somewhere you'll never find it," Zorkin said. He spat blood in Dayan's face. "May you lose an eye for this," he said. "Everyone dies for the gold, and nobody lives." And then he died, just like that. I thought it was all bullshit, myself. Some story the Jews told each other so often some of them grew to believe in it. Like the messiah, I suppose. And then I just forgot about it for a long time.'

'What happened to your friend?' Hassan said. 'This Tashy?'

'He lived,' Burton said. 'Got discharged back to England eventually. I still get a Christmas card from him most years. He has a farm in Kent somewhere and grows apples.'

He wondered if it was him, and not Tashy, who had gotten the short end of the stick in the end. All Tashy lost were intestines. Now he had a home, a family, something to call his own. Whereas Burton – was he just stuck here, all that time? He supposed he was merely doing the empire's work. Someone had to maintain control, someone had to keep order. But then you woke up after twenty years and looked around you and all you could smell was gunpowder residue, and you wondered what it was all *for*.

HQ, the building rising in the muggy light of dawn. The guards waved them in. The courtyard bustling with troops and officers moving equipment. He passed Jack Smith carrying a typewriter out as he went in.

'Seriously?' Burton said.

'Phones are next,' Smith said cheerfully.

'Find Cohen,' Burton said to Hassan, 'and let's get Waldman talking. We're running out of time.'

But they were not in luck; and time had run out. Burton had an inkling of it even before Hassan returned, a shame-faced Cohen in tow.

'Dead,' Cohen said without preamble.

'How?' Burton said. He felt a slow burning anger rise inside him.

'Hanged himself in his cell,' Cohen said.

'How?' Burton said again. 'He should have been kept safe.'

'He was alive when I put him in there, I swear it,' Cohen said. 'But we were out at the Bedouin camp, sir. And he was left alone.'

'Who was the last person to see him?' Burton said.

'I found him,' Cohen said. 'I went to check on him as soon as I returned to HQ.'

'Why would he hang himself, Cohen?' Burton said. 'Why would Waldman kill himself when for all he knew we were all dead already in that ambush he sent us into?'

'Who can fathom the criminal mind, sir?' Cohen said, then fell away from Burton's visible rage.

'I am sorry, sir,' he said. 'It was my fault.'

Burton deflated. 'It's my fault if it's anyone's,' he said. But he looked at Cohen suspiciously all the same. He could trust none of his men now, he thought. Someone got to Waldman, he was sure of it. But none of it mattered now, the only thing that mattered still was finding the girl.

'Where is Paddy?' he said. 'Did he come back with you?'

'He's catching forty winks in barracks,' Cohen said.

'Then wake him up and meet us at the Samuelsohn house,' Burton said. He turned on his heels and marched to the morgue. He stared with frustrated fury at Waldman's corpse. There were ligature marks on his neck. Waldman's eyes stared unseeing into the ceiling, and he had soiled himself in death. The smell hung acrid in the room.

'Hanged himself?' Burton said.

'That's what it looks like,' Huw Jones, the assistant pathologist, said, ambling over. 'We're just waiting for that Jewish burial agency to come pick him up and be done with him.'

'The chevra kadisha?' Burton said.

'That's it,' Huw said.

'Did you examine him?' Burton said.

'Got no time,' Huw said. 'Everything's packed and ready for the ship. We're going home, Burton. Didn't anyone tell you?'

Burton stared at the corpse. Whatever Waldman knew, he was no longer telling. Burton's fingers itched as if wanting to form a fist. He wanted to hit something. Someone. He took a deep breath of cold, dead air.

'Fine,' he said.

The Samuelsohn house looked shabbier in the daylight, the garden untended, the paint beginning to peel on the walls. A young woman went past pushing a baby in a pram, enjoying the sunlight and seemingly oblivious there was a war going on. But then again, the battle for Haifa was already over. No doubt in time these German houses would be occupied anew. There was already talk of Jewish immigration from the Arab countries once the British were gone.

Burton couldn't imagine why anyone would choose to come here, not now, with war about to break out. But then, there were still a quarter million Jewish refugees housed in displaced persons camps in Europe, She'erit Ha-Pletah the Jews called them, the surviving remnant of the six million that perished in the Nazi camps. They were people with nothing left to lose. Coming to Palestine to make a last desperate stand made sense, at least for those not still hoping for a simpler, brighter future somewhere like America. God knew they weren't welcome in Britain.

He parked the car. He should send Hassan home, with his broken arm and future in doubt, but where? Nowhere was safe now. And they still had a job to do.

Once again he walked up the path to the house. Opened the door and let himself in. The houseboy was gone. The house was cool and dim. The light filtering in from the outside illuminated dust motes. There had been no attempt to clean the place after the murder. The corpse was gone, and he imagined they had buried Samuelsohn already, the Jews had a thing about burying people immediately after death.

'Hassan,' Burton said. 'Do we know who buried him?'

'I can find out,' Hassan said.

'Use the phone,' Burton said. 'Find out where, and who turned up. We need to look at this case differently.' He had some ideas now. That fucking treasure. Just the idea of it made people do funny things. He waited as Paddy and Cohen walked in.

'Sir,' they both said, saluting.

'Go through everything again,' Burton said. 'We know Samuelsohn specialised in antiques. Whoever broke in tossed the place from top to bottom. We didn't bother to ask what they were looking for, but now I think it could have been an old map. It might be important.'

He filled them in on Dayan's visit in the hospital, and his own recollections of the Zorkin case in '38.

'A treasure map, sir?' Paddy said. 'Really?'

'Just toss it again,' Burton said. 'See if Samuelsohn had any professional contacts we can talk to. And the girl, if she was in on it.'

'The girl, sir?'

'Yes,' Burton said. 'We've been making too many assumptions. But there's a reason Eva Finer was here, and there's a reason she's gone missing, and if that reason is a story about an old map that, true or not, people *have* died for… Well, it might just lead us to her while we all still have jobs. Alright?'

'Yes, sir.' Paddy and Cohen saluted. Then they got to work.

'Sir?' Hassan said. He appeared from the other room. 'They're burying Mr Samuelsohn in half an hour at the old cemetery. Turns out we only just released the body.'

Burton cursed Huw Jones for not mentioning anything – but then, why would he? As far as everyone knew they were still operating under their first assumption, a random robbery-kidnapping. They'd not given a thought to Samuelsohn before.

'You come with me,' he said to Hassan. Burton tossed the keys up and down. It was a nice day outside. Bright blue sky, not a cloud in sight. The city seemed quiet for now. The smell of honeysuckle growing wild, the Templers must have planted it.

He drove down the hill, past the War Cemetery where some of the Mysore and Jodhpur Lancers who fell in the capture of Haifa in 1918 lay buried. They were joined by others since, fallen in the Great War and the Second World War and all the wars in between. Burton didn't like going there too often, there had been something indescribably depressing about the way the dead kept arriving there, like parcels delivered too late to an empty address. It was a military graveyard, for fallen soldiers; but once, wandering away from the orderly rows of white headstones, Burton came across a large tomb, set in stone and older by far than the wars, and the name on it was of a woman, Alice Oliphant. She was just forty when she died. He'd wondered about her. Her husband had been a traveller and a mystic and, so Burton was given to understand, a spy in the service of the empire. But he was buried far away, in Twickenham, while his wife lay here in the company of dead soldiers. She must have been a real sainted lady, he thought.

The old Jewish cemetery was lower down the mountain. A few cars were parked nearby, and Burton could see the small group of mourners in the distance, the coffin carried by four men in shorts with an air of grim determination. A rabbi was speaking liturgical Hebrew, himself seeming like a doctor ticking off items on a long but required form. Hassan remained in the car to note down the licence plates and description of any mourners in attendance. Burton made his way slowly to the grave.

Dayan was there, he saw. The man turned his single eye on him and regarded Burton thoughtfully before giving him a brief nod. He wore a yarmulke in addition to his eye patch. There were barely enough people in the cemetery for a minyan. It was what the Jews called a quorum of ten, needed to fulfil religious rites. Burton wondered what he'd do with all that useless knowledge next week. By the following month he might be hunting down pro-independence revolutionaries in Kenya or communists in Malaya, and what use would his knowledge of arcane Jewish customs be then?

The coffin was lowered into the hole and the gravedigger, a short squat man with payos – the sidelocks which some Orthodox Jews grew, and go explain *that* to a fellow in Borneo – began covering the grave with dirt. It was all regulation-sized, the hole, the coffin, the final rites neither too long nor too short. Dayan came and stood beside Burton.

'You're still here?' Dayan said. He gave a small little grin at his own joke. Burton wanted to wipe that smug look off of his face. 'We're burying a good man today.'

'Was he a good man?' Burton said.

'What are you implying?' Dayan said.

'I just wonder how he ended up in the ground,' Burton said.

'Good men die violently all the time,' Dayan said. 'You should know. You lost enough of your own trying to hold this country for so long.'

'While you and the Arabs,' Burton said, 'all you do is fight.' He said it with some bitterness, for Dayan wasn't wrong. Too many good men had died trying to hold Palestine for the crown.

'I was born here,' Dayan said. 'I don't have another country. This is my land. Why should I not fight for it?'

'I don't know,' Burton said. 'I don't know anything. Did Samuelsohn really have the treasure map?'

Dayan shrugged.

'You tell me,' he said.

'And the girl?' Burton said. 'This Eva Finer? How is she connected to it?'

'What makes you think she is?' Dayan said, suddenly curious.

'You don't know her?' Burton said.

'Never met her in my life,' Dayan said. 'Didn't even know she was over here until I heard she went missing.' There was a new, calculating look in his eyes, as though Burton had let slip a secret. 'We're looking for her, of course,' Dayan said.

'Of course,' Burton said.

'You don't think she's *connected*, do you?' Dayan said.

'Do you?' Burton said.

'I thought you had it figured out for the Latif gang,' Dayan said.

'You seem well-informed.'

Dayan shrugged. 'The Latifs are not in Haifa,' he said. 'If they were I would have had them in cuffs by now.'

Burton stared at him in frustration. Dayan wasn't even bothering to pretend anymore that the police meant anything. *He* was the authority here now. And they both knew it.

'If you found them, would you give them up to us?' Burton said.

'What would be the point?' Dayan said. 'You'll be gone before it even matters and then this will be a Jewish state. The first one in two thousand years. That means something, Burton. We were on this land before ever a church or a mosque were built, and this time next week the entirety of your mandate will be a barely remembered moment, relegated to a footnote in our history.'

'We're still in charge here, Dayan,' Burton said. 'For a few more days, at least.'

'Sure,' Dayan said, already dismissing him. 'You keep telling yourself that.'

With that he turned and left; leaving Burton with nothing more to go on. Well, not nothing, perhaps. It was interesting about the Latifs. Interesting, too, that Dayan now had reason to question the kidnapping story, something Burton had planted in his mind. Let the Haganah and their intelligence network look for the girl, by all means, he thought.

Burton wasn't looking for treasure. He just needed Eva Finer back and on the next ship home to England.

33

'He was a good man, Isaac,' Mr Hirsch said. Mr Hirsch was old and stooped, with a mane of silver hair and a pair of pince-nez which sat awkwardly on the bridge of his nose. His eyes were lively, a light green the colour of pond scum. 'A good man. If this could happen to him, are any of us safe?'

He took out a pipe and began to fill it methodically. They stood some distance from the grave.

'You knew him well?' Burton said. 'You were friends?'

'As much as anyone could be said to have been his friend,' Mr Hirsch said. 'He was a closed man, Isaac. Never married, you know. No children. No one to mourn him now he's gone. It's a crying shame.'

'You have children?' Burton said.

'Five,' Mr Hirsch said with pride. 'I hope I don't lose them to the coming war.' He added that last with a tone of some dubiousness.

'You think there's a war coming?' Burton said.

'Of course,' Mr Hirsch said. 'They want to kill us, don't they?'

'Who does?' Burton said.

'The Arabs,' Mr Hirsch said. 'As soon as you lot leave they will all invade us. It is on your head, Mr Policeman. Giving those Hashemite boychiks their own kingdoms in Jordan and Iraq – what were you thinking?'

Burton squirmed at that one. It was true, there was no denying it. A deal with the Sharif of Mecca back in '16 for his help against the Turks. The crown gave his sons kingdoms sketched out in pencil on a map in a Cairo hotel room in '23. But this was just the nature of the world. Deals had to be made, order had to be maintained. And the new king in Jordan had British military advisers to guide his hand. It was a good solution. Iraq, too, was stable. No, they had done the right thing there, he was sure of it.

'People will respect the UN decision,' he told Mr Hirsch, and the old man laughed.

'We are ready with our guns,' Mr Hirsch said. 'And with the lives of our children, if need be. I just wish Isaac lived to see our independence. He was a good—'

'Man, yes,' Burton said. 'You said. So tell me about him. How did you know him, Mr Hirsch?'

'We were in the same business,' Mr Hirsch said. 'More or less. I am a numismatist. From the Latin, you know. A specialist in coins. Isaac often sought my advice. I have a small shop in Hadar, and do a modest trade, all perfectly licensed, Mr Policeman, you won't find irregularities in *my* paperwork, no sir.'

He glared at Burton with those disconcerting dirty-green eyes.

'Does that mean,' Burton said, 'that if I check Mr Samuelsohn's… paperwork, as you put it, I might find irregularities?'

'I never said that,' Mr Hirsch said.

'But would I?' Burton said.

'The man is dead,' Mr Hirsch said. 'Can't you leave him alone?'

Burton sighed. 'I just want to catch the people who did it, Mr Hirsch,' he said. 'And find the girl. You do remember there is a girl involved, don't you?'

'Miss Finer,' Mr Hirsch said, and his eyes turned soft and watery.

'You know her?' Burton said.

'Yes, of course. An outstanding young lady. Very good manners. Very pleasant. She often came into my shop. In fact, I introduced her to Isaac,' Mr Hirsch said, the words all but tumbling out of him. Burton thought, the old goat had a soft spot for posh young totty.

'What was her interest in your shop?' he said.

'She was passionate about our history,' Mr Hirsch said. 'Yes, yes. I don't know if you know much about Miss Finer, but she comes from a very good family, very British. You know, in England, nobility is *conferred*, yes, and Jews are rare in that world. Miss Finer was not brought up Jewish, but she became, how shall I put it? The blood runs deep. She became interested, then passionate about her history. Her *people*.'

'She became a Zionist?' Burton said.

'Yes, of course,' Mr Hirsch said. 'That isn't what I mean, though. She read history at Cambridge, you know.'

'I did not know that,' Burton said.

'Not to a degree level, of course,' Mr Hirsch said, 'she is a woman, after all. But she had a real interest, is what I'm saying.'

'In old coins?' Burton said.

'And other things. The past is all around us here, Mr Policeman,' Mr Hirsch said. 'Our coins are still buried in this ground, the ruins of our temple, our synagogues, the very wine jars from which our ancestors drank. All of it is *proof*, if proof was ever needed, of our ancestral rights to this land, and—'

Burton was getting sick to the back teeth of getting lectures, but he had to let the old man waffle on in the hope of something useful finally emerging. He said, 'So she was into that, was she? Miss Finer? Antiquities?'

'Quite right, quite right,' Mr Hirsch said. 'I still remember when she first came into my shop, my, she was a sight, I don't mind telling you. A very pretty girl. Well, not pretty in the conventional sense, perhaps. But *animated*. Her purse being generous, as it were, and her interest so keen, I introduced her to a few people eventually, including dear departed Isaac. They hit it off quite handsomely.'

'Did she always stay with him while visiting?' Burton said.

'No, never, to my knowledge,' Mr Hirsch said. 'She could afford a good hotel, and the family has a villa on the Sea of Galilee, I assume you've already checked there in case she popped up?'

Burton cursed himself, for again, he had not – they had not. He'd forgotten all about the villa. But of course, he had been operating on a different set of assumptions before.

'I will check it myself,' he said.

'I was never extended an invitation,' Mr Hirsch said with a mournful air. 'I hear it's very nice there. Many happy occasions.'

'Tell me about treasure,' Burton said.

'Treasure?' Mr Hirsch said. 'What treasure?'

'You tell me, Mr Hirsch.'

The old man waved a hand dismissively. 'I don't know anything about treasure,' he said. 'Only fools rush for gold, as they say.'

'Do they say that?' Burton said.

'Perhaps it sounds better in German,' Mr Hirsch said.

'The Second Temple,' Burton said.

'Ah, that,' Mr Hirsch said. 'Yes, I heard the stories. The Austrian cowboy, you know.'

Burton had no idea what Mr Hirsch was talking about, but he was suddenly very interested.

'The cowboy,' Burton said. 'Of course.'

Mr Hirsch waved his hand dismissively again. 'An old wives' tale. The Bedouins still tell of Abu al-Bunduqia, the Father of the Gun. His real name was Gustav somebody. He supposedly vanished somewhere east of the Jordan, near the ruins of Jerash. The story says he had an ancient map leading to the treasure, and was killed for it by a wily Ottoman colonel. The colonel would have laid his hands on the treasure, no doubt, but as he and his men journeyed back across the Jordan they fell under attack, or maybe had a falling-out amongst themselves, the details always get hazy at this point. Details usually do when it comes to treasure tales. The map was lost, in any case, if it had ever existed at all. Of course, old documents *do* sometimes turn up. It's why I keep in with the Bedouins, you know. Why, just last year some Second Temple era scrolls supposedly turned up in some caves near the Dead Sea, some Bedouins were trying to flog them in the market in Jerusalem. You have to be careful with this sort of thing, though. One must never forget the whole Shapira Affair. A sorry affair, that was.'

'What's that?' Burton said.

'Moses Wilhelm Shapira,' Mr Hirsch said. 'He was a well-respected dealer back in, oh, well before my time, he died in 1884. Suicide. Claimed to have found some ancient scrolls near the Dead Sea. Caused quite a stir back in the day, as you can imagine. Wanted to sell them to the British Museum for a small fortune. Only problem was, he had something of a reputation for selling forgeries. He was ridiculed in *Punch*, the museum deal fell through, and the poor man ended up shooting himself in Rotterdam, of all places. Terrible tragedy. The scrolls ended up selling for ten guineas at Sotheby's and no one's ever seen them since. I don't deal in documents, myself. There are enough forgeries in coins to keep an honest numismatist busy.'

He was giving Burton a headache. Burton lit a cigarette and the old man, looking at him now in some amusement, finally lit his pipe, letting out a cloud of aromatic smoke over the silent graves.

'Did you tell this story to Miss Finer?' Burton said.

'Told her? She couldn't get enough of it,' Mr Hirsch said. 'And it was the same with poor Isaac. He had all kinds of ideas about it, too. Nothing is lost forever, he kept saying, despite all evidence to the contrary. *Everything* is lost, sooner or later. We antiquarians know that better than anyone. All we ever deal in is the few broken remains. A handful of coins, a faded inscription on a broken piece of masonry. The past might be all about us, Mr Policeman, but it just as quickly turns to dust and vanishes with the desert winds. Well, good day to you. I must return to my shop.'

He doffed his hat to Burton and turned to leave.

'Wait!' Burton said.

'Yes?' Mr Hirsch said, a little impatiently, 'what is it?'

'Did he find it?' Burton said. 'Did Samuelsohn find the map?'

Mr Hirsch shrugged.

'If he did,' he said, 'it was probably just another fake.'

And with that he took his leave.

Burton watched him go, this small, slight figure, trailing a cloud of pleasant-smelling smoke as he hobbled to the gates of the cemetery. The other mourners had all left by now. He hoped Hassan got a good look at them.

As he made his own way out of the gates he saw a Vauxhall saloon parked next to his own vehicle. A familiar woman leaned against the hood smoking a cigarette. She was a not unattractive Jewess, her face harder than conventionally beautiful. She looked like a strict school teacher and she looked up as Burton approached and gave him a thin sort of smile around her cigarette.

'Burton,' she said. 'You've been making a real cockup of things.'

'Mrs Myerson,' Burton said. She looked older than the last time he'd run into her, and there were new, tired lines around her eyes.

'Just Golda is fine,' she said.

'Golda,' he said, 'what do you want?'

'I want you to find Eva Finer,' she said. 'You're running out of time.'

'Don't you run the country now?' Burton said. He tried to smile but it didn't take. 'You find her.'

'We're trying,' Golda said.

'Why?' Burton said. 'What do you care? To us she's a political headache, but what is she to you?'

'Her family is an important supporter of the cause,' Golda said.

'Is that all it is?' Burton said.

Golda cocked her head, considering him. She blew out smoke from her nostrils.

'What are you suggesting?' she said.

'Dayan's been at me,' Burton said, and Golda gave a snort of sudden laughter.

'*Dayan*,' she said. She evidently did not have a high opinion of the man.

'He, at least, seems to think this is about lost Jewish treasure,' Burton said.

'And you believe it?' Golda said.

Burton shrugged. 'People do stupid things,' he said.

'We have lost treasure our entire history,' Golda said. 'We have just lost six million lives in Europe, Burton. *Those* were our treasure. Everything else is just for greedy cunts.'

Burton winced; he forgot Golda could swear like a drunk squaddie when the mood took her.

'If you know anything,' he said, 'it's best you let me know.'

'She is a silly girl,' Golda said. 'She got herself into some trouble, is my guess. Look for a boyfriend and you'll probably find her.'

'Anywhere I should look?' Burton said.

'I heard she likes dominoes,' Golda said. With that, she tossed her cigarette and got in the Vauxhall. Burton watched it driving away.

Dominoes? he thought. Who the hell played *dominoes*?

34

'We checked everything,' Cohen said. They were back in the Samuelsohn house. 'And you were right, sir. There are maps, pieces of correspondence with an archaeologist called Trever, with the abbot of the Monastery of the Cross in Jerusalem, and with one Ibrahim 'Ijha, an antiquities dealer in Bethlehem. They are somewhat cryptic in their nature but it is clear Samuelsohn was looking for something precious.'

'The treasure,' Burton said.

'So you believe it?' Paddy said.

'I believe that *he* believed it,' Burton said. 'And I think the girl did too. But they were not the only ones after the treasure, were they?'

'So the question is, who knew of Samuelsohn's interest?' Cohen said.

'The witch,' Burton said. His men looked at him strangely.

'What witch, sir?' Cohen said.

'The witch in Jerusalem.'

'Have you lost the plot, boss?' Paddy said. Even Hassan stifled a smile.

'She's real,' Burton said, feeling like an idiot. 'I met her.'

'Let's discount a... a *witch*, for the moment, sir,' Cohen said. 'We still believe it was the Latifs who broke in, right? If they have possession of the map they may try to go find it. And they most likely hold the girl hostage, in case we catch up to them.'

'A bargaining chip,' Paddy said. 'It would make sense.'

'*Nothing* about this makes sense,' Burton said. 'But yes, the Latifs are still our best shot. They're probably holed up in the Galilee somewhere right now. We're not the only ones looking for them, the Haganah is also searching for the girl. So they'll be keeping a low profile right now. We'll find them. For now, I want to focus on the girl.'

'You think she was in on it, boss?' Paddy said.

'I have no idea,' Burton said. 'We rushed into conclusions last time and look where it got us. So let's not cock this up a second time, gentlemen. Let's do it like we still remember how this job works. Diligent, methodical. Let's do some actual bloody investigating.'

'Dominoes,' Hassan said. They all turned to look at him.

'Yes?' Paddy said.

'Surprisingly popular game,' Hassan said. 'Everybody likes a game every now and then.'

'Who doesn't?' Paddy said, joining in. 'They play it down at the Diana on Nordau Street.'

'The Diana?' Burton said. 'Didn't we have something there a few months ago?'

'Yes, sir,' Hassan said. 'Some boys robbed the card players of all their money and we had to intervene.'

'That's right, that's right,' Burton said. 'But people don't play *dominoes* for money, do they?'

Paddy laughed.

'You can bet on anything, boss,' he said. 'And what else is there to do in this town, go see the Philharmonic at the Palace Theatre again?'

'Bernardino Molinari was conducting last time, actually,' Cohen said, perhaps offended. 'I had tickets.'

'You don't gamble, Cohen?' Paddy said.

'Never,' Cohen said, and Paddy shrugged.

'If you don't take a chance every now and then,' he said, 'then when will you ever win?'

'So we think she liked to play?' Burton said. 'It's a social thing, I suppose.'

'That, or go out dancing,' Paddy said. 'But if she had we'd know her, Haifa's a small enough place.'

Burton considered. He had not heard of Eva Finer before. By all accounts she kept herself to herself, barely registering a presence when she visited Palestine. Yet the boys were right. She must have done *something*, besides digging into antiques and visiting with people like Mr Hirsch, whose every step shook with old dust.

So what did she do for *fun*?

'Let's check in Nordau, then,' Burton said.

Nordau Street sprawled across the side of the mountain in Hadar, a long avenue populated with shops and cafés. Burton parked by the Technion building, the Jewish university built here back when the Ottomans were still in charge. Tuition was meant to be in German at first, but a dispute broke out and Hebrew became the language of teaching in the end. Albert Einstein once planted a palm tree there.

'Albert Einstein planted that palm tree, you know,' Paddy said, pointing.

'I know,' Burton said.

'I mean, Einstein!' Paddy said.

'I heard the Jews want to invite him to become their first president,' Burton said. 'Once we're gone.'

'You think he'll accept?' Paddy said. 'I mean, he's Albert *Einstein!*'

'I have no idea,' Burton said. 'Let's stick to the present mystery, shall we? And leave Dr Einstein's career choices for a later date?'

'Right you are, boss,' Paddy said cheerfully.

They got out and it was weird, Burton thought, how normal everything seemed; how the birds were at their song and the trees cast pleasant shade, and the cars whooshed past and their drivers only honked on occasion. How children ran along the road, how the greengrocer put out the bushels of red tomatoes, how the butcher hung up the kosher sausages on their hooks, how the dog was barking just then with a juicy bone, wagging its tail at the policemen as they walked past, how the sun shone and a radio played somewhere nearby, Shostakovich on the BBC World Service.

No sign of an impending war, of the clearing-out of Haifa, its de facto occupation complete. Just ordinary people going about their ordinary lives. In the places he passed cakes were baked; women were measured for dresses; coffee brewed and was served with sugar cubes; and the clink-clink-clink of domino tiles could be heard, as though there had been nothing out of the ordinary, as though this city was not tensely waiting for battle as soon as Burton and his people left. What had Dayan said? They'd be nothing but a footnote.

Well, fuck Moshe Dayan, he thought. Fuck that one-eyed, grave-robbing prick. Fuck the Jews, fuck the Arabs, fuck this tiny sliver of a country no one in their right mind would give two shits about – next week he'd be on the beach in Zanzibar drinking gin and tonics as the new police commissioner for the protectorate. Or, well, something.

'Boss?' Paddy said. 'You said something?'

'No,' Burton said. 'No, I was just thinking.'

'This is the place,' Paddy said. Burton could see Cohen and Hassan further ahead, trying the Vienna. Someone on Nordau Street would know something, he was sure. He followed Paddy into the Diana Café.

Tables crowded together. The sound of domino tiles, a group of card players around one table, cash and chips piled between them. At another table two men played backgammon intensely. The air filled with cigarette and pipe smoke, the smell of fresh coffee and strudel. Burton's stomach rumbled. He tried to remember the last time he ate.

'Can I help you, gentlemen?'

A short, dumpy woman approached, drying her hands on her apron. Burton saw with some unease the blue number tattooed on her bare arm.

One of *those*, he thought, chilled.

It was easier to pretend they weren't there, those blue-number survivors of the Nazi death camps. On instinct he wanted to ask for her papers – so many of them smuggled the border into Palestine on board the rickety old ships the Royal Navy hunted in the sea. Then he realised the absurdity of such a request. He looked elsewhere; elsewhere but at her number.

'We're searching for a girl named Eva Finer,' Paddy said.

'Eva?' the woman said. 'Did something happen to Eva?'

'Do you know her?' Burton said.

'Yes, of course,' the woman said. 'A lovely girl. Perfect manners. She's English, you know. Like you.'

'I'm Irish,' Paddy said, and the woman looked at him blankly.

'What's the difference?' she said.

Burton stopped him before Paddy could launch into a tirade on the topic. The Irish could be as bad as the Jews about this sort of thing. He said, 'We're just trying to find her, so anything you could tell us would help, Mrs…?'

'Carlebach,' the woman said. 'It's Mrs Carlebach. Eva comes here often when she visits. She doesn't visit Palestine often, though. Her work in London keeps her busy.'

'Her work?' Burton said.

'Charities and so on,' the woman said. 'She is very engaged with the issues. Widows and orphans, and the soldiers, of course. And the Zionist cause and so on.'

'Do you know *why* she keeps visiting Palestine?' Burton said.

'I told you, she is very engaged.'

'Any other reason?' Burton said. He looked around him at the café, the players. Mrs Carlebach followed his gaze.

'Young people come here?' Burton said.

'Everyone comes here,' Mrs Carlebach said. 'Young, old, Arabs, Jews, you British. Not so many Arabs now, not since, you know.'

'Since they were forced to leave?' Paddy said.

'They weren't forced,' Mrs Carlebach said. 'They chose to leave. We asked them to stay. I hope they come back. Good customers.'

Burton put a calming hand on Paddy's shoulder; though Paddy, he remembered, was on the Jews' side. It didn't matter. Only what they could learn.

'Who did Miss Finer like to play with?' Burton said, the question sounding less innocent than he'd intended. Mrs Carlebach shot him a sharp glance.

'She played dominoes,' she said, not really answering the question. 'Sometimes cards.'

'For money?' Burton said.

'Never for money,' Mrs Carlebach said.

Burton looked at the card players at their table, the stacks of cash and chips – jetons, they called them here, a borrowing from the French.

'But people *do* play for money,' Burton said. 'And money attracts all kinds of people.'

'It's all in good fun, nothing more,' Mrs Carlebach said. 'I also have a lending library.'

'So who did she play with?' Burton said, pursuing the subject despite Mrs Carlebach's evident reluctance. 'Who are her friends?'

'All kinds,' Mrs Carlebach said. 'It's all very casual. There are all kinds of people who come here, like I said, and it's not like I can keep track of everyone. I have a job to do. It's hard running this place. Cooking, cleaning, doing the accounts... I have to do everything myself.'

'What about Mr Carlebach?' Paddy said.

'Mr Carlebach passed away,' Mrs Carlebach said. 'In the other place.'

Burton winced. He'd noticed how the survivors he'd met never talked about the... other place. Bad things happened. You just had to get on with it.

'Did she have any girlfriends?' he said. 'A boyfriend?'

'Why do you ask?' Mrs Carlebach said.

'So she did,' Burton said.

'I don't want her to get into any trouble,' Mrs Carlebach said.

'Who is he, then?' Burton said. He took a stab at it – 'An Arab?'

Mrs Carlebach winced.

'No crime in that,' she said.

'Is he a Latif?' Burton said, taking a second stab at it.

'Sami, yes,' Mrs Carlebach said and sighed. 'He's a lovely boy. Impeccable manners. He likes to gamble but then, who doesn't from time to time?'

'They met here?' Burton said.

'I suppose they must have,' Mrs Carlebach said. 'There was never anything untoward. But of course it can't be serious, you know, a lady like her and a boy like him. Well-respected, old Galilee family and all, but still. I thought it was a summer romance, you know. Well, it's all it could ever be. A shame.'

Burton and Paddy exchanged bemused glances.

'This is Samuil Latif we're talking about, yes?' Paddy said. 'The criminal?'

'He never did anything untoward that *I* could see,' Mrs Carlebach said huffily. Evidently she had a soft spot for the man.

Slowly they extracted the rest out of her. Yes, Eva Finer used to frequent the Diana. Yes, it had a mixed clientele. Yes, she met Sami Latif, a good-looking man, very good manners, with an awakening political conscience – 'That really got them talking, you know,' Mrs Carlebach said, 'Palestine and the Jewish question, and what it means to be a Palestinian, and if Palestinian self-determination was like Jewish self-determination, and so on – it was a bit over my head, and I don't encourage political talk in my establishment. So eventually they went to play dominoes elsewhere.'

She said that with a straight face and Burton stared at her for a while, wondering if it was just that English wasn't her first language.

'Dominoes,' he said at last.

'Yes,' Mrs Carlebach said.

'Do you know where?' Burton said.

'How should I know?' Mrs Carlebach said. 'I run a clean establishment here.'

They asked her a few more questions but got nothing else, other than the offer of a coffee and strudel at the end, which Burton regretfully declined.

Coming out, they ran into Cohen and Hassan returning. Burton shot them a questioning glance and Hassan nodded.

They'd found out something, too.

35

'So what do we know so far?' Burton said. They sat around a table in the canteen. His men stared dubiously at their plates of bully beef and spam. Burton took a big sip from his mug of builders' tea. At least the canteen always got that right. Cohen lathered jam onto a slice of white bread.

'She had a boyfriend,' he said.

'Yes,' Burton said.

'So what do we think now?' Paddy said. 'She was in on it? Or her boyfriend found out about Samuelsohn's supposed treasure map, broke in and she got caught in it?'

'We don't know,' Hassan said. 'But we have to proceed on the assumption that she was kidnapped. Don't we?'

Paddy shrugged.

'What else did you learn?' Burton said.

'There were some old card players at the Vienna Café,' Cohen said. 'They knew Waldman well. My understanding is that both he and Sami Latif spent a lot of time going through the cafés, cultivating...' He hesitated.

'Looking for marks,' Hassan said. 'They played low-stakes games, they bought everyone drinks, they learned everyone's names and eventually they found the ones who wanted – needed – to *keep* playing, at which point—'

'At which point messieurs Waldman et Latif would invite the

lucky few to continue the game elsewhere,' Cohen said, 'having set up their own private establishment, as it were, in a flat on Khouri Street down in Wadi Nisnas.'

'Nice work, boys!' Paddy said. 'You got the address, too?'

'Of course,' Hassan said, mock-wounded, and Paddy laughed. 'Who did you get it from?' he said.

'An old boy,' Cohen said. 'He got in quite deep with the Latif gang near the end. Owed them over a thousand pounds. At which point they said he could pay it back by running drugs to Cairo for them. He did two trips on the train and said he was dead scared the whole way there, but what was he going to do? He seemed very happy to talk, now that they're gone. "That Waldman was a piece of shit, sir," he said. "I'm glad he killed himself."

Burton let that one go; for now at least. He still had questions about Waldman's death.

'Are we sure the Latifs are gone?' he said. 'We can't assume anything anymore.'

'We can check the place on Khouri,' Hassan said. He prodded the bully beef on his plate without enthusiasm and put down his fork. 'Maybe get something else to eat while we're there,' he said hopefully.

They drove down to Wadi Nisnas. The neighbourhood lay in the lower city, below Hadar, and Burton could see the new bullet holes in the walls, a burned car lying on its side, broken windows; but more than all that it was the eerie quiet of a place recently abandoned that got to him, interrupted only by the yowling of the neighbourhood cats fighting each other over a piece of rotting fish from the harbour.

As they parked on Stanton he realised Wadi Nisnas was no longer entirely abandoned. As they climbed out of the cars and stood, stretching in the sunlight, Burton saw a long row of people – men, women and children – all carrying their possessions on their backs, the men in hats and the women in their dresses and the children playing, and looking around them at the houses with big curious eyes. Behind them came cars piled with more possessions, and on and on they went.

'What's this?' Burton said.

An official-looking man in the lead car gestured to him irritably.

'Out of the way!' he shouted. 'Out of the way!'

'British police!' Burton shouted back, and the man made a dismissive gesture and said, 'Pah!'

'Stop the bloody car,' Burton said. 'What's going on here?'

The man cursed, but hit the brakes and came out.

'You got a cigarette?' he said.

'Sure,' Burton said. He extracted his pack and lit them both up.

'Resettlement,' the man said. 'I'm just the schlepper they found to stick this job with.'

'Resettlement?' Burton said.

'The Arabs,' the man said. 'The ones who didn't leave. They live all over Haifa but that causes obvious security concerns, while Wadi Nisnas is more or less abandoned at this point. So, for now, they're being resettled here. I mean, look.' He swept his hand around the empty buildings. 'Plenty of places to bed down,' he said.

'How many are there?' Burton said. He watched them come down the mountain, one by one, like the people of Israel crossing the desert.

'Seven, maybe eight thousand,' the man said. 'Mostly Christians, but not all. Not all the Muslims left. They'll be fine here.'

'And elsewhere?' Burton said.

The man shrugged. 'Jerusalem's under siege,' he said. 'There's fighting in Tel Aviv and Jaffa, heavy fighting in Safed I heard. But those aren't my problems. I'm only here to make sure these guys find a place for now. And then, of course, there's the matter of all the abandoned property. Someone has to make sure stuff doesn't get stolen. It will probably get confiscated for the state once we have a government. But that's not my problem. I'm just—'

'The schlepper they found to stick this job with,' Burton said.

'You get it,' the man said. 'We're both just civil servants.'

'We really have lost control of this country now, haven't we,' Burton said. The man shrugged, tossed out the cigarette, said, 'Cheers for that,' and got back in his car.

'Get moving, get moving!' he shouted. 'We haven't got all day!'

'Bloody hell,' Burton said. 'Alright, where is this den of iniquity?'

They tried to ignore the people milling about, looking helpless, as they searched to settle in other people's abandoned homes. Eventually they found a crumbling old Ottoman palace, somewhere in the maze of streets, with an air of faded grandeur still clinging to it and a bathhouse attached. Remarkably, when they tried to enter it was not empty. An older woman with her face painted blocked their entry, three younger women appearing silently behind her. The women were young, tired-looking and pretty. They did not wear too many clothes.

'Can I help you?' the older woman said.

'Burton,' Burton said. 'CID.'

The woman looked at him blankly.

'So?' she said. 'You want to fuck it's ten pounds, two for a handy. It's five again extra if you want them to watch.' She gestured at Burton's men.

Burton sighed. 'You stayed open all this time, Esther?' he said. 'Even during the battle?'

The older woman cracked a smile. 'Burton, Burton!' she said. 'Now I remember you. You used to be an eager little puppy.'

'What am I now?' Burton said.

'An old dog, looking for a place to lay down and dream,' Esther said.

'What does that make you, then?' Burton said.

'Still the same bitch,' Esther said, and started laughing

uproariously. The laugh turned into a racking cough. Burton waited patiently until it faded away. Esther said, 'Got a cigarette?'

'Sure,' Burton said. He lit up for the both of them. He was going to have to buy another pack. A small boy appeared just then, carrying two heavy buckets of water.

'Ah, Shmuel,' Esther said. 'Darling little boy.' She caught Burton's questioning glance. 'He brings water for the girls to wash with,' she said in explanation. The three girls surrounded the little boy and one handed him a coin. The boy smiled.

'Rana, Fatma, Fortuna!' Esther said. 'We have customers!'

'Hold on,' Burton said. 'We're not here to get our jollies, Esther. I'm on the job.'

'What job, Burton?' Esther said. 'Why are you even still here?'

'We still have the Mandate,' Burton said stubbornly. 'Until Friday.'

'Don't make me laugh again,' Esther said. 'It hurts too much to laugh.'

'We were given this address,' Burton said, 'as a known hangout of the Latif gang.'

'Sami Latif?' Esther said. 'What about him?'

'Is he here?' Burton said. Cohen and Hassan had fanned out into the shadows meanwhile, their guns drawn.

'No,' Esther said. 'Haven't seen him in a few days. He's a nice boy, really. You can take a look for yourself upstairs.'

'You're not lying to me, Esther?' Burton said. 'There's no one up there I should know about?'

'You're the man who took down Ali Siksik, aren't you?' Esther said. 'The Terror of Jaffa! They still tell that story, Burton Effendi.' She smiled but her eyes were sad. 'There is no one upstairs,' she said. 'No one but us girls here.'

The little Jewish boy vanished back out into the street. The whores, too, melted into the shadows. Burton went up the stairs, his gun drawn, memories of hunting down Siksik in the cave filling him with foreboding.

But there was nothing upstairs but a sparsely furnished flat. It smelled faintly of mould and perfume. A card table sat in the middle of a large room, a makeshift bar lined up one wall. An ashtray on the table was filled with cigarette butts. They were cold and dead when he touched them. Tiny soldiers. A pack of cards fanned open on the green felt table. Cohen and Hassan went room to room.

'No one in,' Hassan said, holstering his gun. 'The old whore was telling the truth.'

'Her name's Esther,' Burton said.

'Friend of yours?' Cohen said.

'A long time ago,' Burton said. Remembering dark luscious hair, a saucy smile. Same sad eyes. 'I used to work the beat in Haifa.'

'If they used this place as a safehouse,' Cohen said, 'why go to the Piccadilly where we could catch them that night?'

'Because they were arrogant and didn't think we would,' Burton said. 'And this place is a shithole. Get Esther up here, I have some questions for her.'

But when Esther came up she wasn't much use.

'I don't have anything to do with them,' she said. 'Yes, they were here briefly, but I couldn't tell you much more than that.'

'Was there a girl with them?'

'I didn't see anything,' Esther said.

'Come on, Esther,' Burton said. 'Just tell me the truth for once.'

'What's truth, Burton?' Esther said. 'There was a group of them, five, maybe six men. I didn't see a girl. Maybe. There used to be a girl who came along with Sami sometimes. A posh girl, she was always nice to my workers. I think she enjoyed slumming it down here, it was exciting for her. Waldman and Sami went out at some point, then Sami came back, alone, and they all left in two cars.'

'And the girl, Esther?' Burton said. 'What about the girl!'

'I don't know,' Esther said. 'I heard Waldman's dead.'

'Hung himself,' Cohen said.

'I find that hard to believe,' Esther said. 'He had a real zest for life, that one.'

'Well, he's dead,' Cohen said; a little sharply.

'And whose fault is that, eh?' Esther said. 'He died in your custody.'

Cohen raised his fist. 'What are you suggesting?' he said.

'Nothing, nothing,' Esther said.

'Stop that, Cohen,' Burton said. He turned back to Esther. 'Do you know where they went when they left here again?'

'No idea,' Esther said. 'Sorry. But I got the impression that wherever it was, they weren't coming back.'

Eventually he dismissed her. But he was sure she wasn't telling him the whole truth.

'The girl *was* here,' Burton said. 'I know she was.'

'Why would she cover it up?' Cohen said.

'She doesn't want any more trouble,' Hassan said.

'Yes,' Burton said. He frowned. Cohen's earlier question bothered him. 'Why *did* Sami Latif and Waldman go to the Piccadilly?' he said. 'They were safe here, they had the girl, we presume they had this map—'

'Unless they didn't,' Cohen said. 'Remember how they tossed the Samuelsohn house? Almost like—'

'Like they couldn't find what they were looking for,' Paddy said.

'Did we just assume Samuelsohn kept it at home?' Burton said.

'Why would he?' Paddy said. 'I'd keep it somewhere safe. Like a bank.'

'There's another option,' Hassan said. 'They could have gone to the Piccadilly to meet someone.'

Burton tried to remember who was there that night. The men had been sitting alone at the time, he was sure of it. But there had been plenty of people around.

'Jack,' he said.

He closed his eyes. Yes, there it was – he'd fallen down, there was the sound of a toilet flushing and Jack Smith came out, doing up his belt, red-faced and looking up in surprise...

'A lot of the men go to the Piccadilly, sir,' Cohen said. 'It doesn't mean anything.'

'Where is Jack Smith?' Burton said. He tried to think. 'I saw him in HQ when we got back. I should have asked him about it then... He didn't mention it.'

'You're making assumptions again, sir,' Hassan said.

'I don't know what to think anymore,' Burton said. 'We might just be chasing shadows. The important thing is to find the girl, and if they'd gone then the only question is, where?'

'We don't know, sir,' Cohen said.

Burton looked at his men. They were tired, injured, dispirited, but they'd not given up yet.

'We'll find her,' Burton said grimly.

36

Back in HQ he failed to find Smith. Running into Newman, another old CID hand, the man shook his head and said, 'Jack's out on a case.'

'What case?' Burton said.

Newman shrugged. 'Don't know, old chap. We're more or less done here now. Tying up some loose ends, he said. What about you? Looking forward to going home?'

'Sure,' Burton said. 'Home.'

He didn't really know home anymore. The thought of going back to England seemed somehow preposterous. He supposed he could stay behind, pick a side. On paper, at least, everything should have gone smoothly. The United Nations had carefully partitioned the land the year before under Resolution 181 (II). A Jewish state, an Arab state, co-existing in political and economic harmony, and with Jerusalem under international control.

Haifa and Jaffa were to go to the Jews, Jenin, Nablus and Hebron to the Arabs, the Galilee was to be split between them with Acre to the Arabs and Tiberias and Safed for the Jews... In truth, it made your head hurt just looking at a map.

A patchwork quilt. In reality they were already fighting, Syrian and Iraqi militias were already coming in alongside the Arab Legion from Jordan, while the Irgun and Haganah were shoring up their own military operations. The only thing holding them in check right then was the continued British presence. Which was set to disappear, come Friday night.

'Did anyone check the villa?' Burton said.

'The villa, sir?' Cohen said.

'The one her family owns on the Sea of Galilee,' Burton said. 'Hirsch mentioned it.'

Cohen nodded. 'Of course,' he said. He went to a telephone still sitting on one of the empty desks and tried it, sighed, then located the cable and plugged it back into the wall.

'Need a phone book,' he said.

Eventually they found one. Cohen rang the number for Villa Melchett.

'It's ringing,' he said.

It rang for a while. Eventually Cohen shook his head.

'No one's answering,' he said.

'You don't think they went there, do you?' Paddy said.

'Why not?' Hassan said. 'It's isolated, they have the girl with them... And we wouldn't think to look there. We didn't.'

'We should have,' Burton said, cursing himself silently.

'Boss, there are ongoing battles around the lake,' Paddy said. 'It isn't safe for us to go there. If we do, we'll be alone.'

'We have a job to do,' Burton said. He looked at his men. 'I can't ask you to stick with it. By rights you should be dismissed. Cohen, you should be with your pregnant wife. Hassan, you should be with your family looking after that broken arm. Paddy and I should be getting ready to go home...'

'But we have a job to do,' Hassan said, smiling only faintly.

'I can't ask it of you,' Burton said. 'You won't even get paid.'

'We got our last two weeks' wages already, sir,' Cohen said, also smiling.

'Besides,' Paddy said, 'we can't leave it to you, boss, or you'll just get yourself into trouble.'

Burton nodded, touched. They were good men, he thought. Men you could rely on, at the end of the day.

'We will have to move fast,' he said. 'Fast and quiet. It will be just us. I don't want the special squads involved. Not after last time.'

The men nodded.

'With any luck,' Burton said, with more conviction than he felt, 'we could conclude all this by dinnertime.'

The sun was low on the horizon by the time they set off from HQ. The Carmel rose above them, its evergreen forests darkening and the sky awash in blood-red and pus-yellow light. The sea breeze felt warm and filled with oil and tar. The city was quiet, lights were coming on along the slope of the mountain, burning first in Hadar, then trailing down to Wadi Nisnas and up again to the German Colony.

Beyond the skyline the Carmel sloped on, its forests hiding within them deer and wild boar. In the Druze villages, too, the lights would be coming on, and up on the rise where the Mukhraqa monastery sat, in the place where Elijah slaughtered the priests of Ba'al, the monks were getting ready for evening prayers.

Burton drove, Hassan beside him. Hassan held a pistol in his good hand. Burton knew he was hurting, but Hassan never complained. By all rights Burton should have let him go. But he needed him.

Ahead of them were Paddy and Cohen in the second armoured car, Paddy driving, Cohen holding a shotgun. They followed the contour of the mountain and plunged down to the coastal road. No special squads, not after last time. No more mistakes, Burton thought. He pressed down on the gas. Night fell as they headed to the Galilee.

Along the coast and the Haifa-to-Acre railway line. On their left the sea and the new workers' neighbourhoods under construction, ugly low-rise buildings pushed together between the railway and the sea. A sharp right onto the old Nazareth road, badly maintained, the cars bumping along this ancient Zevulun Valley. Burton was tense, not sure how useful Hassan was going to be with one hand out of commission and only a pistol.

The Jewish blocks were replaced here by the village of Shefa-Amr coming up on their left, a mixture of Christian Arabs, Muslims and Druze. He saw few lights burning, the place felt suspended in anticipation but for the moment peaceful. Bedouin encampments in the distance, the air was fragrant with the blooming flowers in the fields, heavy with a hint of rain.

The sun had vanished. Night fell. The stars spread out across the sky like pebbles in a river, bright and strange.

They drove with no lights, the ground rising as they neared the mountains, the trees thickening by degrees. Then bright floodlights turned on, blinding them, and Hassan shouted, 'Watch out!' as Burton hit the brakes. Paddy in the front car did likewise, turning it round as Cohen jumped out with his shotgun ready—

'Stop where you are!'

Burton was halfway out himself with a gun in his hand when he realised they were outnumbered. Men materialised out of the darkness around them, carrying new-looking rifles aimed at the four policemen.

'Identify yourselves,' the same voice said. It was cool and collected. Burton raised his hands slowly, still holding his gun.

'We're CID, damn it,' he said. 'Show yourself, whoever you are.'

He heard the voice laugh. A shadow appeared from behind the roadblock, turning into a man in the glare of the lights.

'Burton?' he said.

'Allon?' Burton said after a moment's hesitation. The last time he'd seen Yigal Allon he was a young recruit under Wingate. 'My God, man,' he said, 'you still have a full head of hair.'

Allon laughed. 'And you look… older,' he said.

'I feel it,' Burton said. 'Why did you put a roadblock here?'

'Got to protect the road,' Allon said.

'Protect it from what?' Burton said.

'Attacks,' Allon said.

'Attacks by whom, Allon?' Burton said.

'Well,' Allon said. 'Attackers.'

'Attackers,' Burton said. 'Right. You do know we're still in charge here, don't you?'

'Are you?' Allon said. 'Where are you going, Burton?'

'The lake,' Burton said.

'Would advise against it,' Allon said. 'It's dangerous from here on.'

'How come?' Burton said. He started to put down his arms.

'Keep them up, please,' Allon said. 'Arab marauders, Burton. Syrian and Iraqi forces attacking Safed. ALA running wild. We're operating emergency forces to protect the Jewish population.'

'Protect them how?' Burton said.

'To win a war you must strike first,' Allon said.

'You're attacking Arab villages?' Burton said, horrified.

'I can't go into operational matters,' Allon said. 'Turn around and go back to the port and you'll be safe. You have a ship to catch, don't you?'

'I'm doing my job, Allon. And I still have authority here,' Burton said. 'Remove the roadblock and let us through.'

Burton put his hands down. He holstered his gun but left his hand on it. He stared at Allon coolly. British-trained, damn it. He didn't doubt Allon was running a tight ship. Didn't doubt he wasn't lying about the dangers ahead, either. But he wasn't going to let the bastard cow him. They stared at each other, faces impassive.

'Don't make me have to shoot you,' Burton said, and Allon cracked first; he burst out laughing.

'You're an idiot, Burton,' he said, 'I always thought so. I can't offer you protection from here on. Not from our side, not from theirs. What are you looking for, anyway?'

'The treasure,' Burton said, and he was satisfied to see the smirk wiped off Allon's face.

'That isn't real,' Allon said.

'Isn't it?' Burton said. 'You and Dayan were very keen on finding it, once upon a time.'

Allon shrugged. 'It's your funeral,' he said. He shouted commands in Hebrew. The lights cut abruptly. Darkness settled and Burton blinked, trying to adjust. Allon's men melted back into the foliage. Burton got back in the car.

Allon leaned against the open window. His cold eyes studied Hassan, then moved on to Burton.

'Drive safely, you hear?' he said. He straightened and banged twice on the roof of the car, and then he too vanished.

'Fuck off,' Burton muttered.

He floored the gas, overtaking Cohen and Paddy in their car. The road ahead felt darker now, the stars colder. A hare ran across the road and Burton cursed, trying to swerve round it, the startled animal caught in the sudden glow of a flare fired high overhead. The hare's dark eyes reflected the climbing flame as Burton yanked the steering wheel, missing the hare by inches.

'Who fired that damned thing!' he said.

'Don't know, sir,' Hassan said. He looked grim, sitting there with the gun at the ready, and Burton realised they were both waiting for an attack.

But an attack did not come. The flare sailed overhead and fizzled out somewhere in the direction of Armageddon. The car raced down the road and was pursued by Cohen and Paddy close behind. This section of the road, Burton suddenly realised, passed through the proposed Arab state under the UN's partition plan. Allon's roadblock was still in the proposed Jewish state side, yet none of it made any sense, for as they sped along they once more passed through the Arab blob and back into a Jewish blob, and Burton thought, with an abrupt and pained realisation, that the partition was unfeasible, its patchwork quilt interwoven in ways that could not be untangled.

Well, come Friday this would no longer be his problem, he thought. The car slowed as the road climbed up the mountain now, twisting and turning, the wheels fighting for purchase as the car bumped and tested the limits of its suspension. The Arab state was linked between Nazareth and Jenin by only a kissing bridge, at the same time separating the Haifa and Tiberias sections of the Jewish state from each other.

None of it made sense, least of all to the combatants, who understood it wouldn't work. Allon talked of establishing control over the proposed Jewish state's lands in Safed, but surely for it to work then Nazareth and Acre, too, must fall; just as the Arab forces could never accept that Haifa and Jaffa on the coast must belong by decree to the Jews.

The war *had* to come – no, Burton knew. It was already here.

All he could hope for was to rescue Eva Finer before all hell broke loose and the war swallowed her up.

They were somewhere near Al-Majdal, the biblical Magdala of old from which Mary Magdalene came to follow Jesus. No paved roads now, nothing but a dirt track and a clear black sky and palm trees, and the lake growing in the distance like a flat disc mirror lying on the land, holding within it the reflection of all the stars in the sky.

A solitary house rose just ahead, some distance from the shore, two storeys high and boxy, its walls white against the black of night. Burton killed the engine. The second car stopped behind him. He climbed out of the car and checked his gun. His men did likewise.

'I'm dying for a piss,' Paddy said. They waited as he turned his back on them and urinated on the rich dark earth. Burton studied the villa. All seemed quiet. There were no lights. An owl hooted somewhere nearby, startling him. Paddy finished. He hefted up his gun.

'Well?' he said.

Burton nodded. He led his men onwards. They crept silently towards the villa by the lake.

37

Nothing moved and nothing stirred. The villa was encased in a wall, the gates were locked when they tried them. Paddy scaled the wall, waited above as Cohen and Burton pushed Hassan up. He vanished over the top with a slight whoomp. Cohen gave Burton a push up then climbed over as easily as a cat. Burton, feeling his age, dropped down beside his men.

The villa was surrounded by English lawns and tended gardens that went down to the shore of the Sea of Galilee. The air was perfumed with roses and jasmine. It was a rather lovely place, Burton thought. He crouched low, his heart beating fast, feeling the adrenaline course through him. They spread out and moved towards the villa.

Ten steps in he stumbled. As he fell, an awful stench suffused his nostrils. He tried not to gag. Cohen rushed to his side.

'Hold still, sir,' he whispered.

'What is that?' Burton said.

Cohen cupped a torch to mask the light and shone it at the ground. Burton gave a cry of disgust. Staring up at them was the rotting face of an elderly man, a beetle crawling out of his left nostril. The beetle stopped still under light. The man's skin looked mottled and chewed-on. His eyebrows were bushy, his eyes dead and cold, his nose aquiline.

'Who is he?' Burton whispered.

Cohen knelt down and took the man's hand in his.

'Look at his nails,' he said quietly. 'Dirt under them. The gardener, I think.'

Burton nodded. Cohen killed the light. They moved on, past that poor unfortunate, up to the villa. Burton gestured, Paddy and Hassan moved anti-clockwise around the building, seeking out the kitchen entrance. Burton went up to the main doors. He hesitated.

'I've got you, sir,' Cohen said. His gun was at the ready. Burton tried the door. To his dismay, it was unlocked. Unlocked doors in Palestine never meant anything good. He shot Cohen a glance, then pushed the door open and slid in.

It was dark inside, a lovely, roomy hallway cleanly decorated. A few paintings, a tasteful rug on the floor running the length of the hallway, a few cabinets against the walls. No one there. Cohen slid in behind him. They checked doors.

Empty.

Empty.

Empty.

Hassan and Paddy appeared at the end of the corridor. Paddy shook his head. All clear.

Which left only the second floor.

Cohen went first, Paddy behind him. Burton and Hassan brought up the rear. The same eerie silence, Burton expecting the retort of a gun at any moment, a shout to raise the alarm as they were spotted—

But there was nothing there, the bedrooms empty and left in disarray. They went through them rapidly, and at last Paddy said, 'They're not here, boss. There's no one here at all.'

Burton wasn't sure if he should feel relief or disappointment. He holstered his gun and took a deep breath.

'But they were here,' he said. Thinking of the gardener unburied in his garden. 'Outside,' he said, 'now. Maybe there's a shed, maybe they're staying out of the house.'

He felt deep inside it wasn't so. But they had to check.

They crept out. The lake shone, the same lake Jesus walked on. The same lake that Peter and Matthew fished on, that Mary bathed in, that Jairus' dead daughter rose out of onto the shore. The dead did not rise, in Burton's experience, they remained like the gardener, slowly devoured by maggots and beetles, decomposing until only the bones remained. But you had to have a little faith, sometimes. You had to believe a man was once born to God and a mortal woman in this very land, that he could turn water into wine and talk to storms and cast out demons. If you didn't, then what was left for you to believe in? There had to be something more than killings to this world.

They moved cautiously around the perimeter of the extensive grounds, in two teams, meeting again on the shore. Two boats were stranded on the pebbly beach, empty but for the paddles inside them.

'All clear,' Cohen said. Burton nodded and reached for his cigarettes. He lit one with relish and wondered how many more cigarettes he would smoke. He no longer expected to grow old, was afraid of a bullet coming his way from the dark, anywhere he went now. He supposed that at least, if one did, he would never know it. Men did not think of growing old, not in the Holy Land, not these days. He took in smoke and felt it burn his lungs.

'No other bodies,' he said.

'Only the gardener,' Cohen said.

'No lights,' Burton said. 'They might come back.'

But he didn't think they would.

They trudged back inside and went through the villa methodically, room by room again. Nothing much seemed to have been disturbed. In the kitchen they found unwashed plates and dirty cups. Upstairs the beds had been left unmade, and he noted the makeshift cots on the floor, as though several people had slept there.

'So they came here with the girl,' Paddy said. 'Possibly against her will. She gets them in, but the gardener—'

'They don't trust him,' Burton said. 'Or maybe he tries to run.'

'One way or the other they shoot him and leave him where he lies,' Cohen said. 'You'd think they'd dig a grave at least.'

'Why bother?' Paddy said. He picked up an ashtray from the bedside table. It was filled with the stubs of rolled-up tobacco.

'Cold,' he said.

'Same for the food in the kitchen,' Hassan said.

'Where would they go?' Burton said.

'To find the treasure?' Paddy said.

'If they believe it's real,' Hassan said.

'Or to find the map,' Cohen said. 'If Samuelsohn didn't have it.'

Burton rubbed his eyes. 'We won't catch them tonight,' he said. 'Let's get some sleep while we can. Cohen, you take first watch.'

'Yes, sir,' Cohen said without enthusiasm. Burton went into the master bedroom. He plopped himself on the bed. It felt good to be lying down. The mattress was thick and comfortable. He closed his eyes. He heard Hassan and Paddy arguing in low voices over who would take the second bedroom. Paddy lost. Burton smiled to himself.

Then he crashed down into the deep chasm of sleep.

In the dream Burton fled under a red sky towards the place of skulls. He knew it well. He forgot it each time he woke but when the dreams came he re-remembered. He had been there many times, had been running towards that destination ever since he fell asleep in barracks on his second night in Palestine.

And he thought suddenly and with an elated clarity that perhaps he had had it wrong all along, that Golgotha was not a place at all, but a land.

Skulls crumbled underfoot as he trod the hard dry earth. Vultures circled high overhead in silence. Ahead of Burton rose a huge skull-shaped mound, a tel, with two vast caves for the hollow eyes. He came upon two men who sometimes plagued his dreams. One was missing an eye and the other scowled as he tossed a tiny mouse skull from hand to hand. Burton stopped when he came to them.

'Ugly,' he said, nodding. 'One-Eyed.'

'How goes the world of the living?' Ugly said. 'I was shot and then strangled in a copse of old trees, pines and oaks they were.'

'I, too, was shot,' the one-eyed man said mournfully. He prodded his chest, where blood began to seep from a gashing wound. Burton watched them uneasily.

'I had nothing to do with it,' he said.

'Beware,' Ugly said, and waved his hands dramatically. 'Beware of seeking the treasure.'

'It's cursed,' One-Eyed said. Their skins flaked and blew away in the breeze. Two skeletons dropped to the ground and sat there, their bones entwined. Burton fled across the lifeless plain, skulls crunching under his boots.

'Boss? Boss, wake up!'

Burton opened his eyes. Early morning light streamed in through the French blinds. Somewhere in the distance he heard the sound of an engine. He sat up in bed. Paddy was at the window, looking out.

'There's a car, boss,' he said.

'What time is it?' Burton said.

'About seven,' Paddy said. Burton got up, went to the window. A Morris Minor crawled its way along the dirt track to the gates, raising dust. It didn't *look* threatening, Burton thought. It was impossible for a Morris Minor to look threatening. It looked like a cheerful little ladybug. The car came to the gates and stopped, and a short woman in a grey dress came out. Burton was already moving, his men joining him as he went down the stairs taking two at a time. Out of the hallway window he saw the woman park the car, go back to shut the gates she had unlocked, then turn towards the house. A few steps in and she saw the dead gardener.

She screamed. The sound pierced the silence. Burton cursed: he'd forgotten about the corpse. He hurried out, his men behind him. The woman saw them coming, screamed louder and turned to run.

'Stop!' Burton shouted. 'We're the police!'

The woman didn't stop and Cohen ran after her. He reached for her shoulder and the woman, turning, shrieked and began to hit him with her fists, a look of abject horror on her face. Burton ran over.

'Miss!' he said. 'Miss! We're with the CID. Please calm down!'

The woman didn't calm down. 'Cossacks!' she screamed. 'Gonifs, vey zmir!'

'Calm down, you stupid bitch!' Cohen said. He made to slap her and the woman shied away from him in fear.

'Cohen, stop!' Burton said. The woman, shocked perhaps, fell quiet.

'Please, miss,' Burton said. 'Let's go inside, we can have a cup of tea.'

'We have Assam,' the woman said.

'I beg your pardon?' Burton said.

'We have Assam, Darjeeling and Earl Grey,' she said. 'We have it shipped from England.' Some sense came back into her eyes. 'You're really with the police?' she said.

Burton showed her his badge. 'Burton, CID,' he said. 'We're here about Eva Finer.'

'Eva?' the woman said. 'What happened to Eva?'

She looked frightened again.

'We don't know, Miss—'

'It's Mrs,' the woman said. 'Mrs Williams.'

'You're British?' Burton said in surprise.

'Married Mr Williams when I came to England,' the woman said. 'I got out of Poland just before the war. I was a housekeeper and Mr Williams was the footman in Melchett Hall. Mr Williams fell in the war, I am sorry to say. I was offered the chance to come here and look after the villa, but as you can see it is not much in use anymore. I'm sorry, what did you say happened to Miss Eva?'

'We don't know,' Burton said. 'I was hoping you might be able to help us find her.'

They walked to the house. Mrs Williams kept stealing glances back at the dead gardener's corpse.

'His name is Syed,' she said. She started to cry. 'He's a good man. Was. What happened here? Who did this to him?'

'You don't live here?' Burton said.

'I live in Tiberias,' Mrs Williams said. 'I used to live on site back when we used to entertain a lot, but nowadays I stay in town, I have friends there.'

'What is the situation in Tiberias right now?' Burton said.

'Tense,' Mrs Williams said. 'But it will all work out, won't it? I mean we get one part and they get the other, it seems only fair. Surely no one could object.'

Paddy looked at her sideways and shook his head.

'We have biscuits,' Mrs Williams said. 'They're from Fortnum and Mason.'

They let her take control and lead the way to the kitchen. It seemed to calm her.

'This isn't right,' she said when she saw the dirty cups and plates. 'No one should have been here.'

'You didn't hear from Miss Finer?' Burton said.

'She did not telephone. I did not even know she was in the country,' Mrs Williams said. She set about removing the dirty dishes, then put the kettle on to boil. Burton watched her.

'I brought fresh milk,' Mrs Williams said, 'it's in the car. I always stock the villa's pantry, just in case we do get a visit. Not just Eva but the others from the family. We used to have big parties here, everyone came, even the high commissioner.'

'Cohen will fetch the milk,' Burton said. 'Well, get to it.'

'Yes, sir,' Cohen said. He went out sullenly.

'He is not very nice,' Mrs Williams said.

'When is the last time you were here?' Burton said.

'Monday,' Mrs Williams said. 'I dusted, mostly. I had a nice chat with Syed about the roses, he is – he was – a keen horticulturalist. I made a list of stock to be replenished and then I went home. I expect the family will sell the villa eventually. No one really uses it much anymore. Some of the officers from the army come sometimes on weekends, to swim in the lake and so on. But no one's come since the withdrawal started. Ah, the tea.'

She removed saucers and cups and began preparing a tray. Burton eyed the biscuits hungrily.

'You wouldn't happen to have any eggs, would you?' he said.

'Oh, you poor men must be hungry!' Mrs Williams said. 'I could make you breakfast, there's bacon too, and I brought fresh bread in the car.'

Cohen came in carrying two heavy bags. He put them on the counter.

'There you go, Mrs Williams,' he said.

Mrs Williams only nodded. Burton hid a smile. The men sat around the kitchen table as Mrs Williams moved briskly here and there, and soon the smell of frying eggs and bacon arose, of toasted bread and hot, strong tea. Burton's stomach rumbled. Mrs Williams served them china plates. The men ate quickly and quietly. Burton sipped his tea and lit a cigarette and sat back in his chair when he was done.

'Excellent,' he said. 'Excellent.'

It all had an air of sudden domesticity. Tea and cigarette smoke and the windows fogging as it rained outside... Father with his paper, mother bustling around the stove, and little Burton playing with his tin soldiers on the carpet by the fireplace.

'They left so much trash,' Mrs Williams said. 'So much trash!'

Burton stared vaguely into the air.

Then he leaned forward abruptly and said, 'What trash?'

38

The gardener's corpse lay still on the lawn, his eyes staring at the clear blue sky.

'What will happen to him?' Mrs Williams said. 'It's so terrible. I still can't believe it.'

'You'll have to have someone come pick up the body, love,' Paddy said.

'Couldn't you take him with you?' Mrs Williams said.

'Take him with us?' Paddy said. 'Where?'

'He has family in Ein al-Zeitun,' Mrs Williams said. 'It's an Arab village just north of Safed. I mean, you're going there anyway, aren't you?'

'Not with a corpse, we're not!' Paddy said, looking alarmed.

'It'd be a mitzvah,' Mrs Williams said.

'I ain't Jewish, lady,' Paddy said, 'and neither's the corpse. We don't really count in your commandments.'

'Oh, everyone counts,' Mrs Williams said. 'At least, I'd like to think they do.'

They were still arguing when Burton left them. Spread out on the lawn were the contents of the trash cans from the bedrooms and kitchen. Rotting food and eggshells, broken glass, stained newspapers, a bloodied shirt, coffee grounds and orange peel, cotton wool, crumpled cigarette packs and attendant butts and ends—

★

They'd already gone through the trash twice, but Burton wanted to make sure they didn't miss anything. The Latif gang had been here, that was for sure. Probably holed up in the villa since the night Burton and his men surprised Latif and Waldman at the Piccadilly. So why leave? Why now?

It was Cohen who found it. He sorted through food, almost cut his fingers on broken glass, examined the bloodied shirt and cotton wool, brushed through cigarette butts and ash, and scrutinised the stained newspapers, pages stuck together, one by one—

'There,' he said. 'Sir.'

'There where?' Burton said. They crowded around him at the kitchen table.

'We regret to inform our loyal customers that, due to the present instability, the Anglo-Palestine Bank, Safed branch, will close by end of week until further notice,' Cohen read. It was a small item on page five of *Davar*. It meant nothing – only someone had circled it with a deep-etched black pen and stabbed the paper twice as if in emphasis.

'Why the bank?' Burton said.

'The map,' Hassan said. 'Samuelsohn couldn't give them the map because—'

'Because he didn't have it,' Cohen said. 'He kept it safe—'

'In a safe,' Hassan said.

'Anything of hers?' Burton said now, staring at the trash spread out across the lawn. He called over Mrs Williams.

'Not that I can see,' Mrs Williams said.

Cohen, on his knees still sorting through the trash, stood up and dusted himself. He shook his head. 'Nothing else,' he said.

'So that's that,' Burton said.

'Take Syed, please,' Mrs Williams said. 'You're going that way anyway. It would only add fifteen, twenty minutes to your journey. It would mean so much. He who saves a life it is as though he has saved the whole world. Hillel the Elder.'

'Hillel who?' Paddy said, coming over and evidently still smarting over the argument. 'Lady, we're on a case here, we're not taking a stinking corpse to—'

Burton sighed.

'Just do it like she says, Paddy,' he said.

'Boss, what?' Paddy said.

'It's the least we can do,' Burton said.

'It stinks!' Paddy said.

'Put it in a body bag,' Burton said.

'We don't *have* a body bag!' Paddy said.

'Then make one!' Burton snapped. Paddy glared at him, furious, then seemed to catch himself.

'Yes, *sir,*' he said.

The notice of a closing-down bank, circled in black ink. It was a thin clue to go on, but it was the only one they had and time was running out. They had to find the damned girl – find her alive – bring her back before the ships departed and all the dogs of war let loose. Burton stared with some unease at the bundled corpse.

Paddy and Cohen carried the dead gardener, neither of them looking pleased about the fact. They had covered the body in burlap sacks of flour and potatoes, one for the head and torso and one for the legs and pelvis. The corpse was in a bad way. Decomposition had set in and flies circled around the package as Cohen and Paddy heaved. The stench was overpowering and the hot sun, rising fast, accelerated this state of affairs. Cohen and Paddy swore. They carried the corpse into the back of their vehicle.

'I don't get paid enough for this,' Paddy said.

'We don't get paid at all,' Cohen said.

They had trouble fitting the body inside. At last they shut the door on it and stood there with their mouths covered in makeshift masks. They looked like bandits. Burton started to laugh.

The men looked furious but they didn't say anything. Burton said, 'We'll go fast.'

Mrs Williams said, 'It's a mitzvah. And please, find my Eva. She's innocent in all this.'

'No one's innocent,' Paddy said. 'It's Palestine.'

'Go home,' Burton said to Mrs Williams. He tried to speak gently. 'It's not safe out here anymore.'

'What about the villa?' Mrs Williams said.

'It will be fine,' Burton said.

Mrs Williams nodded.

'We had such lovely times here,' she said. 'Such lovely times.'

They rode away from the villa. It was etched against the skyline, a pleasant little place that must have been filled with fond memories for someone. Burton knew he wouldn't see it again. The car raised dust into the air. The lake grew distant in the rear-view mirror and he wondered if he would see it, too, again, this Sea of Galilee, where miracles once happened.

He drove fast, following Mrs Williams's directions, two living men and a dead one following behind in the second car. The mountains rose ahead. There were no other cars on the road. Trees grew by the side of the road. Anyone could be hiding behind them. The sun beat down. He drove down an unpaved road and saw an old Bedouin sitting in the shade of a fig tree, a cooking fire in a ring of stones before him. Burton stopped the car.

'Ahlan wa sahlan, effendi,' the old Bedouin said. He flipped flatbread on the makeshift oven. 'It is a nice day we're having, no?'

'I'm looking for Ein al-Zeitun,' Burton said. The old Bedouin looked sad.

'Got a cigarette?' he said.

'Sure,' Burton said. He passed him one. The old man lifted a burning coal from the ring of stones with his fingers and lit the cigarette with it. He blew out smoke.

'That way,' he said and pointed. 'But there is nothing there now, effendi. Nothing but vultures.'

Burton was startled at this. He looked out. Far on the horizon rose thick black smoke.

'What happened?' Burton said.

The Bedouin shrugged.

'What always happens,' he said, 'and will come back again. Perhaps it was that God should never have introduced man to fire. You want breakfast?'

'Already ate,' Burton said.

'Inshallah,' the old man said.

'Where are your people?' Burton said.

'About,' the old man said. 'We shall go, to the Lebanon perhaps.'

'Why should you go?' Burton said.

Again, the old man pointed to the distant smoke.

'How can we stay?' he said.

Burton got back in the car.

'What is it, sir?' Hassan said.

'I don't know,' Burton said, 'but it's something bad.'

They drove on, the hills rising above them, pleasant in the sunshine. Wild za'atar grew on the slopes. A dove flew up to the skies, startlingly white against the blue. The smoke rose thicker, closer – they could smell it now. Burton slowed. Men materialised from both sides of the road. They were young, armed, and nervous.

'Stop the car! Stop the car!'

Burton obeyed. The second car stopped behind him. Men pointed guns.

'Step out of the car!'

'I'm police,' Burton said. 'I'm with the CID.'

He stepped out cautiously, was pushed to the ground, searched. His badge was examined. Someone helped him up. His men were face down on the ground.

'Burton, is it?' a man said. He handed Burton his badge back. 'You're a bit out of your jurisdiction, wouldn't you say?'

'We're still in charge,' Burton said, and the man laughed, but pleasantly, and put out his hand for a shake. 'Kelman, Third Battalion,' he said.

'Sir!' a young soldier shouted. 'Sir, they have a corpse in the back of their car!'

'Now why would that be?' Kelman said.

'Sir, it stinks worse than the others!' the soldier shouted. Kelman shot him a sharp glance.

Burton said, 'What others?'

'Well,' Kelman said. 'We had a bit of a problem, but it needn't concern you. Where were you heading, please?'

'The village,' Burton said. 'We're taking back this man's corpse for burial. He was a gardener.'

'I see,' Kelman said. He pursed his lips. 'There's a slight problem there,' he said. 'Like I mentioned.'

'What's that?' Burton said.

'There is no more village,' Kelman said.

'Kelman?' a voice said – Cohen, face down still on the road. 'Kelman, is that you?'

'Cohen?' Kelman said. 'You're with this lot?'

'Let me up, you fool,' Cohen said.

Kelman nodded. Two of the young soldiers helped Cohen up. He dusted his knees and glared at Kelman, then broke into a grin.

'What the hell are you doing here?' he said.

'Allon sent us to take Safed,' Kelman said. 'It's hairy up there so we're clearing out the nearby villages first. This place was a nest of vipers, Cohen. A nest of vipers! I only did what had to be done.'

'What... what had to be done?' Burton said, dreading the answer.

Kelman shrugged.

'I'll show you,' he said. 'Yeah, yeah, let the other two up. If they're with Cohen they're alright with me.'

Paddy and Hassan got up slowly. Hassan's face carried a strange, lost look. Paddy just looked furious. Burton shot them a glance – *keep quiet, damn it.*

Whatever happened there, he knew, it wasn't going to be good.

'You know Cohen?' he said to Kelman as they followed a dirt track off the road.

'I mean, sure,' Kelman said.

'How come?' Burton said.

'Oh, you know,' Kelman said, suddenly guarded. 'Here and there.'

'Sure,' Burton said. 'Here and there.'

They followed the track down to the burned-out houses. There had been a village there once, but all that remained were the smoking ruins. Burton saw shell casings on the ground, blood in places the fire hadn't reached. He could draw his own conclusions.

'Why?' he said.

'What, this? I told you,' Kelman said. 'It holds a strategic position over the road and they kept shooting at us. A viper's nest, this village. What was it called?'

'Ein al-Zeitun,' Burton said, and Kelman shrugged.

'We'll change it,' he said.

'What happened to the people here?' Burton said.

'The women and children we let go,' Kelman said. 'And some of the old men. But we couldn't let the fighters go, obviously. And I don't have the facilities to take prisoners of war. You understand. You were a soldier?'

'No,' Burton said. 'I was always a policeman.'

'Ah,' Kelman said. 'Then maybe you don't.'

'What did you do with them?' Burton said. 'These... fighters?'

'What could I do?' Kelman said. He gestured ahead, where a

drop led down to the wadi. 'We had to put them there. You could add your gardener, too, if you wanted.'

Burton went over to the precipice. He looked down and was sick. The smell hit him first, the smell of corpses lying too long in the sun. The young soldier had been wrong, he thought. This *was* worse than old Syed. There were some seventy bodies down there, Burton realised. Tied hands and feet. He threw up again. Hassan came and stood beside him. He said nothing at first.

'So this is how it is,' he said at last.

'This is how it is,' Burton said.

'Kelman, you fool,' Cohen said, coming over too and looking down.

'What's that?' Kelman said.

'You left them tied like this?' Cohen said. 'You're lucky it's only us here. Take off the ropes and bury the bodies or we'll all have problems down the line.'

'I need two volunteers to go down there,' Kelman said. 'Cohen's right. Can I get two volunteers?'

No one stepped forward.

'How about you, Netiva?' Kelman said, pointing to – Burton saw with some surprise – a woman dressed in the same khaki uniforms as the others. She glowered at him.

'Fuck, no,' she said.

'It wasn't a request, Netiva,' Kelman said. 'It's an order.'

'I'll go,' Cohen said. 'I don't mind. Happy to lend a hand.'

'Netiva will go with you,' Kelman said. Cohen nodded. He slid down the slope to the wadi. Netiva stared in apprehension, then followed Cohen down. Burton watched them pick between the corpses. Cohen's knife glinted as he cut rope and destroyed evidence.

Burton turned his face away.

39

From the wadi came the sound of spades digging in the dirt. Kelman, a map spread out on the rock before him, traced a route with his finger.

'This is the main artery into the city,' he said, 'but it's under Arab control. You might get shot at. Your Latif will probably be sheltering in the Arab part of the city. Which is most of the city barring the Jewish Quarter. I can't spare any men to accompany you, but you could—'

'Thanks,' Burton said. 'We'll manage.'

They drove convoy again, Paddy and Cohen in the first car, Burton and Hassan following. Burton gripped the wheel until the blood fled his fingers.

'How can you stand it?' he said.

'I can't,' Hassan said.

'They can see it from the city, can't they?' Burton said. 'They can see the smoke.'

'I think that was the idea, sir,' Hassan said.

'We tried,' Burton said. 'We tried so hard! We're still *here*, damn it! Not that anyone would notice. Thirty years since we liberated this place from the Turks, and all that work of civilising and policing… What was it all *for*? How can you stand it, Hassan?'

Hassan looked out of the window. The cars climbed the steep road to the city.

'I have to believe it will work out, sir,' he said quietly. 'That the guilty will be punished, the just rewarded, that Jews and Arabs can live together in peace like we'd done for centuries. And on Friday I will take off my uniform for the last time, and pick up my gun, and go fight with my people all the same.' He laughed, without humour. 'Cohen already is,' he said.

Burton gripped the wheel and didn't reply. They crawled up and into the city, and he expected gunshots at any moment but somehow it was worse: Safed was as silent as the grave.

The silence was broken with sirens. Two vehicles came rushing towards them then, blue lights flashing: police. The lead car pulled up and a man said, 'Burton? We've been sent to take you to Canaan Station.' He was Irish.

'You got my message?' Burton said.

'It was received, sir. Follow us, please.'

The police car executed a neat turn – and now they had an escort. Up and up they went, the road growing narrow, and still that unnatural silence, as if the whole town was holding its breath until night.

Burton was relieved to see the police station. Canaan sat on top of the mountain, the gates still guarded, the same air of activity within as in the Haifa HQ. The British were leaving Safed. Leaving everything.

'Follow me, sir,' the policeman who'd offered them escort said. Burton followed him into the station, down a corridor and up a flight of stairs. The man knocked on a door and waited.

'Come in.'

The man pushed the door open and waited for Burton to go inside. When Burton did he saw a desk and behind the desk an officer. He saluted.

'General Watson,' Burton said.

'Good to see you again, Burton,' the general said. He stood up and shook Burton's hand. 'This is quite a mess out there, isn't it?'

'It is, sir.'

Burton told him of what he witnessed in the village, and the general shrugged. 'It's had the desired effect,' he said grimly. 'They are fleeing on foot, the ones who don't want to fight. It's the same in Jaffa, Haifa, everywhere. Those who can afford to, at any rate. Everyone could see the smoke from Ein al-Zeitun. But there is nothing I can do. It is hard enough to keep them apart in the city until we leave. And I can only concentrate on a few strategic areas to ensure our smooth withdrawal. No, Burton, I am afraid my hands are tied. They will have to decide this thing for themselves.'

'Yes,' Burton said. 'About the other thing, sir—'

'This Latif gang, yes,' the general said. 'The men still have some informants in place. We used to do real police work here, you know. The Latif family is prominent here in Safed. This Samuil did not come to the family, but you could try them. You want my guess? He'd be holed up with al-Maz, he's the current commander of the local Arab forces. Syrian fellow. Or they could be with Shishaqli, he's the chap commanding the forces of the ALA. I can't offer you protection or men, though, Burton. You're in this on your own.'

'I just need to find the girl, sir,' Burton said. 'Gray's orders.'

General Watson shrugged. 'You have your job,' he said. 'I have mine. To get my men out of here safely. Frankly, the girl is not my problem. Understood?'

'Understood, sir,' Burton said.

'Excellent!' the general said. He slapped Burton on the back.

'Well, best get on with it then,' he said.

It felt strange to go on foot; the narrow winding streets were quiet, but eyes watched them from behind drawn curtains, and men with guns stood tensely on street corners checking their progression. The town crawled with Liberation Army volunteers, men from Syria and Jordan, some British-trained, others more eager than experienced. For the moment they let the four policemen go on their way, had marked their progress down from Canaan.

Burton walked tall, letting them see: *We British are still in control here.* No matter the enormity of the lie, or the fact no one believed it anymore. He still carried a gun and a badge.

The house, when they came to it, was old and comfortable, of weathered stone, and an ancient orange tree grew in the yard. A donkey was tied up near the tree and looked up at the policemen mournfully when they came in. An old man sat in a rocking chair facing the entrance and he watched them come in.

'Salim Ibn Latif?' Burton said. He had been briefed up at Canaan.

The old man regarded him with some amusement and said, 'Who's asking?'

'CID,' Burton said.

'You're Burton Effendi,' the old man, Salim, said. 'Heard of you. You're the man who took down Ali Siksik, yes? The Terror of Jaffa?'

'That wasn't me, but I was there,' Burton said, tired of the old story.

'Zorkin's gang,' Salim said. 'Yes, I like to keep abreast of such matters. Been here a long time, don't plan on going anywhere.'

'I'm looking for—' Burton began, but the old man interrupted him.

'My grandson, yes,' he said. 'He is not here.'

'What if I searched the house?' Burton said, and Salim gave a short, surprised laugh.

'You have balls, policeman, I'll give you that,' he said. 'But you'll have to make do with my word.'

Burton sighed.

'I am simply looking for the girl he's with,' he said. 'I do not care about your grandson.'

'You would spare his life?' the old man said, still smiling. 'But would he spare yours?'

'Tell me where to find him,' Burton said.

'You remind me of a man who came here long ago,' Salim said. 'He died out in the desert.'

Burton nodded.

'Thank you for your time,' he said, and made to leave.

'Wait,' Salim said.

'Yes?' Burton said.

'They're hiding near the citadel,' the old man said. He hesitated. 'I am not sure why I tell you this. Perhaps I wish for you to try to find them and be led to your death. Or perhaps I think my grandson's errand foolish. Do you know why he came here?'

'He's looking for treasure,' Burton said.

'So did the man I was telling you about,' Salim said. 'And he came to a sorry end.' He shrugged. 'My grandson is by the citadel,' he said, 'but I advise you to turn back from looking for him. Only death follows if you tread this path.'

'Thanks, old man,' Burton said. He made to leave again, his men flanking him, when there was a godawful sound of cannon fire and a loud hiss in the skies. Burton raised his eyes and saw mortar flying over the old city, coming from the slopes. He turned instinctively towards the old man when the bomb landed.

The explosion shattered the solid old bricks, raised a cloud of dust and debris into the air and knocked Burton over. He raised himself groggily in the sudden smoke and grasped blindly for Salim Ibn Latif.

He found him lying on the ground, the rocking chair broken around him. The old man was still breathing, but there was blood coming out of his chest and his eyes stared emptily into the sky. Gunpowder stung Burton's nose and he sneezed. His mouth filled with the coppery taste of blood.

'It feels as if just a moment ago I was merely a boy,' Salim said, speaking so softly that Burton was never sure, later, if he had heard him at all. 'Then I woke up and was suddenly old...' He coughed blood. 'Life is a strange thing, policeman,' he said.

'No doubt,' Burton said. He laid him down gently. Salim's chest did not move. Burton would have felt sorry for the old man if there was any sorry left in him.

The dust was clearing; but a new volley of that awful noise erupted from the slopes, and with it came the rat-tat-tat of a machine gun and the panicked shouts of men.

The battle was coming, sooner than expected. Burton recognised his chance. The citadel towered in the distance, its walls imposing but now wreathed in smoke. Cohen came over and looked down dispassionately on the corpse.

'It's just a Davidka,' he said. 'All they make is noise. You have to be really unlucky to get hit by one of these things.'

'It doesn't matter,' Burton said. 'It's our chance now.'

'Yes,' Cohen said.

Burton looked at his men. Hassan, Paddy looking grim. Cohen calm. Another volley from the Davidkas bathed the city in its monstrous noise.

Burton said, 'The citadel.'

Burton said, 'Go.'

Burton ran into the street and the smoke and the screams. He held his gun as he ran.

Paddy, Cohen and Hassan followed.

The citadel stood as it had stood for centuries, always occupied by one army or the other. In the chaos and confusion civilians fled from their homes, men with guns bellowed at each other as they took up positions against the advancing Third Battalion. No one paid any attention to the four policemen. They crept up on the citadel. The Davidkas thundered overhead. Mortar hit the high watchtower and showered down dust. Burton ducked through an opening into the structure, shouting 'British! British!' as ALA soldiers ran past.

'Who's in charge here?' Burton shouted.

'Who the hell are you?' a uniformed man said.

'Burton, CID.'

'Al-Maz,' the man said, saluting. 'You have to tell them to stop attacking, Burton.'

'I have no power to intervene,' Burton said.

'Then what fucking use are you?' Al-Maz said. He turned to go, shouting orders at his men.

'I'm looking for Samuil Latif!' Burton said. But there was no one to listen.

He ventured deeper into the citadel. Crusaders in chainmail had stomped through these halls once, Jewish rebels against the Romans, latterly the Ottomans. It had been rebuilt since, and would no doubt fall into ruin again. For now it was re-fortified, and he trod the flagstones into the dark inside, searching for the people who wouldn't be running out to fight.

He came to a place that might have once been a chapel. It was dimly lit by torches set into the walls. A group of men with guns stood in a huddle, looking nervous and confused. Burton caught the flash of pale skin, saw a woman in the far end, near what could have been a baptismal font. He shouted, 'Don't anybody move!' and raised his gun.

Things moved fast and slow.

The men turned with their guns ready to fire. The girl screamed. Burton fired, his men doing likewise. Bodies fell like snow. The air filled with the stench of gunpowder, death and dust. A bullet grazed Burton's shoulder and he spun, fired again, reloaded, until the men they had hunted finally lay on the ground. He went through the smoke and found Samuil Latif on the floor. Burton squatted, looking into his dying face, saw traces of Samuil's grandfather's face in his eyes and the line of his jaw.

'Been looking for you,' Burton said.

'Well,' Samuil said. 'You found me.' He stared into Burton's eyes helplessly. 'I'm cold,' he said.

'It's the mountain weather,' Burton said. 'It gets cold up on the hills.'

'That must be it,' Samuil said. Then the light went out of his eyes.

'I got her!' Cohen shouted. 'She's safe.' Burton rose. On the far side of the room Cohen was holding the girl. She was sobbing. Cohen had his gun in his hand. He looked around him wildly.

'Give me the girl, Cohen,' Burton said.

'Stand back, Burton!' Cohen shouted. 'I've got her now, she's safe!'

'Give me the girl, Cohen!' Burton shouted.

'I said, stand back!' Cohen said. He pointed the gun at the girl's head and began to drag her across the floor.

'I'll take it from here, Burton,' Cohen said.

40

Burton stood frozen. The sound of the Davidka bombardment echoed outside, made the ground shake and dust fall from the high ceiling. He wondered stupidly if any babies had once been baptised here, in the font. Cohen held the girl with his arm around her neck and the gun to her head. Paddy and Hassan fanned out from Burton, all three of them holding their guns trained on Cohen.

'Put them down, boys,' Cohen said. 'And we all walk away from this just fine.'

'Let Miss Finer go,' Burton said.

'Miss Finer is coming with me,' Cohen said. 'Isn't that right, Eva? You'll be a good girl?'

The girl sobbed. Cohen's face was slicked with sweat.

'Why?' Burton said.

'Because it's too important,' Cohen said. 'You will be gone, Burton, but *we* will have a country. Symbols matter. My boy will be born soon, and he will be born a Judean, not a Palestinian. I will recover the treasures of the temple for *him*, so we would never lose them again. The menorah *will* burn in Jerusalem once more. Now put down the guns.'

'You know I can't let you do this, Cohen,' Burton said. His hand was unsteady holding the gun. He couldn't risk the girl getting hurt. 'It will all be fine, Miss Finer,' he said. 'We'll get you out of this.'

'I won't hurt her,' Cohen said. 'Not unless I have to. I just want to find it, Burton. The treasure.'

Paddy and Hassan kept moving slowly, trying to circle Cohen. He glanced wildly from side to side, his eyes white, the pupils enlarged. Cohen began to press forward, towards the door, dragging the girl with him.

'Move!' he screamed.

'Now!' Burton said. He rushed Cohen, slamming into him and grabbing the girl. She fell to the ground and Burton turned to shield her with his body, but Cohen was facing the door, and Hassan was blocking his way. Their guns were trained on each other.

'Don't—' Cohen said.

The two pistols fired at once. Cohen sagged to the floor, looking bewildered. The girl screamed. Burton touched his face, where shards of hard bone left a trace of pain. His fingers came back bloodied. Hassan stood at the doorway, swaying. His hand dropped to his side and his gun fell to the floor.

'Hassan?' Burton said. 'Hassan!'

He ran to his friend and was just in time to catch Hassan in his arms as the man collapsed. Burton laid him down on the stone floor. Blood stained Hassan's chest. He looked up at Burton and tried to say something, at least Burton thought he did. Then the light went out of Hassan's eyes.

'God damn it,' Burton said. 'God damn it.'

'I'm sorry, boss,' Paddy said. 'I couldn't stop it.' His face was stained with tears. He reached out his hand and Burton took it. It felt solid and warm. Paddy helped Burton up to his feet and together they went to the girl. She cowered away from them, but they put their arms around her and lifted her between them. She felt very light.

'Everything is alright now,' Burton said, the words ringing

hollow. The corpses lay on the ground, Cohen and Hassan, and their blood stained the ancient stones. They left them there. Slowly they helped Eva Finer out of the citadel and back out onto the streets of Safed, and no one paid them any mind at all.

Eva Finer sat in the interrogation room drinking tea from a cup. She stared into the middle distance. Burton watched her through the grille in the door. She seemed oblivious and he slid the shutter closed with a sigh.

'Well?' Paddy said. 'What do you think?'

'I'm not sure we'll ever know,' Burton said. He fell into step beside Paddy as they traversed the corridor and went down to the basement. Cohen and Hassan, retrieved – if somewhat begrudgingly – by soldiers from the 8th Parachute Battalion sent into the citadel, were lying there in wait. No one had time to clean them up or make them decent. Their corpses were simply left there, bloodstains and all. Burton stared down at Cohen, a part of his skull missing, and traced the tiny punctures across his own cheek.

'He murdered Waldman, in the cell,' he said. 'We can assume that now, can't we?'

'You think he knew them, boss?' Paddy said. 'Latif and Waldman and all? That they were in cahoots?'

Burton shrugged helplessly.

'All this for a menorah?' he said.

'It means a lot to them,' Paddy said. 'I suppose it's like the crown jewels.' He sighed. 'What will his kid think of all this when he's born?'

'Who gives a shit,' Burton said. 'I suppose they can tell him he died fighting for his country.'

'Shot by an Arab sniper or something,' Paddy said.

'It's as good a story as any,' Burton said.

They turned and regarded Hassan.

'Who will mourn him?' Paddy said sadly.

'I will,' Burton said.

'Then I suppose that's that,' Paddy said. 'You found the girl, boss. All we have to do now is get her back to Haifa and on the ship home.'

Burton nodded. They left that cold room. The corpses would be shipped back to – where, exactly? Who would bury them? Who would mourn? He supposed it was no longer really his problem, if it had ever been. He went back to the interrogation room. Eva Finer turned when she heard him come in. Her pale face was rather lovely, he thought.

'Am I in trouble?' she said.

'No, of course not,' Burton said. 'We will get you back as soon as I get the all-clear from command.'

'I see.'

'Can I get you more tea?' Burton said.

'Tea?' She looked down at her cup as if she'd never seen one before. 'No, no thank you. Are they all dead?'

'I'm afraid so,' Burton said.

'Poor Sami,' Eva Finer said.

'What happened that night?' Burton said. 'What happened in Samuelsohn's house?'

The girl shrugged.

'It's so hard to remember,' she said.

'You were romantically involved with Samuil Latif?' Burton said. He found himself slipping into an interrogator's mode. It was against his better judgement. But he was all out of good judgement.

The girl shrugged. 'We knew each other,' she said. 'He was fun to be around.'

'He broke in that night?' Burton said. Pushing – if only a little.

'It was awful,' the girl said. 'Poor Isaac – no one meant to kill him. They got a bit rough with him, asking about the map, the map. Then he fell. It was an accident.'

'How did they know about the map?' Burton said.

'I may have told them,' Eva Finer said. 'Sami was always goofing around and, well, archaeology is something of a passion of mine, I may have jokingly told him one day.'

'That Samuelsohn claimed to have found the map?'

'Yes,' Eva Finer said. 'You know the story of it? A Swiss named Hoffman found it in a monastery in Jerusalem. Just think, the treasures of the temple!' Her eyes shone. 'They are not just gold and silver, but it is what they represent. All that is holy to Judaism, and the continuity of our presence in the Kingdoms of Judah and Israel! To find them would be... It would be immortality, Mr Burton. Isaac and I often spoke of it. We were kindred souls in that regard.'

Burton paced. 'But if he had the map, Miss Finer, then why didn't he go looking himself for it?' he said.

'I don't know,' Eva Finer said. 'For a long time I thought he was lying about owning it. Perhaps he didn't want to go looking and come back disappointed. Or perhaps... Men are weak, Mr Burton. Perhaps he wanted the treasure for himself.'

'For financial gain?' Burton said.

'Maybe.'

'So you decided to take it upon yourself to go looking for it?' Burton said. She looked at him in shocked outrage.

'Of course not!' she said. 'I had nothing to do with it. What are you implying?'

'Nothing,' Burton said. 'Forgive me. So where *is* the map now?'

'In the vault of the Anglo-Palestine Bank in the Jewish Quarter of this town,' Eva Finer said without hesitation. 'But we couldn't *get* to it, you see! I mean, Samuil and his, well, men. They couldn't. The Jewish Quarter is well-defended. It is also under siege. Sami's hope was that the battle for the city would soon commence, and of course the Arab Liberation Army would prove victorious. Once the Jewish Quarter was breached, we would be able to freely enter the bank and recover the document. All we – they – had to do was lie low for a little while.'

Burton lit a cigarette. It felt to him like forever since he'd had one. His hand shook a little as he lit up. He thought of Hassan, Cohen, all the dead men leading up to now. This Hoffman too, he supposed, or that Austrian cowboy Mr Hirsch had mentioned. He'd forgotten about Mr Hirsch.

'Would you like one?' he said, seeing Eva Finer's look. She shook her head quickly.

'I never smoke,' she said.

'Right,' Burton said.

'Of course,' Eva Finer said, '*we* could go there.'

'I beg your pardon?' Burton said, startled.

'The Jewish Quarter,' Eva Finer said. 'You're a British policeman. You can move between the Arabs and the Jews. They would let *you* pass.'

'I'm... what?' Burton said, and Eva Finer laughed.

'Don't you want to *see* it?' she said. 'Hold it in your hand, this thing it has all been about? The map is real, Mr Burton. It could lead us – you – to unimaginable fortune. And it would mean me and my people a great deal.'

'If it's there,' Burton said.

'Yes,' Eva Finer said. 'If it's there.'

'How would you get it?' Burton said. 'From the bank?'

'Find a manager,' she said. 'Or just break in.'

He looked at her with new eyes. She was very much at ease, sitting there, studying him patiently.

'You're quite something, aren't you, Miss Finer,' Burton said.

'Well?' she said. She looked at him levelly. 'What about it, Mr Burton? Or else, what was it all *for*? The lives of so many. Aren't you at least curious?'

Burton started to laugh. Black smoke rose over the mountains in the distance, beyond the window. Burton's hands shook. He dropped ash on the bare floor.

'Yes,' he said. 'Yes, I suppose I am.'

★

He tossed and turned on the narrow mattress. The sound of the Davidkas had long died down, and the city was quiet again, waiting and tense. Burton was oblivious. Sleep overcame him, night fell, the road to Haifa was too dangerous. He slept.

The woman in his dream cut into flesh and separated fur with her sharp flint knife. She looked up at the stars. Her child played by the fire beside her. The hills and mountains were alive with vegetation and a giant ibex, its horns caught in the dying sunlight, turned its head and regarded her a moment before vanishing.

Then she too was gone, the flesh falling from her bones, the wind blowing until the bones, too, were ground to dust, and only her skull remained, the furrowed brow, those thick ridges of the eyes, buried in old mud now deep under the ground. The children of her son and of her son's children and on down the generations grew and multiplied across the land, migrating in greater and greater waves across the vast continent, roaming from the cold northlands to the steppes and beyond, then even further, constructing boats out of wood and sailing on to other lands beyond the sea.

Burton came then to the place of skulls, the sun red in the skies, the ground dry and the tread of his feet hollow. He bent down and picked the woman's skull and regarded it quizzically as it looked back at him out of those hollow eyes.

'Mother,' he said, 'what should I do?'

She didn't speak, but others came out of the sands then: Cohen, his eyes blind and an amused fury hovering in the corners of his smile; Hassan, sad and yet defiant, standing beside him; still fresh, the two of them, still unused to the afterlife.

'What will you tell my son?' Cohen said. 'Will you tell him of my years of service, of all my good deeds, of the promise that I kept? For he will be a man in his own country, he will be a man in full.'

'Honestly?' Burton said. 'I'm leaving on the ship come Friday. I will likely never see your son. But did you not wish him to be born into peace?'

Cohen laughed. 'Peace is not his destiny,' he said. Then he, too, crumbled away in the wind, turned to dust, and was gone.

'He was always an asshole,' Hassan said. He patted Burton on the shoulder. 'Good police, though, until the very end there. He was that at least. Go find your treasure, sir. Dead men don't need gold.'

And Burton woke up.

41

It was midnight and some people must have slept, but the town of Safed, used to sieges and wars, kept a wary eye open and men with guns patrolled the streets on both sides of the divided city. Burton and Paddy made their way on foot down from Canaan Station, accompanied by Eva Finer. ALA irregulars watched them pass but did not make to stop them. Burton knew his badge would confer only so much protection. Paddy trod along in uniform to give at least the illusion of force, for whatever meagre use the uniform still had. In his backpack he had five blocks of TNT.

Eva Finer hugged herself. She wore a man's overcoat, too big for her, that one of the officers had given her at the station. If she really had been held captive by the Latif gang she did not look any the worse for it; though her hair needed a proper wash. Burton said, 'Are you scared?'

'No,' she said. 'Excited.'

Burton questioned why he ever agreed. It was not too late to regret his decision, to turn back to the safety of the station. But he had to admit he felt something too. He had followed orders, protocols and procedures for so long. They were ingrained in him. To break them now, when the world had stopped making sense – it felt liberating. He flashed Paddy a sudden grin and the man looked worried – which made Burton smile all the harder.

The entrance to the Jewish Quarter, such as it were, was a

narrow alleyway blocked with a heavy makeshift barrier and guarded on the Arab side by the ALA. Beyond it, Burton knew, the Jewish defences of the Haganah were waiting.

'Burton, CID,' he said.

'What business do you have in there?' the man who seemed to be the commanding officer said.

'That's my business,' Burton said.

The man said, 'Tell them to surrender and we'll let them go in peace.'

Burton thought of Cohen's words in his dream.

'Peace is not their destiny,' he said.

The commander shrugged. Burton went up to the barrier and raised his voice.

'British police!' he shouted. 'Requesting entrance!'

He knew there were people on the rooftops, hidden away and watching him.

'What's your business!' came the reply.

Burton had already thought it through.

'General Watson's orders,' he shouted back. 'Open up!'

A hollow laugh rose behind the barrier. Burton couldn't blame them. But he still had nominal authority.

'Let me through!' he shouted.

Something heavy being moved. It dragged on the ground. A narrow opening in the barrier. Burton hesitated before the gap. Then he ducked through.

On the other side he was surrounded by armed men again. He showed them his badge.

'Who's the girl?' their commander said. He looked much like the commander on the other side. They both had tired eyes and silly pencil moustaches. They both spoke bad English.

'We found her wandering,' Burton said. 'It's lucky nothing happened to her. She's simple-minded. We're taking her back to her uncle.'

'Who is her uncle?' the commander said.

'He's a shoemaker,' Burton said. 'He has a place near the Anglo-Palestine Bank.'

Eva Finer was trying not to laugh. The commander peered into her face, holding her chin in his hand.

'She *is* simple,' he said. 'You should have taken her to Haifa, anywhere but here. It's not safe here.'

'She has no other family,' Burton said.

The commander nodded. He let go of Eva Finer.

'They want to kill us all,' he said grimly. 'They're waiting, just behind the walls. But we won't let them.'

Burton shrugged. 'Can you lend us a man to show us the way?' he said. 'I don't want to get lost here.'

'I don't have a man to spare,' the commander said. He gave a short, sharp whistle. A ferret-faced boy came running over. He grinned up at them expectantly.

'Dudi,' the commander said. 'Take them where they want to go.' He looked up at Burton. 'This is Dudi,' he said. 'He's simple too.'

'It's near the bank,' Eva said. 'It's blue.'

'Everything here is blue,' the commander said in disgust. He turned away from them, already losing interest.

'Can you take us, Dudi?' Burton said.

'My name is David,' the boy said. 'I'm not a baby.' He stared at Eva. 'And I know who you are,' he said. 'I'm not stupid like they are.'

'Then shut the fuck up,' Paddy said, picking the boy up by the scruff of the neck, 'and show us the way to the bank.'

'What do you want with the bank?' the boy said, unconcerned even as he was marched forward. 'It's closed.'

'We're not going to the bank,' Burton said, 'we're looking for this poor girl's house—'

'That's Lady Finer,' the boy said. 'I read about her in the paper. My mother cuts out all the society news in *Ha'aretz*.'

They were away from the guards now, and heading into the quiet, watchful streets.

'Look, kid,' Burton said. 'Just show us the way, alright? You'll be doing your nation a service.'

'What nation?' the boy said. 'I didn't ask to be stuck here. I'd much rather go live in London like Lady Finer, and have a big house and servants, and, and...' His imagination seemed to desert him. 'Nice things and stuff,' he said.

'You could have nice things,' Burton said. He took out a coin and held it out enticingly. 'Just take us to the bank and keep your mouth shut.'

'What's that?' the boy said. 'A pound? I'm not doing shit for less than ten, mister.'

'Ten pounds!' Burton said. 'I'll find the bank myself.'

'Five, then,' the boy said, capitulating quickly. 'That's my final offer.'

'Fine,' Burton said.

The boy shrugged.

'Give it here,' he said.

Burton fished out a five-pound note. He wondered if this money would have any value by Monday. No doubt whoever took charge in Palestine would want to issue their own currency next. But they'd have to keep the pound in some form. People usually did. The boy pocketed the money and smiled happily.

'Come on, then,' he said.

He led them up and down the narrow streets. A pigeon sat on top of a clothes line and watched them from above, its head tilted in mild curiosity. A cat slunk past them and vanished under the awning of a watchmaker's shop. Clocks chimed inside, a cacophony of hours. Then they rounded a corner and saw the bank building, shuttered and dark.

'Closed a few days ago,' the kid said. 'On account of the siege and all.'

Burton stared at the building. It didn't look like much of anything, but the walls were thick and the door was stout. He exchanged a glance with Paddy, who shrugged.

'Is there a manager?' Burton said.

'Mr Abrams,' the kid said. 'He lives just up the road.'

'Is he still here?' Paddy said.

'Sure,' the kid said. 'Where is there to go? We can't escape the city.'

'Can you show us where he lives?' Burton said.

'I mean, I could,' the kid said. 'But why should I?'

Burton sighed and took out a handful of coins.

'This is all I've got left,' he said.

'If that's what it's like,' the boy said, taking the money, 'I'll never become a policeman.'

'Can you show us where this Mr Abrams is now?' Burton said.

'You're not going to hurt him, are you?' the boy said.

'No, of course not,' Burton said. 'We just want to have a little chat with him.'

'That's too bad,' the boy said. 'He's never been nice to me. Everyone calls me simple but I'm not – I'm not!'

He looked furious all of a sudden. Burton stared at this runt of a child, skinny and defiant like an alley cat.

'Maybe we could hurt him a *little* bit, then,' Paddy said; and the boy smiled.

'Mr Abrams? Mr Abrams, open up!'

Still that eerie quiet and the sense the whole world was awake. Paddy banged on the door. No lights. A reedy voice from inside – 'Who is it?'

'Police, Mr Abrams.'

'Police, what police?' the voice said. 'Get lost, hooligans, or I'm going to call the cops!'

Eva Finer stepped up to the door. She rapped on it softly.

'Mr Abrams?' she said. 'I'm Eva Finer. I'm here about Isaac Samuelsohn's effects.'

'Samuelsohn?' the voice behind the door said. 'I heard what happened. Terrible business. Terrible. Finer, you said?'

'Eva Finer,' Eva said.

'Related to the Melchetts and the Sassoons!' the voice said delightedly. A lock turned in the door and then another, and the door was pushed open by an old man wearing pyjamas and a dinner jacket. He peered out at them.

'Who are these goons?' he said, nodding at Burton and Paddy. 'Are they with you?'

'They're here for security,' Eva said.

'Security, well, of course,' Mr Abrams said. 'I was offered to evacuate to Haifa, you know. I said no! I am not abandoning the bank.' He stood up straight, then noticed the kid.

'You!' he said. 'Hooligan! What are you doing here!'

'Eat dirt, old man!' the kid yelled. He stuck his tongue out and waved the five-pound note Burton had given him. 'I ain't putting that in your bank!' He laughed and ran off.

'Hooligan,' Mr Abrams said again.

'Mr Abrams,' Eva said. 'I'm sorry to bother you, especially at this late hour. But it's about Isaac's deposit box.'

'His deposit box? Yes, of course,' Mr Abrams said. He peered at her. 'What about it?'

'I need to access it,' Eva said.

'Access his deposit box? But why?' Mr Abrams said. 'The bank is closed. Closed until further notice. Because of the, well...' He waved his hand. 'The situation,' he said.

'Please, Mr Abrams,' Eva said.

'What please? Even if I could open the bank, Miss Finer, you must have authorisation, paperwork, I really am very sorry, but – oh.'

He stared at the barrel of Burton's gun.

'I'm sorry, Mr Abrams,' Burton said. 'But it's important.'

'What are you doing, man?' Mr Abrams said, and the look in his eyes – hurt? disbelief? – cut like a knife through Burton's soul.

What *was* he doing? he wondered, dazed. He had crossed a line he never meant to cross.

But it all seemed so meaningless now, here on the cusp of the world he knew falling into a senseless war. They were all fighting over a land the size of a postage stamp.

'If you could just let us in to the bank,' he said, hating himself.

'I'll get my keys,' Mr Abrams said coolly. Paddy escorted him inside, came back with the man still in his pyjamas and slippers. They followed him down the street to the bank building and Mr Abrams unlocked the door. Inside it was dark, the counter empty of tellers and the stone floor's polish dimmed with a thin layer of dust.

'Well?' Mr Abrams said. 'What do you want?'

'Could you take us to the safe, please?' Burton said.

'Sure,' Mr Abrams said, 'why not.' He led them behind the counter, unlocked another door, then into an office room and down a small flight of stairs. Beyond that sat a metal vault door.

'Well, this is it,' Mr Abrams said. 'It's a Chubb.' He patted the door affectionately.

'Well, then, open it,' Paddy said.

'Oh, I can't do that,' Mr Abrams said.

Burton levelled his gun at the old man.

'Open it,' he said.

'I wish I could,' Mr Abrams said, not looking upset in the slightest. 'But I can't, you see. It can't be done.'

'Why not?' Paddy said. Eva stared at them, biting her lower lip.

'Why not?' she said. Her voice was soft, but it carried in that quiet place.

'It's a two-key lock,' Mr Abrams said. 'I don't have the second key. It's at head office.'

'Head office?' Eva said.

'Of course. In Haifa. We couldn't take a chance of someone

having the bright idea of robbing the bank, could we?' Mr Abrams said. 'Not with all this going on. We have a duty of care to all our customers, whether they're Arabs or Jews.'

'Open it!' Eva said. The old man looked at her in defiant amusement.

'I can't,' he said, almost regretfully. 'Nobody can. Not without the keys.'

Burton held back Eva, who looked ready to leap on the old man.

'It was always a possibility,' Burton said. He nodded to Paddy, who grinned and reached for his backpack.

'What... what are you going to do?' Mr Abrams said, looking suddenly worried.

Paddy took out the blocks of TNT.

'We'll just have to blow it up,' he said.

42

Burton had seen his share of bank robberies during his service in Palestine. There was the attempt on the Feuchtwanger Bank in Haifa a couple of years back, foiled by security guards as the gang of six robbers, equipped with an oxygen tank and safe-cracking tools, were about to get away with several thousand pounds in cash.

There was the notorious robbery of the Ottoman in Tel Aviv, by a gang of armed Jewish youths, aligned no doubt with one of the resistance movements and equipped with a Tommy gun. They had taken the British manager, Mr Denham, hostage, before making a daring escape in a getaway car. The Ottoman branches were frequently subject to robberies: Arab robbers in Haifa murdered a bank teller and stole some six hundred and fifty pounds before escaping in a taxi only three months earlier. And in August of the year before another gang, also Arab, got away scot-free with a cool ten thousand pounds.

The truth was that any lawbreaker who needed quick money sooner or later made for the bank. The Stern Gang were particular repeat offenders on this score.

Burton could have gone on; but he had never been on *this* side of a robbery, nor had he ever expected to. He felt ashamed as he covered old Mr Abrams with his gun. They were in the main hall. It was still dark. It was still quiet. Paddy was alone in the cellar with the safe. Burton wondered what was taking him so bloody long.

'You are making a terrible mistake,' Mr Abrams said.

'It is for the greater good, Mr Abrams,' Eva Finer said.

'Him I am not surprised,' Mr Abrams said, 'he's a cop and all cops are crooks. But you, Lady Finer? That I would not expect.'

'We are not robbing you, Mr Abrams,' Eva Finer said. 'All I want is what's inside Isaac's deposit box. I do *have* the slip.'

'You do?' Mr Abrams said. He peered at her. 'Then why didn't you say so?'

Eva dug in her bag and brought out a small piece of brown paper. Burton stared at her, with the awful realisation that if she'd had it on her all along, it put the rest of her story in some considerable doubt, and Mr Abrams said, 'Well, of course, it is no good to you under the usual circumstances, with poor Isaac being dead and without his authorisation, but sure, for you, I can go and open the safe after all,' which meant he had *also* lied, when—

Paddy came barging out of the office door and screamed, 'Get down, now!' and threw himself on the floor, covering his head with his hands—

The ground shook and the bone-breaking, skin-tearing sound of an explosion rose like a thousand screaming men being tossed into a communal grave. Burton threw himself to the ground as the office walls, teller counters and the door blew apart like matchsticks, and an enormous force of heat pushed through, as though a giant's hand punched through the building. Debris flew through the air as the walls shook and Burton curled into a ball and closed his eyes, trying to protect his head with his arms.

'Come on!' Paddy shouted, sounding strangely exhilarated, and Burton opened his eyes again as the world settled. Dust masked the air. Mr Abrams was curled on the floor under a thick, unbroken slab of the counter. He did not move. A hole in the ground led directly to the cellar now, and Burton followed Paddy down, where the door lay flat on the ground, exposing the dark confines of the safe beyond.

'You did it!' Burton said. 'Good man!' He slapped Paddy on the back.

'You just want to watch out it doesn't—' Paddy began to say when there was a second explosion, coming from inside the safe, and Burton jumped. The contents of the safe were illuminated in the sharp sudden glare: an Aladdin's Cave of secure boxes of various sizes, piled rather haphazardly, one of which must have contained illegal explosives. Burton watched in dismay as the box burned. The fire, perhaps of a chemical nature, began to spill and crawl towards the nearby objects and he panicked.

'Where is it?' he screamed. He dashed inside, a hot stench of TNT and hot air and fire. He began picking up and discarding boxes, finding Abdallah, Amin, Adelman, Becker, Cohen, Darwish, Freud, Frankel, Hadid and Hamdi, Goldfarb and – 'Where the fuck is it?'

The fire hissed, outside he could hear sirens and shouts. Eva Finer came and joined him, her hair singed and her eyes burning with excitement. Together they picked and tossed boxes—

'Samuelsohn!' Eva said. She grabbed the box and dashed out with it. Burton cursed and followed, Paddy bringing up the rear. They ran back into the main hall to find the doors wide open and a troop of men in khaki shorts and armed with guns staring at them in perplexed hostility.

'Police!' Burton shouted. He pointed to Mr Abrams's prone body on the floor. 'Can't you see he needs help? Paddy, help me lift him!'

'They went that way!' Eva Finer said, speaking Hebrew, her eyes brimming with newfound tears. She pointed helplessly – 'They were armed, there was nothing we could do – go, quickly!'

Paddy grabbed Mr Abrams by the legs, Burton by the arms. They lifted the poor man up and began moving to the door, a crying Eva Finer behind them. The armed men, caught up in the story, parted for them. Burton could hear shouted orders, and a bulk of the men went running up the road in pursuit of the supposed robbers. He and Paddy moved quickly, and as soon as they turned the corner they put down Mr Abrams and began to run, Eva and the box following.

The city was dark. Burton was afraid of getting lost but first he wanted to get free of any pursuit. They took a turn into a narrow alley and there, sitting on a crate marked *Gherkins*, his feet dangling from the crate nonchalantly, was the boy, David.

'Can you take us to the nearest exit?' Burton said.

'There are no exits, mister,' the kid said. 'We're under siege.'

'There must be a way out,' Burton said.

'There's the way you came in,' the kid said.

'That won't work anymore,' Burton said.

The boy hesitated.

'There's maybe a way,' he said.

'So take us!' Burton said.

'Well,' the boy said, considering. 'I *could*, but…'

'Oh, just—' Burton said. He rummaged furiously in his pockets. 'Does anyone have any cash?' he said.

'There,' Paddy said, tossing the boy two notes and a handful of coins. The boy didn't make a move to grab them. The coins fell in the gutter and the notes fluttered down to the ground.

'I don't want your money,' the boy said. 'It's just that it's dangerous to try to leave.' He looked older then, older than his age; and when he turned his face Burton had the impression of a faint halo, like a golden wreath surmounting the boy's head.

Eva Finer knelt beside the boy and took his hand in hers.

'We have no choice,' she said. 'Please, help us.'

'You're a nice lady,' the boy said. 'Well, follow me. Did you blow up the bank?'

'Wasn't us,' Paddy said. 'Honest.' He picked up the money from the floor.

'I like it when things blow up,' the boy said wistfully.

He led them through the alleys and in short order they came to a wall hanging with vines. The boy knelt on the ground and reached for the bricks, which came out one by one. A small hole formed and the boy crawled through it. Burton followed, and found himself in a secluded garden. An ancient apple tree grew in its centre, and although it was not the season it was laden with fruit. The air was warm and scented with the heavy perfume of flowers Burton didn't recognise. A snake rustled in the grass and the boy, with a cry of rage, picked up a rock and smashed it against the creature's head until it went limp. Burton stared with sorrow at the dead snake. The boy tossed the rock away and reached for an apple, but it was too high overhead and he jumped up and down in frustration. Burton plucked an apple from the tree and handed it to him. The boy smiled. The apple was red. When the boy bit into the fruit the juice ran down his chin.

'No one comes here,' he said.

Burton looked around and realised this tiny garden must have formed accidentally, bordered in between walls. Perhaps it had been a plot left empty, or more likely an error of calculation that merely left this curious gap in the density of houses. He noticed a cigarette butt on the ground and the boy, following his gaze, said, 'I like to come here sometimes to get away from it all.' He motioned Burton to follow him. Against the far wall he knelt again and pushed aside a thorn bush to reveal an opening.

'This will take you out,' the boy said.

'Thank you,' Burton said, and the boy shrugged, a little uncomfortably, and said, 'Go, you're just a foreigner here anyway.'

Burton crawled through the hole. The others followed him. When he looked back he could no longer see that there was ever a breach there, and the wall stood seemingly whole. They were back on the Arab side of Safed. All was quiet. Eva Finer held the deceased Mr Samuelsohn's strongbox in her hand. Inside it would be a treasure map. Burton thought of gold, but it didn't seem to mean that much to him. The garden – there had been a garden. He couldn't quite remember it now anymore. Smoke and fire and shouts and death, and a moment of peace – he thought he could remember that.

He lit a cigarette. That was something real. And he hurried his steps through the night streets of Safed, and up the hill to the police station.

'Why are you still here?' General Watson said. 'Are you insane, man? You were supposed to take her back to Haifa hours ago!'

'I fell asleep,' Burton said. The stupidity of the remark caught the general off-guard.

'Well, then,' he said. 'We're pulling out, man. They'll be at each other's throats come daybreak. Get out of here and make just one less problem for me, is that clear?'

'Sir, yes, sir,' Burton said.

'Dismissed,' General Watson said.

Burton hadn't been planning to hang about. It was just bad luck he'd run into Watson. The station was a hive of activity, rooms emptied methodically one by one, vehicles loaded, soldiers and police officers moving hurriedly to finish the final preparations for the withdrawal. Burton stared out at the city below. The sun was rising over Safed. The Arab forces held the citadel, the Jews were bunked down in the Jewish Quarter, and both Arab and Jewish forces were moving beyond the city, jostling for position for the end of the Mandate. Might as well light a match and toss it on pine needles in the forest.

'Paddy, you take the second car,' Burton said. Eva Finer stowed the strongbox in the first car.

'Boss, yes, I mean—' Paddy said. He hesitated.

'What is it, Paddy?' Burton said.

'We did it, sir,' Paddy said. 'You rescued the girl. You found the map to the treasure. All you've got left is to get to the port on time. But there's nothing left for me back in Britain, sir. We could play policemen all day long, year after year in this country and not make a difference. Or we could pick a side.'

Paddy stood there, not contrite but earnest, standing tall, the keys to the armoured car in his hand.

'You still have some of that TNT, don't you?' Burton said.

Paddy smiled.

'I do, sir,' he said. 'And a couple of Sten guns from the armoury no one was going to miss. And a few grenades and things. You know.'

'That kibbutznik girlfriend of yours?' Burton said.

'I like her, boss,' Paddy said. 'I like her just fine. I think the Jews deserve their shot.' He looked suddenly shy. 'I hope I'm not overstepping,' he said. 'But there's nothing for me in Piccadilly, boss. It's not quite the same as the one on Mount Carmel.'

Burton smiled, despite himself.

'Are you deserting, Paddy?' he said.

'No, sir. I've been given my papers, remember? There's no more job.'

'That's right,' Burton said. 'That's right. Well, if they ask, I'll just tell them you got lost on the way back.'

Paddy smiled too.

'They won't ask, boss,' he said. He put his hand out for a shake, and Burton shook it.

'Thanks, Burton,' Paddy said. 'You weren't a bad guy, for an officer.'

'I'll see you, Paddy,' Burton said, and Paddy turned, already climbing into the car, and said, 'No, you won't.'

'No, I suppose not,' Burton said, but Paddy was already gone. Burton turned to Eva Finer.

'Are you ready?' he said.
'I am ready,' she said.
Burton got behind the wheel of the armoured car.
'Then let's go home,' he said.

43

You could have left it there, with Burton and Lady Finer driving off into the sunrise. The wind in their hair, the open road, the sea in the distance. The smell of salt and wild sage if you were into the whole sensory thing. Gulls crying.

Cue credit sequence.

Didn't quite go that way.

Back in '73, '74, around that time, a producer called Nat Cohen got interested in Burton's memoir. The book, *Golgotha: True Recollections of a Colonial Detective*, was published in hardcover by Hodder & Stoughton. Burton received a modest advance, which never earned out, and the book soon went out of print. A favourable mention in the *Telegraph*, which his wife, Ophelia (they had met while he was serving in Nyasaland), framed for him to put on the wall of his study in Twickenham. Then one day came Nat, then at EMI, flush with cash from the *Carry On* films but also doing more edgy fare like '71's *Get Carter* – 'Genre stuff, you know, it pays the bills,' he'd said. A tough-looking little Jew with a pencil moustache, the son of an East End butcher made good. He'd owned the Savoy Cinema in Teddington back in the day. Nat had it in mind to make a film adaptation, but it never came to aught.

He'd put enough in to develop a treatment, though, which is what movie folks call a broad outline of the story. No one ever quite filled in the dialogue, they never got that far. But it got Burton talking, rehashing the old story again, he'd take it out for a spin after a few pints down the Swan.

'What happened to the treasure?' was always the question he got. Everyone had heard about the Dead Sea Scrolls by then, the ones from the Qumran Caves, and might even have heard of the copper scroll from Cave 3, the one with the lengthy listing of the temple's lost treasures. But Burton always just smiled an enigmatic smile and said, 'Well, who knows?'

Some things, he thought, should remain buried.

Burton lived to a ripe old age. He never went back to Palestine – Israel, as it was called now – though he sometimes thought about it, and more than once Ophelia hinted that perhaps they should go. He'd laugh and say one should never revisit the places of one's youth. Sometimes he still thought of Ruth.

Back in '65 he got a telegram informing him that a John Cooper, who everyone called Paddy, had collapsed and died from a heart attack as he was exiting his apartment that morning. After he left Burton in Safed, Paddy had driven straight to his kibbutznik girlfriend, and formally enlisted in the newly formed Israeli Defence Force, where he served in 'B' Company of the 89th Mechanized Command Battalion. He always did like driving. He lived through the war, remained with his girlfriend, and opened a kiosk at a busy traffic junction in the sands of the Negev.

'Now I've left all my men in the dirt there,' Burton told Ophelia. She helped him tie his tie and said, 'Stop being maudlin.'

Nat Cohen had talked of casting Albert Finney for the Irishman's role. He'd wanted Jon Finch for Cohen. For the aristocratic girl he talked about getting Jenny Agutter – 'For that English rose quality,' he said, 'and, of course, you've got to be able to show some tits.' But the movie never came to anything. Most movies don't.

Burton had served in Trinidad and then Nysaland, where he rose to the rank of a deputy police commissioner. After his retirement he went back to England, finally a married man, though he and Ophelia never had children. He worked for a car company for the next fifteen years, kept a dog named Bucky, who he was very fond of, and even took up golfing, though never enthusiastically. But he enjoyed the social aspect of it, and being outdoors. He never did quit smoking, though he swapped the cigarettes for a pipe late in life. Perhaps it was a lifetime of smoking that killed him, but as Burton would have been the first to point out, death came in all shapes and forms and there was nothing you could ever bloody do about it. He died and was buried in Twickenham, by a curious coincidence only a few rows behind that old rogue and dreamer of Palestine, Laurence Oliphant.

It happened in 1995. The same year the Israelis and Palestinians signed the Oslo peace accords; same year Rabin was assassinated, too, which put an end to *that*. That same year a Russian astronaut orbited the Earth in a space station for 366 days; a doomsday cult in Japan attacked a subway station with a lethal nerve agent called Sarin; an American terrorist murdered 168 people in an Oklahoma City bombing; the serial killer Fred West hanged himself in prison, the Queen Mother had a hip replacement, and the Grateful Dead played their final concert.

It was, in other words, a year like any other year; worse than some, better than others, and the roses bloomed in his garden the night Burton died. He woke up just before dawn, disoriented, Ophelia slept by his side. Rain pattered softly against the double-glazed windows.

They say that when your heart stops your brain keeps firing neurons. For as long as six minutes after you've stopped breathing your brain comes alive, no longer constrained by the body, lighting up across the two hemispheres of grey goo on an EEG screen. Time loses its meaning. Perhaps at that moment you are always alive.

What did Burton see? A shower of falling stars like sparks against the black sky, Eve by the fire watching the omens. The wind changed. He saw Cohen and Hassan rise back from the dead, become young as they went back through the stream of time, became babies who were loved, and then were swallowed back inside their mothers, who grew young in their turn. He saw the horseman with his rifle ride across the barren lands. He saw a great forest grow back where it had been cut down.

He ran across the plain with the red burning skies, and he came at last, and for the final time, to the place of skulls.

'I'll find a locksmith back in Haifa,' Eva Finer said. They were down on the Esdraelon, the hills of the Galilee mercifully behind them, and only Armageddon rising in the distance ahead of them. All looked peaceful, the fields brimming with life and a fine haze laying over the ancient valley. A butterfly hovered motionless in the air.

'In London, you mean,' Burton said.

'What?' Eva said.

'In London,' Burton said. 'You are getting on the ship.'

'Yes,' she said. 'Yes, of course. Only...' She bit her lower lip. 'I could stay behind,' she said. 'Do you really think there'll be a war? I mean, the UN said we're both getting countries. Jews and Arabs, side by side. It shouldn't be so, well, so *hard*. And I could find a locksmith, hire men for an expedition. It's somewhere near the Dead Sea, I'm sure of it. They took the treasure from Jerusalem using the underground water tunnels, the monks.' She turned her head. The sunlight caught her hair. 'You could come with me,' Eva Finer said. 'You could be a part of it, too.'

Burton gripped the wheel and stared ahead at the empty road. No, not empty. A vehicle was travelling towards them, far in the distance still but gaining speed. 'You're getting on the ship,' he said.

'Yes, of course,' Eva said. 'That is probably the sensible thing—'

The car came towards them awfully fast. It was a police vehicle,

Burton saw, speeding along the narrow road, and he wondered where it was heading, whether it was to Nazareth or another hotspot, when he realised the car wasn't going to pass them by, it was aimed directly at the—

He pressed on the brakes as hard as he could as he turned the wheel, instinctively if uselessly putting his arm across Eva Finer—

Metal screamed. The car shuddered, *rose*, the pit of Burton's stomach *dropped* as though he were suddenly weightless—

He slammed into the windshield glass. The glass cracked but held. Burton lost control of the wheel. He fell back in the seat. The car flipped sideways. Eva fell on top of Burton. He couldn't breathe. His vision went dark. His head throbbed with pain. Is that how he was to die? he thought, dazed. He tasted blood. The car rolled and came to a stop. The sudden silence was somehow worse than the noise. He pushed against soft flesh and found that he could breathe and he was still alive.

'What in God's name?' he said. 'Eva? Eva, can you hear me?'

A groan. She was alive. He reached for the door but it was under him and he couldn't get out. He pushed Eva, past her, the door was there. The door opened.

A friendly, familiar face looked into the car in concern.

'Jack?' Burton croaked. It was Jack Smith, his buddy from CID. 'Jack, I found her.'

'You sure did,' Jack said. He held his hand out to Eva, pulled her up and through the open door. Burton heard her flop onto the ground outside. 'Can you move?' Jack said.

'Help me out,' Burton said. 'Why did you... Why did you hit us, you damned fool?'

'Couldn't be helped,' Jack said. Burton held his hand out to him but Jack seemed in no hurry to pull him out. And now there was a gun in Jack's hand. It pointed at Burton.

'Don't try anything stupid, now, Burton old boy,' Jack said.

'Oh, Jack,' Burton said. 'Not you, too.'

Thinking – it was Jack who was called first on the Samuelsohn case. Jack at the Piccadilly, coming out of the bathroom as Waldman and Latif ran—

'Oh, no, Jack,' Burton said.

'It's just business, Burton,' Smith said. He kept the gun on Burton, rooted in the back, came back with the Samuelsohn strongbox. 'You're a good officer, Burton,' he said. 'I knew you'd find her for me.'

'You,' Burton said. 'You killed Waldman? In the cell.'

'Nah,' Smith said. 'That was Cohen. Though neither of us wanted that cunt singing. Anyhoo, I'll be going now. Won't shoot you or the bird, for old times' sake.'

He vanished from the window. Burton pulled himself up, saw his arms were bloodied and cut, but he barely felt it. A slow fury rose inside him. He saw Jack walking back to his own, barely damaged car. He was going to get away, and take the treasure with him—

But Eva Finer, with a roar of rage, rose from where she lay in the damp grass. She ran at Smith, low and hunched, more animal then human, and tackled him to the ground. Smith, surprised, hit her with his gun as he fell and Eva howled, then grabbed the strongbox and spun like an Olympic discus thrower and tossed the strongbox into the air. It flew high and true and vanished into the vegetation by the roadside.

'What did you go and do *that* for, you stupid bint!' Smith said. He smashed the butt of his gun across her face and she fell from him with a cry. Smith ran into the vegetation. Burton heard him searching. He pulled himself out of the door and fell to the ground. He tried to reach for his gun but could not muster the will even to move. He could only stare helplessly as Smith raised his head above the shrubbery, a huge smile plastered on his face, and held up the strongbox high for him to see.

'What do you think of *that*, you fuck!' he shouted. Then he looked down, and a puzzled expression came on his face. 'What's that,' he began to say—

The explosion, when it came, was surprisingly muted. Burton flinched as Jack came apart, his torso opening and his head exploding in a cloud of bone and blood. Eva howled again, in sheer rage, and ran into the bushes.

Burton screamed, 'It's mined, god damn it! Don't!' but she paid him no attention, and Burton rose to his feet and hobbled after her.

The strongbox lay open and smoking on a patch of grass, and Eva knelt beside it, sobbing and cursing.

Inside the strongbox, a small sheet of what might have once been ancient vellum curled softly into ash.

The lights glimmered over Haifa harbour. Burton stood unsteadily on the deck of the ship, his bandaged arm aching uncomfortably as he held on to the railing. They had stood by the side of the road on the Esdraelon until a convoy of trucks, departing Nazareth, passed by and he flagged them down. On the drive back to Haifa he saw other convoys join them, from all corners of Palestine, from the reaches of the Dead Sea and the Hermon, from the Judean Hills and the Negev. The British were departing at last, leaving whatever could not be carried behind. In some police stations mortar had been left. Some fell into Arab hands, some went to the Jews. It was going to be someone else's problem now, was the consensus. Perhaps a UN peacekeeping force, perhaps... Well, no one knew for sure. It was somebody else's headache now.

There was a logjam of trucks on the way into Haifa. Soldiers and old policemen smoked and chatted good-naturedly, and the natives came out of their houses and stared, and some waved and shouted and others scowled as though to say, the British couldn't leave fast enough. Eva Finer said nothing the whole way. Burton kept his eye on her. She, too, was going home, and that was just the way of it. A medic with the Nazareth unit bandaged them both up. Burton lit a cigarette, watched the mountain, remembered being young here once, when all he had to do was shout at taxi drivers to keep down the noise of their horns. Recalled, too, the Zeppelin impossible in the skies, and he remembered lying in the bed with Ruth, and feeling something that was more than affection, a little less than love.

A story gets written and you think you're the hero, only to discover yourself, at the very end, relegated to the margins. The story would go on without him, he realised, and perhaps never needed him at all. He was just a passer-by. He smoked his Woodbine and waited as the trucks edged forward, on and on, until they reached the port gates and were allowed entrance.

Here he safely deposited Eva at the hands of a couple of sympathetic NAAFI girls; made a brief report to Stockwell, the MG, who merely nodded tiredly, as though nothing would surprise him anymore; and then went in search of his own berth on the ship.

It was organised chaos. He found a sandwich and a cup of black coffee. He smoked another cigarette. Night fell, and the stars came out over the ancient mountain. To the Carmel, the British occupation had been a mere blink in time. It had stood there before the first people came, and would no doubt stand when the last of them were gone. Maybe to the stars, Burton thought, like in those American pulp-magazine stories.

Trumpets blared. In the port the flag was lowered, for the last time, then folded neatly and taken away. Everyone sang 'God Save the King'. And that was that.

One by one the ships pulled out of the harbour, and in the distance Burton could hear sporadic gunshots erupt, punctuating the waiting silence. When he turned his head he was surprised to see Gray.

Seagulls cried. The wind blew humid against Burton's face.

'What now?' he said. 'What do we do with them, sir?'

Gray shrugged. The light caught his weathered, austere face as though it were of some ancient seer captured in stone.

'Let them kill each other,' he said.

He turned and left. Burton stared at the sea. Then he flicked his cigarette into the air, where it flashed once, brightly, like a star, and vanished into the dark water. He turned his back on the receding shore and went into the bowels of the ship to rejoin his people.

About the Author

LAVIE TIDHAR's work encompasses literary fiction (*Maror, Adama* and *Six Lives*), cross-genre classics such as Jerwood Prize-winner *A Man Lies Dreaming* (2014) and World Fantasy Award-winner *Osama* (2011) and genre works like the Campbell and Neukom prize-winner *Central Station* (2016). He has also written comics (*Adler*, 2020) and children's books such as *Candy* (2018) and *The Children's Book of the Future* (2024). He is a former columnist for the *Washington Post* and a current honorary visiting professor and writer in residence at Richmond American International University London.